"Traveling together like this has thrown us into an intimacy that isn't proper for an unmarried couple." Tarquin sought the right note: sensible, cool, restrained.

"I'm sure in the past we were always chaperoned," he went on. "A kiss under those circumstances can't go too far. You probably don't understand what I'm talking about, but we must be careful we don't let nature take its course." He feared he sounded like a pompous idiot. Better that than a blackguard.

"We never kissed," Celia said.

"Never?"

"No," she said. "You always treated me with the greatest respect."

Instead of relief he felt an irrational indignation. "It sounds to me like I was—am—a prig."

She looked up and her gray eyes seemed huge and bright. "I wanted you to kiss me," she said.

An invitation he ought to resist. Just one kiss, he reasoned. To refuse would be to insult a lady.

"I'll give you a thousand kisses," he croaked just before he completely lost his senses and toppled her to the ground.

The Amorous Education of Celia Seaton

MIRANDA NEVILLE

AVON

An Imprint of HarperCollins*Publishers*

This is a work of fiction. Names, characters, places, and incidents are products of the author's imagination or are used fictitiously and are not to be construed as real. Any resemblance to actual events, locales, organizations, or persons, living or dead, is entirely coincidental.

AVON BOOKS
An Imprint of HarperCollins*Publishers*
10 East 53rd Street
New York, New York 10022-5299

Copyright © 2011 by Miranda Neville
ISBN 978-0-06-202304-9
www.avonromance.com

First Avon Books mass market printing: August 2011

Avon Trademark Reg. U.S. Pat. Off. and in Other Countries, Marca Registrada, Hecho en U.S.A.
HarperCollins® is a registered trademark of HarperCollins Publishers.

Printed in the U.S.A.

10 9 8 7 6 5 4 3 2 1

To my father, Edmund

Chapter 1

Never get into a cart with a strange man.

Yorkshire, England, July 1820

"**T**ake off your clothes."

Celia's mouth fell open. "Why?" she managed to articulate. Stupid question perhaps, but nothing had indicated lascivious intentions during the two or three hours since her kidnapper had picked her up in the lane, tied her up, and driven her off to this obscure moorland cottage. He'd handled her with insulting indifference.

"I most certainly will not," she said, gathering courage.

She backed away from him, rubbing her wrists, still sore from the bonds he'd removed. Her head hit the sloping roof. "Ow!"

"Do it or I'll have to do it for you." The man sounded more bored than threatening. He reached under his laborer's smock and metal glinted in the dim light.

"And I'll shoot you first." The words lacked any trace of the rustic burr which, along with the smock, had fooled her into believing him a local farmer when he offered her a lift in his cart. "Get on with it. I don't have all day."

Definitely not from Yorkshire. His accents carried a hint of something far more exotic that matched his olive complexion and suggested an origin or sojourn in foreign parts. Coming from foreign parts herself, Celia would normally have been interested in conversing with him. But she hesitated to bandy words with an armed man, especially one whose pistol aimed straight at her heart. In the tiny attic, she couldn't believe he'd miss. Raising trembling hands to the buttons of her pelisse, she summoned her most ferocious scowl, with the hope of making herself repulsive.

At first it seemed her grimace had the opposite of the desired effect. His eyes held a hungry gleam as they fixed on her bosom.

"Give me that." He held out his free hand. With relief and reluctance she offered him the cloth reticule that hung from her left wrist. "That's right. Now the coat." The serviceable gray garment slid from her shoulders. "Lay it on the floor there. Do you need help with the buttons of your gown?"

Celia shook her head. A governess dismissed for moral turpitude does not merit the attentions of a maid. She'd dressed herself that morning, in undergarments and a dress that could be fastened without assistance.

She kept a wary eye on the kidnapper, though she

couldn't imagine the act of rape would be conducted in such a nonchalant atmosphere. Robbery seemed more likely his motive, not that her clothes were worth much. Keeping the barrel of the gun trained on her, he loosened the laces of the reticule and shook its contents onto the rough floor: the miscellaneous clutter of a traveling lady and the princely sum of fourteen pounds, thirteen shillings and fourpence. Princely to her, anyway. It represented her entire worldly worth.

Princely enough for her abductor too. He gave a little grunt of satisfaction as he squatted to gather up the notes and coins, stuffed them into a pocket of his breeches, and the other things back in the reticule.

By now she'd unbuttoned her dress but couldn't bring herself to remove it. "Off with it," he said. "And the rest. Shoes, stockings, and whatever's underneath."

"Why?"

"I have to leave you for a while and I don't want you escaping. You should be safe up here, but if you managed to get out I reckon you'll think twice about wandering off over the moors naked."

Reassured that violation was not to be her immediate fate—for once she could be glad she wasn't the kind of woman who drove men to madness—she did as bidden until she reached the last layer. Saving on cloth, she made her shifts short. Showing her knees to this man was bad enough. Celia couldn't bring herself to expose her breasts and other private parts.

"Please," she said, hating to have to beg. "Let me keep this on."

He looked her up and down with, she feared, a grain more interest than he'd previously displayed.

"Please." She crossed one arm over her chest, the other lower, in a vain effort to protect her modesty. "Please don't make me take this off. I'd never go outside dressed in so little."

Whether from pity, or conviction that the cheap linen had little value, he agreed. He made her gather up the rest of her clothing and lay it over his free arm.

"I'll be back later," he said from the ladder as he climbed down into the cottage below. He paused before he disappeared from sight, looked her up and down. She hugged herself closer and pressed her thighs together. "You know, you're not so bad after all. Maybe we'll have time for a little fun before." She could guess what kind of fun he meant, but before *what*?

The swinging hatch closed and she heard the wooden bolt driven home. Celia Seaton was alone. She no longer had employment, a future, a reputation, or a penny to call her own. All that remained was a too-short shift and a healthy indignation.

She heard him banging around below as she took stock of her surroundings. There wasn't much to see. Sunlight leached in through a spot in the roof where a tile had broken. Lucky it wasn't raining, or perhaps not. She was thirsty and her stomach rumbled. And very hot, even in her scanty garment. She knelt and lowered her ear to the floor, the better to discover if her captor had left.

Instead she detected the approach of hoof beats outside, followed shortly by a knock at the door below, an unintelligible exchange of male voices. Then a thud and more sounds she couldn't interpret. No more voices. A few minutes later horses—more than one—leaving.

She turned her attention to the floor of crude beams with a plastered ceiling below. She could probably break through the plaster, but the beams were spaced too closely for her to slide through them. During her investigation her fingers encountered a familiar object that had fallen from her reticule and escaped the thief's notice.

It was made of silver and worth something, probably a pound or two. More important, the baby's rattle had been her mother's before it was hers and was dear to Celia's heart. Grasping its handle she brought it to her ear and shook it. It didn't sound quite right, making a dull clunk instead of a lively clatter. She found a new dent in the always battered old toy. The lack of noise together with dark tarnish accounted for the thief's failure to notice it.

Since it was the only thing she possessed that belonged to either of her parents, the serendipitous discovery gave her heart and strengthened her determination not to wait around to be raped, and whatever unknown horror came afterward.

There must be a way out of the attic.

Tarquin Compton hated summer.

Most of all he hated summer in the country.

London might be hot, dusty, and malodorous but at

least the familiar streets surrounding Piccadilly were paved. The back roads of northern Yorkshire, the location of his seldom-visited estate, tended to be mired in mud. Instead of handsome terraces and well-dressed women there was nothing better to look at than rustic cottages, stone walls, and endless flocks of noisy, smelly sheep.

But everyone left London for the summer. Not literally of course. Most of the million or more souls who called the great city home remained there. Only the rarified precincts of Mayfair and St. James's were silent and neglected in the hot months. Alas, despite the influence he'd achieved over the inhabitants of those quarters, Tarquin hadn't yet been able to dissuade the English aristocracy from their underlying preference for country life.

Only one of his intimates felt as he did: Lord Hugo Hartley. Fond as Tarquin was of his octogenarian great-uncle, he was a little wary of him at the moment. A month earlier Hugo had ambushed him.

It started innocently enough, over brandy at the Burgundy Club and a comfortable chat about Tarquin's latest rare bibliographic acquisition. He laughed off Hugo's contention that Tarquin's passion for poetry proved him a romantic.

"There's nothing," he protested, "remotely romantic about my relations with women."

Instead of the usual gently deprecatory remark about Tarquin's latest mistress, Hugo suggested that, at the age of twenty-seven, it was time he married. Tarquin couldn't have been more astonished if the elderly dandy had suggested he wear a coat made of homespun. Though it wasn't something they ever discussed, his uncle, to put it politely, had no interest in females.

"Do you imagine it is by choice that I never married?" Hugo asked.

"I assumed . . ."

"I could have. Most of those who share my tastes do. But I discovered early on that I was incapable of performing with a woman. It didn't seem fair to wed a lady and have her discover she was doomed to a barren bed."

Tarquin couldn't think what to say. He regarded Hugo almost as a father and this was not the kind of thing one wanted to hear from a parent. Or anyone else.

"Eighty-two years is a long time to live alone with no lover, no companionship, and no children." The old man's voice sounded bleak, so different from his customary mellow tones.

"You always seemed happy." Never had it occurred to Tarquin that Hugo, who possessed such joie de vivre and generosity of spirit, might be lonely.

"I've led a good life. I enjoy society and my collections. But the greatest joy came quite late in my life: your companionship. You are like the son I could never have."

It took all Tarquin's control not to shift in his chair at this uncomfortable exchange. "All I wanted was to make you proud by attempting to equal you in the art of elegance."

"And in that, my boy, you have amply succeeded. But

now I think it's time for you to set your sights elsewhere. I don't want to see you grow into a middle-aged exquisite with a taste for dirty books."

"Ouch."

"I'd like to see you happy with a family of your own before I die."

Tarquin never forgot the debt of gratitude he owed his uncle. Unable to resist Hugo's plea, Tarquin agreed to consider a match. A particular match with a lady who, on the face of it, was perfect for him.

And then immediately left town.

Standing invitations and the best spare bedchambers awaited him at a dozen country houses. While Belvoir, Blenheim, Osterley, and other aristocratic mansions could hardly be described as rustic, their surroundings were nevertheless rural.

Tarquin hated rural, but since rural was his only option, he heeded the pricking of his dormant conscience and returned to his ancestral acres. His land agent thought Tarquin might be able to head off an expensive lawsuit threatened by a quick-tempered neighbor. And since the litigious fellow was away from home visiting his daughter, Tarquin had to undertake another thirty-mile journey to settle the business.

He rode off with a sense of relief. Revesby Hall, which he'd visited but a handful of times since his parents' deaths, had a gloomy air, mocking the memories of his childhood there. He trotted up the steep drive and at the crest of the hill, just before descending out of sight, he glanced over his shoulder. The house, a solid, unpretentious mansion, looked just the same; the neglected grounds, once his mother's joy, did not. His parents had loved to stroll together in the gardens, arm in arm, surrounded by their children and dogs.

Tarquin turned his eyes to the road ahead and kicked his horse to a canter. His spirits rose as he rode away, shaking off disquieting recollections of happier times and the guilt of the absentee landlord.

Since England was enjoying an unusually fine summer, the continuing sunshine had dried up the mud. His lightweight pantaloons, made from a special knit cloth secretly developed by his tailor, were far better suited to the unwonted heat than old-fashioned leather. Nevertheless, after twenty miles Tarquin was glad to stop at an inn to refresh his mount and himself. Following a meal of cold beef, bread and cheese, and a pint of home brew, he sauntered out into the high street of the small market town. The swinging sign of a bookshop attracted him.

Tarquin collected exceptional editions of English poetry and unusual erotic works, most but not all of them French. He didn't expect any astounding rarities from a country bookseller, neither did he find them. One small volume caught his eye, a slim octavo with the title of *The Genuine and Remarkable Amours of the Celebrated Author Peter Aretin*. It was doubtless a bawdy novel of dubious literary merit that would help him wile away an hour or two before he slept tonight. He stowed it in the inner pocket of his coat and continued on his journey.

Two hours later he was hot, tired, and hopelessly lost. At some point he'd taken a wrong turn. Cursing the ambiguity of his directions, he tried to retrace his steps but the effort only led him deeper into deserted moorland. Finally he sighted a small stone cottage, probably a shepherd's abode. Hoping the lack of smoke from the chimney was attributable to the warmth of the day, he steered his horse along the rough track, dismounted, and knocked at the door.

That was the last thing he remembered.

Chapter 2

*While telling the strict truth is always
commendable, slight prevarication may be
excused when confronted with a half-naked man.*

The wooden hatch refused to budge but a rough door
in the gable at one end of the attic looked more
promising, if only the aperture wasn't nailed shut or
bolted from without. After a hard shove with all her
weight the door fell open, and she almost fell out. It was
some six or seven feet to the ground below but Celia
could swing herself down. As she calculated the best
method of descent she made a vow.

Since the day she'd awaited her father in Madras and
instead received the news of his death, she'd done her
best to please people and live according to the rules of
English society. And at every point, through no fault
of her own, she'd failed. By coincidence her twenty-
first birthday was just two days past. Not that it meant
much, since there was no one to whom she belonged or
owed obedience. But she embraced the symbolism of

her majority. From now on Celia Seaton was going to exist on her terms without bending to the whims and rules of others.

And the first person she'd foil would be her kidnapper, who thought she'd never dare escape clad so scantily. Had he left her naked, he might have been correct. But in her new mood of defiance she wasn't going to worry about showing her legs. She got down on her hands and knees, took a deep breath, and prayed.

She made it down with nothing more than a scratch or two and a small rip near the hem of her garment. It was as well no one could see, because in the process of escape she had bared just about all of her rear. With luck she'd find something inside the cottage to cover her.

The door to the humble structure was blocked, by a body. The body of a man lying unconscious, wearing nothing but breeches and a pair of riding boots. It had been some years since Celia had seen the bare torso of a grown man, and never a white man. He was pale, as befit a man who was always dressed up to his neck, but the smattering of dark hair, covering the chest and descending in a vee over his flat stomach, didn't disguise the fact that the skin covered well-formed muscles. This interesting masculine form distracted her only a few seconds from the astonishing fact that she knew him.

And although he was one of several men who had bedeviled her life, she did not actually wish him dead.

Kneeling on the ground she set her fingers to his temple and found a pulse. "Mr. Compton," she said. "Mr. Compton, wake up. Are you well?"

Nothing. She rested her head on his chest. Judging by the strength of his heartbeat, Mr. Tarquin Compton would live to cause further distress to awkward arrivals on the London marriage mart. She supposed she'd better try to revive him. And much as she detested the creature, she was curious to discover why the *ton*'s most fashionable gentleman lay half-naked next to a deserted Yorkshire cottage.

She couldn't think of a less probable milieu for a man adored and feared by London's ladies for his exquisite taste and poisonous tongue. She'd been the victim of the latter.

Like every other girl, she'd yearned for a word of approval from a man who could make or break a reputation. She'd admired the supreme elegance of his figure, his clever hawkish face that made softer and fairer men seem clumsy and commonplace. And as a nervous aspirant to the beau monde, from her stance on the fringes of the ballrooms she'd envied the way he seemed not to give a damn for the opinions of others.

That was at first. Later her pride rebelled against his determined ignorance of the very fact of her existence. Nevertheless she'd been pleased when his aunt, the Duchess of Amesbury introduced them, again. But then his careless insult had destroyed her slender standing and ruined her hopes of making a suitable marriage. The fury and humiliation of that moment burned as though it were yesterday.

The most influential gentleman in London, a nonpareil adored by all, had compared her to a cauliflower.

Only concern for her unshod foot restrained the urge to kick the man while he was down.

Balked of revenge, she considered her next move as a reluctant Good Samaritan. Water. Cold water on his forehead ought to revive him. Since she couldn't get into the cottage while his body blocked the door, she went around the building to check for an alternative entrance. While contemplating the possibilities of the single window, a groan summoned her back. Mr. Compton had woken on his own and risen to his knees. He looked up at her approach, stared at her for a few seconds, shook his head as if to clear it. Then he tried to stand and swayed, extending an arm to the ground to retain his balance.

"Do you think you ought to stand?" she asked.

If he noticed the grudge in her tone he gave no sign of it. "I'm not doing any good down here." He felt the back of his head. "It appears someone hit me."

"You're bleeding."

He examined the red stain on his fingers. "So I am. No wonder it hurts. I would be in your debt, madam, if you would lend me your arm. Without it I fear I may ignominiously fall back into the dirt." The words might entreat but the tone reeked of arrogance. As he regained strength he sounded like the Mr. Compton she knew and loathed.

"Here," she said. "And try not to get blood on my shift. It's all I have."

With fastidious care he wiped his fingers on the grass. Then, with the commanding grace that befitted the lion of the London drawing rooms, he placed the clean hand on her arm and rose to his feet.

She'd forgotten how tall he was, one the few gentlemen she'd met who towered over her. He looked down at her and she blushed. She was, she recalled, decidedly underdressed for the encounter. He was, too, but still managed to look disgustingly elegant naked from the waist up. His breeches and boots, though dusty, fit perfectly while her shift was shabby and torn. At least it was made of solid cloth. For once her slender means turned to her advantage. Finer, dearer linen would reveal far more.

Whether from good manners, genuine indifference, or a derangement of judgment caused by injury, Mr. Compton showed no discernable emotion as he took in her appearance. Instead he managed a creditable bow.

"Madam," he said. "Thank you for your assistance. We are not, I believe, acquainted. Perhaps introductions are in order."

Any impulse to forgive his past transgressions dissolved. Six times in London Celia had been presented to Tarquin Compton. Six times he had expressed his obviously insincere pleasure at making her acquaintance. He never remembered her. Even after they'd danced and he'd spoiled her prospects he couldn't identify her. It was particularly insulting that he could so heedlessly destroy someone's future without even knowing her name. She refused to humiliate herself by reminding him of their previous meetings.

She tilted her nose a few degrees higher, engaged his haughty eye, and prepared to deny any prior acquaintance when he spoke again. "I am . . ." He stopped. For the first time in the strange encounter he seemed unsure of himself. "I don't know," he said slowly. "I don't remember who I am. I don't remember anything."

"You don't know your own name?" she asked.

He shook his head, wincing with pain at the motion.

Celia had heard of such effects of a blow to the head but could scarcely believe it. That this should happen to Mr. High-and-Mighty Compton, that the man had no idea he was an arbiter of fashion, the darling of the *ton*, the terror of the unmarried maidens, was too bizarre. About to inform him of both their names she caught herself and stopped to give some thought to her predicament.

It was too perfect.

She was stranded in the wilderness, she knew not where, with no money, no friends, and no clothes. Aside from one offer of assistance, which might not still be open to her, she was alone in the world, in dire need of help and protection. Nothing she knew of the odious Mr. Compton suggested that, were he in his right mind, he'd give the time of day to a penniless governess with a soiled reputation. But he didn't know he was Mr. Compton, had no idea of his paramount position in London society. He could be persuaded to be of use.

"My dearest," she said, letting her voice break on a dry and entirely spurious sob. "Surely you know *me*!"

"Er. No. Have we met before?"

"Alas! You have forgotten." She flung her arms about his neck and inhaled the merest hint of his scent, a subtle, complicated essence lingering beneath the musky, and by no means disagreeable, overlay of sweat and horse. In the instant before he drew back she learned his chest was hard and the light mat of hair covering it almost silky.

"What have I forgotten? Who are you?"

"You don't know me?"

He narrowed his eyes and scanned her face carefully. "You do seem familiar."

"Thank God! The evil thief has not robbed you of all your wits. It must be beyond the power of any villain to make you forget what we are to each other."

"Perhaps you could give me a little hint."

"You will recall as soon I remind you. You must recall."

"What must I recall?" Testiness blended with confusion.

"That I am Celia! Your betrothed wife!"

He didn't believe her, that was clear. "We are engaged? To be married? Are you quite sure?"

"Of course I am sure. Can you have forgotten the sweet moment when I promised to be yours?"

"Apparently, yes." His eyes seemed more black than brown as they met hers in the gaze that had reduced a hundred debutantes and a thousand parvenus to sniveling idiots. "I can't remember anything else, either. Why don't you remind me? And you can start by telling me my own name."

Celia stiffened her spine and refused to be intimidated. She needed help and Mr. Tarquin Compton owed her recompense. She might as well enjoy herself a little. She shrugged off any slight qualm about her next lie.

"Your name, my dearest, is Terence Fish."

Chapter 3

Amnesiacs can't be choosers.

When he discovered the hole in his consciousness where his own name ought to be, the woman stared at him, seeming as bemused as he. From the neck up she looked like a lady, a young lady, with reddish hair arranged neatly, if not fashionably, and pinned up on top. This proper coiffeur framed a strong face with high cheekbones, gray eyes, a straight nose, and a wide mouth.

Propriety ended at the neck. Her only garment was a linen shift ending above the knees. That was it. Not a stitch more. And since he had no idea who he was, where he was, or why, the presence of a lady so garbed explained everything. Obviously he was asleep. The scanty chemise was less diaphanous than the under-garments favored by women who might be expected to invade his dreams, but it did reveal long and shapely legs and he was quite partial to long legs. How unfair that in such a promising dream his head continued to ache. A steady pounding in his brain spoiled the erotic possibilities of this illusory encounter.

Then she began to speak and his headache worsened. She claimed to know him—that made sense. Why else would they be together in this place, each so woefully underdressed? Her face seemed faintly familiar, like that of a slight acquaintance encountered out of his or her usual sphere, whose name one cannot place. But any illusion of sleep was shattered when she flung herself at him. She was a tall woman, and strong, and her fierce embrace almost knocked him down, proving their corporeal reality beyond doubt.

He drew back in alarm, fearing she might be deranged, an impression strengthened by her next claim.

Betrothed? They were betrothed? He might have forgotten his identity, but instinct revolted at the notion of impending matrimony.

"Can you have forgotten the sweet moment when I promised to be yours?" she cried.

Good God. Could he possibly be the kind of man who went in for sweet moments?

"I can't remember anything else, either. Why don't you remind me? And you can start by telling me my own name." Surely that would recall his wits.

And then he knew. Perhaps he had, in a moment of madness, agreed to wed this demented female. But of one thing he was sure, to the very depths of his being. His name was *not* Terence Fish.

"I don't believe it," he said. "I cannot be named Fish."

Continuing in dramatic vein she wrung her hands

before her bosom. "You are indeed my Terence!" Then her expression changed to one of horror. "Unless you lied to me! But that cannot be so. When we met you were staying with the vicar."

"What was I doing there?"

"Studying for the church."

He felt on firmer ground. "No," he said. "I am not going to be a clergyman."

"Of course you are. You are a most pious man with a promising career before you."

"Huh? Then what on earth am I doing in this benighted place?" He looked around at a landscape of steep hills, scraggly grass, low shrubs, few trees, frequent crags, and no human habitation in view, aside from the rough cottage in whose shadow they stood. "At a guess I'd say we are on the Yorkshire moors, hardly a suitable launching point for a career in the church."

"I will explain everything later. We must leave before our attacker returns. Unfortunately he took all our possessions as well as," she added with a blush, "most of our clothing."

He frowned. "Why would the thief return if he already has everything?"

She sounded a little irritable. "Because it wasn't just a common robbery. I was kidnapped and brought to this place. My abductor shut me in the attic of the cottage and said he'd come back later."

His head ached even worse. "Let me get this straight, er, what did you say your name is? Celia?"

"Celia," she said in a resentful tone. "Celia Seaton."

She actually dropped a curtsey which he could have sworn was ironic. Why on earth? She could hardly blame him for forgetting her name when he didn't even remember his own. Although Celia Seaton chimed a familiar note in his brain. Unlike Terence Fish.

"A man kidnapped you, Celia."

"Yes."

"And brought you here?"

"Yes."

"How did I get here?"

"I don't know, but I think you must have followed us and come to rescue me. Then the villain knocked you down and stole your horse and your clothes." And the blasted woman flung her arms around him again. "Thank you, my dearest Terence. You are a hero!"

Some hero, managing to end up half-naked, horse-less, and no doubt penniless too. He felt for his pockets and found none. The snug cut of his breeches didn't allow for such a convenience.

Celia heaved an inward sigh of relief when Mr. Compton stopped asking questions and agreed to enter the cottage in search of water. Inventing "Terence Fish's" background was going to be a challenge. She knew next to nothing about the workings of the Church of England. This was the trouble about coming up with a lie without time to plan ahead. She wished she'd made him a prospective East India Company clerk instead. Thank the Lord, she could claim ignorance of the path that had brought him to this place.

It astonished her that he managed to reek of arrogance, even under circumstances which should have reduced the proudest man to a proper sense of humility. The way he'd accused her of making no sense reminded her of his officious opinions, used to depress those who didn't live up to his standards. He didn't like his name, that was for certain. Too bad, she thought smugly. She had no idea how long he would remain ignorant of his true identity. She hoped for her sake it would be long enough to keep his escort to Mrs. Stewart's house, and for his that it wouldn't be much longer than that. In the meantime Tarquin Compton, the second coming of Beau Brummell, was going to live as Mr. Fish.

The cottage showed signs of recent but not immediate habitation. The stone hearth was cold though a heap of ash and charred wood gave evidence of use. Celia snatched up an old-fashioned metal tinderbox.

"We'll take this," she said. "And this." She tugged at the blackened kettle hanging on a chain over the fireplace. "I can't get it loose. Will you try?"

Silently he tried to free the utensil. Celia was pleased to see him so obedient. Perhaps the loss of his memory had softened his disposition.

"It's forged together. I can't remove it without tools." He regarded his now-sooty hands with distaste. "Did you happen to discover any water?" The supercilious tone told her his improved manners were only sporadic and he'd lost none of his fabled fastidiousness.

It took but a minute to search the cottage: a narrow bed, a rustic table and chair were the principal furnishings. A small cupboard contained a tin cup and a small knife but not a crumb of food. An earthenware pitcher on the floor stood empty. "There wasn't anything to eat or drink upstairs, either," she said. "Either the villain intended to leave me thirsty, or he'll be back soon. I think we should hurry. Let's take everything we can." A small burlap sack with a strap hung from a hook on the wall. A dusting of seeds fell to the floor as she shook it out. She stuffed the tinderbox, cup, and knife into the bag, and threw in a couple of rags she found in a corner.

Mr. Compton looked at her with disapproval. "You cannot travel dressed like that."

"I'm so sorry but I missed the wardrobe of ladies' clothing. Perhaps you could direct me." Their betrothal had slipped her mind and she let her underlying hostility show. "I would certainly prefer not to walk across the Yorkshire moors in my undergarment," she said, moderating her tone, "but I don't see the alternative."

He eyed her person with a glint in his eye that might almost be appreciative. Then his glance shifted to the bed.

"Here," he said. "Use this."

"This" was a crude homespun blanket of undyed wool. She wrapped it around her waist and, after some trial and error, succeeded in tucking it in to form a skirt. While not very secure, the makeshift garment at least covered her legs.

"What about you?" she asked. "You'll get a sunburn without anything on top and later you'll be cold."

"I'll have to manage." Even though the light told her

evening fast approached, there was no hint of chill in the air. "Wait."

She saw it at the same time, lying on the floor behind the open door. "Perfect! The kidnapper must have left it behind."

"And no doubt replaced it with my coat and shirt. I trust they were more elegant than this . . . thing."

"You always dress well, Terence, considering your limited means."

He fingered the rough cloth. "I suppose I should be grateful he left me my breeches and boots. It's better than nothing."

Celia hid her smile and slung the seed bag over her shoulder. She couldn't wait to see Tarquin Compton dressed like a yokel. "I'll leave you to your toilette and await you outside."

The first thing she saw was her mother's rattle. She'd dropped it when she knelt to tend to Mr. Compton. Finding it a second time, quite by chance, boosted her confidence; luck might finally be on her side. Not far from its resting place, against a tussock of grass, she spotted a small book bound in marble paper covers with a leather spine. At the creak of the cottage door, she thrust both rattle and book into the sack. The latter very likely belonged to her companion and might bear his name, or some other clue to his identity.

At the sight of him she couldn't contain her grin. "You are quite à la mode," she said and dropped a mocking curtsey. Yet, much to her annoyance, the man was incapable of wearing anything, even this humble garment, without a certain air. The impeccable fit of his breeches and knee-high boots helped, as did dark hair cut in the short Brutus style that kept its shape under duress. A faint shadow on his chin and jaw lent him a raffish air that only added to his attractiveness. With his piercing dark eyes and aquiline nose he looked less like a farm laborer than a pirate.

"Will I start a new fashion?" he asked.

How ironic that if anyone saw him so garbed he most likely would.

"I'm not sure they'd allow you into Almack's."

"Have I been to Almack's?" he asked with a frown. "I don't believe the patronesses welcome humble clergymen." Why did he have to remember that fact?

"No," she said coolly, "but I have."

"I thought you were a governess."

"Not always. I fell on hard times."

"I wish you'd tell me about it. Hearing your story might jog my memory. For that matter, you must tell me everything you know of *my* history."

"Later. We must leave."

"Where shall we go?"

"I don't know where we are, but if we follow the track we'll come to a road eventually. I wish to reach the town of Stonewick where we can be sure of a welcome from an old friend of my father's. When we meet someone we can ask for directions."

Mr. Compton surveyed the landscape with a frown. The cottage, though isolated, overlooked a gentle vale. A few hundred yards down the hill, the rough track joined a stream, and accompanied the silver ribbon of water into the horizon. "I don't like that idea."

"Why not?" Celia tried to contain her irritation. She felt quite strongly that she was in charge of the party since her companion was, in his present state, almost an idiot. "Have you a better one?"

"You said your kidnapper planned to return. I imagine he will come that way. While I am anxious to meet the fellow who abducted you and attacked me, I would rather do so when I am feeling stronger and my head doesn't ache."

The alternative was a steep rise behind the hut, leading who knew where. She looked wistfully at the downhill grassy track and back at the rocky hillside and had to admit he made sense. "He had a pistol," she acknowledged. "Are you able to walk?"

"There's nothing wrong with my legs."

Chapter 4

*A gentleman without his valet is
like a fish without a phaeton.*

Whatever the state of his legs, it appeared his riding
boots had not been designed for a tramp over
rough terrain. Before they reached the crest of the hill,
he had a pain on one heel that echoed the continuing
throb in his brain. But he could hardly grumble when
his companion was barefoot. She never uttered a com-
plaint as she picked her way up the rocky slope. He concentrated on placing one foot in front of another until he
heard shouts from below. Without forethought he fell to
his knees, pulling Celia down with him, and rolled them
both behind a rocky outcrop.

"Ow!" she complained, when he landed on top of her.

"Shh!"

"Why did you do that?" She shoved at his chest.

He put a hand over her mouth. "There happen to be
at least two men down there," he hissed, "and my guess
is they are looking for us, so be quiet."

She nodded and he released her. "I heard them," she whispered, "but do you have to lie on top of me? There's something sticking into my leg."

"Sorry." He shifted his lower body so his hip rested on the ground. "Better?"

"Not really."

Once again he adjusted his weight but they were on a steep hillside and gravity pulled him down, squeezing her recumbent body between his and the rock. "I can't move further back without exposing myself to view." Stretching his neck, he peered around the side of their shelter. "I can see down the hill," he said. "There are two men and they're searching the area. We'd better keep quiet and keep still."

They lay together for many minutes listening to the ebb and flow of their pursuers' voices. His concentration on their location was disturbed by the sound of his own breathing, and more especially that of his companion. As he strained to make sense of the men's shouting, the gentle undulations of her chest beneath his took on an outsized importance. One fact kept penetrating the mingled concerns of physical pain, mental bewilderment, and present danger. That the body lying against his was undoubtedly a female one. And that the female in question was—perhaps—his betrothed wife. Through his confusion, the thought added piquancy to their situation.

He wondered if he'd ever kissed her. Tilting his head he observed a generous mouth. Whatever else he forgot, surely he'd remember its touch. Slightly ajar, it emitted a soft warmth that tempted him to taste. But the stormy expression in her eyes belied the invitation. His beloved's temper, if the experience of the past hour or so was anything to go by, didn't match the sweet promise of those lips.

How could he blame her? She'd endured a day every bit as trying as his own. On the other hand she did, at least, know who she was.

Hoof beats down the hill put paid to his musing.

"What's happening?" she said, wriggling to escape.

"They're riding off. Their horses must have been behind the house."

"Most likely one of them is yours."

"What color is my horse?"

"A bay."

"Those two looked like a gray and a chestnut."

"Can you be certain from so far away?" For some reason she sounded defensive.

"No."

"You see? It may easily be a bay."

"Is it important?"

"No," she said. "I suppose not."

After two hours hard trudging, a broad, swift stream halted their progress. A nearby stand of trees offered shelter from the still-powerful evening sun. With matching sighs of relief they cast themselves down in the shade.

"Let me look at your head," she said.

He fingered the tender spot on his skull. It didn't

feel too terrible a wound and the walk had diminished the throbbing. "It's all right," he said. "The bleeding stopped."

"I'm going to clean it. Wait." She scrambled down the slope to the water. Glad to rest, he sat and leaned back against the trunk of an oak tree. Closing his eyes, he tried to contemplate his bizarre situation. Since deep cogitation made his head ache more, he gave up until Celia returned and fell to her knees beside him.

"Tilt your head forward," she commanded. She probed through his hair and gently palpated the sore spot with cool, soothing fingers. "It's quite a lump," she said, "but the area of broken skin is small and a scab has formed. Head wounds always bleed a great deal, even slight ones."

"Are you an expert?"

"As governess in a family of four boys I have vast experience with all kinds of minor injury."

"Did any of your charges ever lose his memory?"

"Only for the multiplication tables. And the dates of the kings of England."

"I assume such memory failure was temporary."

"Intermittent, but in some cases likely permanent, I fear. I was never a very good teacher."

He laughed. "Ouch."

She drew back. "I'm sorry. Did I hurt you?"

"Only by making me laugh."

"I want to give you a compress. Bend your head and keep still."

The cold wet cloth felt wonderful. As the dull throbbing in his brain faded he realized Celia had pulled his head almost into her bosom. He jammed his eyes shut but that didn't help since he became aware of her scent: a little musky, not surprising after a strenuous walk in hot weather, but far from disagreeable. When they'd lain together hiding from their pursuers, his impression had been that her small breasts, under the sensible shift, were well-shaped and pert, practically perfect. He ventured a quick look, just to make sure, but the range was too close. All he could see was linen and shadowed skin so he closed his eyes again, with a feeling of virtue, and concentrated on the blissful soothing of his wound.

"There," she said after several minutes. "The cloth is warm now. Shall I soak it again?"

"Later perhaps. Thank you for your care. If only your ministrations had cured my more vexatious injury! But I still can't remember a thing. Please tell me everything you know about me."

She fussed with the damp rag, spreading it to dry before returning to sit beside him on the ground. "I don't know where to start."

"How about when we met," he said with a touch of impatience. "Surely the reminder of such an important event will jog my memory."

Celia certainly hoped not.

During their long walk she'd had time to invent a few details of her romance with Mr. Fish, so she began with a degree of confidence. "Soon after you came to lodge with Mr. Blyth, the vicar of Sedgwick."

"To study for the church?"

"As I said before. Soon afterward we met at a ball."

"A public assembly?"

"A small private ball given by the squire's wife, Mrs. Wilkinson, to celebrate her daughter's engagement."

"Is it usual for a governess to be invited to such a private party?"

How typical of Tarquin Compton to detect the flaw in her story. She had decided to stick to facts, as far as was possible, in the invention of their courtship. It so happened that she *had* attended Mrs. Wilkinson's ball because she *had* lately become betrothed, to her employer, Mr. Baldwin. Apparently the blow to the head hadn't dulled his instinct for social nuance.

"I may only be a governess," she said with a touch of hauteur, "but my family is not without distinction. Miss Baldwin, my employer's sister, chaperoned me." Much against her will, she could have added. Miss Baldwin had loathed her brother's promised bride. Celia was sure she'd done everything she could to make Bertram believe the evidence of her misbehavior. "Shall I continue?"

"I was merely trying to understand the situation. Why was I invited to the ball?"

"Because you are a gentleman, and Mr. Blyth's pupil."

"Not because I come from a family of distinction?"

"Will you stop interrupting and let me tell the story?"

"I beg your pardon. Go on."

"I wore my best evening gown, a pale yellow silk left

from my London season. I believe I looked very well for Yorkshire."

If any doubt remained that Tarquin Compton was not himself, his reception of this statement dispelled it. "I'm sure you looked charming, but could we pass over the fashion folderol and get to the point?"

This was where her account departed from the historical into the fantastic. "The dancing had already begun but I had no partner because there were too many ladies." She frowned. "Why are there never enough gentlemen at balls?" This question evoked a groan which Celia read as a demand that she get on with the story. "As soon as you came through the door I noticed you. All the ladies did, you understand, since there weren't enough partners to go around."

"Is that the only reason?"

"You are very tall."

"How gratifying to be noticed for something beyond the mere fact of being male."

"Male and able to dance. The vicar entered with you but he can't walk without a cane." Realizing she needed to put a little effort into her depiction of their courtship, she edged around to look him in the eye. "I noticed you particularly because you are so handsome."

"Am I?" He sounded surprised. "I don't know what I look like."

This part was easy. She had only to describe Mr. Compton as she'd first seen him in a London ballroom. "Oh yes! Though in an uncommon way. Your nose is quite prominent, your chin firm, and your eyes so dark a brown as to appear almost ebony. But what struck me most is the way you present yourself. You always hold yourself so proudly, and your attire is faultless. Your clothes fit perfectly without any flaw. Your neck cloth is a work of art. And even with black hair and a dark complexion, I have never seen a cleaner-shaven man. People always wonder how you do it. Mr. Baldwin, my employer, is a dark man and by midday he almost has a beard."

While she described his features, Mr. Compton examined his face with his hand. He rubbed his chin. "Not so smooth now. I fear by the morning I *will* have a beard."

Celia gave into temptation and ran the tips of her fingers over the rough bristles forming on his jaw. "I like it," she said truthfully. "It makes you look a little like a pirate in a storybook."

"I'm pleased to hear it. The way you portray me makes me sound a blasted dandy. Did you just choke?"

She snatched away her hand. "Frog in my throat. I would never fall in love with a dandy."

"I wish I could say I remember any of this, but none of it seems familiar. What happened after I entered the ballroom?"

"You looked across the room and saw me. As soon as our eyes met I fell in love, and later you told me you had felt the same way. Although Mrs. Wilkinson—"

"Remind me, who is she?"

"Our hostess. Mrs. Wilkinson tried to present you

to other young ladies but you declined to meet anyone but me."

"That seems shabby behavior."

"I thought it excessively romantic. You asked me to stand up for the country dance and afterward you fetched us lemonade."

"What a thrilling entertainment."

"It was the most wonderful night of my life. The next day you called on me at Mr. Baldwin's and a week later we were betrothed."

"How could I afford to offer marriage? Are the Fishes a family of means? Where do they come from?"

Celia repressed a sigh of exasperation. Instead of being carried away by her tale of love at first sight, Mr. Compton insisted on asking a lot of boring, practical, and highly inconvenient questions, as though he were her father instead of her lover. Of course he wasn't her lover, but he didn't know that. She scrutinized a mental map of England for an area far from Yorkshire.

"Your home is in Cornwall. Near Falmouth, on the sea."

"A very suitable location for a family of Fishes. Are we big Fish or little Fish?"

"You told me your family is highly respected."

"But the question is, how big is the pond in which we swim? And how many are in the shoal? Am I an orphan Fish? An only Fish? Do I have living parents or close relations?"

"You never told me very much about your family," Celia said cautiously. "You must at least be acquainted with big fish in Cornwall. You have a promise of an excellent living near . . . Truro."

"Then why am I studying for the church in Yorkshire? It seems a long way to go. I should think I could find a situation closer."

He looked haughty again, reminding her that this was still Tarquin Compton, the toplofty terror of the *ton*. For a few minutes there she'd almost believed in Terence Fish, her charming half-dressed fiancé who made jokes about his own name. To avoid his inquisitive gaze, she shifted around and sat beside him, sharing the backrest of the sturdy tree trunk.

"I don't know why you came to the north, but I'm glad you did. Perhaps it was fate that we both ended up here. I lived in India until two years ago."

"How in the name of Zeus did you end up a governess in Yorkshire?"

Changing the subject from his invented life to her (mostly) true one had definite appeal. "It's a long story."

"Before you begin, we should decide whether to go any farther tonight. It will be dark in little more than an hour."

"My feet would prefer to stay here, yet they might be persuaded to walk another mile or two if there was a meal at the end of them." Her stomach growled horribly.

"I suppose nothing edible has magically appeared in that bag?" he asked.

She picked up the sack and peered in. "I can smell roast chicken. No, I'm mistaken. Just a pile of rags. And a cup."

Across the stream rolling moorland stretched for miles ahead. "I think," he said, "we should resign ourselves to fasting tonight. Here we have water, and the shelter of this tree. I also doubt we can cross the stream without getting our clothes wet and I'd rather do it in the morning when we have time to dry off." He reached for the bag. "Let me fill that cup."

Remembering the book, Celia retrieved the cup herself and thrust the bag behind her. "Here. Or let me." She stood and winced when her foot hit a stone.

"Are you injured? Let me look. You tended to my wounds, now let me return the favor." He knelt before her, his dark head bent low. His touch on her ankle gave her a shocking little tingle.

She pulled away her foot. "Thank you but there's no need. My feet are sore but no skin broken. I bathed them when I soaked the rag."

"A foot bath is an appealing idea. I'll go and do it now and fetch us some water. Will you give me a hand up?"

The touch of his fingers, the brush of his body as he stood, sent a tremor through hers. "I look forward to a serving of Eau de Yorkshire brook," she said hastily. "An excellent vintage, I am sure."

He smiled at her. "I'll be back in a few minutes. We'll toast our escape and our betrothal and then you can tell me the story of your life."

Celia had never seen Tarquin Compton smile. It made his harsh, characterful face appear incredibly handsome. As she settled back against the tree, she began to feel quite guilty for deceiving him. He was being such a good sport about their predicament. The thought of confessing her lies was daunting. It was bad enough to spend the night out in the wilds with an almost strange man. She had no doubt that if she confessed the truth now he would become an exceedingly angry man. Once they reached Mrs. Stewart's she'd have to tell him who he was, and hope the knowledge would bring back his memory. If not, her friend would find him a doctor and they could contact his relations.

"Ahem." The subject of her thoughts stood over her.

"That was quick," she said.

He looked sheepish, another expression new to Mr. Compton. "My boots fit so well I can't get them off. I daresay that's why the thief didn't take them with the rest of my clothing."

Naturally Tarquin Compton wouldn't be like lesser mortals, whose boots tended to wrinkle, or even sag, around the ankles. His were perfectly smooth, molding his calves almost to knee height.

"Let me try," she said. "Sit down."

Removing a man's footwear was an oddly intimate business. In the few hours spent in his company, nothing else had seemed more indecent. Absurd since when they met they'd both been half-naked. Even lying together, hiding from their pursuers, hadn't troubled her as much: it had been necessary. And at that point her indignation was still fresh while now her feelings toward him had shifted. She was still angry at Tarquin Compton but she found she almost liked Terence Fish. Avoiding his eyes, she knelt before him and yanked the proffered boot. She'd never felt such butter-soft leather.

"It won't budge," she said.

He leaned back and braced himself on his elbows. "Try now."

"Nothing. Not an inch. They fit like gloves."

He stood and offered her a hand to help her up. "I was afraid of that. We'll have to do it the other way." Celia didn't think she liked the glint in his eye.

Not far off he found a boulder of the right height. Once seated he extended a leg. "Straddle my knee. If you don't mind, of course." She minded all right, but it would be churlish to object. He did need to remove his boots. "Not like that. With your back to me." She was sure she didn't imagine the amusement in his voice.

Following his instructions required some adjustment of her "skirt." The blanket's tendency to slip had given her a good deal of annoyance during the long walk. When she got herself into position, balanced over his leg, she was aware of the view she presented of her bottom. This, she discovered, was only the beginning of her humiliation.

"Grasp the heel with both hands, and pull."

He hadn't thought to inform her he would be playing an active part in the proceedings. It came as a nasty shock when his other booted foot pushed against her rump. She shrieked. Seconds later she found herself on the ground, on her knees, clinging to one free boot.

She glared back at him. "Why didn't you warn me?"

"I thought you might not agree."

"I most certainly would not."

"It did the trick," he said with unbecoming smugness. "Now for the other."

"Very well," she said. "You are going to owe me a huge favor for this. Stretch out the other leg."

Just her luck that this one didn't come off as smoothly. It truly did seem molded to his limb. She tugged away, all the time aware of his stockinged foot braced against the small of her back, warm through the linen of her chemise. As she pulled she couldn't help but raise his leg so that it sawed between her thighs, giving her a funny feeling in her private parts.

"It's coming." She panted, whether from exertion or some other cause she'd rather not examine.

"Harder," he said.

With a groan she stiffened her spine, leaned against his thrusting foot, and put all her strength into one more effort. The boot released his ankle with a jolt and slid down the length of his calf.

Expecting the force of the release this time, she managed to land with a degree of grace. She pivoted and stood before him, offering the boot with a nod of the head and a curtsey. The dignity of the gesture was marred when her makeshift skirt loosed its shaky moorings and descended to the ground in a heap. He sat back and stared at her legs with unabashed interest.

Gritting her teeth, she pulled up the blanket and in her haste the hairpins, which had performed sterling work under adverse conditions, gave up and her hair descended around her shoulders. "Don't you dare laugh," she ground out.

It took some effort to comply, she could tell, but he managed. "I wouldn't dream of it. I promise you look no more absurd than I do, garbed like a yokel. If you'll excuse me, I'll go down to the stream now."

He lined the boots up neatly next to the boulder and, not forgetting the tin cup, sauntered down the grassy slope. When he reached the water he stripped off his stockings then discarded the linen smock. Quickly she turned away, then twisted her head for another look at the well-sculpted back. Embarrassed curiosity turned to fascinated mortification when he undid the buttons of his breeches. As the garment descended she whisked herself around. She needed to take care of her own needs during his absence.

After a quick trip behind a nearby bush, she returned to their oak tree and did her best to arrange her clothes and hair. Thriftily she retrieved every hairpin and stowed them in the seed bag. The sound of splashing told her Mr. Compton was occupied. A quick glance at the little book she'd picked up revealed no signature or other mark of ownership. The name of the so-called "celebrated author" Peter Aretin was unknown to her, but the title *The Genuine Amours* suggested a novel and a love story. She tucked her legs under her and began to read the tale, narrated in autobiographical fashion, of one Francis Featherbrain.

"Where did you get the book?" She hadn't even noticed his return. He must have bathed thoroughly. Damp hair clung to his scalp and he'd donned his smock over his wet torso. The cloth clung a little.

"It was on the ground near where I found you. If it was yours, the robber must have left it."

"Perhaps he isn't a lover of literature. What is it?"

"Only a novel. I just started it but it's quite dull so far. About a boy of fourteen, an only child, living in the country with his parents. Judging by his name he's not very intelligent."

"May I see?" She handed it over. A very odd expression crossed his face as he opened the volume to the title page.

"Do you recognize it?"

"No. I doubt it was mine."

His remark struck her as strange. If he couldn't remember his own name, why would he expect to recall possession of a book? She had the impression he was withholding something. "Give it back then."

"You promised to tell me about India," he said hastily.

"Very well. It's almost too dark to read, anyway. We may as well try to get comfortable."

Chapter 5

Things always seem better in the morning.
Unless there's nothing for breakfast.

Getting comfortable on rock-strewn Yorkshire soil proved difficult. Northern England was enjoying a rare, brief period of uninterrupted heat so Celia could dismiss her compunction at not offering to share her blanket. It occurred to her that as her betrothed husband, Mr. Compton, or rather Terence, might feel the urge to kiss her goodnight. Largely to her relief he made no such offer. While not actively repulsed by the idea, it made her shy. Spending the night alone with a man was contrary to anything she'd been taught of the proper conduct of an English lady.

Instead they lay in the deepening gloom, a few feet apart, and she told him the story of her life. The mostly truthful but carefully edited story. Mr. Baldwin remained her employer and never progressed to fiancé. And her childhood and youth in India, as the daughter of an East India Company officer, were described with much local color of a largely unsensational nature.

Fortunately Mr. Compton showed some curiosity about Indian life while asking not a single question about her widowed father's household. She'd become quite adept at skirting the issue since she arrived in England.

"My mother's sister married a gentleman from Lincolnshire," she explained. "After my father's death I sailed for England and arrived to discover my aunt had been dead a year. But my uncle, Mr. Twistleton, welcomed me. He sent me to London to come out under the wing of Lady Trumper."

He showed more interest than she would have liked in her truncated London season. She confined her account to public entertainments such as plays, the opera, and Hyde Park. Of particular private balls, a certain rude dandy, or his aunt the Duchess of Amesbury she said not one word.

"You mentioned you attended Almack's, so you moved in circles of high *ton*."

"My uncle was a man of influence and connection. He also implied I was to be his heiress. A respectable fortune, you know, will open many doors."

"How then did you end up a governess? Did you not receive offers?"

"There was a gentleman who showed interest, but it came to nothing." She feared she sounded like a sad spinster who'd lost her one chance at marriage. *Because,* she added silently, *a certain busybody of a dandy took it into his head to call me a cauliflower.* All her resentment returned in force.

Only to be disarmed by his gallant reply. "What a fool. But I suppose his hesitation was my good fortune."

How could this possibly be the same man?

She concluded the sad story of her brief, inglorious history as an heiress. "Soon afterward my uncle died and I was called home, before the season was over. He never changed his will and his entire fortune went to a cousin who had no connection to me. All I had was my London clothing. I sold most of it and looked for a post as governess."

He lay on his back and gazed at the stars, listening to the soft murmurs of the night on a cool breeze. Hunger, chill, and the hard ground weren't all that kept him awake. A few feet away lay his supposed betrothed wife, the quiet rhythm of her breathing letting him know she slept. Why not? She apparently had nothing to disturb her conscience.

His own doubts wouldn't allow his body and mind the rest they needed to recover from the demands of the day. Over and over he went through Celia Seaton's story, a sad tale narrated without a trace of self-pity. He couldn't help but be affected by the hardships and setbacks she'd endured, culminating in her apparently pointless disgrace and kidnapping. Tomorrow they might have to face the forces that threatened her.

But what most exercised his mind was the account of their meeting and courtship, which he distrusted with every fiber of his heart. A young, innocent girl, disappointed in love, would so easily believe the protestations of a man who claimed to have become enamored in a single glance across a country ballroom. He knew better. Men, he thought cynically, didn't think like that. Lust at first sight, perhaps; love, never. And neither was at all likely with this girl. True, her features were tolerable and her figure pleasing: breasts small but firm, a narrow waist and rather wide hips, but not ungracefully so, and those wonderful long legs. But she wasn't handsome enough to tempt Terence Fish.

Or whatever his name was.

Some things he'd seen or discussed seemed familiar, others not. Cornwall, for example, meant nothing to him. Yorkshire, he knew. The rugged landscape felt recognizable and somehow comfortable. Not surprising if he'd lived nearby for some months. But London he knew even better. There wasn't a site in the capital Celia had mentioned that failed to arouse a mental image. Even Almack's. It was strange enough that he had recognized the name of the assembly rooms, odder still that he knew them to be highly exclusive and he envisioned their appearance, inside and out.

Cornwall, however, was a blank. He could not believe he'd ever visited the place. Then this notion that he'd ever studied to be a parson was patently absurd. He shuddered at the thought of clerical dress and laughed at sermonizing. Not to mention his apparent taste for indecent novels. Celia might not recognize the name of Aretino but he did. If he had any scruples, he'd remove that volume from the bag and hide it, before she read some very shocking stories.

Scruples were something he feared he lacked. Judging by his behavior he suspected that he was an adventurer, winning Celia's confidence with an assumed name and false history. Why a female so lacking in worldly advantage would attract an adventurer was a mystery. But he couldn't ignore the fact that someone else was interested in her, someone who'd gone to considerable trouble to disgrace her in the eyes of her employer and kidnap her.

In his state of forgetfulness, his instinct was to assist and protect her from those who wished her ill. Once he recovered his identity, he would likely find himself their rival in infamy.

As he drifted off to sleep a deep memory emerged. Someone had once told him things, no matter how bad, would seem better in the morning. He didn't know who. His mother? A nurse? Was his mother alive? He'd have to ask Celia and hope he had told her the truth. He felt alienated enough with so much of his mind a blank. The fact that the one person who knew him, the one person he could cling to for sanity, might not know the truth of his identity, frightened and depressed him. Supposing he never regained his memory and spent the rest of his life living a lie?

It didn't matter who had voiced such optimism about the beneficial effects of a new day. It was the kind of folksy adage he instinctively dismissed.

And yet, roused from a few hours' sleep by an unharmonious concert of birdsong, his spirits lifted. It was a spectacular early dawn, all blue and green and pale misty sunlight, promising another scorching day. His head no longer ached and he felt at home.

How odd. Last night he would have sworn he was a Londoner.

He checked his memory. Nothing else had changed. Knowledge of anything personal remained shrouded in a mist thicker than that rising off the nearby brook. Celia, one cheek on the ground between outstretched arms and her hair spread about her, slept on despite the avian chorus. He wondered if she could be deaf in one ear.

Leaving her to rest, he went down to the stream to look for something edible. Was any wild fruit in season? He didn't know. Walking a few hundred feet along the bank he observed bubbles in the water, heard the splash of a jumping fish.

Fish. He might not be called Fish but he had no objection to eating them. Too bad he lacked rod and tackle. Then another memory, of the same vintage as the nursery platitude, sparked in his brain. Some yards farther on, the brook widened to a pool. The perfect spot.

On hands and knees he approached the tarn in dead silence, eyes searching the sun-dappled water. Brown shadows swayed in the depths. Trout. In a minute he found what he sought: a shallow rocky outcrop at the edge of the water, ideal for a drowsing fish; a telltale tail barely protruding.

It had been a long time, but he remembered.

Balanced on one elbow, he slipped his hand, fingers

turned up, into the water and under the rock until he felt the firm kick of the fish's tail. Then he began to tickle with his forefinger, gradually running his hand along the fish's belly further and further toward the head. The trout basked in the attention, dozing its way to doom. When his hand reached the gills, his fist closed like a trap, grasping the struggling creature, wrenching it out of its element.

Poor fish. It flapped helplessly on the grassy bank for a moment or two before he dashed its head on a rock and ended its happy life and brief misery.

Terence Fish, if that was indeed his name, spared it no pity. Whoever he was, he had been revealed as very useful sort of fellow. A man capable of providing breakfast for his sweetheart.

Celia wasn't appreciating the beauty of the morning. Finding herself alone, she panicked. Either Mr. Compton had recovered his memory and had abandoned her in a snit. Or worse (and she acknowledged it was worse) wandered off in a mindless haze and fallen over a precipice.

Her relief at his reappearance turned to rapture when she saw what he carried. She hadn't forgiven Tarquin Compton for comparing her to a large vegetable. Terence Fish was a man she could fall in love with.

And, if she said it herself, so aptly named.

"Breakfast," he announced.

"I always knew you were brilliant, Terence."

"Do you have to call me that?"

"It's your name."

"I don't like it."

"I could just call you Mr. Fish. Or Fishy."

"No, thank you."

"Terry?"

"Instead of amusing yourself with variations on my name, why don't you help me gather wood for a fire?" He faltered. "Do you know how to build a fire? I'm not sure I do."

"What do you think? I'm a governess."

"Is that a yes?"

"Yes. And put that fish somewhere safe. What a tragedy if some passing fox or weasel should steal it."

They took opposite directions along the bank and in short order collected the makings of a fire. Blessing the hot, rainless week, Celia gathered dry grass and struck the tinderbox. While she nursed the spark and blew carefully on a burgeoning flame, Mr. Compton contemplated the next step.

"Can you cook?"

"I'm a governess."

"I take it you mean yes again."

"Unfortunately this time I mean no. Governesses don't cook. In fact I've barely set foot in a kitchen in all my life."

"I thought young ladies were taught housewifely arts."

"Not in India. There's no shortage of servants there. Even the poorest English can afford them."

"That's a pity. Shall we eat the fish raw?"

She shuddered. "I'd much, much rather not."

"Nor me. Let's think about this."

"We can't just lay the fish in the fire. It would get all ashy, or burn."

"Hmm."

She looked up from her task of delicately feeding ever larger twigs to the flame. "Do you have an idea?"

"I've seen food cooked on a gridiron."

"Of course. How foolish of me not to think of that. And how lucky that we have a gridiron with us."

"There's no need for sarcasm. I'll see if I can cobble something together. Don't we have a knife?"

"In the bag."

Fifteen minutes later he returned with a very respectable gridiron, woven from the thick green stems of bulrushes. "It'll burn eventually but let's hope the trout will cook in the meantime. It is, unfortunately, not a very large fish. I wish for our sake it were a salmon."

"I could eat a whale."

"How's the fire?"

"A few more minutes and it'll be nice and hot."

Cross-legged on either side of the fire, they sat in companionable silence. Mr. Compton, it emerged, was a man who liked to think things through. With narrowed eyes he stared at his catch, laid out on the rush trellis. "I am envisioning a cooked fish on a plate," he said. "There's always a cavity in the bottom part." He pointed at the place. "There."

"You are right. I wonder why."

"Sometimes it's stuffed with something, but not

always. Even when there's no stuffing, the hole is still there." He made thinking noises. "Entrails. We need to remove the guts."

Despite acute hunger, Celia felt a little queasy. "We?" she asked. Was fish-gutting a woman's job? She'd made the fire but, to be fair, he'd caught the fish and worked out how to cook it. Should she offer?

"I'll do it by the stream so I can wash off the smell afterward," he said. Fishy or not, she would gladly have kissed him.

He poked it carefully with the point of the knife and found it white and flaky. "I do believe it's ready."

"I've never smelled anything so delicious in my whole life," she said.

"I cannot of course remember my whole life, but if I did I venture to guess I'd feel the same way. How shall we do this?"

Celia jumped up and plucked a couple of shiny dock leaves, shaking off pearls of dew. Despite their busy morning it was still very early. "Here are the plates. Will you do the honors?"

As though he were a jeweler cutting a precious diamond, he sliced into the humble trout, parting the flesh from the bones and dividing it evenly between the two green "plates," careful not to lose so much as a sliver.

Despite his hunger, he hesitated, seeking suitable words to mark the occasion. They were a couple betrothed to be married and this was the presumably the first time they'd shared breakfast, the most intimate of meals, à deux. To him at least it felt momentous, an irrational sentiment given his doubts about his own sincerity.

His suspicions of the night before returned and he again examined the woman with whom he had reportedly fallen in love at first sight. In the morning light the only new detail he could add to the picture of a lady neither plain nor pretty was the color and quality of her hair. Freed of its moorings and lit by the sun it was definitely more red than brown, but on the gingery side of Titian gold. And though he could hardly expect shining locks when she was out in the wilds without a comb, her hair, springing energetically from her head in wild kinks, probably never gleamed. And he liked to be able to run his fingers through a woman's silky tresses . . .

Yet while dispassionate examination told him she was nothing out of the ordinary, he had to admit she possessed a certain appeal, an almost animal energy that made her a perfect companion for an adventure in the wilds. Most women, he had a feeling, would not be enduring the situation with such equanimity. He found her to be quick-witted, humorous, and uncomplaining, three excellent qualities. But not qualities that were revealed at first sight. If she'd told him he'd fallen in love with her after a normal acquaintance he'd have believed it. But that meeting of strangers' glances across a crowded room was too far-fetched.

His scrutiny went on too long when food awaited the starving. She raised her brows—quite elegantly arched ones—in question. As befitted an aspiring parson, he murmured a quick grace. "Let's eat."

By silent mutual agreement they made it last, savoring each ambrosial mouthful. Only an occasional sigh of appreciation competed with the hum of insects and the occasional bird call. All too soon, the dock leaves were wiped clean. Celia eyed the carcass hungrily.

"Go ahead," he said.

"I'll split it with you." She snapped the spine and handed him half.

Following her example he sucked every flake of flesh from the bones. He couldn't believe he was doing anything so crude. When nothing was left they tossed the remains in the fire. He offered her the cup he'd filled with water from the brook and their fingers brushed. Their gazes met as they held the crude tin vessel between them. Time stopped.

" 'Drink to me only with thine eyes, And I will pledge with mine,' " he said softly.

" 'Or leave a kiss but in the cup, And I'll not look for wine.' " She capped the quotation in a throaty whisper. "Ben Jonson."

He remembered the title of the poem. " 'To Celia.' "

Her awkward laugh broke the spell. Their gazes parted and he relinquished the cup. "I always liked the poem," she said. "I imagined it was written for me."

"It's one of my favorites too."

"How do you know?"

"Just another of those things I recall. There's no pattern to it." He frowned. "I know I like poetry."

"So do I. I always read a lot of it."

"In India?"

"I never had much of an education but my father liked to read and ordered books from England."

"Do they have schools in India?"

"None that I ever attended. Until I was twelve we lived in Madras and I took lessons with the wife of another company official. My formal studies stopped at that point so I never learned to play or draw."

"How did you manage as a governess?"

"I was lucky to get a position in a family of boys who only needed reading, writing, and elementary figuring before they went to school."

She had been, he thought. Despite her season in London, her background in India had given her little of the knowledge usually required by a governess of well-bred English children.

"We should toast the trout," he said.

"To a most excellent, noble fish!" She took a draft and returned the cup to him.

"May he find a special place in watery heaven for sacrificing his life for the needs of others."

She laughed. "Much choice he had. Yet I do wish him well in the afterlife, for that was easily the best meal I ever had."

"Let's hope we have another one soon."

She stood up and pointed. "You see that hill? I predict that a delicious dinner awaits us just over the ridge."

Chapter 6

The way to a lady's heart is through her stomach.

C rossing the stream presented a problem. They had to walk several hundred yards in each direction before they discovered shallows they could ford without soaking their clothing. As it was, his pantaloons were wet below the knee. On the positive side, he cheerfully ignored her request to look away and enjoyed another glimpse of Celia's legs when she removed the blanket to make the crossing.

It proved impossible to get his boots back on and he lacked the incentive to try very hard. The blister on his heel was sore and he couldn't think of a way to have Celia help him that would involve her raising her bottom to him. Seeing her like that, vainly trying to suppress her indignation, was his favorite moment on the journey so far. The view had been nice too.

So he stuffed them into the sack which he, like a gentleman, insisted on carrying. In his own mind he needed to brush up his gentlemanly credentials because, as he wrestled with the footwear, one of those visions flashed through his mind: a well-appointed shop staffed by the most superior of tradesmen; plaster casts of his feet; obsequious attention to his demands; the magical name of Hoby, boot maker to the *haut ton*. He began to fear he was no gentleman. On the other hand he might be a *nobleman*. A member of the aristocracy up to no good.

The hill grew steeper, the sun higher and hotter. The day that had started so well descended into sullen discomfort. What should have been an hour or two's brisk walk stretched out as they picked their way, bare-footed, through prickly shrubs over the rocky moor. Judging by the sky it was near noon when they reached the top of the hill. Celia let out a brief moan of disappointment at the sight of unrelieved gorse, grass and rocks disappearing into the horizon.

"I was wrong," she said. "There's nothing to eat here."

"I can't tell you how sorry I am."

"Not as sorry as I." She smiled without humor. "I hate to be wrong."

"Somehow I guessed that."

"You don't like it, either."

"Do I not?" He frowned. "I don't feel like the sort of person who insists on being right."

"Well, you are."

She rubbed the soles of each foot against the opposite calf, looking comically annoyed as she hopped from one to the other. With a sigh, for the dozenth time that morning, she adjusted the blanket that served as her skirt. "This wretched thing won't stay up and the cloth is scratchy."

"Let's sit and rest for a few minutes," he said, drawing her down onto an unbrambly patch of grass. "Perhaps later we'll find a stream and I can tickle another fish."

Hugging her knees, she glared at the endless moors. Oddly, the discontented expression suited her: with the strong bone structure of her face she looked haughty and handsome while the pout of her generous mouth had him thinking about kisses again. He found her perfectly justified ill-temper endearing.

"I'm sorry I am grumpy," she said after a few minutes. "I'm footsore but you must be too. How's your head?"

"Still empty but it doesn't ache anymore."

"I'm hungry again. That trout wasn't very large and I ate nothing all day yesterday, either, except a bite of breakfast."

"I'm sorry," he said and put an arm about her shoulder with no intention to do other than comfort. She stiffened under his touch, confirming his impression that their relations had included little physical contact.

"Many have suffered far worse than a missed meal and a blister or two," she said briskly. He could imagine her addressing her charges thus. Whatever she might say, he'd wager she was an excellent governess. "I just remembered something my ayah said, my Indian nurse. When we eat and drink the water and food of a place, we draw strength from the land."

"In that case, what are we waiting for? That one small

trout must have imbued us with the vigor of giants. We should be able to walk all day."

Then her face changed. Her mobile features registered every shift in emotion, though he couldn't always interpret them. "I forgot. She said it's the food of our *home* that gives us strength. Indians like to eat food from home, even when they travel."

"Is India your home?"

"I was born there and lived there most of my life," she said. "But I don't think I really belonged. How could I? How could any English? It isn't our country."

"I don't think that fact troubles the East India Company, or the British government."

"No. In fact many of the English try and build their own little corners of England on Indian soil. From what my father told me, their efforts can be quite comical, given the climate."

"You didn't live like that?"

"After we moved from Madras my father's situation was obscure. We saw very few English."

He wanted to probe further but something told him, not for the first time, that she found the topic of her life there distressing. She had, after all, lost both her parents in that distant land. "Where is home, then?" he asked.

"Not Lincolnshire. I only spent a few weeks at my uncle's house and since he died there's nothing for me there. I've been in Yorkshire for a year so it must be home." She shook off the air of melancholy that had settled on her when they spoke of her past. "Splendid.

I've had half a fish and a cup of water. I should be ready to walk ten or twenty miles today."

"It won't do *me* much good. I'll have to work hard to keep up with you. I'd have to have brought something from Cornwall, wouldn't I?"

For a moment he thought she was going to argue with him. That one of her expressions he knew, because he'd seen it before. Instead she shrugged. "So you would. Perhaps you could eat those boots."

Idiot. Celia had been about to contradict him, tell him that he was at home. For as she spoke she remembered something about Mr. Tarquin Compton. The Duchess of Amesbury had commended him to her London chaperone with the information that his estates were in Yorkshire, not far from the duke's secondary residence. She'd implied that the duke's sister had made something of a misalliance when she'd wed Mr. Compton's father. At the time Celia had found it amusing that the duchess was apparently the only person in London to speak of the reigning dandy with what bordered on contempt. Of course the duchess hardly accorded her, Celia, much respect, either. But that was to be expected. Anyway, the fact that the Duchess of Amesbury despised her nephew wasn't relevant. What mattered was that her companion was a Yorkshireman, unlike any inhabitant of the doughty county she'd ever met, but nonetheless a local. He must have been visiting his lands when he was robbed.

Perhaps they were even on his lands. The first person they met might recognize him and her lies would be exposed. She watched him stand and survey the rolling moorland, fearing every second he would recognize a landmark and come to his senses. He stroked his chin thoughtfully. As he'd predicted, dark bristles covered his jaw. She found the disheveled, faintly disreputable appearance far more attractive than the sleek perfection of his other self.

"I believe I see smoke," he said. "Some distance off, but the air is so clear now I don't think it's mist. There must be a house or a village over that rise."

With mixed feelings and because there was, after all, nothing else to do, Celia agreed they should head in that direction. Perhaps she faced exposure the other side of the hill, but why expect the worst? They might find a square meal and directions to her destination.

Civilization at last!

Of a kind. It wasn't a village, or even much of a hamlet: a handful of small gritstone houses nestled in a shallow vale, a shepherding community judging by the white blobs that dotted the surrounding fields. There was no inn and it was likely several miles to the nearest mail stop or post road. Nevertheless, someone there should be able to point them in the right direction. Perhaps they could even beg a ride in a cart with the promise of reward at the other end. Celia assured him that Mrs. Stewart would take care of things. Best of all, the inhabitants there, however poor and rustic, had to eat.

A disadvantage of livestock was the gifts of dung they left in the fields. By the time they scrambled over the last stone wall at the end of the village street—if the single narrow earthen track could be so dubbed—his feet were soiled by substances he'd rather not identify. He wondered if the place would run to the comfort of a hot bath. Without ready money it seemed unlikely. Still, he was prepared to exercise the considerable powers of persuasion that instinct told him he possessed.

He never had the chance.

A small child emerged from one of the buildings, stared at the pair of them, and started to cry.

"Gypsies, Ma!" the urchin shrieked.

Half a dozen doors burst open to release a crowd of women, children, a couple of men, and several dogs. All were barking, shouting (the people) and waving sticks (again the people). At them.

"Be gone! You dirty heathens."

"Stealing varmints."

"Horse thieves!" That one rankled.

He made one attempt at reasonable discourse. "Good people, we are not Gypsies. We are the victims of robbery."

The dictum that a soft word turneth away wrath was proven eminently false.

"Set the dogs on them!"

The dogs, each one large and loud with enormous teeth, didn't need any setting. At least six were headed in their direction.

He grabbed Celia's hand. "Run!"

He learned that he could run fast and so could she. Only a slight moderation of his pace was needed and she kept up. Not that the hounds snapping at their heels couldn't have caught them. But once clear of the hamlet their owners called them back. No one was looking for trouble.

Celia collapsed on the grass, emitting great gasps of breath. She'd done well but with the danger passed she appeared to be suffering an attack of the vapors. Perhaps she was terrified of dogs. Kneeling, he took one shoulder in a firm grasp and raised her chin with his other hand. "Listen, my dear. We are safe now. The dogs have gone."

She shrieked. With laughter. She was *laughing*.

"What, may I ask, is so amusing about our current predicament? I for one am disappointed not to be enjoying a meal, a bath, and a carriage."

That set her off even worse. He sat back on his heels, stared at the sky, and waited for the restoration of her wits. A final splutter, a quick back of the hand over her wet eyes, and she looked almost rational. He raised an eyebrow. "Yes?"

"It's you. Being mistaken for a Gypsy. It's so funny."

"Not just I. You were too."

"But I am a kind of Gypsy, if you think about it. A wanderer, anyway. But not you. You are such a very proper man."

He still didn't understand what merited such excessive mirth. Mildly amusing, he'd call it, at best. Even if he were a very proper man, a fact he had every reason to doubt.

She stood up. "Come on, Terence, let's go."

By Zeus, he hated that name. But until his memory returned it was the only one he had.

Chapter 7

Beware of Greeks following bloodhounds.

Nick Constantine despised the countryside. He been born in a Greek village and once he reached London, after a few years' detour around the oceans as a sailor on a ship of dubious legality, he'd left the comfort of fog and pavement as rarely as possible. The Governor had brought him to this benighted part of northern England for what promised to be an easy job. How hard could it be to snatch and rob a governess?

But everything had gone wrong. He blamed the rolling moors and rocks and endless green stuff. The way he figured it, if God had intended man to live in the wilderness, He would never have created pavement. The Governor, of course hadn't come with him on the chase. He'd stayed comfortable at the inn, enjoying the local ale, while Nick did the dirty work. That was the Governor's way.

They walked for hours behind the hideous, sniffing, slobbering dog and his boots hurt. The trail from the cottage led them to a deep brook. The bloodhound appeared baffled.

"He can't smell naught. Reckon she must have gone in the water," Hobbs said. To add insult to injury, Nick had been landed with a local as a guide, a rustic with an almost impenetrable brogue. "Give him that hankie again. See if the man was still with her."

With great reluctance Nick pulled the handkerchief from his pocket again. Oversized and of the finest cambric, he expected to get several shillings for it when he found a customer with the initial C. He didn't want any canine tooth marks reducing its value.

The dog drooled on the linen square and took off along the bank, downstream.

"He's got the scent," said Hobbs. "Happen we'd have her by now if she didn't have the fellow with her."

Nick didn't need to hear any cheek from Hobbs. He'd taken enough grief from the Governor when they arrived at the cottage and found her gone. The ruby wasn't in her baggage and Nick reckoned she'd lost it long ago. But the Governor wanted to question her himself.

He had not been amused when he learned she now had a companion.

Yet Nick couldn't regret robbing the gentry cove that had come to the door. He'd got a fine horse, a fat purse, a gold watch, and some first-rate togs out of the deal. If the handkerchief could be sold for shillings, the coat and waistcoat were worth pounds. Too bad he hadn't been able to get the boots off. They might have fit him, better than his own. His only slip-up was leaving the man alive. He wouldn't make that mistake again.

The stupid animal lumbered up and down the bank several times until they found a place that looked fordable. Crossing the stream ruined his damn boots, but on the other side they picked up the trail again.

Chapter 8

Never underestimate the importance of cheese.

A t least, she remarked cheerfully, it was a road of sorts. And a road must eventually lead somewhere. It wouldn't make any sense to build one otherwise.

Mr. Compton informed her that English roads, except those built by the Romans, derived from cow paths, thus their meandering habit. And since he didn't put much credence in the logical powers of female cattle, he wouldn't be surprised if this particular rutted, weed-infested trail led them over a cliff to their deaths.

She pointed out, with the brilliant logic of female humans (a trait she specifically mentioned), that since they were on the Yorkshire moors and nowhere near the sea, there weren't any cliffs for them to fall over.

He gave her the distinct impression that, though he was too polite to mention it, he would be happy to assist her in her descent should they find themselves in the vicinity of, say, Dover, a place famous for cliffs.

To put it bluntly, Mr. Compton was out of sorts,

grouchy even. She wasn't quite sure why. Not that being hungry, dirty, and chased by vicious dogs wasn't enough to try a man's temper. But she thought something else had upset him and nobly forbore from nettling him. A shame because, even when grouchy, Mr. Compton was fun to spar with. It would have made the journey go faster. Instead she plodded on in silence, thinking about every meal she'd ever eaten and wishing she'd appreciated them more at the time.

They'd barely exchanged a word in an hour when they reached a crossroads.

"Any preference?" he asked.

"I wish we had any idea which way is Stonewick. We may be going in the opposite direction."

"Very likely."

At that moment they heard the clop of hooves coming toward them. "Shall we hide?" she whispered. "It may be the kidnappers."

He straightened his back, folded his arms, and frowned. "If it is, I am not in the mood to run. I have a few questions I'd like answered."

That seemed rash to Celia, who had no desire to face even one man with a gun, let alone two or more. On the other hand it might be a harmless stranger who could help them. The lack of a suitable hiding place decided her. She took up position beside him in the road and tried to imitate his fighting stance, learned, no doubt, at Gentleman Jackson's Bond Street Saloon, and the way he brandished his fists.

"Thumbs out," he murmured. "On second thought, if it comes to a fight, leave it to me."

He looked very dangerous with his dark eyes and darkening jaw. Perversely, Celia found the situation exciting.

The horse came closer and rounded a curve into view. It was almost a disappointment when a cart followed. The driver wore a rustic smock, similar to that worn by Mr. Compton, but there all resemblance to either her kidnapper or her companion ceased. Fair, thinning hair, long whiskers and a red shiny face topped the largest man Celia had ever seen. Even Mr. Compton was dwarfed by him. Though he might not be taller, he was twice as broad. She hoped very much it wouldn't come to fisticuffs. She feared this giant would pound poor Mr. Compton to pulp.

"Not him," she murmured. "I've never seen him. But may I suggest I do the talking? *Good people, we are not Gypsies.*" She mimicked his condescending tones.

Mr. Compton smiled. "Be my guest. I can't wait to see you apply the common touch."

"Good afternoon, sir," she said with a friendly wave.

The giant made a noise. His horse understood and stopped. "Afternoon."

She smiled. "Fine day."

"Aah."

"Would you be good enough to tell us how to reach Stonewick. Is it far?"

He scratched his balding pate while he gave the

matter some thought. Like many Yorkshiremen, he seemed a man of few words. He did, however, have eyes and they were surveying her person with noticeable interest. She tugged at her shift to make sure it covered both shoulders and tried to lengthen the blanket to cover her ankles.

After a lengthy perusal he glanced at Mr. Compton, whom he found less worthy of examination, then back at Celia. He scratched his shoulder.

"East."

"You mean Stonewick is to the east?"

"Aye." He pointed to one of the four roads.

"If we take that road will we reach Stonewick?"

"Maybe."

"How far is it?"

The question provoked him to eloquence. "Don't rightly know."

"Do you have any idea? I'm sure you must know the moors very well."

"Over Revesby way." She gave him an encouraging smile. "Ten, fifteen miles mayhap."

"Oh dear! That is a long way. Do you know anyone who could drive us?"

He thought some more and scratched some more, his stomach this time. "Nay. But I can take you partway."

"Oh, would you? How kind? Shall we get in the cart?"

The giant looked at Mr. Compton and waved his thumb. "Him in the back. You ride with me."

As she sat squeezed next to the driver on the bench,

Celia's nostrils were overpowered by a smell she preferred to identify only as rural. To be fair her own scent was likely less than fragrant.

"I am Celia and that's Terence back there," she said, trying to speak and breathe through her mouth at the same time. "What's your name?"

"Joe."

"Are you married, Joe?"

"Nay."

"Do you have a sweetheart?"

"Nay."

"Do you have a farm?"

"Aye."

"A sheep farm?"

"Twenty sheep in t' flock."

"So many! Do you have many lambs? I love lambs."

Terence grasped the sides to save himself from being bruised black and blue by the jouncing cart and listened to Celia prattle on to their laconic host. He hoped the oaf wasn't misinterpreting her interest in him. He hadn't failed to notice a gleam of interest in Joe's eyes. Women, he guessed, weren't in plentiful supply out here on the moors. Then something riveted his attention: a wheel of cheese, resting in a pile of straw next to him.

Ask him about food. He willed her to hear his thoughts as his stomach clenched.

After a while Joe ventured an inquiry of his own. "You Gypsies?"

"No indeed. Terence, Mr. Fish, is a gentleman. We are escaping from an evil villain. A *foreigner.*"

Joe responded with a grunting noise that might have been sympathy, but more likely dismissal of anyone born outside the North Riding of Yorkshire.

"That's why we need to reach my friend at Stonewick. We've been walking for a day and a night and had almost nothing to eat. Do you think you could spare us some supper?"

In his lengthiest communication so far, Joe allowed that he could, if they came to his cottage.

"Oh, thank you! Joe." Celia patted the giant's arm.

Terence's mouth watered even as he wondered how they'd pay for their meal. Perhaps Joe would like an erotic novel. That would be a handy way to dispose of it before Celia got to the good bits.

Joe's horse was built for endurance, not for speed. The sun had almost descended by the time they reached his cottage, an isolated cote similar in size and design to the site of Celia's imprisonment. The dwelling and a small barn in matching stone were set in a walled barnyard in which a few mangy chickens scratched among the weeds in dusty earth.

Celia jumped down from the cart. "What a fine place, Joe. And you have a well in the barnyard. Do you mind if we draw some water to drink?"

While Joe unharnessed the horse and led it out to pasture, they conferred over a thirst-quenching bucket.

"Will you stop making up to that fellow?" Terence said, keeping his voice low. "Lord knows what he thinks."

"I'm doing nothing of the kind! I'm being nice to

him. You may not have much notion of agreeable conversation, but I do. Please note that Joe has brought us
part of our way in comfort."

"Some comfort!"

"And is going to provide us with food." A look of
something like ecstasy lit her features. "Did you notice
the cheese? Thanks to me, we have a chance of getting
a good slice of it."

"How much remains to be seen when he realizes we
have no money."

"Joe won't charge us. He's a sweet man!"

"Joe is a Yorkshireman."

His own instinct that he knew a good deal about
Yorkshire was confirmed when Joe, having produced
a loaf of bread, a good wedge of cheese, and half a
dozen wrinkled apples, asked for a shilling. Informed
by Celia, in her sunniest tones, that they had no coin, the
farmer prepared to return the provisions to his larder.

Before Celia could begin to weep—the agony on her
face far surpassed anything he'd so far observed—Terence entered negotiations. As expected, Joe was unim-
pressed by *The Genuine Amours of Peter Aretin*. Pity.
He'd probably enjoy the book, if he could read it.

Which left one pair of gentleman's boots, possibly
made by Hoby and certainly costing more than a shilling. More than many, many shillings. Not practical
footwear for farm life, and Joe's feet were enormous.
But even in a small market town they'd fetch a guinea
or two.

Celia held her breath as Joe subjected the stylish

footwear to a careful examination. Finally he nodded, but she couldn't contain a moan of grief when Joe removed three apples from the pile and brandished his knife to cut the cheese wedge in half. Mr. Compton, proving himself a canny Yorkshireman when it came to bargaining, pushed the blade so only a sliver would be lost. After some back-and-forth they settled on three quarters of the original amount. The loaf of bread remained intact. He stowed the bounty into the sack as Joe described a shortcut over the moors that would bring them to Stonewick. But before they could take leave of their host, they heard the bay of a hound from the direction of the road, echoed by a furious bark from Joe's sheepdog.

"Strangers." Joe muttered the single word with a ferocious frown.

Celia's heart sank at the word. She might be wrong but she had a premonition about a visit that, judging by Joe's face, was unusual. She seized the countryman's arm and spoke in a fast near-whisper.

"Can we hide? It may be the foreigner I told you about."

Mr. Compton flexed his fists. Joe appeared undecided.

"Please, Joe," she said urgently. "He wants to capture me again. He'll take me away if you don't help us."

"Go in the barn."

Chapter 9

*Though not the best manners, sometimes
you have to hit and run.*

Not a moment too soon they pulled the barn door
closed. Agreeing in sign language, she climbed
a ladder to a hay loft, Mr. Compton following behind,
his body crowding her up the narrow wooden ladder. In
case Joe proved incapable of fobbing off their pursuers,
they burrowed into the hay.

It was dark and cool and the hay smelled fresh and
sweet. They lay on their sides, Mr. Compton behind
her with one arm draped loosely over her waist. They
seemed cut off from the world, the distant melody of
birdsong and their soft breathing the only sounds. She
was acutely sensible of his beating heart, his chest
pressed against her back.

A cacophony of barking dogs and flapping hens shattered the stillness, then a counterpoint of male voices.
Celia strained to hear through the open window of the
loft and sensed Mr. Compton angle his head for the
same reason.

Her instinct had been good. A familiar, slightly exotic voice asked—rather rudely—if a man and a woman, scantily clad, had passed that way. Thieving Gypsies, they were. Celia smiled. The man had no idea how to manage Joe. Predictably he received no answer at all.

The other man spoke for the first time, revealing a local accent and a better notion of how to make friends and gain information. "Our hound lost the scent at the crossroads. Followed you then. There's a half crown for you if you tell where they'rt."

Joe hemmed and hawed. "Might remember for five shilling."

"Three."

"Four."

A pause. "Four then, but only if your news is worth it."

"The brass first," Joe said. "I know where."

Mr. Compton's arm tightened, heavy and comforting. His whisper buzzed in her ear. "Stay up here and let me do the fighting."

A moment's silence as Celia imagined rather than heard the clink of coins.

"I were driving home. Met Farmer Thorpe coming from crossroads. Man and a lass in his cart. Never seen them before. Reckon they be the ones."

"And where's Thorpe's place?"

"Over to Bracewell."

Their release of tension was mutual and simultaneous. So were their movements. Somehow she was on her back in the hay and he lay over her. A flutter of excitement rippled under her ribs. His mouth came down on hers.

She'd never been kissed before. Bertram had too much respect for her to take liberties beyond a salute on the back of her hand. She had imagined it a static experience, a mere meeting of stationary mouths. Instead his lips were warm and firm and very alive, nibbling at her own, coaxing her to open and admit the hot mist of his breath. Initial uncertainty quickly turned to pleasure. What a lovely feeling it was! She moved her own lips in return.

Good heavens! His probing tongue came as a shock, but one soon adjusted to. Caressing inside her mouth, it set up a tingling that somehow shot to her breasts, her hardening nipples, down through her torso and lower.

More than the physical reactions, delicious as they might be, kissing Mr. Compton gave her a feeling of intimacy, of knowledge of the man at a deeper level than the little she knew of his real person, or the false one she'd invented.

Tarquin. No, Terence. And her pleasure was marred by a twinge of genuine guilt, the worst she'd suffered, that she had robbed him of his identity.

She thrust aside such inchoate thoughts. Leaning back into the bed of hay, she sensed her whole body soften, almost melt with blissful sensation. Without conscious knowledge, she parted her lips, welcoming his invasion. Her entire body relaxed into openness, ready for whatever came next.

What came next was a banging at the barn door. With a muttered oath Terence pulled back onto all fours. She lay still, staring at him, her brain void of a single sensible thought. He settled back on his heels and offered a hand to pull her up, then brushed off her hair and shoulders.

With trembling fingers she removed a handful of hay that clung to the crown of his head. "More of a scarecrow than a pirate now," she murmured.

"And what do you think you look like?" Pale golden rays from the late afternoon sun came through the window, caught the swirling dust and lit his features. He smiled at her with an unguarded expression, perhaps a tender one. Her heart turned over. She cupped his bristly jaw and gazed into his eyes, trying to read the message in their basalt depths.

Then the barn door opened to admit a bath of light. "You can come down now," Joe said. "They've gone." She lowered her hand.

"Thank you, Joe," she said, once they'd returned to the barnyard. "You saved us." And gave his beefy arm a grateful squeeze.

"They'll be right busy in Bracewell. Half the folks there are Thorpes."

"That's very clever!"

"We are most grateful for your assistance," Terence said, holding out his hand. "We should be on our way."

Joe ignored the hand. "I have coin now."

"That was clever of you, too," Celia said, "to make them pay you for false information."

"I'll give you three shilling," Joe said. What a kind man, she thought, determined to reward him well once she had the means. He pulled the coins from his pocket and offered them to Terence. With his other hand he grasped her lower arm. "Three shilling and I keep the woman."

Well, really! He didn't even offer the full four shillings. Was that all she was worth? She couldn't believe she'd been so mistaken in her gentle giant.

Terence seemed less flabbergasted than she by this turn of events. He stepped forward and pulled her away from Joe. "The lady is not for sale."

Joe grinned. They already knew he enjoyed a negotiation. "Three and sixpence," he offered.

"I'm afraid I am unable to oblige you, at any price." Terence drew her close. He sounded as disinterested as Tarquin Compton refusing a glass of wine offered by a footman.

"Three and six and the boots."

"No."

"And more cheese." Joe's brow wrinkled with pain as Terence shook his head. "Four shilling then."

"I'm sorry, but Celia is my woman and she stays that way." She felt a little thrill of joy at being so claimed, at the sinewy strength of his arm about her waist.

His staunch refusal baffled Joe. He applied his powers of persuasion to her instead. "See what I have." A sweep of his arm indicated the scope of his riches which were, to a country fellow, quite considerable. Come to think of it, they were quite considerable to her, too, her worldly value being precisely nothing. Half seriously she contemplated his offer. It wouldn't be the first time she'd accepted a proposal for mercenary reasons.

"You can have the chickens for your own," he coaxed.

Bertram had proposed to her because he had four sons to care for. A handful of chickens was a less burdensome gift, but still required attention. Why did men never offer her anything that came without responsibilities?

She looked at Joe's ruddy complexion and rotting teeth, thought about kissing him, and shuddered. She breathed the odor of the sheep that she guessed sometimes shared his living quarters. When she accepted Bertram Baldwin's proposal he hadn't been a handsome man, nor was he young. But he did bathe.

"I'm sorry, Joe," she said softly. "Thank you, but I don't love you and I don't believe I could." She leaned into the shelter of Terence's less earthy embrace.

Joe's eyes shrank, slitted and blue in the florid folds of flesh. They surveyed the dandy's trim figure, lingering below the waist. He no longer looked friendly. When compared to the farmer's beefy shoulders, barrel chest and massive thighs, Terence, even at some inches over six feet, seemed puny. "You'll be better with me. He's but a small man, happen with a tiddly little pillock."

Celia clapped a hand over her mouth; though unfamiliar with the phrase, she guessed its meaning and intent. Terence gave a snort of laughter. Immediately she knew that was an unwise reaction.

"I'll fight you for her!"

Showing no sign of a very sensible terror at the prospect of engaging a man who outweighed him by several stone, Terence bent his knuckles and studied his fingernails. "You'd better get out of the way, my dear," he said in a bored tone.

With a bullish bellow Joe charged. Considering and abandoning the idea of getting between the combatants, Celia stepped back, shut her eyes, and resigned herself to the demise of Tarquin Compton, alias Terence Fish, and her own future as Mrs. Joe.

A crack, a groan, and a crash followed in quick succession. When she dared look she saw Joe flat on his back and completely still.

"My goodness! How did you do that?"

Terence rubbed his knuckles. "I am an extremely skilled pugilist."

"I had no idea. Did you?"

"Not until just before I hit him. Did I never mention to you that I was in the habit of boxing?"

"Not that I can recall."

"Odd."

"Perhaps you decided to give it up when you became a clergyman. Fighting is not a suitable occupation for a man of the cloth."

"Perhaps," he said.

"Shall we leave, or do you think we should do something for poor Joe?"

"Poor Joe tried to buy you from me. I shouldn't feel too sorry for him." He bent over and felt the fallen farmer's pulse, eliciting a faint moan. "He'll be fine. Let's go before he wakes up." He picked up the sack containing the wonderful, precious food.

Chapter 10

However much you've learned from
books, reality can still surprise.

Celia had spent quite a lot of time over the past year feeling sorry for herself. But real hunger and not knowing where her next meal would come from lent perspective to her misfortunes. There were many people in the world—and she'd seen hordes of them in India—far worse off. She and Mr. Compton savored each bite of their meal, and prudently refrained from wolfing down every crumb. Enough remained for tomorrow, even though she felt pleasantly full and reasonably clean.

Terence wandered downstream in search of another trout pool. Whoever would have imagined the elegant man about town would be such a competent countryman, or such a brilliant fighter? Shamefully, she'd found the moment when Joe crashed to the ground exciting.

And then there was the kiss. Neither said one word about it as they trudged another hour or two over the hills in the long summer evening. Nor over bread and cheese. Yet the knowledge of that intimate encounter hung heavy between them. She'd found herself staring at his lips as he bit into an apple, and recalling their texture against her own. Perhaps it meant little to him; after all he must have kissed many women and it wasn't as though she was a beauty. Of course he couldn't remember any of those others. She tried to remember if she'd ever heard any whispers about Tarquin Compton's amorous exploits. The fact that she couldn't meant he probably didn't dally with ladies. He probably consorted with women of the demimonde, beautiful and alluring.

Perhaps he had been carried away by proximity and would have kissed any woman with whom he'd been buried in the hay. Worse still, he might have felt he *had* to kiss her, because they were betrothed.

That line of thought was likely to make her feel sorry for herself again. Looking for something to divert her thoughts, she remembered the novel. What could be better than to curl up on the ground under her blanket and follow the adventures of Francis Featherbrain, which must surely be about to improve after a slow start.

He goes for a walk. Yawn. He meets the vicar's wife. He walks and talks with the vicar's wife. Even Celia's life hadn't been this dull. Surely *something* would happen soon.

The vicar's wife wears scarlet fringed petticoats. Now that was unusual.

Oh my goodness! And scarlet silk garters! Celia's eyes popped as she read the consequence of this discovery: "I put both my legs between hers . . ."

Celia's knowledge of mistresses wasn't confined to the forbidden gossip of well-brought-up English virgins. Although it was a fact she'd been frequently told to forget, she'd shared a house with her father's native Indian consort. The nature of her upbringing had made her informed about relations between a man and a woman, yet she couldn't help being fascinated by the details. She felt a thrill of recognition at reading about the lady's "coral bud of sensuality." It came as a disappointment to discover that the youthful protagonist merely dreamed the encounter. She began the next chapter eager to discover if young Mr. Featherbrain managed to "swive" outside of his imagination.

Peter Aretin, whom she assumed was the author, was no master of English prose. As she read about Francis's enrollment at Eton, his lodgings, and his study of the Latin classics, she quickly became bored and skipped to where he became interested in his landlord's daughter and a maidservant. To the former he promises marriage.

Don't believe him! she wanted to shriek. *He may swear eternal love but he has been spying on you while you undress. There's only one thing he wants from you.* She was right, of course. Over the poor girl's protestations he sat her on the edge of a table and . . . oh dear! Amazingly she ended up enjoying it. *Her critical period arrived sooner than I expected. A tremulation possessed her whole frame—her eyeballs rolled as if convulsed, and her eyelids quivered, shook, opened and shut . . .*

Celia tossed aside the book in disgust. The villain

had seduced the unfortunate girl with promises that must surely be false. Featherbrain was a gentleman and never going to marry the daughter of a tradesman. And then, when the girl had very sensibly resisted his blandishments, he'd taken her against her will. To Celia's mind the encounter was very close to ravishment, despite the girl's eventual pleasure.

How could Terence—Mr. Compton—possess such a dreadful book? Was it really his?

Of course it was, hence his peculiar demeanor when he'd found her reading it before. He'd known exactly what it was. She ought to get rid of it, bury it in the ground perhaps. And yet . . . it intrigued her, despite, or perhaps because of the crude unfamiliar vocabulary and exact descriptions of private acts. Reading it made her feel hot and needy and damp between the thighs. She had enjoyed "critical periods" through her own ministrations, but reading about them provoked by the attentions of a man made her hungry for knowledge.

One thing was certain. She couldn't let Terence know she'd been reading the book. Her face burned. Having buried it in the bottom of the sack, under the food, she walked the short distance to the brook. A little cold water on her glowing cheeks wouldn't go amiss.

It felt good on her feet, too, sore from two days walking barefoot. She left her blanket skirt on the bank and wore only her shift, now a little grimy. She'd like to rinse it but recoiled from being left with only the blanket for coverage.

The shallow water ran swift, throwing up spray as

it divided about the larger rocks in the streambed. She amused herself hopping from stone to stone, tickling her toes in the foam. Rounding a gentle curve that had been concealed by a stand of bushes, she stopped dead.

She'd had occasion to admire Terence's bare chest. Nothing had prepared her for the sight of the whole man in his naked perfection, standing in midstream. Breathless she watched the contours of thighs and buttocks clench as he bent to scoop water between his palms. Then the muscles of his shoulders and back came into play as he raised one arm and splashed water down its length, rubbing the armpit and shoulder with circular motions of the other hand. He repeated the motion on the opposite side and her throat went dry.

Her feet clung to a damp boulder but she couldn't retain her balance and she teetered, arms flailing. She tried to do it quietly and managed to remain upright, but made the tiniest splash as one foot landed in water. He turned to face her.

Hastily he lowered his hands over his groin but not before she was able to confirm, with some surprise, that Joe had been correct. Tarquin Compton, though unusually tall, had a tiddly little pillock. Not that she had any basis for comparison, but based on her recent reading she would have expected it to be larger. Stammering and blushing she took to her heels, floundering back upstream and out of sight and giving him, she feared, a good view of her retreating bottom.

Terence already knew Celia had beautiful legs and when she'd removed his boots he'd seen her shapely behind. It looked even better bare, firm cheeks revealed by the movements of her shift as she ran away. He wanted to call her back.

When Joe had insulted his manhood he hadn't been bothered since he knew it wasn't true. This was an item of personal knowledge that apparently survived memory loss. Besides, he'd checked at the first opportunity.

But being caught shriveled by a cold water bath, he wanted to assure Celia it wasn't always like this. Especially when the sight of her had him rapidly regaining length and girth. He repressed the urge to chase her, absurd since an innocent like Celia wouldn't even understand the significance of what she'd seen. Surely she wouldn't. She'd have no reason to think ill of him.

He needed to face a fact that had become obvious since the kiss in the hayloft, a kiss that might have led to something more had they not been interrupted: he desired her. More than that, he found her extremely appealing. And if that was so, perhaps their engagement was a real one and there was no nefarious ulterior motive involved in his pursuit of her. And yet, there was still the mystery of his name and background. The ache from his assailant's blow prickled in the back of his head, not enough to hurt, merely to impede his powers of reason. It was time, he decided, to find out a little more about his betrothal and his past relations with Celia. Even if it meant holding a conversation on an intimate subject when all alone with a woman he wanted to bed.

As well as washing himself, he'd rinsed out his fine

knitted drawers, a task he performed with no sense of familiarity whatsoever. However he loathed the feeling of soiled linen and hoped the garment would dry overnight. He spread it over a bush and pulled his calf-length pantaloons over his bare arse.

He found her seated under a tree, those long legs folded primly and covered. But something had changed. She no longer looked like a prim governess, nor an ungainly girl. Under the worst of circumstances, clad in a grubby chemise and a blanket, uncombed hair rioting over her shoulders, she looked like a siren, made to lure him to his doom.

Taking a deep breath, he wrestled for control. To take advantage of her under these circumstances would be highly dishonorable. He was certain she had no notion of the effect she had on him. He sat down near her, one leg folded beneath him, the other bent against his chest.

"That was a rather awkward encounter," he said, hoping his voice projected tranquility and reassurance.

"It's all right," she said in a small voice. Her gaze darted back and forth between his limbs and the ground. Naturally she was embarrassed. It was up to him, as the man, to take the lead and put her at ease.

"We find ourselves in an unusual position. Traveling together like this has thrown us into an intimacy that isn't normal or proper for an unmarried couple," he said, seeking the right note: sensible, cool, restrained. She nodded, her eyes now fixed on a spot next to her knee.

"I'm sure in the past we were always chaperoned, or at least there were other people nearby. A kiss under those circumstances can't go too far. You probably don't understand what I'm talking about, but we must be careful we don't let nature take its course." He feared he sounded like a pompous idiot. Better that than a blackguard.

"We never kissed."

That took him aback. "Never?"

"No," she said. "You always treated me with the greatest respect."

Instead of relief he felt an irrational indignation. "I do not believe it shows any lack of respect to kiss the woman one is to marry. The woman one purports to love." He frowned. "It sounds to me like I was—am—a prig." Perhaps he was going to be a parson, after all. Or perhaps, whatever his motive in lying to her, he had some sense of honor.

She looked up and her gray eyes were huge and bright. "I wanted you to kiss me," she said.

An invitation he ought to resist. Just one kiss, he reasoned. To refuse would be to insult a lady.

Leaning over he put one hand to her chin. Her wide, plump mouth opened. Kissing, like all lovemaking, improved with familiarity and practice. Last time he hadn't known what to expect. Now he knew her to be both inexperienced and willing. So he took her mouth gently and firmly and was stunned by his own reaction at her eager response to his invasion.

"I'll give you a thousand kisses," he croaked just before he completely lost his senses and toppled her to the ground.

Any notion of gentlemanly restraint faded. Somehow they stretched out on the straggly grass, mouths devouring, bodies straining against each other. He cupped a breast, firm beneath his hand and he felt his erection swell as his thighs straddled her hip. Pushing aside the linen shift, questing fingers found plump peachy skin and a taut nipple. She gasped at the touch and thrust her chest forward, begging for his caress. He obliged her by taking first one nipple and then the other in his mouth and sucking hard, eliciting further pleasured moans. Her hands cradled his head and tugged it back to her lips. "Kiss me again," she said greedily.

"A thousand kisses," he repeated, "and then a hundred more," and recognized the origin of the sentiment. The fact that a student of the church knew the erotic poetry of Catullus was a reflection that could only distract him for an instant. His brain emptied of anything but Celia's kisses, her soft strong flesh under his hands, his raging desire to possess her, and her keen response to his attentions.

Getting rid of her "skirt" was laughably easy, a most convenient fashion. Then he pulled back onto one elbow and pushed up the too-short chemise. Reverently he stroked the deep curve of her hips and brushed her smooth belly, feeling the gentle ripple of muscles at his touch. Her responsiveness fascinated him. Her pelvis lifted in invitation or command and he felt his cock leaping in reply, straining against cloth. He placed his palm over her mound of Venus, sensing its contours through the reddish-brown curls, pressing against his hand. Her breath came faster. A delicately inserted finger found her wet. A little more foreplay and she'd be ready, ready to take his swollen, aching cock into her hot quim.

Her hot, virgin quim. *Damn, damn, damn.*

With supreme effort and a growl of pain he rolled over a full turn and landed three feet from her.

"What?" Her exclamation combined confusion and indignation as she struggled to a sitting position.

"That," he said with a coherence that astounded him, "was what I meant by going too far."

Her gaze was on the full of his pantaloons. "Joe was wrong. You don't have a tiddly little pillock." She clapped her hand over her mouth. "I shouldn't have said that."

"Probably not." Nevertheless, he was glad she knew. He couldn't help but grin at the rueful expression on her face and she caught his humor and laughed with him. He relaxed onto his elbow, suddenly at ease, despite his physical frustration. The combination of his memory loss and their being stranded together in the wilds made this very improper conversation seem acceptable.

Celia couldn't believe she was having this conversation. There was something about Terence, relaxed, wry, humorous, that impelled her to boldness. Though she'd long known the basic facts of human reproduction, reading that naughty novel had given her more detailed information and made her anxious for more, not to mention eager to experience the real thing. Though she knew she should be grateful to him for breaking off their embrace before she was ruined, she also regretted it.

"Its size seems to—er—vary with the . . . circumstances," she said.

"That's true. It gets larger when a man becomes excited by a woman." He paused. "Cold water makes it smallest."

"And when it's stiff"—that was the word Francis Featherbrain used—"it's ready to . . ." Her voice trailed off. She couldn't use *that* word. Schoolboys were birched for letting it pass their lips.

"Engage in marital relations," he said helpfully.

"And you were, just now?" She felt a thrill of pride that she'd roused him to that point.

"I certainly was. But they are called marital relations for a reason. You shouldn't do it before you are married."

"You mean you've never done it?"

"I can't remember for certain, of course, but I'm reasonably sure I have. It's different for men."

Celia was well aware of that fact, from her own father's history if for no other reason. It was always different for men. She crossed her legs in front of her and leaned forward. Terence lounged on the ground, perfectly at ease with the tenets of custom and morality. Why not? He was a man after all, even if incognizant of his supremely privileged status. "It seems most unfair. I am expected to come to marriage untouched but you can have as many women as you like."

"I've forgotten all of them, I assure you."

"It isn't funny."

"Actually it is. As with all my abilities—boxing and trout tickling to name two—I know I can do it, but have no idea how I learned." He leaned over and pulled one of her clenched fists toward him, dropping a kiss on the knuckle. "Aren't you glad you are the only woman to occupy my mind?"

In a way she was, though she'd be gladder if their entire relationship hadn't been invented by her. She also wanted to continue her argument. In two days of walking over the hills she'd had time to do a lot of thinking. She'd come to the conclusion that her life would have been very different had she been born a boy. She'd been subject to the whim of others since her father's death. Before her father's death if she were honest. Algernon Seaton had never put himself out for the sake of his daughter.

"At least you have learned," she said. "Ladies are kept in ignorance."

"I am not going to argue with that. But there's a good reason for them to wait for marriage. The legitimacy of children. Getting with child is the frequent result of marital relations."

"If men don't have to wait, what of the women they 'learn' with. Are they not in danger of getting with child?"

"Unfortunate accidents do occur. But women of loose morals often know how to prevent them."

Celia knew for a fact this wasn't always true. But she

couldn't reveal her personal acquaintance with children born out of wedlock without speaking of aspects of her past that must never be mentioned. Besides, thinking of her father's "other" family made her sad.

"Perhaps you have a child or two somewhere," she said with some asperity. "But of course you will have forgotten them."

"It's not my fault I can't remember. Besides, I'm a respectable future member of the clergy. *Women of loose morals*," he mimicked himself. "Sounds like a sermon. How can you abide such a staid prig?"

That drew a chuckle. "You weren't behaving like a staid prig a few minutes ago."

"No," he said, "I was not. And don't look at me that way or I'll start my misbehavior again and then we'll be in trouble."

Chapter 11

A conscience is not innocent until proven guilty.

The best cure for uncontrollable lust being, as recently discussed, cold water, Terence excused himself and returned to the stream. Were he truly betrothed to Celia he'd be pressing for an early wedding.

Perhaps he was. His certainty that somehow the story of his background was an invention had been shaken by the realization of how deeply he was attracted to her. That he cared for her. That his falling in love and proposing marriage no longer seemed implausible.

Yet his brain continually refused to accept the life story of Terence Fish, student of the church. The fog clouding his memory was thinning, but when he struggled to penetrate the mist it grew denser. Only when his conscious thoughts were elsewhere did he perceive glimpses of what he believed to be the truth. He needed to sneak up on it sideways, catch it by surprise. Logic informed him that were he a villain, he must somehow be involved, either as cohort or rival, with the men pursuing Celia. He needed to hear her tale again. The first time she'd described her misadventures his head had ached too much for good judgment. It wasn't a bad idea anyway. The men and their bloodhound, balked of their prey at Bracewell, would return to Joe's farm. It was unlikely Joe would cover for them again. It would be as well to learn as much as he could about them.

He returned to their camp, reclined on the ground with a good five feet between them for safety, and asked her to recount the story of her dealings with the man who'd kidnapped her.

"Three days ago . . . Was it that recently? How much has happened since then! The two younger boys and I walked over to the vicarage to fetch the older ones who have Latin lessons with Mr. Blyth."

"Was I there? Did we meet?"

"No, you were not. Shall I continue?" He gestured his assent. "While I was out with my charges, a man called on Mr. Baldwin and asked for me. He introduced himself as Nicholas Constantine and said we were old friends from Lincolnshire days."

"But you weren't."

"I had never heard of the man, and so I informed Mr. Baldwin and his sister upon my return. I now know he was the man who later kidnapped me: a dark man of about thirty with a hint of a foreign accent. I knew no one who fit his description. He declined the invitation to wait, said he had business in the neighborhood and would call again."

"Were you not suspicious?"

"Puzzled rather. I wondered if the Baldwins had misunderstood him and he was acquainted with my late uncle, rather than me. Later I learned he persuaded the kitchen maid to tell him where the bedrooms were located. That night I was awakened by a noise in my room. I am not easily disturbed so it must have been a loud one. Indeed, it aroused Miss Baldwin in the next room. From my bed I sensed the presence of someone in the room. 'Who's there?' I asked, not worried but thinking perhaps one of the boys wanted me. A voice called my name. 'Celia,' he said."

"A man's voice."

"Yes, and not Mr. Baldwin's. I was astonished and alarmed but before I could react the door burst open and Miss Baldwin came in carrying a candle. I hardly got a look at the intruder in the flickering light, just enough to catch him in the act of buttoning up his breeches, before he ran to the window and disappeared. As we learned, he'd come up by means of a ladder and escaped the same way."

"Was your window open when you retired?"

"Wide open. You know how hot it has been. Miss Baldwin set up a screech for her brother and accused me of admitting a lover to my room."

"And they believed it? Even though you were betrothed to me?"

"Mr. Baldwin would have given me the benefit of the doubt but she wouldn't allow it. She never liked me. She insisted I be dismissed without a reference. I was told to pack my bags and leave first thing in the morning. They wouldn't even let me say goodbye to the children." For the first time the matter-of-fact tone of Celia's narration became tinged with emotion. "I was fond of them. I'd been with them over a year and I've always enjoyed the company of little boys."

"I cannot believe these people. They didn't even arrange a ride to the nearest coach stop?"

"No. I had to walk."

Something struck him, an oddity that had eluded him the first time he heard the tale. "Why were you going to the coach at all? Why didn't you come and find me at the vicarage?"

"You were away."

"Away from the vicarage overnight?"

"Yes. So I decided to leave and write to you once I reached Mrs. Stewart's house."

"Did you fear I might not believe you?"

"No, I didn't think that."

Despite her denial, Terence was sure that was the reason. Poor Celia, so alone in the world. She must have felt all at sea. He wished he could have offered her comfort. Instead he'd been away on some unexplained business, and he feared it wasn't a coincidence.

The rest of the tale was much as he remembered it. A man in a smock—probably the very one he now wore—offered her a lift in his cart. Believing him a harmless yokel she'd accepted. "He didn't say much but I'm used to that with the local folk. If he had I'd have known his Yorkshire speech was feigned. He turned off the high road into a lane, telling me it was a shortcut. Then he overpowered me." A couple of hours later, bound and gagged, she was brought to the moorland cottage where she and Terence had met.

"Why?" he asked. "Do you have any idea what the purpose of this crime might be?"

"None at all, apart from robbery and I had so little worth stealing."

"You say Constantine seemed foreign. Could he be connected with your life in India?"

She shook her head. "I never met anyone like him there. I have thought about it, but I cannot see how anything that happened half the world away could cause someone to kidnap me in Yorkshire. I am perplexed."

As darkness fell and Celia slept, he revisited the tale a dozen times and came to only one positive conclusion about his own role in the drama. He and the so-called Nicholas Constantine were no friends. The man had knocked him cold and robbed him of his horse, most of his clothing, and whatever else he carried.

But one question begged—no, shouted—for an answer. How did Terence Fish, who was away from the vicarage for the night, know where to come to his fiancée's rescue? How did he know she even needed rescuing? The most likely explanation he could come up with was that he had ridden to the cottage to meet Constantine, who was his accomplice. The robbery had been a case of thieves falling out.

Celia had complete faith in him. It hadn't occurred to her that his arrival at the cottage might have been for nefarious rather than heroic purposes. He wished it were so, longed to find evidence that his suspicions against himself were nonsense.

His feelings about his future bride had taken a radical turn. Not a shadow of reluctance remained, though he still had reservations about a future career in the church. He made a vow as he lay in the dark, listening to Celia's soft breathing a few feet away. When he regained his memory he would extract himself from whatever criminal toils ensnared him. He didn't sense that he was a man steeped in infamy, incapable of reform. He would make himself a man worthy of her and give her the protection she needed and deserved.

"Terence . . . ?" The whisper told him she wasn't asleep after all. "Are you cold? Would you like to share my blanket?"

Not the best idea if he intended to retain his honor, and hers. With some misgiving, he put trust in his self-control and rolled over. It was warm. She was warm. And almost naked. He kept a couple of inches of air between them and his hands to himself.

"Terence . . . ?"

"What is it?"

"Would you kiss me goodnight?"

Five minutes later he dragged himself away and scrambled by starlight in search of cold water.

She ought to tell him.

She ought to confess her lie. Though *lie* seemed a tiny little word, inadequate for her massive deception.

Terence Fish had turned out to be so very different from Tarquin Compton as she had known him. It was impossible to believe that the man striding at her side, unshaven and shabby, had ever been a dandy. And appearance was the least of it. Terence bore no resemblance to the haughty, critical, and reserved gentleman of the *ton*. He was in a wonderful mood this morning, cheerfully anticipating the end of their journey. Shared fantasies of meals, baths, and soft featherbeds kept them laughing.

He also displayed perfect civility and thoughtfulness in the way he was ever prepared with a hand to help her over a rough patch, two hands at her waist to lift her up a steep incline. Not that she wasn't capable of managing alone. She always had before. Even during the short period she'd lived as a proper English lady of means, she'd never been the kind of woman who inspired a man to chivalry. She enjoyed his courtesy, and his touch. Each contact gave her a little thrill. Especially once she perceived his frequent assistance was deliberate and not called for by his assessment of her needs. When he added a light kiss to her lips as he swung her over a stone wall, she was certain of it. The low hum of desire that had woken her several times in the night grew stronger. Their glances clashed in an exchange that scorched her to her toes.

She had, she feared, fallen hard for Terence Fish.

To try and rid herself of such an inconvenient sentiment, she replayed in her mind her various encounters with Tarquin Compton. Instead of rekindling her wrath she found excuses for his behavior. She now had to admit he wasn't the only man in London to snub her. As a debutante she'd been a dismal failure. Her anger at his consistent inability to remember her name faded.

But there had been that night.

She'd anticipated the evening with some excitement. Mr. John Jocelyn, a gentleman from Devon, had asked her to dance with him at three balls in a row. He'd evinced no shock at learning she'd grown up abroad, neither was he interested in her former life. He was a little dull but he paid her attention, more than could be said for anyone else. By this time Celia had invented a nice little story, implying that her family in India had been one of total respectability and, though she was much too modest to boast of it, some social prominence. Mr. Jocelyn liked social prominence. He enjoyed instructing her about the relative importance of various members of the *ton*. Celia didn't love Mr. Jocelyn, or even like him very much, but she needed to marry and he was her only prospect.

Her chaperone, Lady Trumper, was excited too. Deciding Celia might present a better appearance if her hair was less red, she'd summoned a new hairdresser for the evening. Monsieur Alphonse combed some powder through the thick locks, guaranteed to make her look more blonde than redheaded.

Celia's pleasure in her improved appearance seemed justified. Mr. Jocelyn complimented her as they danced. And then the most extraordinary thing happened. The Duchess of Amesbury came up and presented her nephew, Mr. Compton. Tarquin Compton, the darling of the *ton* and despair of matchmaking mamas, asked Celia Seaton, whose standing was so low as to be virtually subterranean, to stand up with him. He, of course, denied all prior acquaintance but she didn't care. She knew Mr. Jocelyn would be impressed and enjoyed envious glances from girls who'd always ignored her. She couldn't now remember what they'd talked about. Country dances, with all the back-and-forth between partners, were never conducive to coherent conversation.

Some time after the dance was over, she stood with some ladies next to a large potted tree when it happened. "Remind me, Jocelyn." Mr. Compton's arrogant voice was unmistakable. "What is the name of the young lady I danced with earlier? The duchess presented us. The one with a head like a cauliflower."

Hateful, hateful man! Humiliation stung anew, as it had so often over the last year when she'd remembered the moment.

She scowled at her companion who met her glare with a whimsical quirk of his brow and a quick smile, flashing white in contrast to the tan he'd acquired during two days in the sun. All at once her resentment washed away.

After hearing the fatal words she'd rushed off to find a retiring room and a mirror. Disaster! The powder had all risen to the surface of her hair. A bubble of mirth formed low in her chest. A cauliflower was a polite way of describing it. She looked like someone whose head had been dipped in a flour sack.

As for the architect of her mortification, look at him

now! No model of elegance he, in his dusty smock and bare feet. Although, she had to admit, he also looked nothing like any species of vegetable or fruit. She laughed out loud.

"What?" he asked.

"Nothing," she said. "It's just that you look so funny."

"I hate to break it to you, but your own appearance is quite odd."

"That's not a nice way to address a lady. Try for a little flattery."

"I believe in total honesty. You look odd and also beautiful."

A flush of pleasure suffused her chest. "Thank you. I'm not used to hearing compliments."

"You should be. And I intend to make sure you become so used to them you'll shrug them off. Positively blasé as Byron put it."

At that moment Celia knew she'd fallen in love: certainly with Terence Fish but also, she feared, with Tarquin Compton. She no longer believed they were two separate beings. In fact it was absurd to think so. Terence was merely the true man stripped of his worldly accouterments. Her heart lurched and her breath felt thick. Ignoring a niggle of doom in her brain, she wanted to laugh with joy and throw herself into his arms.

"Celia." His voice grew serious. "How long have we known each other?"

"About three months."

"Did you ever think I might not be the man I claimed to be?"

She stumbled and immediately he was there with a steadying arm. "No, of course not."

As she spoke the words she knew she'd missed, or deliberately avoided, an opportunity to tell him who he really was. But she shied from the confession. Let her enjoy her loving, attentive fiancé for a little longer. Time enough to tell the truth when they reached Stonewick which might, if Joe's directions were good, be only a few miles further on.

She hoped so. Clouds had been gathering all morning, promising an end to the dry weather. The air grew muggy and oppressive. At the same time, she willed the moors to extend before them and prolong her time with Terence. Tarquin, when he learned the truth, was going to be very angry.

She clung to his arm shamelessly, enjoying his closeness while she could. "I always knew exactly who you were," she said.

"Do you think I could have been on this part of the moors before?"

"It's possible, I suppose," she said cautiously. "Does the landscape seem familiar? Everywhere we've been looks much the same to me."

"Every so often I get the feeling my memory might return. As though it were pushing against a heavy curtain in my head, seeking a way out of the dark. It's happened several times this morning, but if I try to find the opening in the curtain, it closes tight."

"What an interesting way of describing it."

"It's happening now, looking down into this vale. Do

you see that cottage there, or perhaps it's a barn? I think I've seen it before. And the road beyond it. I *know* where it leads."

"Where?"

"That's just it. I know and I don't know."

Celia had a sick feeling in her stomach. They must be close to his home, perhaps on his land already. The end of their idyll was imminent. *Idyll* was an odd term for two days spent under such uncomfortable conditions, but it was the right one. In all her life she couldn't recall a happier time and she yearned to prolong it, if only for an hour or two.

"Let us sit for a while," she said. "If your body relaxes, your mind will be diverted and perhaps your memory will open." And hoped for the opposite result.

Chapter 12

*Since to err is human, it's safer to
avoid the occasion of sin.*

The presence of stone walls between fields, absence
of gorse, and evidence of numerous sheep, told him
the land was more intensively used for husbandry than
the moors they'd crossed. Perhaps they were on land
belonging to a prosperous estate. Terence noted with
interest that he was able to interpret the signs. His brain
quickened, asking whether he might be acquainted with
the owners. He beat back the questions. Such calcula-
tions, he'd discovered, thickened the fog of his memory.
Celia was right. *Relax.*

She seated herself beside him on a patch of grass,
hugging her knees. A tilt of her head gave him a view
of her wide, smiling mouth. She'd learned a lot about
kissing in the past day. He looked forward to giving
her another lesson. Not the best way to relax his body
perhaps, but it would certainly divert his mind. The significance of animal husbandry receded by the second.

"Would you kiss me good morning?" he asked.

Her lips compressed to an *O*. The glimpse of hot pink within sent a message to his southern regions that was the opposite of relaxing. But he was confident of his power of self-control. Had she not survived the previous night with her virginity intact?

"I thought I already did," she said, low and soft like a stroke of velvet.

"A mere peck. I want another. This time make it last."

He loved the way she rose to the challenge. Shifting to kneel between his legs she surveyed him gravely, cocking her head to one side. She trailed her fingers down his forehead, then just the forefinger along the length of his nose. He raised his own hand to join hers and felt the slight bump in the bridge. He had an aquiline nose. How odd that he had no more notion of what he looked like than a blind man did. He didn't know if he was handsome, though from Celia's description and her expression now she didn't find him repulsive. Glowing gray eyes followed her hand's examination of his face with absolute concentration: the ridges of his cheekbones; the brackets on either side of his own smiling mouth; a fingertip tracing the length of his lips, one after another, making them glow. His breathing accelerated.

Palms cupped his lower face, massaging his jaw.

"Bristly," she murmured.

"I beg your pardon."

"I like it. It makes you seem . . . wicked."

And though that was exactly what he feared he

was, he reveled in it. What man wouldn't wish to seem wicked when being kissed by a pretty girl? Who, incidentally, hadn't yet done the deed.

"Kiss me," he growled and her pupils expanded, darkening her eyes. Her mouth swooped in, then stopped. Pulled back.

"Make me," she whispered.

He placed his right hand at the angle of her neck and shoulder, extending his thumb to caress the bump of her collarbone. Her skin was warm and smooth and slightly moist in the humid air. She edged a little closer on her knees and one part of his brain noted the blanket skirt came untucked during the maneuver. His hand descended, pushing down her chemise. He stopped when he reached the shallow mound of her breast, firm beneath his palm, and applied a gentle squeeze. Her breath quickened.

"Do you like that?"

"Yes."

"Would you like me to continue?" Even as he framed the question his left hand gave the same treatment to the breast's twin.

Her eyelids dropped and her only response was an "aah" he took for assent. His hand stilled. "You know what to do."

She did and it was wonderful, the best kiss yet. It started soft, a sweet friendly skirmish of lips nibbling at his, then proceeded to full engagement. As their mouths and tongues clashed, Celia's arms went round him and she pressed her breasts against his chest. Struggling to get closer, she moved her knees to straddle his thighs. His cock, already on guard, leaped to rapt attention.

Danger. The part of his brain that governed virtue and responsibility shrieked for him to stop before his control slipped away. His mouth retreated a little. His animal senses yelled back. *Just a few more minutes. Just one more kiss.* Virtue struggled and succumbed. *Oh, very well,* it said. *Just one more kiss, then stop.*

Since it was going to be just one, Terence gave it all he had. He knew it was going to end badly and he hadn't even noticed a source of cold water nearby. But there was a contentment in pleasing a woman, *his* woman, while knowing that he was about to sacrifice his own ultimate pleasure for her protection. Innocent that she was, she had no idea how arousing he found her enthusiastic response, the growing skill of her kisses, the sounds of approval in her throat. His hands clasped her waist, to hold her steady and in preparation for thrusting her aside. *Just one more minute.*

Then one of her hands came down, inserted itself between their bodies, and rested on the bulge in his pantaloons. The heavy cavalry of his animal senses roared in and virtue was tossed aside, unconscious if not dead, defeated on the battlefield of passion.

If she'd thought about it she wouldn't have dared, but Celia wasn't in a state where careful consideration of her actions and their consequences was an option. From the moment he caressed her breast, her mind and body had been driven by desire: to touch and be touched; to give and receive; to be as close as possible to the man she adored. Deep, damp, devouring kisses were easily the best thing she'd ever done and they made her want more, much more, to feel the same bliss in every part of her. Acting by instinct and without a thought of shame, she parted her knees, moved over him and pressed herself against the length of his body so not a bubble of air separated them.

And felt that part of him hard against her lower belly: the pillock, according to Joe, or pintle, the word preferred by Francis Featherbrain. Like one of Master Featherbrain's inamoratas, she reached for it. It swelled and stiffened through his clothing as her own private parts throbbed back.

The effect was once again remarkable—and delightful. In a matter of seconds her shift had vanished and she was on her back, stark naked. Terence tore off his own clothing with the same desperate urgency with which he'd removed hers and gathered her into his hot hard embrace. Awash in sensation she reveled in the texture of skin, muscle, and hair against her body. Being outdoors, naked to the sky in broad daylight, made her feel deliciously exposed and vulnerable. She yearned to open herself to him, to entrust herself, body and soul, into his keeping. With the desperate knowledge that this happiness could not last, she seized the moment and held on tight.

Between her legs she ached and knew herself damp with longing. And his time when his fingers penetrated through the nether hair he didn't stop. Her coral bud of sensuality—Francis had taught her some useful vocabulary—throbbed in anticipation and when his probing digit found it she cried out "yes" and raised her pelvis. She could bring herself to the "critical period" quite efficiently, but oh, how much better it was when Terence did it. Clinging to his shoulders and kissing him wildly, too mindless for any finesse, she urged him on with movements and sound until she dissolved into ecstasy, feeling great shudders of joy ripple through her hidden passage and out along her limbs.

She wanted more—it wasn't enough. His pintle rested hot, silken, and smooth against her hip and she felt an emptiness, a sensation, new to her, that she was a void needing to be filled and only he could do it.

He was breathing hard, half on top of her, his eyes closed and his mouth resting on her shoulder. "Come in," she whispered, the only way she could think of to express her wish. "Come into me. I want you."

"I shouldn't." His voice sounded strangled, as though he suffered the cruelest torture.

He was right. He shouldn't, for reasons he didn't even know. But she didn't care. She wanted him and the consequences be damned. Groping between them she clutched his pintle, hard, feeling it twitch like a wild animal in her grasp. Imitating the vicar's wife in Feath-erbrain's fervent imagination, she guided it toward the entrance of her privies. He groaned again and resistance ceased.

He took over and any doubt she might have enter-tained of his experience dissolved. Lying over her, he rubbed his pintle up and down along the crease of her entrance. It was wet and slippery and her excitement reanimated under the friction. At the same time he worked her breasts. Tweaking her nipples, firmly but not enough to cause pain, sent sharp sensations shooting through her body to enhance the wonderful ache of her inner passage. With some effort she raised her head, pecking at his mouth with hers, to encourage him and wordlessly communicate her pleasure and her affection. They kissed messily, then her head flopped back and their eyes met in an exchange that pierced straight to her heart. She closed hers tight to hide the tears that arose unbidden, testament to the bitter truth that marred the sweetness of the moment.

"Now!" she cried. "Come to me now."

It wasn't what she expected. There was a little pain at his entrance, over quite quickly, then a feeling of being overly filled, not comfortable but not unpleasant, either. She also had a feeling of being possessed, of belonging, something she hadn't enjoyed in more years than she could remember. His splendid body encompassed her and shielded her from the neglect and dangers of the world. Joined in this primitive act of man and woman, she no longer felt alone.

She was wet down there and when he began to move, hard and slippery, she could sense herself stretching to accommodate him. Discomfort faded and she began to like it. Their eyes met. His gaze was intense, reflecting his utter concentration on the matter in hand, but also, unless she imagined it, affectionate. She surrendered to the luxury of believing herself loved.

Wishing to reciprocate in physical form and actively participate in their congress, she put her arms around his waist, stroked the contours of his back then, acting purely on instinct, raised her slightly bended knees and hugged his hips. She caught the rhythm of his movement and rocked her hips to meet them. As the conscious world shrank to the few square inches of their joining, delicious tension swelled up again. Squeezing her eyes shut she focused her mind on the sensations he aroused, drawing him in with her hidden muscles, praying for completion. It came in a rush, less intense than her earlier peak but somehow more satisfying for being shared. Her incoherent benediction to him for making her feel that way elicited a moan of pleasure and he increased the speed of his thrusts. She opened her eyes.

His own were closed now, and the concentration on his face echoed hers. She realized he must be going through a sensual progression similar to that she'd just experienced. She was fascinated, empowered by her ability to assist in such delight and fiercely happy that she could do so for him. As his crisis approached he threw back his head in an agony of joy. A new warmth flooded her and he collapsed, the weight of his heaving chest welcome on hers, his breath heavy against her shoulder.

Determined not to let anything ruin the moment, she lay still and emptied her mind.

All too soon he rolled off and upright. "Here," he said gruffly, holding out her chemise, as though he, like her, was suddenly aware they were stark naked in the rapidly cooling air, with some kind of dwelling, possibly inhabited, within sight. Then, with a gentle smile that sent her heart tumbling, he sorted out the garment himself and slipped it over her head, giving her a quick kiss on the cheek while he arranged the neck. Greatly to her regret, since she loved the sight of his bare chest, he pulled on his own smock. It was such a silly piece of clothing with its floppy collar, rough gathers, and crude stitching. That she found it heightened the brooding masculinity of his face was a measure of her infatuation.

His expression grew serious. "That was not well done of me. You deserved a bath and a bed and a wedding ring."

What could she say? She wanted them, too, especially the last, though she supposed wedded life wouldn't be much fun without the other two. Yet a vision of the two of them living like Gypsies on the moors forever had a certain appeal. She shook her head to clear her thoughts. She was procrastinating, postponing an unwelcome task.

Perhaps this was the moment. When he was satisfied and happy and regarding her with an expression that could be love. She might find him in a forgiving mood. Or perhaps she'd discover that Tarquin Compton, as well as Terence Fish, could love Celia Seaton. She opened her mouth . . . *Now.*

"What?" he said, with another quick kiss. "You look as though you have something momentous to say."

"Not really." *Coward*. She couldn't bear to drive away that look. Just a minute more, then she'd tell him. "I'm glad we did it," she blurted.

"I'm glad we did it, too, although we shouldn't have."

They grinned foolishly at each other in suspended time. A fat drop of water landed on her forehead and she realized the sky had grown dark.

He snatched up his breeches, her blanket and her hand. "Run!"

Stumbling, shrieking, laughing, they charged down the hill. He wrenched open the door of the stone building and they were inside before the rain came down in earnest and soaked them. They found themselves in a low barn, empty of inhabitants, either human or animal, though a distinct odor gave evidence of the latter. Celia wasn't anxious to explore the contents of the floor. At one end of the small room was a hayloft, about as high as her chest.

"Help me up," she said, reaching for the loft edge since there was no ladder.

His touch on her waist and the cool air on her bare bottom as she struggled up had her thinking about "doing it" again. Might as well be hung for a sheep as for a lamb. She giggled softly at that thought in a sheep barn. Once she'd scrambled into the loft she arranged herself on the hay in an alluring pose, or so she hoped.

"Come and join me," she cooed. The speed and determination with which he swung himself up indicated a willingness to accept her invitation.

Then a tingling in the back of her nose presaged an

enormous, noisy sneeze. The place wasn't just dry, it was thick with dust. And that wasn't all.

"Oh lord," she shrieked and twisted bolt upright onto her knees, slapping wildly at her back and shoulders.

"What is it?"

"Insects. Or something. I can feel them crawling down my back." She thrashed around in a panic.

"Keep still," he said, half laughing. "Here. It's just a little spider."

"Ugh! I hate spiders."

"All gone now." He dropped the offending creature over the side. "You're covered in hay and dust."

She could sense it all over her skin. Joyful lust had dissipated to be replaced with a sense of being grubby and charmless. Yet looking back at Terence she didn't find *him* unattractive. "I must look a fright," she said.

He leaned back to examine her with exaggerated portentousness. "The dust has made your hair look almost white. Rather like a cauliflower."

She was watching his face as it happened. Affectionate teasing faded to confusion. He swayed and clutched his head. A new consciousness dawned.

"Miss Seaton," he said.

Chapter 13

It's always best to own up before you are caught.

The curtain parted and he was in a ballroom. The scraping of fiddles mingled with the unmistakable babble of the chattering *ton*. Quite normal. A young woman stood before him, looking anxious. That was normal, too, Tarquin made sure of it. He never gave marriageable females, or their chaperones, the chance to get the wrong idea. He knew this girl: she was a little older than some, though it was her first season. Lady Trumper, who discreetly charged handsome sums to the rich and unconnected for introducing their daughters to London, had attempted to foist her in his direction several times, trying to win his approval and help the chances of a lady lacking beauty, elegance, or wit. He'd even been bullied into dancing with her once, though he couldn't recall how such an anomaly had come about. What was her name? He always forgot.

She looked even less prepossessing than usual. Un-kempt was the only word. Why on earth had her chaperone let her out with her hair in such a mess? Not even pinned up, it framed her face in a wild dusty halo. He blinked twice.

Apparently Lady Trumper had also let her out without her gown.

A sharp pain pierced his skull. The music and voices faded as the curtain closed behind him. Then, for the first time in a while it disappeared. His memory no longer had closed off rooms: it felt clear and complete. He even remembered her name.

"Miss Seaton," he said. "Why are you dressed like that? It is most improper. And what are we doing in this . . ." he glanced around " . . . *barn*?"

She regarded him with a wary expression. "Do you know who you are?"

"Of course I do. Why would I forget my own name? I am Tarquin Compton. What an absurd question! I wish I knew what I was doing in this place, however."

She smiled. "You don't remember anything about how we came to be together? Nothing at all?"

He thought about it. Clearly they weren't in London. That established, he remembered traveling to Yorkshire to visit his estate, then making a trip away from Revesby on business of some sort, getting lost. Involuntarily he touched the back of his head and found a bump and a scab.

It all came flooding back, every bit of it, up to and including making love to Miss Celia Seaton in the open air. An act of indiscretion he'd committed in the belief that he was Terence Fish and she was his promised bride.

He's always known there was something fishy about the story, but it had never occurred to him, fool that he was, that the whole thing had been invented by *her*. He wasn't the villain of the piece, she was.

"My God! You knew." His breath was taken away by her effrontery. "Don't even pretend you didn't know exactly who I was, right from the start."

He jutted his head at her and she shrank back against the wall, hugging her knees to her chest. "I won't," she said quietly.

"Why? *Why?*" He was yelling and he wanted to strangle her. Rather than risk yielding to temptation he jumped down from the loft and berated her from the floor below. "You had me wandering around the moors like a damned idiot for three days, believing I was Terence bloody Fish." The fact that he'd believed no such thing just made him angrier.

"I'm sorry."

Not good enough. He wanted her to weep but her eyes were dry and flat.

"You said we were engaged. My God! We lay together. How could you? What were you thinking? You're a lady of breeding. How could you allow something so improper?"

"I don't remember you being so reluctant," she said with a show of spirit.

She was correct and it made him more furious. He'd known he was doing wrong. In his shame he lashed out at her. "You were a virgin. You should have guarded your virtue."

Celia had been cringing with guilt, prepared to grovel at his feet and beg his forgiveness, but that riled her. She crawled over to the edge of the loft and glared down at him. "I know about men like you. You seduce innocent girls, force them to your will, then blame them." He was no different from Francis Featherbrain, only older and not fictional. And probably taller. And not stupid.

"I beg to inform you, madam," he sputtered, "that I have never forced a woman, neither have I seduced an innocent, in my entire life. And I certainly wouldn't have seduced you—and I beg leave to dispute that I was the seducer—had I not believed us to be betrothed." He put his hand on his hips. "Why did you do it? To trap me into marriage? Well, madam, you fail. I refuse to fall victim to your scheme."

Celia wanted to scratch his eyes out. Tarquin Compton had returned just as supercilious and nasty as he'd ever been. What a fool she was to believe him different, to fancy herself in love. The man she'd fallen for, Terence Fish, had never existed.

"Your arrogance is overweening," she said, low and deadly. "How could any woman want to live with a man like you? I'd sooner starve than marry you."

He raised his hands in clawed supplication to some higher power. "Then why in the name of all that's holy did you claim we were engaged?"

"Because I needed your help getting away from my kidnapper."

"And you didn't think I'd give it unless you made up your farrago of nonsense?"

"No," she said bluntly. "You never seemed like the kind of man who would help a stranger."

"An outrageous conclusion to make about a gentleman." His eyes narrowed. "And why choose such a ludicrous name for me? That, madam, has the odor of spite."

"Well, Mr. Tarquin High-and-Mighty Lord-of-All-He-Surveys Compton. Maybe it was spite and maybe it was fair recompense. You never remembered my name, not once in all the times we were introduced in London. Not even when you destroyed my prospects and doomed me to a life of drudgery as a governess."

"What nonsense! You became a governess because your uncle failed to change his will. Unless you lied about that too."

"I would have married Mr. Jocelyn if it wasn't for you."

"John Jocelyn? He's a pompous fool. No one would want to marry him."

"Mr. Jocelyn," she said with a complete disregard for truth, "is a man of good sense and character and I would have been proud to be his wife. But he never offered because *you* told him I looked like a cauliflower."

"You did look like a cauliflower and you still do."

That was enough! Celia let out a squeal of rage and would have stalked out of the barn, except she was perched on the edge of the hayloft.

She gritted her teeth and prepared to drop. "I'm coming down. Get out of the way."

But instead of moving, he held up his arms, caught her, and lowered her gently to the ground. For a moment he was Terence again, strong, gentle, and chivalrous. But Terence was dead and Tarquin was only strong. The touch that made her chest thump and her skin tingle was devoid of inner softness: his heart was as hard as his muscles. Once she was safe on the floor he released her and folded his arms over his chest.

"I'm leaving," she said, gathering up her blanket and heading for the exit without bothering to say thank you.

"You have nowhere to go."

"I'll find Mrs. Stewart on my own. Or I'll return to Joe. He appreciated me."

She pushed open the door and was greeted by a howling gale and sheets of rain. So intent had she been on their quarrel she'd ignored the thunderstorm that raged without.

"Don't be a fool. You can't go out in this weather. Besides, what about the kidnapper and his cohort? There's no reason to think they've given up the pursuit."

Undecided, she stood and let the rain blow in and wet her shift.

"I am *not* the kind of man who abandons a woman to her fate, even if she is a stranger."

"I don't want to marry you." She continued to stare out at the sodden landscape.

"I don't want to marry you, and I won't," he said. "Unless you are enceinte. Did you even consider that outcome? But I'm not leaving you until you find your father's friend. That would be the act of a scoundrel."

She should, she supposed, be glad he was prepared to stand by her if she was with child. Any impulse to gratitude was quashed by the condescension of the offer. Both offers. They were inspired by pride and the need to do right in the eyes of others. For the opinion of the *ton* was what mattered most to a dandy and Tarquin Compton was the consummate dandy. He'd do nothing—father a child out of wedlock or leave a helpless woman—that would expose him to worldly censure.

Much as she'd like to spit in his eye, she had to be sensible. "Thank you. I accept."

"Good. Now that nonsense is out of the way, shut the rain out."

The crude planks were heavy and the door had blown wide open until it banged against the stone wall of the barn. Already wet, she didn't hesitate to step out, but the wind was too strong. She couldn't move it.

"Get inside," he yelled over the storm. "I'll do it."

She continued to tug but her fingers kept slipping on the wooden latch. He came out to help and they stood, each naked from mid-thigh and below, as water soaked through the linen of her shift and his smock.

He wasn't helping her. Instead he gazed out at the hills, rain plastering his hair flat and making his forehead gleam. She yelled something and he came to his senses. Together they backed into the barn, dragging the door with them. It slammed shut to leave them in eerie quiet.

A sweep of hands over his head wiped the water from his short hair. Hers hung in wet matted hanks. At least the powdery dust would have washed out. Her blanket, luckily, she'd dropped on her way out and it was only a little damp. She wrapped it around her like a shawl and shivered. She'd been stupid to attempt to leave. Not only were they stranded in a barn together, barely on speaking terms, they were also likely to catch a chill. Yet Mr. Compton looked less angry than he had since regaining his memory, and also less human. She wasn't sure how he managed it, something about the way he held his head at a slight angle, his chin tilted upward and his eyes peering down his aquiline nose at her. Mr. Tarquin Compton, the terror of the *ton*, was back.

"I know where we are," he said, the ice in his voice matching that in his eyes. "I recognize the landscape. We're on my land, less than a mile from my house at Revesby."

"Joe said Stonewick was near Revesby."

"Three miles away. As soon as it stops raining we'll go home and I shall take you to your friend by carriage. I shall remain in the neighborhood until you know whether you are with child."

She understood the unspoken corollary: if she wasn't he'd never willingly see her again.

His valet stropped the razor to a fine edge and applied it to Tarquin's face, warm and softened from his bath. With deft passes over lathered cheeks and jaw, upper lip and chin, his three-day shadow was scraped away. As each stroke of the blade left a path of smooth skin, Tarquin felt Terence Fish recede into history. The man who had walked barefoot, tickled for trout, brawled with a yokel, and fallen in love with an impertinent governess disappeared with his beard. By the time the servant rubbed a soothing tonic into his skin, all that remained of him was black bristles wiped onto a white towel.

A clean shirt of finest linen lay soft and crisp against his skin, so different from the crude homespun smock. Taking the strip of starched muslin draped over the valet's arm, Tarquin began the practiced ritual. As he wound it twice about his neck and tied the elaborate knot, arranging the folds so they framed his clean chin in frothy precision, a pang of regret assailed him, a fleeting dread that he returned to prison and the neck cloth was a chained collar.

He shook off the fanciful illusion. "Waistcoat," he said.

And with each garment and layer he felt more himself until Tarquin Compton, the best-dressed man in England, stood before the cheval glass in all his tastefully restrained magnificence. One last twitch to the cravat, an adjustment of his cuff, and he was ready. Once he left the room, confident in the perfection of his dress, he wouldn't give it another thought. Man and appearance were united in aesthetic harmony.

Chapter 14

You cannot always rely on the kindness of strangers.

"Forgive me, Miss Seaton," he said, "for conveying you in a closed carriage. It isn't quite proper."

Celia took a sidelong glance to see if he was joking. The words were the first he'd spoken to her since leaving the barn that weren't necessary to the practicalities of consigning her to the care of his housekeeper and finding her something to wear. Her bath had been blissful and she should be grateful. But he probably wouldn't have let her have it, she thought darkly, except that he wouldn't wish to share a carriage with a woman who reeked of sweat and sheep. Then she thought of presenting herself at a strange lady's house in her state of dirt and managed to scrape up a little gratitude, mostly to the servant who'd carried the cans of hot water upstairs.

In contrast to the elderly carriage, exhumed from the Revesby stables and still bearing traces of cobwebs around the windows, he was impeccably dressed in buff trousers, glossy Hessian boots, and a blue coat that fit his powerful shoulders like a glove. Beneath his high crowned hat his face, shaved of every trace of bristle, seemed harsh, almost ascetic.

Mr. Compton did not appear to appreciate the irony of his remarks. Since arriving at Revesby Hall he'd been very much Mr. Compton. Not Tarquin and most certainly not Terence. "Your dress is somewhat eccentric and your situation irregular. It would be better if you were not seen in my company."

"Compared to the eccentricity of my dress and irregularity of my situation in the past three days, I would call myself a model of decorum."

"I am thinking of your reputation. I believe I can trust the discretion of my staff. My valet I can vouch for and the Wardles have been with my family for decades and they are the only servants in residence at Revesby. Luckily Yorkshire folk do not in general care for gossip."

Celia would have liked to make a joke about Joe, but he looked so forbidding. She stiffened her spine and resisted intimidation. She had seen this man in the most undignified circumstances. She'd rather not think about how he looked in the grip of ecstasy; that incident needed to be forgotten. But she did think about him standing in the stream with his tiddly little pillock. He didn't have to be so superior.

Yes, she'd behaved badly. But it was clear to her now that Tarquin Compton was just as unpleasant as she'd always believed. It mitigated her guilt and made her deeply thankful that she'd most likely never have to see him again.

Please, please, she prayed. Let Mrs. Stewart be home and still willing to offer her assistance.

Mr. Compton perhaps shared her thoughts. "Tell me about Mrs. Stewart," he said. "I know you have never met the lady, but how much do you know of her?"

"Until two months ago I was unaware of her existence. I received a letter from her offering me a home. She claimed to be the widow of an old friend of my father's from India who had learned of my misfortunes."

"Did your father have many friends you never met?"

Celia chose her words carefully. "We lived in a small place with few English, and my father traveled on business a good deal. So yes, I imagine he must have. I was a trifle surprised he'd never mentioned Mr. Stewart, but it's not impossible and I might have forgotten."

"Why did you refuse? Not," he said grimly, "because you had just become betrothed to Terence Fish."

"No," she said, hiding her trepidation at revealing one of those little facts she'd kept to herself. "But I was engaged to my employer, Mr. Baldwin."

She turned her head away and spoke so softly Tarquin wasn't sure he'd heard her. "What did you say?"

"I was engaged to Mr. Baldwin."

Of course, he thought. Another surprise courtesy of Celia Seaton, and something told him it wouldn't be the last. The girl was proving to be a congenital liar. "No wonder he was upset at finding a man in your room."

"There's no need to be disagreeable. It's not as though I let him in." Since she wore no bonnet, he saw indignation possess her features. "My goodness! You don't believe me. I told you the truth about that. Constantine was not my lover."

He knew that. He knew she'd been a virgin. His responsibility for the loss of her maidenhead hung heavy on his conscience, however often he told himself it was as much her fault as his.

"Did you love him? Mr. Baldwin?"

"No. He only offered because he had four sons and I was the first governess who could manage them. He didn't want to lose me. His sister, however, hated me. She persuaded him I was guilty."

Why he should be glad she hadn't loved her betrothed, he wasn't sure. Why should he even care? Yet he wondered what the man looked like, and whether she'd ever kissed him.

She continued her story. "I wrote to thank Mrs. Stewart for her kindness and told her of my good fortune and she replied with her felicitations. Her letter was stolen with the rest of my belongings, but I remember the address. Moorland House, Stonewick."

"Let's hope she's still living there."

She wasn't. Moorland House, a respectable stone house on the High Street, was empty. Inquiry at the inn quickly revealed that the most recent tenant had taken a year's lease, but stayed only a month or two before leaving with no forwarding address. Yes, said the publican.

Mrs. Stewart was her name. He thought it just about two months ago she left.

Another strange occurrence related to Celia Seaton and not, Tarquin would wager good money, a coincidence.

Chapter 15

*A lady should never leave her
chamber improperly dressed.*

He finally got rid of his land agent, who had joined
him at the breakfast table. Tarquin didn't want
Truman to know of the existence of Celia, let alone that
she'd spent the night under his roof.

The man had been worried when Tarquin went missing. But instead of instituting discreet inquiries, Truman
had gone too far. Learning the Duke and Duchess of
Amesbury were in residence at Castle Hartley, some ten
miles away, he'd sent Tarquin's uncle a message.

It wasn't the duke so much as the duchess. Tarquin
shuddered to think what she'd do if she got wind of this
escapade. Finding a solution to the problem of Celia
was now urgent.

The only thing he could think of was to throw himself on the mercy of Lady Iverley, his best friend's new
bride. Diana was kindness itself and Tarquin didn't
think she'd refuse to help. His head ached a little. He

found he still had some gaps in his memory, mostly relating to recent, and he hoped relatively trivial, matters. One of these was the exact location of the Iverleys. Sebastian's family seat was in Northumberland but they also owned a house in Kent. He'd better send letters to both places right away.

He got up to pour himself more tea and found the pot almost cold. He preferred coffee in the morning, but Mrs. Wardle's notion of the beverage was undrinkable. He'd wait and order a fresh pot when Celia appeared. His unwelcome guest was in a spare bedroom, presumably enjoying a prolonged sleep, though not that of the innocent. His own rest, despite exhaustion and the joy of a feather bed, had been disturbed by the dozen difficulties she presented. Her lack of suitable clothing, for instance. The girl had nothing, not a thread to her name aside from that tattered shift. His mother's twenty-year-old ball gowns, the only feminine garments in the house, fit her well enough, but she couldn't be seen abroad in them. The throb in his brain intensified.

The previous day's storm had abated the heat only for a few hours and the sunshine brightened the dining room. Like most of the seventeenth-century house, with the exception of a fine wood carved mantelpiece in the drawing room, the decoration was plain but well executed: white painted paneling setting off bad ancestral portraits and agreeable landscapes, and solid, unpretentious furniture. As a child he'd often eaten here since his parents liked to share the morning meal with their children.

The sounds of birdsong through the open windows were interrupted by the crunch of carriage wheels on the gravel. Rising to look, a quick glance identified the crest on the carriage door and the passengers within. Much to his disgust, the duchess had accompanied her husband.

With Wardle away from the house on an errand and Mrs. Wardle in the kitchen quarters, there was no one to answer the door and Tarquin had no intention of doing it himself. But that wouldn't keep the duchess out for long. Sure enough, he heard her harrumphing her way through the hall, opening and slamming the doors of empty rooms while her mild-mannered husband offered unheeded demurs. All too soon she made her way to the dining room.

As a child Tarquin had been terrified of her. She reminded him of a parrot belonging to a friend of his mother's: sharp and beaky with clashing plumage, ready to peck a boy's eyes out when disgruntled. Considering his aunt's ghastly taste in clothes, Tarquin never understood why she was the one person in the world who made him feel like a scrubby schoolboy. Perhaps because when he'd first come to live with her at Amesbury House, the ducal mansion in London, that's what he'd been.

"So you're here," she snapped without preamble. "That fool of a man of yours said you were missing."

Tarquin rose politely at her entrance. He'd given up offering her verbal defiance when he discovered she reveled in the excuse to retaliate. She'd hadn't owned the right to chastise him for many years, but his flawless demeanor always irked her, along with the power and respect it had won him among her peers.

And he never traduced her. Her dress sense, for example, would be an easy target for his wit. If he wanted he could have all of London repeating a bon mot about the imperial taste in color that matched her nature. She knew it, too, and must wonder why he never attacked her. He was rarely tempted anymore. His disdain and loathing were too great. A playful epithet on her person would be like fighting a tiger with a chicken skin fan.

"Good morning, Duchess. Good morning, Uncle. What a surprise to see you."

The Duke of Amesbury cast him a look of mute apology. Tarquin was fond of his mother's brother, who had done his duty as a guardian with a measure of affection and now showed no inclination to interfere with his life.

Unlike his wife.

With exquisite punctiliousness he bowed over her hand. She flared her nostrils and emitted a sound halfway between a sniff and a snort, eloquent with derision. "Compton." Her fingers clenched as though itching to wield the birch. That, at least, he no longer had to suffer at her hands. "I've heard nothing from your sisters," she continued, holding him responsible for the dilatory letter writing habits of two ladies who were older than him, married, and living far away.

"Mary writes that her family is well. Claudia is increasing again."

The duchess's mouth thinned to what passed for a

smile. "It's to be hoped she does her duty this time."

"Indeed."

"Six girls! Was ever anything so mismanaged?"

In Tarquin's opinion the only mismanagement was expecting his sister to endure so many pregnancies in twelve years of marriage, but he said nothing. He never bandied unnecessary words with the duchess.

"Such a thing would never be allowed in *my* family. The Bromleys always have boys."

"Really, Duchess? I thought you were born a Bromley."

"Well, of course there must be some girls, or whom would men marry?" Magnificently immune to logic, she turned to the subject at hand. "Where were you?" she barked.

"Truman took unnecessary alarm when I decided to spend a night or two away from home."

"You have a mistress, I suppose. You should be married. When you return to London I shall present you to my niece, Miss Belinda Bromley. She came out this year but she didn't take. She is perfect for you."

And would, being a Bromley, presumably breed many sons. If it was possible to feel amusement in her presence he would have laughed. She'd been trying to marry him off for years, always presenting him with the most insultingly dismal marriage candidates. Including, he reflected with grim irony, Miss Celia Seaton. And since she mustn't discover an unmarried lady staying under his roof, he needed to get rid of her as soon as possible.

"It was thoughtless of you, Compton, to make me come all the way here."

Tarquin gritted his teeth and raised his eyebrows. "Had I known you would be concerned, or even that you were in Yorkshire, I would have been sure to inform you of my whereabouts."

"I loathe Yorkshire but I had to come up on a matter of business." She looked around the room. "I haven't been in this house since the day we came to tell you about your parents' death. It hasn't changed."

"Why would it? It's been largely uninhabited since that day."

"I never liked it. Old and badly arranged."

"In that case don't let me keep you here for another minute."

The duchess never took a hint. Instead she took a seat. "Pour me some tea. Coming out so early was highly inconvenient. I scarcely had time for a bite of breakfast."

Without a word, Tarquin went to the sideboard and poured her a cup, adding milk and sugar at her demand.

"It's cold," she said. "Ring for fresh."

He was growing anxious. Celia might descend at any moment. "The bell is broken." True. "And I believe all my servants are out. That's why you had to let yourself into the house."

"I'll find someone." Ignoring his protest she swept out of the room and he prayed she wouldn't decide to look upstairs.

"Taking the opportunity to nose around," the duke

said, confirming Tarquin's fears. "I'm sorry to intrude on you, my boy, but you know what she's like. She's particularly vexed at the moment."

"How can you tell?"

The duke winced. "I can tell. She's been balked."

"Jewelry?"

"The Mysore ruby again. She first heard of it a year ago—over a hundred carets and pigeon blood red—then it disappeared."

"If I remember, you bought her the Hohenstein emeralds instead." With a shudder he remembered the sight of the huge parure adorning the duchess's scrawny neck, clashing horribly with a purple satin gown.

"Forty thousand, they cost me. They kept her quiet for a month or two, but then she heard a rumor the ruby had resurfaced, in Yorkshire of all places. Nothing for it but to leave Brighton and come up here. Then she meets her London agent and he tells her he doesn't have the jewel yet. But when—if—he finds it she's going to make me pony up and the emeralds will seem a bargain." He leaned closer and lowered his voice to a whisper. "You don't know how lucky you are not to have a wife."

Tarquin looked down at the rather pudgy duke and backed away as tactfully as he could. Subscribing to Mr. Brummell's dictum that a gentleman should smell of unobtrusive cleanliness, his only scent was a special soap, ordered from a Parisian shop and custom made for him in the south of France. He abhorred the duke's unfortunate addiction to perfume. Of course his uncle was rich and powerful enough not to give a damn what anyone thought of him. The only person he feared was his wife. "It's not as though she can make you, Uncle."

"You know what she's like. A man does prefer peace in his own house. I don't suppose you'd tell her you'll propose to Belinda, would you? She'd be so pleased she might forget about the ruby." The duke's expression recalled a dog who knows it isn't dinnertime but asks anyway.

"Forgive me, but I wouldn't be inclined to choose anyone related to the duchess."

"I daresay you are wise. Belinda's a little dab of a chit, that's why she hasn't found a husband yet. And I expect she's not as amenable as she appears." His mournful expression was comical. "They hide their true natures until after they catch you."

The duchess stormed back into the room, her true nature on flamboyant display.

"I can't find anyone. Your kitchen quarters are a disgrace, just like the rest of this house. Your mother was a fool to marry Compton, and a bigger one not to raze the place to the ground and start again. I suppose she couldn't afford it. A duke's sister should have done much better than a Yorkshire gentleman. I blame your uncle for making us spend Christmas here that year. They should never have met."

"Shall we leave my mother and father out of it?"

His father may have been a country gentleman and only an adequate match for a duke's daughter, but to Tarquin's mind there was no question his mother had made a wiser choice than her brother.

The duchess reclaimed her seat at the table. "She had no notion of family dignity. Lucky for them that *I* was in charge of your sisters' presentations. I made sure they made decent matches, better than they could have expected."

He waited, letting her invective roll over him.

"When I had to take the three of you in, the last thing I needed was more children. I'd just married off my youngest. But I spared no effort to ensure your sisters were well established and I shall do my duty by you as well."

"I cannot tell you how grateful I am, Duchess, but there's no need. Now let me escort you to your carriage."

Ignoring his offered arm, she remained planted in her chair. "Grateful! If you were grateful you would have offered for one of the unexceptional young women I have introduced you to."

One of those unexceptional candidates occupied a spare bedchamber and might appear at any second. Tarquin clenched his fists at his sides, wondering how on earth he was going to dislodge the mulish duchess. He stared at her for a minute, contemplating drastic measures. Would his uncle feel bound to object if he slung the beldame over his shoulder and carried her to the carriage?

Too late. Celia burst in, wearing his second-best dressing gown.

The house was an agreeable surprise. Celia knew little of architecture, but from her first sight of the interior she found Revesby Hall appealing. A well-proportioned square of gray stone, it was the perfect size for a no-nonsense country family with many children and lots of dogs and horses. Mr. Baldwin's house had been on the small size for his four boisterous sons. Keeping the place, and the boys, in order had been a constant struggle. The Baldwins could have used a room like one she'd noticed off the hall at Revesby: a big messy depository for boots, coats, fishing rods, bats and balls, and the like.

It was hard to equate Mr. Compton with this informal paradise, but Terence Fish would have been quite at home here.

The view from her bedchamber revealed rolling moorland, stone walls, and sheep, arousing memories of events better forgotten. She needed to look ahead and face her terrifyingly empty future. And since she had no idea what she would do next, she put her mind to the immediate problem of getting dressed. The evening gowns belonging to the late Mrs. Compton, or Lady Something Compton rather, were lovely with very high waists, tiny bodices, and floating skirts. Unsuitable as it was for breakfast in Yorkshire, she had a mind to wear one in blue silk with a tunic of embroidered silver tissue. Celia laid the delicate stuff over her hand and admired the glistening beadwork.

Realizing she could manage neither stays nor gown alone, she pulled on the red brocade dressing gown her host had lent her over her shift and went downstairs to find a human being. She wandered along a promising

corridor and found the kitchen, but Mrs. Wardle was
nowhere to be seen. Trying the other side of the staircase, she caught a glimpse of Mr. Compton through an
open door.

"I need help with my stays," she said. "And my gown.
It fastens at the back with laces and I can't manage them
alone."

By the time she noticed the visitors it was too late
to withdraw.

"Miss Seaton, isn't it? I never forget a face."

Neither did Celia, certainly not this one. She'd never
seen a human being with a greater resemblance to a
parrot than the lady seated at the table. Her impulse to
flee she suppressed with regret. The Duchess of Amesbury had recognized her. Across the table from his aunt,
Mr. Compton stood like a statue. Celia didn't mistake
his glacial expression for indifference. He'd spent most
of the previous evening, before they retired to the separate bliss of beds with mattresses, impressing upon her
that no one—*no one*—must ever learn she'd spent the
night under his roof without a chaperone.

Just her luck she'd been caught at Revesby by someone who knew her. She looked down at the floor and
wished her ankles weren't exposed. Mrs. Wardle had
found undergarments and shoes for her, but not a single
item of hosiery.

Slightly to her surprise she had the presence of mind
to summon a curtsey and her knee poked through the
opening of the robe. "Your grace," she murmured,
straightening hastily.

The duchess's eyes bored into her. "I had no idea, Nephew, that your habits included the seduction of well-bred ladies."

"You misunderstand, your grace," Celia cut in quickly. "Nothing of *that* kind happened. Mr. Compton rescued me from a very difficult situation. He has behaved like a perfect gentleman."

"I see. How very chivalrous of him. Did you spend the night in this house?"

"Yes, but . . ."

When the duchess smiled, Celia learned, she ceased to resemble a parrot and turned reptilian. "When is the wedding?"

"There's no need for him to offer for me, I assure, your grace."

"You and he are alone here?"

"Yes, but . . ."

Mr. Compton cut off her protest. "Miss Seaton is a young lady of unimpeachable virtue." She had to say that for him: he knew how to lie with conviction. "So virtuous, so innocent, that she doesn't understand how the impure minds of others will perceive her situation." If their plight weren't so grave she'd have giggled. "I have not yet had an opportunity to broach the topic since we hadn't yet met this morning. Naturally I shall offer her my hand in marriage."

Celia broke in. "There's no need . . ."

A stern glance bade her be silent and she thought she'd better obey. They could find a way out of this fix later.

"Come here, girl." The duchess summoned her with a nod.

"Her name is Miss Seaton."

His aunt ignored the interruption. "If you are to join our family I need to know more of yours than that foolish Trumper woman told me. She's been known to present some odd birds to the *ton* but she charges a pretty penny so I imagine your fortune is more than respectable."

"I have none." Celia disdained to lie to this rampaging elephant of a woman.

"How can that be true? Did you lie to Trumper?" The duchess's eyes gleamed with avid curiosity. "I never thought she could be deceived about money."

"My late uncle," Celia answered with as much dignity as she could summon when clutching a man's dressing gown closed at the front, "sadly died before he made provision for me."

"Such carelessness about business would not be permitted in the best families. I know some Seatons in the north. Are you one of them?"

"I have no idea. My father lived in India and that's where I grew up."

"Not a nabob, I take it. A pity. Inferior connections may be eradicated by a truly large fortune."

Celia hadn't thought Mr. Compton had anything in common with his formidable aunt until she was on the receiving end of this set down. But he surprised her by coming to the rescue.

"Don't be vulgar, Duchess. There's nothing the

matter with Miss Seaton's connections. She was the niece of a most respectable man in Lincolnshire. Her lack of fortune was an accident, and my own is adequate to our needs."

His chivalry touched her. He knew little of the respectability or otherwise of her late guardian, while the unpretentious shabbiness of Revesby Hall made her wonder about the truth of his second claim.

The duchess looked as if she'd like to argue, but even she, without actually quailing, retreated before Mr. Compton's icy rebuke.

"I shall take my leave then," she said, getting to her feet, "and give you a chance to come to an understanding. Miss Seaton, I have no idea why you disappeared from town last year, or what you've been doing since, but you will do very well for Tarquin." She walked to the door, leaving Celia with the feeling she meant something quite different, then paused at the threshold. "I do recommend, dear Miss Seaton, that you put on some clothes before hearing my nephew's proposal. You wouldn't want him to get the wrong idea."

"I should go upstairs," Celia said weakly, as she watched the duchess's retreating back, trailed by her husband, a man so insignificant in appearance that Celia had only noticed his presence when he offered hasty felicitations. "My attire . . ."

"Stay." Mr. Compton gripped her arm. "Sit."

"I am not a dog." He glared at her. She sat.

They shared an uneasy silence until they heard the duchess's carriage depart.

Mr. Compton's eerie calm was fraying at the edges. "Do you make a habit of entering dining rooms in a state of dishabille?"

"I needed help with my gown. Mrs. Wardle was nowhere to be found. I had no idea you weren't alone."

"Don't you have ears? Didn't you hear us speaking? Didn't you think before you stumbled into a public room in a dressing gown? A *man's* dressing gown?"

"There's no need to shout."

"And when you realized someone was with me, why didn't you have the wit to flee? If the duchess hadn't known who you were, we wouldn't be in this mess. She'd have assumed I'd brought home a woman of easy virtue."

"That's what I am, isn't it?" She swiped the back of her hand across her eyes to dispel a prickly weakness.

"No," he said, moderating his pitch. "That is not what you are. The blame for our actions is equal. And now we've been caught, we must marry."

The words were generous, gallant even, but they didn't sound that way. While no longer shouting he clearly remained furious.

"I don't want to marry you and you don't want to marry me."

"Of course I don't."

"The duchess is the only one who knows. Can't you explain to her what happened? I find it hard to believe she'd welcome me to her family if she knew the truth. She'd be glad to save her nephew from a disastrous match."

"If the duchess knew the truth she'd broadcast it to the world."

"But surely she cannot wish to put you in a difficult position?"

A short humorless laugh was his only response.

"My goodness, you mean she would!"

"The Duchess of Amesbury likes to make people dance to her tune. In recent years I've managed to avoid putting myself in the position of having to. If we don't marry she'll make sure I suffer public embarrassment. And you will be ruined. Not that she bears you any ill will beyond the general malice with which she regards the world. You are merely an irrelevant bystander caught in the crossfire of our lifelong mutual loathing. Your ruin would be my fault as much as hers."

Irrelevant bystander or innocent victim, Celia rejected either role. She hadn't escaped from that cottage and lied and cheated her way across the dales to find herself back where she started, at the mercy of fate and the whims of others.

"You forget," she said. "I am already ruined."

"That is why our marriage is your only option."

"I could return to Mr. Baldwin and explain." Even as she made the suggestion her voice faltered. She saw herself telling the tale under Bertram's confused gaze and his sister's scornful one. Kidnapped by the man they thought her lover; locked up without her clothes; escaping across the moors, almost naked, in company with yet another man. Only a simpleton would believe such a tale.

"If he wouldn't believe in your innocence before, he certainly won't now." Unspoken but ever present was the fact she was no innocent.

As she stared at the table a chill seeped through her veins and she faced the truth. There was no one to whom she could turn. She'd love to spurn his grudging offer, made only to save face in the eyes of the world. *I shall go to my father's cousin Sir Lordly Baronet. I have no need of your help.* She might have any number of baronets, even a peer or two, among her kin. But if so she didn't know them. Other than her former guardian Mr. Twistleton, her mother's sister's widower, she possessed not a single connection. And, worse still, not a single penny and no means of earning one. Needless to say, the Baldwins weren't going to supply her with a reference. The mysterious disappearing Mrs. Stewart had been her only hope. She was absolutely alone in the world.

"There's no alternative, Celia," he said. "I don't see a way out."

His use of her Christian name, for the first time since he remembered his own, comforted her a little. While he still seethed with barely suppressed rage, the slight effort to be civil was to be commended. If she had any sense, she ought to accept his offer with relief and gratitude. He risked only the loss of his reputation; her life was at stake.

She hadn't been in love with Bertram Baldwin, even a little, but she'd been ready to marry him and be a good wife. He offered his name and home, she'd be a mother to his four sons; it was a fair exchange. But with Mr. Compton, Tarquin, the condescension was all on his part. And perhaps it would be easier to contemplate wedding him without affection if there hadn't been a few hours—impossible to believe it was only yesterday when it seemed a lifetime had passed—when she'd fancied she loved him.

He loomed over her, frightening in the perfection of his person. Not a wrinkle, a snagged thread nor the slightest blemish marred his clothing. His hair was a sculpted masterpiece. And how did he get that jaw so smooth? His forbidding expression killed any impulse to touch it. The man she'd loved had been a temporary product of a blow to the head and never really existed. The idea that she, with her lack of prettiness, unruly reddish hair, no fashion sense (and lack of wardrobe of any kind, modish or otherwise) should wed this haughty paragon was absurd. She'd spend the rest of her life feeling inadequate, a shabby wraith in the shadow of his magnificence.

Tired of having him tower over her, she stood and moved to the other side of the table. "Mr. Compton," she began. "I am sensible of the honor you do me, but I'm not overcome by joy at the prospect of our marriage. I'm sure you feel the same way."

"That is of no importance. We have no choice."

"We have a choice, as long as we haven't stood before a clergyman and spoken our vows. Let's not do anything hasty. If we wait, some other course will occur to us."

"I highly doubt that."

"I am trying to save us both from a lifetime of misery and you're making no effort to help."

"What makes you believe we are condemned to a lifetime of misery?"

"The expression on your face, for one thing. You look as though you'd stepped in something odious." She threw up her hands. "I'm going upstairs to dress."

"You can't fasten your stays, remember, which is why we find ourselves betrothed."

It was the thought of her wardrobe that almost brought Celia to tears. If she wanted to wear anything other than twenty-year-old ball gowns, she would have to ask him for money. She detested her utter dependence.

"Now sit down, there's a good girl."

She blinked furiously, gritted her teeth, and sat.

"I have a plan. I shall take you to stay with Lord and Lady Iverley. Sebastian Iverley has been my closest friend since Cambridge. He married a few months ago and his wife can chaperone you. We must make sure everything appears proper before our marriage. I don't want a hint of scandal."

"Oh no! Everything must appear proper," she muttered mutinously.

"They are visiting her family in Shropshire, less than two days away by post. Mrs. Wardle can come as your companion for the journey."

"Would Lady Iverley help me find a position? Perhaps she could be persuaded to furnish me with a reference."

"You'd rather be a governess than marry me?"

Instead of a blunt *yes* Celia strove for a measure of tact. "I think our lack of enthusiasm is mutual."

"Let's not start that again," he said. "The best thing is that Diana Iverley has perfect taste. There's no better-dressed lady in London. She is the very person to make you presentable."

Wonderful. She was no doubt one of those haughty beauties of the *ton* who had regarded Miss Celia Seaton as less than the dust beneath their feet. On the other hand, she'd hardly be pleased to see her husband's friend make a misalliance. Lady Iverley might be turned into an ally. Celia decided her best course was quiet acceptance while she examined her alternatives.

Chapter 16

One betrothal may be a misfortune.
Two looks like carelessness.

He was engaged to be married. To the wrong woman.
When he remembered the summer plans of
the Iverleys another lost memory resurfaced, and not a
trivial one: the existence of the Countess Julia Czerny,
to whom he might or might not also be betrothed. His
predicament was bad enough, without adding a malfunctioning brain to the mix. Concentrating fiercely, he
traced the history of his dealings with Countess Czerny.

Lord Hugo Hartley had shared a settee with the
English-born widow of an Austrian count at the Amesbury rout-party late in the season. She was some kind of
cousin of the duke, and thus of Tarquin, too, but the connection was obscure. As usual every aspect of Hugo's
person, from his well-cut white hair to his evening slippers, was impeccably groomed, his clothing the height
of current fashion in the best of taste. In the countess
his uncle might have met his feminine equivalent. Her

bronze satin gown could only have been made in Paris, its deceptive simplicity designed to enhance the lady's exotic beauty.

"My dear boy," Hugo greeted him. "Have you met Julia yet? Countess Czerny, my nephew, Mr. Tarquin Compton."

"'When as in silks my Julia goes, Then, then methinks how sweetly flows, That liquefaction of her clothes,'" Tarquin quoted, brushing his lips over her gloved knuckles. He encountered golden eyes, almond-shaped and distinctly amused.

"What do you say to ladies when the poets fail to provide you with apposite lines?" Her low voice seemed quite English yet held indefinable overtones of some unknown, alien song.

"I've never encountered such beauty as yours, Countess. I fear I'd be struck dumb if Herrick had not supplied me with the text."

Her laugh was music itself. "You haven't complimented my beauty at all, sir, only my dress."

Clever too. And well read.

He'd called on her a couple of times, taken her driving in the park, danced with her at a ball. Then Hugo made his plea and suggested the countess as a suitable bride. For the first time in his life, Tarquin considered marriage. She was a year or two older than him, but that was an advantage. If he had to marry, a sophisticated widow with money of her own who shared his taste for fashionable life would be perfect.

Much to his relief, he was sure nothing had been

said, though they both knew the game they were playing. They'd been acquainted a bare fortnight when they left town, each for different parts of the country. Tacitly they'd agreed to let Hugo negotiate the union, one that wouldn't, he supposed, now take place.

He wasn't heartbroken. That he'd waited almost a day to remember Julia's existence after the return of his memory was testimony to his relative indifference. But he wasn't sure if he was in some way committed to her. At the very least, becoming betrothed to Celia without breaking with her first seemed bad *ton*.

Tarquin did not like to be guilty of bad *ton*.

He looked at Celia, standing with her hands on her hips, her face a mask of angry defiance, her hair a wild halo clashing with the deep red silk brocade of his dressing gown. The contrast between her and Julia was not flattering. Why had he felt bound to defend her when the duchess had accused him of debauching her? Because, he supposed, when it came down to it he had.

"We don't have to marry," she continued to argue. "We can find a solution."

He thought about Julia's sleek elegance, her understanding of the way the world worked, her lack of noisy, messy emotion.

"We must marry," he said and wished for once he didn't have to act the gentleman.

But far worse than the loss of Julia was the fact that he'd been compromised or bullied into marriage with Celia through the interference of the duchess. How he hated to let her get the better of him!

Chapter 17

*Rabbits are known for long ears
and excessive fecundity.*

Most of the journey to Shropshire was spent apart, Tarquin on horseback, Celia in the post chaise with Mrs. Wardle. His valet and their baggage (mostly his) followed in another vehicle. Hiring two speedy vehicles was an extravagance. Used to spending without much thought, he would have to be more provident once he had a wife. He habitually lived up to the limits of his healthy income.

Dinner at the inn where they stopped for the night was eaten almost in silence. Only for the last leg, after they were alone, did he join her in the carriage, wanting to present a united front to anyone who saw them arrive. His recitation of information about the Iverleys was received quietly.

He had no idea what Celia felt about their situation: anger, nerves, acceptance, triumph, or none of those. She seemed almost cowed and he found her passivity irritating. Where was the impertinent, argumentative governess who wore her feelings openly? He wanted her to rage so that he could rage back, smile so he could turn her glee to misery, grovel so he could reject her apologies.

"That must be the wall around the Mandeville park," he remarked. "The Duke of Hampton's house is very close to Wallop Hall."

"I see," she said without notable interest.

"We must be close." Much to his relief they turned into a drive lined with ancient oaks.

All the way to Shropshire, Tarquin had the uneasy feeling he'd forgotten yet another thing. When they reached Wallop Hall he thought he knew what it was. While aware that Diana Iverley's handsome fortune came from her first husband, he hadn't appreciated the relative humbleness of her family, the Montroses. They pulled up in front of an ivy-covered manor of considerable antiquity. Both building and grounds had a frayed appearance and the house was a small one. Though not doubting their welcome, he wondered whether the Montroses would have room for them. He was thankful for his foresight in leaving Mrs. Wardle at Much Wenlock to return home by stagecoach.

As he handed Celia down from the post chaise, three squealing piglets sped across the gravel, running perilously close to his boots. Reflexively he checked that his footwear remained unsullied and finally drew a reaction from his companion.

"Don't worry," she said. "They didn't leave a single mark."

Ignoring her smirk, he turned his attention to the rusty door pull, half expecting it to come away in his hands. He heard the bell clanging within and waited. And waited.

"Is there anyone here?" Celia asked.

"There must be." He rang again and almost at once the door was opened, not by a servant but by Minerva Montrose, Lady Iverley's younger sister, looking harassed.

"Mr. Compton?" she said. "What a surprise!" And not a welcome one apparently, though he'd always been on cordial terms with Miss Montrose. She was unusually sensible for a seventeen-year-old and he'd never needed to depress her pretensions. "Oh good heavens! The pigs are loose again. I'm afraid you find us at sixes and sevens. Not," she added with a deprecating grimace, "that there's anything unusual about that, but today's worse."

"I'm sorry to arrive at a bad moment. May I present Miss Seaton? We are engaged to be married."

Minerva's eyes widened as she and Celia exchanged curtsies and polite greetings.

"Are Lord and Lady Iverley here?"

"Yes, but they're rather busy. Or at least Diana is. She was brought to bed this morning."

The missing puzzle piece in Tarquin's memory dropped into place. Diana Iverley, who'd been the size of a small pony last time he saw her, was due to give birth any day. This very day, it appeared. The timing of their arrival couldn't be worse.

Minerva saved him from the uncomfortable experience of an insoluble social quandary. "You had better come in." Once in a dark hall, she indicated a room next to the entrance. "Sebastian's in the study with my father. Why don't you join him? I'll take Miss Seaton to tidy herself."

Abandoned by the ladies, Tarquin opened the door and found a scene of debauchery in a book-lined office. Competing with an array of papers and mysterious metals objects on the big desk were two empty bottles and another half-full. A bewhiskered gentleman of middle age sat slumped on one side of the desk, his substantial belly straining a half-buttoned waistcoat. Hunched on the other, elbows on desk and head in hands, the picture of misery, was the tall, rangy figure of Viscount Iverley.

"Tarquin!" he moaned, looking up without evincing any surprise. "I've killed her! I've killed Diana!"

"My child!" The other man, presumably Diana's father, began to weep. "My little goddess. I should never have let her marry you! She's going to die and I've killed her."

"It's all my fault and I didn't mean to do it. I didn't mean to hurt her."

Surveying the scene with equal parts alarm and disgust, Tarquin was tempted to pour himself a glass from the open bottle but decided the addition of a third drunk wouldn't be helpful. He'd arrived unannounced, with an unknown lady, at a strange house. Without Diana or Sebastian to introduce him—the latter was obviously incapable of polite observance—he'd have to navigate an awkward situation alone.

"Y'know, Tarquin," Sebastian said. "A great head has to come out of a teee-ny hole. You know how small the hole is. At least," he frowned, "you don't with Diana but with other women. It's small. And heads are hu-u-ge."

"And most women survive it. I knew you shouldn't have been reading that book about childbirth. It's made you worry too much. Leave it to the women and the doctors."

The attempt to bolster his friend's spirits had no effect. "She's going to die. What am I to do without her?" He banged his head on the desk and his spectacles slid down his nose. Adjusting them, he spotted the bottle but found it just outside his grasp. "Pour me some wine."

"More wine," echoed Mr. Montrose.

"For God's sake, don't give either of them another drop!" The new arrival, a tall fair woman, was identified as Mrs. Montrose by her resemblance to Minerva. "William, you are a fool," she said to her husband. "I survived childbirth six times, not that you were any help."

"But this is Diana," he moaned. "My little goddess. I remember the day she was born. The most beautiful child I ever saw."

Their hostess turned away in exasperation. "You must be Mr. Compton," she said briskly. "Minerva told me you were here. I'm sorry I'm too busy to welcome you properly." She quelled Tarquin's apology with a brisk "Nonsense" and addressed her son-in-law. "If you want to be useful, Sebastian, ride over to Mandeville House and fetch some ice. The icehouse here is empty but the duke's is much deeper. Diana's feeling the heat badly."

"How is she? Will it be long?" Sebastian wasn't as drunk as Tarquin had first thought.

"She's fine and it'll be hours. Run along now and take Mr. Compton with you. Minerva will look after his fiancée. William," she said to her spouse. "Go and put your head under the pump then find someone to round up the pigs."

Sebastian led Tarquin to the stables. "It's terrible, this waiting. Knowing what Diana's going through and not being allowed to be there. There's not a damned thing I can do to help."

"You are helping," Tarquin said bracingly. "You're going to get her some ice. Has there ever been such a summer?"

Quarter of an hour later they headed up the drive on horseback.

"Did Mrs. Montrose say fiancée?" His allotted task had, for the moment, diverted Sebastian's mind from his fear of widowerhood and reminded him of the existence of the rest of the world. "What's going on? You never said anything to me about marriage." Though he'd come far from his old scorn for all females, he still didn't have a very high opinion of the sex, with the exception of Diana and Minerva.

Tarquin had great respect for Lord Iverley. Sebastian was well read in a wide range of disciplines, a loyal friend, and there was no one with better judgment when it came to an antiquarian book. But the knotty issues of social custom and human relations had never been his forte. Though Diana had brought him a long way from the scruffy, misogynistic bookworm he used to be, Tarquin would never have believed he'd need Sebastian's counsel on a social matter. Nuances of good *ton* fell into his own area of expertise. Yet he needed to talk to someone and there was no one he trusted more.

They were almost at Mandeville House, the mansion of Sebastian's uncle the Duke of Hampton, by the time he finished telling his story. He had to put up with a good deal of laughter from Sebastian who found the name Terence Fish immensely amusing.

"I look forward to meeting Miss Seaton," he said. "She sounds like a lady with a sense of humor and there are worse attributes in a wife. Diana never lets me take myself too seriously."

"Do you agree that I must marry her?" Tarquin said hastily, not anxious to hear another outburst about Lady Iverley's diverse perfections and imminent demise.

"She sounds as though she's in a tricky spot without much choice. Does she want to marry you?"

"Why wouldn't she? I'm an excellent match. Much better than she could ever have expected."

"I can't think of anything worse than being married to you if you despised me. You think I don't notice these things, but I'd have to be even blinder than I am not to be aware you've a nasty way with a set down."

"I believe," Tarquin said with a touch of hauteur, "that I know how to treat a wife correctly."

"Lucky her."

"I refuse to allow, after a few months marriage, that you are such an authority on the subject."

"You asked my opinion, Tarquin. Marry her, don't marry her. It's your affair."

"And what of Countess Czerny. Am I engaged to two different women?"

Sebastian gave the matter his usual thorough consideration. "Not in any legal sense. You and she have never discussed marriage directly and you haven't proposed to her. What her expectations may be based on Lord Hugo's intervention, I could not guess. You may have a moral obligation."

"A greater one than I owe Miss Seaton?"

"I think you owe her something, certainly if she is with child. I wouldn't set too much store by the Duchess of Amesbury's gossip. You can survive it. But you cannot abandon Miss Seaton without making some provision for her future."

"I know that. We came together by accident and she deceived me badly, but if she doesn't marry me I can't see any alternative for her other than ruin. With her reputation gone she is alone in the world with no means of making a living, or prospects of any kind."

"And let us not forget," Sebastian said, "that she is under immediate threat from someone for a reason neither she nor you understand. Time enough to worry about her future when she has survived the present. Have you made any arrangements for her protection?"

"You are quite right. I fear my brain isn't working as well as it should. I don't see how anyone would know where we are, but I also forgot Diana was expecting to be brought to bed." He laughed at Sebastian's exclamation of indignant disbelief that anyone could lose track of such an important event. "We should ride back and make sure Miss Seaton's all right. She mustn't go out alone and perhaps she should be armed. I wonder if she knows how to use a pistol. She's quite an enterprising young woman. She'll probably wield a weapon with as much dexterity as she spins a tale."

"Ice first. We're here to get ice for Diana."

As they rode up to the great entrance front of Mandeville House, a man emerged from the rusticated arches on the ground floor, beneath the towering central portico. Tarquin braced himself for the deployment of tact, or more extreme measures to keep the peace, when he identified the Marquis of Blakeney, the Duke of Hampton's heir and Sebastian's cousin. Not only did the cousins share a lifelong mutual loathing, Blakeney had been a rival for Diana's hand.

Today he greeted the new arrivals amiably enough. "Of course," he said when he heard of their errand. "Anything for Diana. I'll have a cartload delivered to Wallop Hall. But knowing how long servants take to do anything, I suggest we ride over to the icehouse now and get some for you to take with you. It's devilish hot and I wouldn't want to keep Diana waiting."

Sebastian threw Blakeney a skeptical look but managed to respond with equal if curt cordiality.

"What brings you here, Compton?" Blakeney asked. "I don't often see you out of London."

"Tarquin," Sebastian said, with commendable presence of mind, "has been good enough to come and offer me support. I'm very anxious about Diana."

The icehouse was almost half a mile from the house, quite inconvenient for the kitchen, Tarquin couldn't help thinking, and extremely grand for such a utilitarian building. Surrounded by trees for extra shade, it was designed like a squat classical temple with Doric pilasters adorning the protruding front and a shallow dome. The door, partially below ground level, was approached by a short flight of sunken stairs.

As soon as they entered a small entrance hall, spontaneous sighs of relief went up at the cool contrast to the blazing sun. Blakeney lit a lantern and led the way down a passage some ten feet long into a central brick-lined chamber with a deep round pit dug into the floor.

"I haven't been here in years," Blakeney said. "We weren't supposed to, but I'd come with my friends in the summer to cool off. We were always in danger of being shut in and freezing to death. Added a little spice to the visit."

"I doubt that," Sebastian said. "It's above freezing point up here. The ice doesn't melt because it's packed in tight and protected with straw. As it's used up, the temperature rises and the melting rate increases."

"You never were any fun, Owl," Blakeney said, using

Sebastian's childhood nickname. "I always thought this would be a great place to keep a prisoner. No one outside would hear him scream and as a rule the servants only fetch ice in the early morning. You could hide someone for hours."

Seeing Sebastian's tolerance, never great when it came to Blakeney, stretched to breaking point, Tarquin put a halt to these boyish reminiscences and called them to the task at hand.

He couldn't remember the last time he'd engaged in manual labor, the kind of task seen to by servants. Aside from his recent foray into the art of cookery, that is. He enjoyed climbing down into the pit with the others and scouting out a suitable block of ice in the meager light. "Does the ice come from the lake?" he asked.

"No, the springs flowing into it stop it freezing thickly," Blakeney explained. "There's a string of shallow ponds on the other side of the estate dug specially for the purpose."

"When do you run out of ice?"

"Never, unless the winter is unusually warm. We bring the older ice up and use it first."

Tarquin thought the icehouse at Revesby was usually empty by late summer. He should think about improvements so he could enjoy iced confections year-round. Then shook his head in bafflement at the idea he should spend any time on his estate at all, let alone live there permanently. He was still not himself.

Sebastian's nerves wouldn't permit any further discussion about the construction and use of icehouses.

They stuffed three blocks, each the size of a couple of bricks, into a sack and raced their horses to Wallop Hall to get back before it melted. Taking the stairs two at a time, the prospective father carried one block up to the lying-in room. Tarquin followed directions to the kitchen to deliver the rest of the ice to the cook.

There must be something about a lying-in that raised the drama level in a household. The scene was reminiscent of the recent one in Mr. Montrose's study, only with tea-drinking females instead of drunken men. Celia and Minerva, each clutching a cup, sat at the long deal kitchen table, on either side of a very large woman wearing a mob cap over gray curls and a red face. The two young women listened to her with round eyes.

"Three days, three days she was in labor, poor thing." The woman, presumably the cook, appeared to be coming to the end of a long story. "And after all that time, the child was born with webbed feet and the head of a rabbit." Tarquin sent up a silent prayer that Sebastian hadn't come to the kitchen. He could only imagine what a tale like that would do to his friend's tenuous sanity. "And that should be a warning to young ladies not to let gentlemen get too close."

"Ahem," he said. Three pairs of eyes looked at him with a certain hostility, as though he might be in the habit of impregnating women with coneys. He held up the sack. "I have ice. Where shall I put it? Lord Iverley has taken some upstairs but it won't last long in this heat."

The cook bustled over and bore it off to a pantry,

taking Minerva with her. "One of the maids broke her wrist yesterday," Celia explained, "and the other is visiting her dying mother. Minerva is helping the cook."

"Let's go outside," Tarquin said. In this household he wouldn't be surprised if the cook ordered him to peel vegetables or scrub pots. "The best we can do is keep out of the way. I'm distressed that Lady Iverley's confinement slipped my mind."

"They didn't expect her to begin her labor for at least another two weeks. The doctor hasn't even arrived yet. He was away from home last night. Luckily the midwife is in attendance and Minerva says Mrs. Montrose knows just what to do. But little wonder the household is in disorder."

She appeared to have learned the layout of the house and led him down a passage to a back door. They were on their way out when Minerva caught them. "Here," she said, handing Celia a basket. "Would you mind picking some peas for dinner? You'll find the kitchen garden round the corner and to the left."

"I suppose," he said, when they were alone again, "there's no point inquiring what happened to the gardener."

"Probably suffering from the plague. I'm glad there's something we can do to help."

"I'm at my wits' end to know what to do with you."

"Minerva says we shouldn't worry. I can sleep with her, and only one of the Montroses' four sons is at home so there's a room for you too. According to her, the family always welcomes guests and the only thing that ever bothers Mrs. Montrose is a sick dog."

Though he should be relieved that the solecism of arriving uninvited at such a time was to be overlooked, he couldn't feel comfortable. Not for the first time, he heartily wished he'd never left London. Celia seemed quite at home in a kitchen garden. Was he really going to marry this woman?

He shook his head at her appearance in the simple gown Mrs. Wardle had found her in Stonewick, a loosely constructed garment without the slightest pretension to fashion. The dull green suited her red hair, now improved by a good brushing and neatly confined by hairpins at the back of the head. The days outdoors had imparted a healthy glow to her eyes and complexion and he had to admit her lips were a good color. Nevertheless she looked exactly what she was, a governess.

Nothing could be further from the elegant woman he'd envisioned as his bride. Yet when he thought about the Countess Czerny, he couldn't quite remember her face.

"The Montroses are very kind," he said. "I'll send my valet to an inn. I doubt there's room here and he complained enough about the conditions at Revesby."

Celia's face lit up with an evil grin. "You should have him brush the straw off you before he leaves. Or is rustic adornment the new fashion for gentlemen?"

He hadn't even noticed the wisps clinging to his coat after the exploration of the icehouse, eloquent proof of his disordered brain and the sorry state to which acquaintance with Celia had reduced him.

"Well," he said, delicately removing a straw from his sleeve and trying to make the best of things. "A gentleman's attire should always suit the occasion. We'd better pick those peas. Do you suppose we need to pod them too?"

Chapter 18

*A thirst for knowledge is not always
healthy in a young woman.*

They shelled peas and tried to keep Lord Iverley
distracted. Mr. Montrose and his youngest son,
Stephen, joined them on the shady terrace once all the
piglets had been rounded up.

Celia loved the Montrose family. Every member
seemed utterly unaffected, speaking fearlessly without
thought of criticism or judgment, and accepted her in
the same spirit. She had never, since leaving her father's
household, felt so much at home. More so, in fact. Not
that Ghazala had ever treated her unkindly, but the gulf
between Algernon Seaton's native "bibi" and his daughter by his deceased English wife had been deep and un-
bridgeable. She might have shared her recollections of
awaiting the birth of Ghazala's sons, but experience had
taught her to keep that time in her life buried. She did not
believe the Montroses would condemn her for her past.
Mr. Compton—Tarquin—was another matter entirely.

Her so-called betrothed did not, in her opinion, show

to advantage compared to the lively Montroses. He kept stealing glances at her and she could feel the weight of his disapproval. Scorning her appearance, no doubt. She didn't care. Her simple gown was entirely appropriate for her company and surroundings and he was overdressed, especially since he'd somehow disposed of all the straw.

She admitted, grudgingly, that Tarquin showed a certain skill in keeping his friend from becoming unhinged. When the doctor made his appearance, Lord Iverley had to be restrained from strangling the man for his tardiness.

The next time the bell rang, Minerva was elected to answer the door. Judging by Lord Iverley's reaction to the caller, it was just as well. Celia couldn't think what there was to inspire his comical look of loathing, unless it was the newcomer's extreme beauty. Celia had never seen a better-looking man. Much of an age with Tarquin and Iverley, he possessed golden hair, blue eyes, and perfection of face and figure that said *Greek god*.

"What are *you* doing here?" asked Lord Iverley, who had been pacing around the seated group but now stopped and glared at the caller.

"I accompanied the ice cart over from Mandeville," he replied. "Naturally I wanted to inquire after Diana in person. We are, after all, old friends."

"There is no change in Lady Iverley's condition," her husband snarled.

"Sebastian," Tarquin said, leaping to his feet. "Let's go for a little walk. It'll take your mind off things."

"Just as well," Minerva said once the two men were out of earshot. "You provoked him."

"Me?" the god asked with an air of astonished innocence. "I just brought the ice."

"Well, there was no need. It's not as though you drove the cart yourself."

Celia knew Minerva to be frank, but she hadn't seen her rude. In fact she'd learned the girl burned with ambition to become an influential political hostess. The animosity between this pair was comical, especially since Minerva, tall and fair like her mother, almost matched the visitor in beauty.

"How gracious of you, Miss Minerva," he said, "but you are always so charming."

Minerva flushed at his sarcasm and remembered her manners. "I beg your pardon. You haven't been presented to our other guest. Miss Seaton, this is our neighbor, Lord Blakeney."

So in addition to resembling a deity, he was also heir to a dukedom. Celia felt quite out of her depth. Much to her relief he excused himself and Minerva escorted him back through the house.

By the time she returned, Tarquin and Iverley had rejoined her on the terrace. "We've got so much that Cook has decided to make raspberry ices," she said happily.

"Why did *he* come asking after Diana?" Iverley demanded, straightening his spectacles which had fallen halfway down his nose. "None of his business."

"Calm down, Sebastian," Tarquin said. "He brought ice and he meant well."

"I wouldn't go that far, "Minerva said. "Blakeney is selfish to the bone. But I honestly don't think he's interested in Diana anymore. He was more curious about Mr. Compton, surprised he'd deigned to appear in the rural fastness of Shropshire."

"That doesn't sound like Blakeney," Tarquin objected.

"I paraphrased. I told him you'd escorted Celia here for a visit."

"D . . . dash it. We told him earlier I'd come to support Sebastian. I wouldn't want to harm Miss Seaton's reputation by having it known she was traveling the countryside in my company." He looked his formidable haughtiest but Minerva was unquailed, if apologetic.

"I do beg your pardon. I didn't realize it was a secret." She grinned. "Don't worry. Blakeney never takes much interest in other people's affairs. He'll have forgotten by the time he gets home."

"Isn't his father a powerful politician?" Celia inquired. "I would think he'd be a good connection for you."

"The duke and duchess have been very gracious to me since Sebastian married Diana and we became relations. But Blakeney is a complete idiot. I used to be bored to death listening to him drone on about hunting. I am so thankful Diana didn't marry him."

Celia grew curious to meet the elder Montrose sister, who had turned down the heir to a dukedom to marry the bespectacled and understated figure of Lord Iverley. True, the viscount was not perhaps seen to advantage with the wild hair and disordered garments of a man driven to the brink of madness. She thought his anxiety for the health of his wife, whom clearly he adored, spoke well of him.

She'd like to drive a man to madness. It was quite impossible to imagine Tarquin so deranged. Terence Fish receded further into her memory.

Sometime after ten o'clock Mrs. Montrose brought the news that Lord Iverley had a son. Leaving the family to celebrate, Celia retired to the room she was to share with Minerva. Too agitated to sleep after the day's anxious vigil, she looked for something to read. Minerva's taste in literature was astonishingly dull: historical memoirs, political treatises, and *The Reformist* magazine. Luckily she'd retrieved *The Genuine Amours* and tossed it into the small valise Tarquin had provided.

Francis Featherbrain continued his adventures; Celia continued her education and enlarged her vocabulary. She felt a certain sympathy for the boy when his father lost his fortune and his studies came to an end. She did, however, find it hard to credit the way he claimed to be heartbroken by his separation from Nancy, the girl he'd forcibly seduced. His protestations of love would have impressed her more had he not continued to enjoy himself with several other women in a fascinating variety of postures.

When Minerva joined her she stuffed the book under a pillow. Chattering away while she undressed and prepared for bed, Minerva sang the praises of her as yet unnamed nephew, the first Montrose of a new generation.

"I'm much too excited to sleep," the girl said, jumping onto the bed and hugging her knees. "Tell me about your engagement. I would never have expected Mr. Compton to fall in love with someone like you."

"What kind of woman would you have expected?"

"Please don't be offended. I meant that you seem quite sensible. I'd think he'd require someone much more *tonnish*. Someone like himself."

"Someone like your sister. I haven't met her, of course, but from the way he speaks of her she sounds excessively elegant."

"That's only her clothes. Underneath she's ordinary, like the rest of our family." Minerva thought about it. "Well, not ordinary. I wouldn't call the Montroses precisely ordinary." Celia nodded her emphatic agreement. "But sensible compared to most people I've met. That's why Sebastian is perfect for her. He doesn't conform to the world's expectations, either. Lord Blakeney would never have done."

"Would you say Mr. Compton—Tarquin—conforms to those expectations?"

"He doesn't just conform to them, he creates them! And according to Diana he can be quite rude to those of whom he disapproves."

"Yes, he can."

"Celia! Has he been unkind to you? Why then did you accept his offer? I'm sorry. I shouldn't have asked. It's not my affair."

The temptation to confide to a sympathetic ear was too much. Sitting cross-legged opposite, Celia found herself relating the whole story, omitting only the degree of her intimacy with Terence Fish. While shocked at the gravity of Celia's plight, Minerva found much of the story highly amusing and Celia enjoyed dramatizing her tale. This must be what it was like to have a sister, she thought. Never in her life had she stayed up at night, sitting on a bed in her nightclothes, confiding in another girl.

"Mr. Compton is behaving quite honorably to insist on guarding your reputation," Minerva said at the end of the tale.

"I know," Celia said. "I'm very grateful, truly I am."

"I can't imagine anything worse. Gratitude is so fatiguing. Think of having to suffer it for the rest of your life."

"I am thinking about it."

"Yet I've always liked Mr. Compton. And he's Sebastian's friend. I trust my brother-in-law's judgment better than that of anyone I know."

"They seem a mismatched pair. But I assumed Lord Iverley wasn't himself today."

"Poor Sebastian. Since the beginning he's been far more concerned about Diana's condition than she ever was. Childbearing seems to be a very unpleasant business. I think it's a good thing a man should feel some compunction."

"I quite agree."

"It doesn't seem fair that the woman has to do all the suffering while the man enjoys himself."

Celia wondered if Minerva understood how and how much the man enjoyed himself. And the woman, too, at the beginning. "Er, Minerva. How much do you know about marital relations?"

"Not as much as I would like. I've seen dogs and horses. And you?"

"A little."

Minerva bounced on the mattress. "Tell me! Please! I've begged Diana but she says I must wait until I'm betrothed. How did you find out?"

"I probably don't know much more than you," Celia said hastily. "Do you think Tarquin would be a solicitous husband?"

"I should think he would find a woman far gone in pregnancy quite lacking in grace."

"I think so too."

"Even Diana wasn't elegant the last few weeks. She reminded me of our old pony who's too old to be ridden and fat as butter."

"I don't think Tarquin would have much use for a pony. He's much too tall to ride one."

Minerva found this exquisitely funny. "His legs would touch the ground on either side," she shrieked, and rolled over and hid her head in the pillows. "Oh, what's this book?"

Celia lunged for it. "Give me that! It's nothing."

"Nothing? Really?" Minerva held it out of reach. "It looks like a book to me."

Celia saw that having a younger sister might have its annoying moments. "You shouldn't open it. It's not suitable for young girls."

"In that case I'm most definitely going to open it."

Minerva slid down from the bed, carried *The Genuine Amours* off in triumph to the far side of the room and settled on the stool next to her dressing table. Celia waited in dread as the girl opened the book to the bookmark and began to read aloud.

"'A man who seeks pleasure in casual f . . .' Oh my goodness. I can't say that word!"

"Then don't. Stop now."

"Never! This is fascinating. 'He can never find it but in the senses, while he who has love on his side, is stretched on the rack of delight, by those able ministers of pleasure, passion and imagination.'" She looked up. "That seems a proper sentiment. The author advocates the act of you-know-what only when love is present."

"Believe me," Celia said. "He does *not* practice what he preaches."

Minerva read quickly down the page. "No, I can see that. Now he is engaging his master's daughter. How very interesting. They are doing it outside on a downward slope. Listen to this. 'This posture greatly enhances the pleasure, as it admits of the most perfect entrance that possibly can be conceived of every inch of a prick.'"

"Truly?" Celia asked, torn between interest and the conviction that Minerva should not be using words like *prick*. Not at least in that particular meaning of the word. "I didn't get to that bit."

"*Where* did you get this book?"

Celia felt her face heat up. "I believe it belongs to Tarquin." She explained how she found it.

"I knew he collected books, but not this kind. I didn't even know this kind of book existed. How fortunate that you found it. Finally I can learn something useful." She flipped a page. "What do you suppose this means? 'A deluge of spermy rapture.'"

Celia gave up trying to argue Minerva out of further reading and the pair of them laughed a good deal over phrases like "hills of delight" for breasts. The younger girl, exclaiming with almost academic interest over a description of a sexual position where the man held the woman as he would a wheelbarrow, was principally impressed by the educational value of the book. Celia, on the other hand, found herself growing warmer with every warm paragraph. Her private parts—or the "arched cloister of Cupid" as Mr. Featherbrain would put it—grew wet and achy and offered the best argument yet for accepting Tarquin's offer. She had a notion, hastily suppressed, of joining him in his room. Even if she could do it without Minerva's knowledge, he would likely not welcome her.

"You know, Celia." Minerva looked up from her reading. "I don't think you should marry Mr. Compton. I don't think you want to do any of these things with a man you do not love."

As nothing else could, Minerva's opinion made Celia realize she was not, and perhaps never would be, a properly brought up English girl. She did not love Mr. Compton, but felt no reluctance about doing any or all these things with him.

Chapter 19

A friend in need is often another woman.

The next afternoon Tarquin and Celia were invited to attend Lady Iverley in her chamber. Less than a full day after giving birth, her appearance was flawless. Propped up against a mound of pillows in a gorgeous lace-trimmed dressing gown, her dark brown hair was arranged in perfect glossy waves. Tarquin's appreciation of the skills of her maid deepened. Sebastian gazed at her with a more than usually infatuated grin, but Diana's attention was all on the swaddled bundle she held in her arms.

"Tarquin," she said, looking up. "What a lovely surprise to see you. Please introduce me to Miss Seaton. And accept my felicitations."

He presented Celia, who curtseyed very properly. "I do apologize for our intrusion at this time, Lady Iverley."

"It's no trouble to me. If Tarquin needs our help, naturally he has it. Would you like to see the baby?"

Celia showed great, and apparently unfeigned, enthusiasm for the new arrival. "What a beautiful boy."

Tarquin, taking a squint without getting too close, thought he looked like a rouged walnut. "Does he have a name yet?" he asked.

"We're still arguing about it. Sebastian wants to name him after one of his favorite fifteenth-century printers, but I draw the line at Wynkyn de Worde. He'd be dreadfully teased at school."

"I should say so," Tarquin said, appalled. "What's wrong with something ordinary, like John?"

"Or Sebastian?" Celia asked. "Or Tarquin?"

"The bane of my childhood," he said. "My father was fond of Roman history."

"We're not naming him Tarquin," Sebastian said. "But we would like you to be godfather."

"And Miss Seaton—may we call you Celia?" Diana asked. "Will you be his godmother?"

Celia looked pleased but diffident. "Oh, thank you. I don't know . . . you scarcely know me. And who knows what we . . ."

Tarquin cut her off with a squeeze to the upper arm. "We would both be honored," he said firmly. "You'll have to inform me about the duties of a godparent. I don't remember my own godfather doing anything for me. I certainly didn't go and live with him after my own parents died."

"Don't you know?" Sebastian said. "You will be in charge of his religious education."

"Are you quite sure about that?"

"I expect you to take him to church every Sunday when we are in town."

"I never go unless I'm accompanying Hugo."

"And you must teach him every one of the Thirty-Nine Articles."

Diana came to his rescue. "Stop teasing, Sebastian. Poor Tarquin is terrified. It will be nice if you—both of you—take an interest in our son. I hope you will be providing friends for him soon and that our families will always be close."

Tarquin didn't know if Sebastian had told his wife about the complications relating to their engagement, nor whether his friend was showing his support for Celia or applying subtle pressure on Tarquin to stick to his resolve. He wasn't sure how he felt about that. Yes, he was set on doing the right thing. But on another level he couldn't truly accept that he might, in a matter of weeks, be tied to this woman for life. Was he expecting to be rescued from the consequences of his own good intentions?

His betrothed blushed at the hint of their future progeny. Astonishing really that she should be capable of shame.

He found himself looking at her a great deal and the more he looked the less he was troubled by her appearance. He decided her bold, expressive features transcended mere fashion, and was astonished to discover fashion *could* be transcended.

Perhaps his strange reaction resulted from their setting and company. Accustomed to being perfectly at ease in the highest of *haut ton* circles, among the Montroses Tarquin was nothing special. He could draw a belly laugh from Mr. Montrose for a jest or a serious response from Minerva for an observation on politics. But none of them cared a whit for the cut of his coat. Mostly he remained a silent listener to a constant stream of badinage about children, books, medicine, the cultivation of vegetables, the breeding of dogs, and any other subject that crossed anyone's mind. And Celia was there with them, bantering back and forth as though she'd known the family forever. Her face alight with laughter and interest, she was a handsome woman.

Lady Iverley diverted his attention from Celia's face, softened almost to prettiness as she smiled at the baby. "I know how you can be helpful," Diana said. "When he is old enough you may take our son to your tailor."

"That I can do. And perhaps in return you could help Celia with her wardrobe. She has almost nothing to wear and is in need of some advice."

"I would be delighted. And it will give my maid something to do. She's dying to start planning new clothes for when I have my figure back, but I'd much rather just play with him." She lifted the infant for a kiss and while she made the kind of silly noises people use for young children and small dogs, Tarquin planned his escape from this dangerous location.

"Would you like to hold your godson before you go?"

"Thank you, no," Tarquin said hastily. "Another time perhaps. When he's a little older." Much older, he swore silently, if ever. He suspected babies of exuding undesirable secretions. Extremely glad to be told to leave his betrothed with Lady Iverley, he retreated with his dignity intact before being landed with any new duties. Sebastian went with him, under orders to send in his wife's maid.

"Funny little fellow," he said of his newborn son. "I wonder when they start looking like people. I'll have to find a book about it."

"I should leave it to the women. They know what to do with infants. Diana looks well."

"Doesn't she?" Sebastian said with his rare wide smile. "It's remarkable how she has come through the ordeal."

Tarquin shook his head in silent amazement at the way his friend had changed since his marriage. And yet he hadn't really. He was the same old earnest bookworm. The only difference lay in his undoubted happiness.

Celia remained behind with Diana Iverley who, though groomed to an inch, appeared otherwise un-alarming. They spent a few more minutes admiring Master Iverley who was tiny and sweet in a red, wrinkly way. Celia had always been fond of babies, but she thought Indian ones, with their darker skin, were prettier.

"Now," said Diana, "before Chantal comes in. Tell me, do you want to marry Tarquin? Sebastian and Min have both told me some of your story."

"At the moment," Celia replied, "I don't have a ready alternative. I hoped perhaps you could help me find a position as a governess."

"If it comes to that, I could try. But I really think

you should consider marrying him. He's a good man underneath that exquisite exterior. And I should like having you as a friend."

"You don't know me."

"I wouldn't admit it to her, but my little sister is a good judge of character. She likes you very much."

Celia wondered if Minerva had told her about their previous night's readings, and if Diana would feel the same way if she knew she'd introduced a young girl to improper literature.

"He's still very angry with me."

"Of course he is. You made a fool of him." Diana laughed. "Terence Fish! We are never going to let him forget it."

"Please don't bring it up. Things are awkward enough between us."

"Very well, much as it pains me, I shall refrain from teasing him until you and he have resolved your differences. Let's talk about clothes."

"Thank you. I do need something to wear, even though I never look right, however I'm dressed."

Diana narrowed her eyes and looked her up and down. "Your figure is good," she said with a nod. "That kind of thick curly hair can be troublesome but I like the color. It must be dressed in a way that enhances your face, particularly your cheekbones which are your best feature. You have a strong face and you need gowns to match it. Demure muslins such as young girls wear will not show off your looks to advantage."

"Thank you." This dispassionate and honest assessment gave Celia far more confidence than indiscriminate and insincere praise.

"When Chantal comes we'll make you modish enough to hold your own in any company."

"Perhaps it's wrong of me, but I'm quite reluctant to make an effort to improve my appearance just so that I won't shame Tarquin. It rubs me the wrong way to transform myself just to try and win the approval of a man who'd probably strangle me if he could get away with it."

Diana gave a crow of satisfaction. "I knew you had spirit. But let me make one thing very clear. We don't dress to please men. We dress to please ourselves and annoy other women. You'll feel much better when Chantal has finished with you. Men don't care. I could put on rags and, if he noticed at all, Sebastian would ask me if I have a new gown."

"Tarquin would notice."

"True. He's quite unnatural that way and therefore should be ignored."

For a moment Celia succumbed to temptation and a secret ambition to dazzle Mr. Tarquin Compton into stunned adoration so she could proceed to trample on his heart. Reality intruded. "I have no money."

"That's all right. I have all the clothes I've worn while I was increasing. My maid shall cut them down to fit you."

"Won't you need them for next time?"

"I never wear the same thing for more than one season. Chantal would give notice."

The Iverleys, Celia decided, must be very rich despite their lack of pretensions. She'd never heard of anything so extravagant.

"If we need to buy anything," Diana continued, "and I expect we shall—shoes, stays, that kind of thing—you can repay me when you are married."

"I am very grateful, Diana, but I'm not comfortable with the arrangement. It's bad enough that I may be forced to marry a man who dislikes me, without burdening him with my debts."

"In that case, you must marry someone else. You have no idea what a genius Chantal is. I used to be quite ordinary-looking, you know. By the time she's finished you'll have no trouble attracting suitors. Tarquin will have to fight for you."

The next morning she found Tarquin in the garden, staring at the seedy shrubbery in such a brown study he didn't hear her approach. Her eyes were caught by something in the middle of his back. She plucked it off and he swung around.

She held up the short white hair. "I'm just trying to be helpful. This was clinging to your coat."

He half smiled at her, for the first time in several days. "Thank you. With Mrs. Montrose's dogs, it's hard for a dandy worthy of the name to maintain his standards in this household."

"Will your reputation be sunk beyond reproach?"

"I shall have to resign from my clubs."

"You may rely on my discretion. I promise not to

tell a soul that the perfection of Mr. Tarquin Compton's person was marred by canine shedding."

The elusive grin broadened and her heart banged against her ribs. She'd missed that smile. It would be easier for her if he remained resentful and morose.

"Thank you. I don't know what Uncle Hugo would say if he knew."

"Who is Uncle Hugo?"

"My great-uncle, Lord Hugo Hartley. He taught me how to dress."

"I always wondered how you became a dandy."

This glimpse into his past seemed to offer a hint of his private self. She wanted to know more, but she had no right to press. He didn't further enlighten her.

"We need to talk about your safety," he said. "We can't assume Constantine has given up."

"How would anyone know I am here?"

He thought about it. "They probably don't, for now, but a really determined pursuer will track you down eventually. I don't want you to go anywhere outside alone. And if I can ever get Sebastian to pay attention for more than five minutes, we may be able to come up with an idea of what else to do about it."

"I've thought and thought and I still can't imagine what anyone wants with me. But if they catch up with me, I think we ought to try and catch them. It may be the only way we'll find out."

Tarquin frowned. "I don't want to put you in danger, but you may be right. Shall we walk?"

She nodded and took his arm. "Lady Iverley is delightful," she said, after a while. "I didn't know where to look when they asked me to be godmother."

"It's quite suitable that they should ask my bride to share my godparental duties." He pokered up again and looked down his nose at her. There'd been moments when she'd been unsure if the information she had to impart was good news. Now she knew: good news for her and certainly for him.

"Mr. Compton."

"Don't you think the formal address is rather absurd? You call me Tarquin in public."

"That's because our public relationship is a lie. In private let us be honest with other. There is no need for us to marry and in future we shall be Miss Seaton and Mr. Compton to each other under all circumstances. I came out to inform you that I am not with child."

He responded with a stiff little bow. "My felicitations. It is better that way. A rushed marriage and early birth always causes talk."

"There's no need for a marriage at all."

"I say otherwise. My honor demands it."

"Keep your honor. I am breaking off our engagement."

"You can't do that."

"I can and I do. The only reason I agreed to it was that I had no money and nowhere to go." She sounded churlish to her own ears, but it was better to make a clean break, even if she added discourtesy to her list of sins.

"You still don't."

"Lady Iverley has offered to help me find another

position as governess, or even a different husband."

"The devil she has! What business is it of hers?"

"I thought you'd be relieved."

He towered over her, with his most formidable glare, his wrath as great as when he first discovered her deception. She raised her hands, palms out.

"What do you want?" she almost shouted. "You ought to jump at the chance to get rid of me."

Then he kissed her.

There was no sweetness to it. His hands gripped her shoulders painfully; his mouth on hers was hard, punishing. And she loved it.

She loved the instantly familiar touch of his lips, his spicy taste now overlaid with a hint of tooth powder. She loved his subtle untraceable scent, and the feel of his shaved chin against hers. She seized his head between her hands and pulled him closer, opening to his kiss and returning it.

All too soon she was free again. He stepped back, softly panting and looking more furious then she'd yet seen him.

"Why?" she said, catching her breath. "What was that for?"

He ran his fingers through his hair and she recognized that his state of agitation must equal her own. Normally Tarquin was so physically controlled.

"I don't know," he said. "I don't understand. You are *not* the kind of woman I am attracted to."

She stood there with her hands on her hips, hair disarranged, glaring up at him with wild eyes. She was letting him off the hook, tossing him back into the pond, and Tarquin knew he should be happy.

She wasn't pregnant and she'd been embraced by his friends who would help her get settled without him. And instead of feeling pleased, all he could think was that he'd never make love to her again. What was it about this tall, flat-chested, ill-dressed governess that he found irresistible? Why had he spent the previous night wishing she wasn't sharing a room with Minerva so he could join her in bed? When he thought about being married to Celia, about sharing his life with her, he shuddered with horror. But when he thought about sleeping with her his heart pumped and his body stiffened.

Good manners slipped away. "You are an impossible woman. I don't know what I see in you."

"In that case," she said, "it's a good thing we do not have to be married. I shall inform our hosts that our engagement is over."

"Fine," he said and stamped off.

Chapter 20

*Gentlemen are not, as a rule,
interested in young children.*

Chantal, Diana's maid, terrified Celia. The French-
woman was middle-aged, tiny, and dressed entirely
in black. She had strong opinions and no compunction
about expressing them. To Diana's suggestion that Tarquin should be consulted about Celia's attire she replied
with a single French-accented word.

"English." It emerged like an expletive and Celia
took malicious pleasure in her scorn for the arbiter of
fashionable London.

Draped, pinned, and poked, she watched her wardrobe take shape. Not even during her London season had
she possessed such finery. Lady Trumper had dressed
her in the youthful, pale garments of a debutante but not
even the genius of Chantal could make Diana's sophisticated gowns simple. Neither did she wish to. The maid
agreed with Diana's assessment that Celia needed to be
dressed in rich colors.

The details of cut and trim baffled Celia and she accepted whatever Chantal and Diana suggested. But she loved the materials. She had a weakness for the caress of silk, velvet and fine muslins and linen on her skin. She mourned her yellow silk, lost when Constantine stole her possessions, the only evening gown from her London wardrobe she'd kept. Everything else she'd sold when her guardian's death left her penniless.

Deeply grateful for Diana's generosity, she couldn't but remain uneasy at the uncertainty of her position. While wonderful to have found friends, it was humiliating to have nothing of her own. She kept wondering if she should have held Tarquin to his reluctant engagement. At least he offered security.

Or did he? Without knowing much about the law, she had the impression a wife had little power of her own. From the conversation of other girls in London she'd gathered two things about marriage among the upper orders: that a girl without a fortune found it hard to find a husband, and without a marriage settlement a married woman could find herself without pin money during her husband's lifetime or a jointure at his death. With no guardian to act for her, no money to bring to the marriage, she could wed and be left a neglected wife and a penniless widow. To be on her own and know so little of English customs was infuriating. Low burning anger at her father flamed up.

As she knew only too well, reliance on the support of men didn't always work out. Deliberately or not, one by one her father, her guardian, and her fiancé had abandoned her and left her helpless.

In the end, she suspected, she was going to have to find a way to support herself. Meanwhile she thrust her worries to the back of her mind and enjoyed the company of the Montroses.

The end of her engagement to Tarquin had been greeted with the same easy acceptance from the Montrose family as her unexpected arrival as his fiancée.

"I don't blame you in the least," Diana said. "Tarquin is much too unyielding in his habits to make a comfortable husband. Although," she added with a tinge of doubt, "no one was more set in his ways than Sebastian when I married him."

"What do you think is important in a husband?" Celia asked.

"Reliability, I suppose. It's good to have a man there when you need him. And not when you don't." Diane looked mischievous. "Take me, for instance. I love to rearrange my houses and find new furnishings and bibelots. But Sebastian, as long as I don't interfere with his library, doesn't care. I'd find Tarquin with his everlasting opinions quite tiresome."

"To me a room is just a room, as long as it's comfortable and contains the necessities for its function."

"Just as well you aren't married to Sebastian then. The pair of you would live in squalor." Diana liked to exaggerate. Lord Iverley, though by no means a dandy, dressed with a neatness and propriety that matched his character. Once recovered from the terror inspired by his wife's lying-in, he displayed a measured and heartfelt consideration for her that inspired Celia with envy.

As for the mixture of bafflement and pride with which he approached his infant son, always studying the tiny creature to discover his secrets and needs, Celia found it funny and touching.

"What about love?" she asked. "Do you think it matters?"

"It matters most of all," Diana said, "for those of us who are lucky enough to find it."

Tarquin saw little of Celia for several days. Except when they met at meals, she was closeted upstairs with Diana and her maid. One day, with Minerva for company, she went shopping in Shrewsbury. Since their hosts had accepted the end of their engagement without concern and seemed to have appointed Celia an honorary Montrose, he considered leaving Wallop. But no other destination appealed to him.

He should return to Yorkshire and finish the business that had been interrupted by his assault and memory loss. While there he might call on Celia's former employer and fiancé and look for clues to their mystery from that end. But for now he preferred to remain where he was. The idea of leaving her without his protection made him uneasy.

So he stayed on and lack of occupation frayed his temper. Normally he would have passed the time with Sebastian, boxing, riding, conversing about their mutual interests, especially their libraries. Since first meeting at Cambridge, they'd shared adventures in bibliophilia and co-founded the Burgundy Club, an exclusive association of young book collectors. But between his wife, his new son, and extensive business correspondence, his best friend hadn't leisure to spare for him, as he had before acquiring a peerage and a family.

Sebastian found time one afternoon to accompany him on a visit to the Duke of Hampton's library at Mandeville House. To Tarquin's surprise they spent as much time discussing their estates as they did the rare treasures in the collection. Talking through a couple of the problems raised by his land agent helped Tarquin make decisions regarding the future development of his property.

They returned to Wallop Hall to find the house invaded by Vikings, although invaded was perhaps the wrong word when the two arrivals were sons of the house, big, fair men, male versions of Mrs. Montrose and Minerva. William, the eldest of the family, was very brown, as befitted a man who had just returned from two years in South America and a summer sea voyage across the Atlantic. His brother Henry was a medical student in Edinburgh and correspondingly pale, neither the Scottish climate nor the habit of study being conducive to a tanned complexion. The family ran to good looks and this pair was no exception. Very handsome devils, though a trifle unrefined if one were to ask Tarquin, which no one did.

William Montrose had reached London only in the last week. Though news of his sister's marriage had reached him when he emerged from the Amazon jungle where he'd been gathering botanical specimens, this was the first time he had met his new brother-in-law. Henry and Sebastian were already friends.

Tarquin had observed Sebastian's rapport with the Montrose family and was glad for his friend, who'd had a lonely childhood. Seeing him embraced into the society of his brothers-in-law, who were chaffing him on his new state of paternity, didn't upset him exactly. But after years of being Sebastian's closest, almost his only friend, Tarquin was disconcerted to find himself on the sidelines.

He stepped back from the scene and quietly wondered which of these Norsemen he'd have to share a room with, when Minerva and Celia appeared at the doorway, Celia as he'd never seen her before. The pomona green round gown in jaconet muslin appeared simplicity itself, if one ignored the three layers of French work on the skirt, but Tarquin knew better. Diana Iverley had tricked his erstwhile betrothed in a garment that spoke eloquently of Bond Street. And her hair! The bushy locks had been tamed into gleaming curls that would pass for auburn. They framed the face, making her complexion look creamy and sending her high cheekbones into relief. Diana's maid had lived up to her reputation. The new Miss Seaton was highly presentable as well as damnably attractive.

The Montrose brothers seemed to agree. Acting as one, they made a beeline for the new arrival and demanded introductions. In no time Celia was swapping tales of Indian flora with William and folk remedies with Henry. Tarquin leaned against the mantelpiece feeling disgruntled.

Minerva came over to join him. "Celia could have been born a Montrose," she observed. "She fits in perfectly."

Tarquin strove for politeness and barely succeeded. "You mean she's naturally boisterous?"

"I meant unconventional. Our family is quite mad. But I suppose we are a bit noisy, especially when the boys come home." She looked at him curiously. "Do you have brothers and sisters?"

"Two sisters."

"And was your family always sane and quiet? Even three children can make quite a din."

He remembered that, in the nursery at Revesby, or tearing around the garden. Before London and the regime of the duchess, where any expression of emotion might be repressed or punished.

"At Amesbury House exuberance was not encouraged," he said.

"I don't know if it's precisely encouraged here. It just seems to happen. As you've probably noticed, we live on the edge of chaos."

As if on cue, a dog rose from its peaceful repose on the hearth rug, barking and nudging at Celia's skirts. The animal quieted at once when she patted it but the oldest Montrose, quite unnecessarily, went down on one knee. Celia laughed down at the genuflecting giant and their hands brushed on the canine head.

To crown his irritation, Diana made her first appearance downstairs since the birth of her son, now gloriously named the Honorable Aldus Manutius Iverley after the celebrated Venetian printer. Not that he was unhappy to see her, but she had young Aldus with her and the infant made Tarquin profoundly nervous. He'd always avoided close contact with his sisters' babies and had no intention of changing his policy now.

The boy's uncles had no such reluctance. The Vikings took turns holding and rocking him, attention the baby accepted with good-natured tolerance. Tarquin tried to fade into a corner but Celia, curse her, spotted him, just as she had taken Aldus from Henry and was cooing at him.

"Mr. Compton," she said, with a glint in her eye he swore was malicious. "Wouldn't you like to hold your godson? Aldus, meet your godfather."

There was nothing for it. He let her place the baby across his arms and prayed he wouldn't drop him. Aldus stared at him with unfocused blue eyes and opened his tiny mouth like a fish's. "I think he's about to cry," Tarquin said.

"No," Celia said. "It's just wind."

What the devil did that mean?

"Hold him upright, like this." She adjusted the child in his arms. "There."

Aldus blinked once and opened his mouth again, ejecting a milky emission over the lapel of Tarquin's superfine wool coat.

Celia knew the baby would spit up. She was only sorry it was so little. A gallon of sour milk soaking Tarquin's coat would have been cause for celebration.

She hated him.

He hadn't said a single word about her appearance, not one. All the time she was talking to the Montrose brothers she watched him out of the corner of her eye. She'd been dying to see what he thought of her now that Diana and Chantal had pronounced her presentable. Well, she had the answer.

Nothing. He thought nothing. The lovely new Celia wasn't worth a smile or a comment from the Grand Panjandrum of London style. She might have guessed she'd never be good enough for him and she scolded herself for caring.

The admiration of the new arrivals soothed her bruised sensibilities and she'd be inhuman had she not enjoyed their pointed admiration. Never in her life had she been the recipient of gallantry from not one but two very handsome young men. Sitting on either side of her at dinner, both showered her with compliments. But she began to sense a more pointed interest on the part of the elder.

He eagerly listened to everything she had to say on the subject of Indian botany. William knew a great deal more than she, having conducted extensive correspondence with botanists at the gardens in Madras and Calcutta. He had been engaged by an aristocratic patron to design and oversee the construction of a large hothouse for tropical plants.

"I hope to travel to India myself," he told her, "and bring back specimens. It's far more satisfying to gather them *in situ*. And I would like to see a giant banyan.

They can grow over three hundred yards in circumference. Did you ever see such a thing?"

She denied acquaintance with such a monstrous tree and, though she'd lived in Madras for a few years, had never visited the botanical garden there. But she did her best to describe the plants in the luxurious gardens surrounding her father's house.

"Do you wish to return to the land of your birth, Miss Seaton?"

"I have no connections remaining there," she said, though not sure if this statement was true, "and the journey is long and uncomfortable."

"To one whose whole life was spent there, the climate in England must appear very cold."

"Cold, Mr. Montrose? After this summer we shall all be grateful for a little temperance. Even a snowflake or two."

"During two years in the jungle I dreamed of snowdrifts every night. What do you miss, if not the heat?"

"Why, vicious biting insects and poisonous snakes. The English countryside is so tame and lacking in challenge."

"I can see you are a lady of great intrepidity, an excellent trait."

His attentions to her were quite marked and she ought to feel excited at the prospect. With his career well launched, William Montrose could afford to marry. He was a great blond giant with eyes that appeared startlingly blue in his tanned face. He had intelligence, kindness and a sense of humor. And his family, the unconventional Montroses, would accept, and quite possibly revel in the shadier elements of her own background. After a few hours' acquaintance Celia felt that William, with his easygoing temperament and ready laugh was a man she could confide in. She imagined telling him the truth without condemnation.

What she couldn't imagine was being married to him, and the intimacies she knew that entailed.

Once again, as happened all too often, her eyes were drawn across the table to where Tarquin conversed politely with Mrs. Montrose about horses. He was the antithesis of the Montroses: dark, sleek, reserved, self-contained.

Utterly devastating, and completely beyond her touch.

Chapter 21

Be prepared to shop.

"**W**ill likes you," Minerva said the next morning as they walked to the village of Mandeville Wallop to buy sweetmeats.

"I like him. I like all your family. You've been so very kind to me."

"I think he's interested in you. Perhaps we shall be sisters. I'd love that."

There and then, Celia decided to forget Tarquin Compton. How hard could it be to fall in love with William Montrose? With her resolution set, she asked Minerva the kind of questions a lady would want to know about a suitor she wishes to encourage. Will's sister did her best to present him in a flattering light.

"One thing about Will that I think would be very useful in a husband," she said, drawing to a halt outside the only shop in the village, "is that he never cares what he eats or what time meals are ready. He's quite undemanding." She lowered her voice to a near whisper.

"Look. Mrs. Phelps has the most hideous new ribbon. Would you call that mustard or egg yolk?"

Mandeville Wallop was a poor sort of place, without much commerce save a small inn and the shop that carried a meager and miscellaneous selection of necessities. Minerva found it a source of amusement, though she was fond of the hapless proprietor and would never let Mrs. Phelps overhear her mockery.

Celia peered at the narrow window, groping for a word to describe so ghastly a shade. The reflection of a face in the glass caught her eye and she spun around to find a man on the other side of the street, staring at them. Seizing Minerva's arm she wrenched open the shop door and pulled her inside.

"What?"

"Shh," she hissed and slammed the door behind them. "It's him. The man who kidnapped me."

"No!"

They jostled to look out of the window. "Is that him?"

Celia would never forget those dark curls and thick lips. "I have no question. He's the man who calls himself Nicholas Constantine."

"Did he see you?"

"I think so. No, I am sure. He was looking straight at us. How did he find me? And how are we going to get home?"

Although they both kept their voices low, they inevitably drew the curiosity of Mrs. Phelps. "Miss Minerva, Miss Seaton. Is there anything I can do for you ladies? You look upset."

With great presence of mind, Minerva walked over to the counter affecting a limp. "Oh, Mrs. Phelps! I have turned my ankle." She sank into the chair provided for customers and emitted a piteous moan. "Oh dear! It is very painful."

"Poor Minerva," Celia said. "I begged you to step carefully, but you would insist on jumping over that dog."

Minerva moaned some more to cover her laugh, and gave Celia's ankle a surreptitious kick. Mrs. Phelps, who hadn't the brightest of wits, wrung her hands and complained about the plenitude of stray animals.

"Do you think, Mrs. Phelps, that Jim could go over to Wallop Hall and let them know I need the cart to carry me home? And have my brothers come to collect me. At least two of them."

Mrs. Phelps looked a bit dubious. "My Jim's not too bright in the head. He might forget the message. If the other young lady goes with him I'll stay with you."

Celia panicked. "I'm afraid I'm subject to fits. I never go anywhere without another adult in attendance."

"I'll write a note," Minerva said quickly and scribbled a few words for Mrs. Phelps's slow witted son to deliver. Both she and Celia then succumbed to giggles which they tried to disguise as cries of pain and sympathy, respectively.

"Fits, Celia?" Minerva asked while the shopkeeper went upstairs to find Jim. "It's lucky Mrs. Phelps is gullible."

"It was all I could think of. What did you write?"

"I said you'd seen your kidnapper. I think we can expect a crowd."

Tarquin wasn't convinced a show of force was the best tactic. His instinct told him just he and Sebastian alone had the best chance of catching Constantine unawares. But he was grudgingly prepared to admit that the two elder Montrose brothers looked like good men to have one's back in a fight. And the matter was moot. As soon as they understood Celia was in danger there was no persuading them. Without going into more detail than they had time for, Tarquin couldn't explain his special interest in the capture and interrogation of Mr. Nicholas Constantine. Mr. Montrose and his youngest son, Stephen, insisted on joining the party too.

Tarquin had never seen their quarry, only heard his voice when hiding in Joe's barn. The others hadn't even heard Celia's description of her kidnapper, but the Montroses could tell at once that none of the men in the village street was a stranger. Tarquin, with Sebastian at his heels, tore into the shop.

Was that sobbing he heard? Had the bastard injured Celia?

Fear abated when he saw that the only occupants of the shop were female: a harmless-looking shopkeeper, sorting the contents of a box behind the counter, Minerva, seated on a chair, and Celia bending over her. She straightened at his entrance.

"Are you harmed?" he asked, taking both her hands

and inspecting her face. Alarm melted into irritation when he perceived that if either girl was hysterical it was with mirth.

"We are perfectly well," she said, "apart from Minerva's ankle." Her face crumpled with the effort not to laugh.

Minerva didn't even bother. "And Celia's fits." At least, that's what it sounded like but she could hardly speak.

"What?"

"I suffer from fits," Celia said, grinning broadly. "That's why I was unable to accompany Jim to fetch help."

He dropped her hands and raised his eyes to the ceiling. "Zeus! What nonsense will you spout next?"

She shrugged. "It was the best I could come up with at short notice."

"I'm intimately acquainted with the lies you invent on the spot."

Celia pushed past him to the door. "Let's discuss this outside." She turned back and called a farewell to the shopkeeper. "Minerva," she said. "I am sure Lord Iverley will help you."

She stalked out onto the street and confronted him. "Why are you being so unpleasant?"

He didn't know. Once it was apparent she'd come to no harm his temper had been on the rise. "I told you not to go out alone."

She stared at him. "I wasn't alone. I had Minerva with me."

"Minerva is a foolish young girl and no protection. You need a man to look after you."

"Excuse me. First, you didn't say anything about not going out without a man. Secondly, that *foolish young girl* and I managed very well."

"You obviously weren't aware of the gravity of the situation. You were laughing!"

"I am so sorry. Clearly everything would be much better if I had the vapors."

She really was the most infuriating woman. Tarquin's hands clenched in the effort to keep them at his sides. The exit of Sebastian from the shop with Minerva in his arms quite possibly saved her from strangulation.

"Are you going to carry me all the way home?" Minerva asked.

"Not if I can help it. I thought your twisted ankle was feigned."

"It is, but we don't want Mrs. Phelps to know that."

"As soon as we get out of sight you're walking. Diana's the only woman I'm prepared to carry about."

One by one, the Montrose men joined them to report on their canvass of the village. William, the first to arrive, bent over Celia with an air of concern. "Are you all right? You must have been alarmed."

Tarquin snorted.

"Celia was quick as a whip," Minerva said. "The moment she saw him she dragged us into the shop."

"I'm sure she was," William said, pouring on the butter. "I can tell you are a lady of great presence of mind and fortitude."

"Oh no," Celia simpered. "Minerva was the clever one, with the ankle."

Tarquin couldn't stand any more. "If you can bring yourselves to postpone this orgy of mutual adulation, I think we should continue our discussion at the Hall."

Quarter of an hour later, gathered in the drawing room, the Montroses reported on what they'd learned from the villagers. "The fellow rode out of the village about ten minutes before we arrived," Henry said. "Headed to the main road, no doubt."

"He can't have been in the village for long," William reasoned. "According to the innkeeper he arrived only an hour or so ago and made inquiries about where to find Lord Iverley."

"About me?" Sebastian asked. "That's odd. Why would he connect Miss Seaton with me?"

"No reason," Tarquin said. "But it's common knowledge *we* are friends. Somehow Constantine must have learned my identity and assumed Celia was still in my company."

He'd been careful to call her Miss Seaton since the end of their engagement but the Christian name slipped out and William noticed. "How came she to be in your company? I thought she was a friend of Diana's." He gave Tarquin a hard look. "If you don't mind my asking."

Tarquin thought it none of his damn business, but he obliged with a brief and heavily edited account of their adventures.

"So this man stole everything you had on you? Did you carry a card case?"

Tarquin felt a fool. That William Montrose had been the one to make the connection was especially irritating. "Of course," he said. "I should have thought of that."

"I'm not surprised you didn't," Celia said. "You're likely still affected by the blow."

Better and better. Now she thought him weak in the head. "He would only learn my name from my cards. But anyone in that part of Yorkshire would recognize it and direct him to Revesby."

"Where he must have learned you'd come to find me." Sebastian frowned. "I don't like this. I'm concerned for Miss Seaton's safety, obviously, and I don't like the idea of such a scoundrel coming anywhere near Diana and the child."

"What about me?" Minerva asked. "Aren't you concerned about me?"

Sebastian's face relaxed. "You, miss? I'd be sorry for any villain who tried to tangle with you."

"Did he know you'd seen him, Celia?" Tarquin asked.

"I'm almost sure he did. He was looking straight at me when I spotted him so he must have noticed my surprise."

"That's a pity. When he makes the next approach he'll be more circumspect. You must redouble your vigilance and we must all be on guard."

"If he shows his face in Mandeville Wallop again, someone will tell us immediately," said Mr. Montrose. "I shall inform the magistrate too. The man should be locked up and tried for kidnapping and robbery."

"But what does he want?" Celia cried. "I've thought

and thought and cannot come up with a reason for any of this."

"That's why we need to apprehend the man. Questioning him is the best way to find out." Tarquin's knuckles itched. Having Constantine arrested and placed in the hands of the law seemed a tame solution. He looked forward to going a few rounds with him and next time *he* wouldn't be the one with a sore head.

"There's the other man too," Celia said. "The one with the bloodhound. We don't even know what he looks like."

"I don't think Miss Seaton should stay here," Sebastian announced. "The house is too small and easy to break into and she can't have male protection in her room at night. I'll ask Blakeney if she can stay at Mandeville House. She'll be safe there."

Tarquin was impressed. For Sebastian to ask his cousin Blakeney for a favor, he must be truly worried. That his concern was likely as much for his own family as for Celia was forgivable. Sending her to the Duke of Hampton's house wasn't a bad idea. The mansion sat in a walled park and swarmed with servants; no stranger would easily get access. Since the duke, a prominent politician, entertained a steady stream of visitors all summer long, Celia would be surrounded by people.

"I'm going too," he said. "If Constantine turns up, I want to be there."

Who knew what foolishness she'd get up to without him to stop her?

Chapter 22

Dressing well is the best revenge.

"**A**re you quite sure you can spare Chantal?" Celia asked.

"For the dozenth time, yes. You'll be doing me a favor. She loves Mandeville and was quite disgusted when I didn't marry Blakeney." Diana patted her son's back and he dribbled milk onto her shoulder. "Look at this. As long as Aldus emits a constant stream of drool there's no hope for me. I look dreadful and I don't care."

"Hardly dreadful. Perhaps your hair is a little less perfect than usual."

"You'll get much more respect at Mandeville if you have your own maid. And she'll make sure you look your best. The Duke and Duchess of Amesbury have dozens of guests every summer and these gatherings of the *ton* can be intimidating."

Celia nodded. "I remember all too well from my brief London season."

"I do too." That the elegant Lady Iverley had ever

been an awkward debutante was hard to fathom, but Diana assured her it was so. "Even later, when I was a wealthy widow, I received frequent snubs. Remember you are just as good as they are and never let them see you care about their scorn. Being beautifully dressed is the first line of defense."

"I can't thank you enough for all your help."

"I've enjoyed it, and I'll miss you. We all will. You'll come back for the christening, of course."

Celia reached into her pocket. "I have a present for Aldus. It's not much, I'm afraid, but it's all I have. It was my mother's when she was a child and she passed it on to me."

The cook had provided her with a rag and some silver whiting, a paste of tartar and water with a little wine spirit. She'd sat at the kitchen table and rubbed every scrap of tarnish off the battered rattle, polished it until it glowed. Alas, the cleaning revealed every flaw: scratches in the small handle, just the right size for a baby's chubby fist; several dents and a crack in the side of the sphere containing the rattler.

"I'm afraid it's rather the worse for all its travels. It doesn't even make much of a noise."

Diana took it and shook it near the face of her son who now lay quietly in a cradle next to her chair. He regarded it without apparent interest. "He's too young but he'll love it later. And I love it now. Old toys have so much character. Every blemish tells a story from a child's past. Perhaps you cracked it fighting off a poisonous Indian snake."

"You wouldn't want your infant anywhere near a cobra. I don't remember playing with it, any more than I remember my mother. I was too young."

Diana touched her hand. "Are you quite sure you can spare it? I'll understand if you prefer to keep it."

Celia's eyes welled up. "I want Aldus to have it as a small token of my gratitude. You've welcomed me like a family. Or at least as I imagine a family does."

"You told me your mother died when you were four. Who brought you up? Was your father an attentive parent? Mine was, as you may imagine, but gentlemen aren't always like that."

The questions were too close to things never spoken of and better forgotten. "My father traveled on business a great deal. The rest of the time I lived with the native servants." An answer repeated so often she almost believed it to be the whole truth.

"Did your father never think to remarry?"

"There were few English ladies available." Another truth.

"You must have been lonely."

"Sometimes." It was impossible to explain the nature of her situation in her father's household, though for once she was tempted to try. Mr. Twistleton and Lady Trumper were the last of a line of advisors who'd strongly cautioned against frankness. "I shall miss you all," she said instead.

"Perhaps you will be a member of our family one day. Oh dear! I may start weeping."

"Me too."

The entrance of Lord Iverley put paid to the impulse to either confidence or lamentation. "The carriage is ready. Your luggage has been loaded and Tarquin is waiting."

Celia hadn't imagined a house as large as Mandeville. The Palladian mansion with its massive central portico and two sprawling wings was as big as a town and the front door large enough to admit a carriage. As they passed through the hall into a huge oval receiving room, topped with a high dome, Tarquin's presence was a comfort. She resisted the urge to clutch and crease his tailored arm.

The splendor of the surroundings appeared not to affect him. Why would it? He'd grown up in such a house, under the guardianship of the Duke of Amesbury. For all she knew that particular ducal home might dwarf this one.

Liveried servants brought their bags from the Montroses' elderly carriage and led them up a grand staircase, the beginning of a long journey to their rooms. Celia tried to take note of the route, imagining herself lost in the endless maze of corridors. Much to her relief, she was told there would be a footman on duty all day in the guest wing, should she need assistance. They reached her room first.

"I'll see you downstairs later," Tarquin said and left her feeling small and lonely.

Luckily she had Chantal, who made no secret of her delight at being in a house worthy of her status as a first class dresser. The maid was less pleased when she saw the size of her room. "When I came with milady last year," she complained, "we had one of the best rooms with a view of the *grande allée*. That was when I thought milady would wed Milord Blakeney. This is a closet."

"I'm sorry, Chantal. I believe there are a great many people staying here so perhaps nothing better was available."

"It doesn't matter, but there is no dressing room or place for me. I shall have to sleep in the servants' quarters."

Though there'd been times in India when she enjoyed considerable luxury, in England Celia was accustomed to small bedchambers, first in Lady Trumper's cramped Mayfair house and then as governess with a family of respectable but modest means. She found her Mandeville quarters more than adequate. The furnishings, including a washstand, wardrobe, chest of drawers, dressing table, and small escritoire, seemed lavish to her. The floor was carpeted and the bed and window curtained in chintz that had certainly been imported from India and made her feel quite at home.

After a carriage journey of three miles she was hardly travel-stained, but Chantal subjected every inch of her apparel to a minute inspection and tidied up her ever-unruly hair. The maid wouldn't allow her to be seen in public until pronounced *impeccable*.

Half an hour later, when a footman led her downstairs, she was grateful. She might not be the prettiest or most elegant of the ladies, but at least she looked good enough not to embarrass anyone. If she'd had to see to her own toilette she'd have appeared the country bumpkin she was. The knowledge that her attire was in fashion and her grooming flawless gave her the confidence to face a palatial saloon filled with the rich, the powerful, and the beautiful. She had a fleeting fancy that Tarquin's exquisite appearance was inspired by a similar need to face a critical world in full armor.

What nonsense. Tarquin Compton had no need of armor. He was born to this world and had never known a moment's doubt in his pampered life.

Tarquin settled into his large and luxurious chamber with a sense of relief, delighted to be reunited with his valet and not to be sharing a room with Henry Montrose. It wasn't London, but he was on home territory, a haunt of the beau monde. He stood at the tall double windows and looked out at the vista of Mandeville's famous Grand Avenue, leading up a hill to a triumphal Roman arch. The grounds contained an artificial lake and half a dozen classical follies, set amidst carefully arranged plantations. If he had to be in the country, this was as it should be: nature tamed by art and subordinated to the service of mankind.

An excellent setting, come to think of it, for a dandy. Some fifteen years ago Lord Hugo had found him cowering beneath the steel slipper of the Duchess of Amesbury and introduced him to the art of the tailor. Hugo's kindness had taught the unhappy schoolboy a lesson he never forgot: that being well dressed was the best defense.

Hard on that thought came another vision: the freedom of striding the hills barefoot and laughing at the open skies, the wild beauty of Yorkshire. Of home.

Ridiculous. He thrust it aside and descended to the *piano nobile* and the state rooms, symbols of the Duke of Hampton's wealth and power and thrown open to impress a large gathering of the nation's most influential subjects. He had a duty to see Celia comfortably settled.

He found her alone in the corner of a crowded drawing room, looking anxious, the fearless Amazon of the moors cribbed, cabined, and confined by society.

"Are you acquainted with anyone here?" he asked.

"Not a soul but you," she said. "I suppose you know everyone."

"Probably." He looked around and didn't find a single unfamiliar face.

"You are lucky to have so many friends."

Friends? Were they friends? A few of them were better than acquaintances, people he liked: men he boxed and fenced and dined with; ladies who invited him to their parties and eagerly consulted him on matters of taste. But none of them was an intimate. Sebastian Iverley, the Marquis of Chase, and above all Hugo were the only people in the world worthy of that designation. In the loftiest circles of the English *ton*, where he was universally accepted and admired, few people were important to him.

He found the idea unsettling and unwelcome.

"Have you met your hostess?" he asked. "I'll take you to her."

Although he didn't particularly mix with the political set, he of course knew the Duke and Duchess of Hampton. The latter, a clever woman whom even Tarquin found a little intimidating, received them without a great deal of interest, beyond inquiring after the health of the Iverleys, and her neighbors the Montroses.

"Where is the duke?" Celia whispered as they departed the regal presence.

"No doubt closeted with some gentlemen, deciding the fate of nations."

"Wouldn't Minerva love to be there!"

"She'd set them straight in no time."

"Cousin!" Their conversation was interrupted by a fashionable couple, approaching him arm in arm. "What a surprise to see you!"

Bowing politely, he introduced them to Celia. He never could remember how this particular pair was related to him but the young matron with an unfortunate penchant for lavender and lace always claimed him enthusiastically. She wouldn't, of course, dare to openly solicit his praise of her gown. But she preened and adjusted her gauze shawl, clearly angling for his opinion. She should count herself lucky he didn't give it.

Her husband possessed less self-preservation. "What do you think of my waistcoat?" he asked as they exchanged greetings, gazing hopefully up at Tarquin from his eight-inch disadvantage.

Tarquin surveyed the offending garment, made

prominent by too many good dinners settling in its wearer's stomach. "I do believe it matches your wife's gown," he said with a polite bow toward the lady. "The pair of you could start a fashion. Please excuse me. I see someone I know."

He wondered if they felt complimented and if so, whether they would persuade any of their friends that his-and-hers matching clothes were the new thing.

Celia, who had lost the pinched look she'd worn when he first joined her, regarded the departing couple with a mischievous smile. "So you think they will? Start a fashion, I mean."

"Perhaps. Last year Sebastian set off a rage for peacock feathers in bonnets when he told someone I'd said they were the latest mode."

"Good Lord. Just because *you* said so?"

"Just because *he said* I said so."

"I don't believe it!"

"I'm afraid it's true."

"I knew you were powerful but that is absurd."

"Quite absurd," he agreed. "It lasted two weeks before some intelligent lady realized it was all nonsense."

"I should like to meet *her.*"

They laughed in cautious amity.

The peacock feather affair had been an amusing episode. Even more amusing had been the challenge of turning Iverley from a shabby bookworm into a man of fashion. But otherwise, Tarquin realized, in the last couple of years he'd found *ton* entertainments tended to get repetitious. Climbing the ladder to the pinnacle of fashionable power had been fun. Ruling from on high lacked variety and spice. Perhaps he needed a new challenge.

Celia looked about her, bright-eyed and smiling. He had never seen her bored, and he'd never been bored by her. Infuriated, certainly. Fascinated and entranced even, when he wasn't in his right mind. The picture of her naked to the winds, her face transformed with bliss, swam into his brain. He beat it back.

That was not the new challenge he needed.

With relief he greeted the approach of half a dozen ladies and gentlemen. He presented Celia to the party, concluding with Lady Georgina Harville and her sister, a dim girl wearing over-trimmed yellow muslin and a hopeful smile.

"Excuse me, ma'am. I do not believe we are acquainted."

The young woman's face fell. "Oh, indeed . . ."

"Lady Felicia Howard," said one of the gentlemen.

Tarquin bowed. "Lady Felicia, your most humble servant."

"You knew that girl perfectly well! How can you be so callous?" Celia hissed at him once the party drifted on. "You are rude."

"I never encourage unmarried girls. I wouldn't want to give them ideas."

"Do you have any idea how arrogant that statement is? You insulted her by pretending not to know her. If she knows you were pretending. If not, if she really thinks you have forgotten her, her feelings must be hurt."

"Really? How do you know what Lady Felicia feels?"

"Because, Mr. High-and-Mighty . . ."

"Enough! I remember now. I ruined your life by forgetting your name . . ."

"*Pretending* to forget my name."

"And you called me Terence Fish."

"It served you right, *Fishy.* I shall never apologize for *that.*"

Their squabble, conducted a couple of tones above a whisper, was beginning to attract attention. He placed a warning hand on Celia's arms and raised his voice. "I am sure you are right about that, Miss Seaton. Let me accompany you to the tea tray."

He meant that he believed she'd never apologize. But perhaps it did serve him right. The idea that the reverence of the *ton* gave him the right to be unkind aroused his conscience. He'd noticed how unhappy Celia was, standing alone in this vast room full of indifferent strangers. Many who lacked the birth and connections, or even just the beauty and personality, to impress the leaders of the beau monde must feel like that much of the time. Why, even he could recall feeling awkward and out of place as a youth, before Hugo took him in hand.

Fishy. His lips twitched. Inventing a silly name for him wasn't such a terrible crime. And Terence Fish was a funny one.

But the comic christening was only the beginning of

Celia's deceptions. Far worse was the way she'd misled him into behavior unbecoming to a gentleman. Worse still was that he would very much like to repeat the misconduct and he no longer had the excuse that they were betrothed.

Chapter 23

*When a gentleman offers advice,
pretend to consider it before doing
whatever you originally intended.*

In three days as a guest of the Duke and Duchess of
Hampton, Celia learned two things. Young ladies
had a very dull time of it at gatherings of the politically
prominent; and she, Celia Seaton, was virtually invisible. The two facts were not necessarily connected.

No one quite knew what to make of her. She was
accepted as being a slight acquaintance of Lord Blakeney's, invited as a courtesy to his eccentric neighbors
the Montroses whose house was too small to accommodate their entire family. To be an excess visitor of such
an undistinguished family put her beyond anything but
the most perfunctory of notice.

To her surprise she didn't much care. The previous
year she longed to be one of the inner circle; now she
was a disinterested and often bored observer. Had she
any knowledge of politics, she might have found mean-

ing in the machinations of the Members of Parliament who spun in the Duke of Hampton's orbit. Most of the men and a few women, older friends of the duchess, were gripped by weighty matters of state or wallowed in the shallows of patronage and political jockeying.

When in London she'd heard people boast of being invited to the great country houses, she'd been curious and envious. But once she got over the beauty and splendor of the mansion and became accustomed to the army of servants, there wasn't much to do. The gentlemen may have been having fun; she wouldn't know; they were absent most of the day. The ladies sat around and talked, dabbled in genteel accomplishments, and waited for the next meal when the gentlemen would join them.

Tarquin, needless to say, didn't share her invisibility. She doubted most of the three or four dozen guests at Mandeville even connected her with him. They were simply too thrilled to have the famous dandy among them. Hearing the ladies flutter like deranged doves in his presence, preening and flapping to win his attention, reminded her of the miserable days of her London season. The third morning of her stay, the younger members assembled in the Yellow Morning Room, a modest designation for a large and elaborately decorated chamber. At breakfast there had been some talk of cricket among the gentlemen and to Celia's surprise she gathered Tarquin was to take part. Despite firsthand observation of his prowess as a boxer, not to mention direct knowledge of his muscles, seeing him in this milieu made it difficult to recall his appearance and behavior in those other circumstances.

As happened far too frequently, her glance was drawn across the room to where he stood with two or three of the gentlemen. Always the center of attention in any group, regardless of sex, he said something that raised a crack of laughter. A response from one of the men drew a brief smile. Celia remembered that smile, all too rare but transforming his face from stern judgment to irresistible warmth. Her knowledge of Tarquin as a very different man from the social peacock came flooding back as her heart thumped, heat suffused her torso. Oh yes, indeed. Under the perfect grooming Tarquin Compton possessed a physicality that was belied by the tailored shell. She felt a little short of breath as she remembered what lay beneath the exquisite clothing.

"Do you think Mr. Compton handsome, Miss Seaton?" She'd been caught staring, luckily by Lady Felicia Howard. Celia had become quite fond of the youngest, kindest, and dimmest of the female guests.

"I don't believe anyone denies that his appearance is perfect in every way," she replied.

"Do you think so? Of course, he is very well dressed. Everyone says so, though I like to see a gentleman wear a little color. He is so severe, and satirical too. I find him quite frightening."

"Do not, I beg you, Felicia, say anything foolish in front of Mr. Compton." Lady Felicia's dominating married sister, Lady Georgina Harville, joined the conversation. Or rather she joined her sister, whom she was desperate to wed to Lord Blakeney. Celia, she ignored. "He may say something to Blakeney and all your prospects will be dashed. Why must Mr. Compton come here at this time? He rarely accepts invitations to country houses. I didn't even know he was a friend of Blakeney's."

"I wonder whom Mr. Compton will marry," Felicia said. "I can't imagine any girl being good enough for him."

"Do not even think about him," her sister ordered, mostly unfairly, Celia thought, since Felicia's question had been driven by idle curiosity rather than the least interest in Tarquin as a potential husband. "He is to wed Miss Bromley."

"Belinda?" Felicia giggled. "She must be two feet shorter than him."

"I had it a month ago from the Duchess of Amesbury herself. As his aunt and hers she is in a position to know."

Celia wasn't aware she'd tensed up, till she found herself relaxing. It amused her to be privy to knowledge the so-fashionable Lady Georgina lacked: that his aunt the duchess was the last person Tarquin Compton would take into his confidence, and any niece of hers the last girl he'd marry. She'd love to hear Lady Georgina's reaction to the information that Tarquin had preferred to marry *her*.

Another lady entered the discussion. "*I* heard that he is all but betrothed to the widowed Countess Czerny. She is a connection of the duke and very wealthy. Mr.

Compton has no need to settle for a lady of lesser fortune and I daresay Miss Bromley has no more than twenty thousand pounds. Lord Hugo favors the countess and his influence is great. They are to be wed before Christmas."

"Don't say! I met the countess at Devonshire House. I never saw a more elegant gown. Straight from Paris, I swear on my honor. It seems that skirts are to be much wider next year."

Don't talk about skirts, Celia silently begged. She wanted to hear more about this countess. The minute her name was mentioned she'd had an ominous feeling.

Lady Georgina's brow creased. Clearly she was torn between pique at having her own gossip contradicted and fascination with this new tidbit. "I must admit they would be well suited. I cannot imagine a more elegant pair. Are you quite certain?"

"My mother had it from her cousin Lady Juno Danvers."

"Of course, Lady Juno is almost as old as Lord Hugo and they've been acquainted forever."

"Came on the town in the reign of George II, can you imagine?"

Don't talk about Lady Juno.

"I believe Lord Hugo once offered for Lady Juno but the old earl, her father, wouldn't hear of it."

"She would have been better off than with Danvers. Bad blood there."

"Lady Juno was heartbroken. On the other hand

it's difficult to fancy Lord Hugo wed, the dear old gentleman."

Celia was ready to scream. She had no interest in a putative and long-forgotten romance between two people she'd never met, but was consumed with curiosity about Countess Czerny and Tarquin. While she could dismiss the power of the duchess, she knew of his affection for his Uncle Hugo.

It had never occurred to her that he might have an understanding with another woman. Not a formal engagement, for surely he wouldn't then have offered for her. But if he had courted this countess, come close to making her an offer, her own deception was all the more shameful.

Perhaps Tarquin was in love with Countess Czerny. Celia envisioned her: beautiful, dressed in the height of fashion, possessed of an intriguing foreign accent and a fortune that made twenty thousand pounds seem contemptible.

She scarcely noticed when the ladies drifted off into recollections of other ancient alliances and never returned to the present day before the arrival of Lord Blakeney. Lady Georgina nudged her sister, who tried to look enticing. At least that was Celia's interpretation of an expression that put her in mind of a friendly mouse. Felicia needn't have bothered.

"How are you, Miss Seaton? Are you being looked after?" Blakeney made a point of inquiring at least once a day. He even, with a little effort, remembered

her name. It was likely the only reason anyone bothered to speak to her at all, his attention and that of Mr.
Compton. Though after the first day Tarquin had spoken
to her very little.

"Very well, thank you, my lord. I am quite
comfortable."

"Excellent. We're having a cricket match tomorrow.
Some of you ladies must come and watch."

"I'd rather play than watch."

"A lady who plays cricket? Compton, come here!"
Tarquin, who had ignored her throughout breakfast,
excused himself from his conversation. "Did you know
Miss Seaton is a cricketer, or a cricketress, rather?"

"A cricketrix, perhaps? How very Amazonian." He
bowed to her. "Is there no end to your accomplishments?"

Foreign countesses, she was quite sure, never played
outdoor games with small boys. The thought made her
surly. "Don't put yourself out to compliment me," she
said, "if you can't sound as though you mean it."

Tarquin knew he didn't and he knew he was being
unfair. Abandoning Celia to the mercy of the fashionable ladies staying at Mandeville was not the behavior
of a gentleman. A little more attention on his part would
make her life easier. He never underestimated his own
power. Yet it was all he could do to exchange a few
civil words when the whole party gathered at breakfast
or dinner. The rest of the time he avoided the ladies
and, despite the heat, spent most of his time joining
the sporting pursuits beloved of Blakeney and his cro-
nies: riding, sparring, and fencing, or playing tennis in

the court built in imitation of Henry VIII's at Hampton Court.

He'd always cultivated his physique, but generally he balanced his sporting and intellectual interests. Now he was spending several hours a day pushing his body to the limits of its endurance so that he could make it ignore its primary urge: to indulge in what was perhaps his favorite physical activity.

But it wasn't the current lack of a mistress that was driving him to distraction. It was the presence of one maddening woman whom he was determined to avoid. Celia Seaton had nothing—*nothing*—to recommend her as a wife. No fortune, no connections, no *ton*, and a dubious character. Since the minute he'd woken up without an idea of his own identity, her only honorable act had been to release him from the engagement his own honor had demanded of him. He'd narrowly avoided being tied to her for life and he ought to get down on his knees and thank God in his infinite mercy for sparing him that fate.

And yet. And yet she had something, something that drew his eyes to her when they were in the same room. Something that made him itch for her company and her impertinent conversation. Something that kept him awake at night as he contemplated finding her bedroom, now empty of Minerva's shielding presence.

Fearing loss of control he kept away from her, relying on the presence of the swarms of guests and servants to keep her safe while he awaited the report from his Yorkshire agent whom he'd ordered to discreetly investigate Constantine's visit to the Baldwin household, and the character and movements of the mysterious Mrs. Stewart.

"Don't forget," he began, drawing her away from Lady Georgina's group.

"I know," she said. "Don't go outside alone or with fewer than two gentlemen or half a dozen ladies. Try never to be alone. Stay in the house as much as possible. I could hardly forget. You tell me every time we meet." She folded her arms and curled her wide mouth in a sulky—and tempting—pout.

He wanted to strangle her. Or kiss her. "It's for your own safety."

"I am deeply grateful." She didn't sound even shallowly grateful. "Now excuse me. You have cricket to practice and I have embroidery to admire." She turned her back on him and took a seat next to an elderly lady famous for her devotion to tent-stitch. Tarquin stamped out of the room in search of a cricket bat.

An hour of knocking Charles Harville's bowling all over the field calmed him. Having washed off the sweat and changed his linens, he descended in a conciliatory mood, determined to say something nice to her, pay her a little attention to encourage the other ladies. It took him five minutes searching to establish that she was nowhere to be seen.

On a couple of occasions he'd noticed Celia—lucky woman—in company with Lady Georgina Harville and her sister. Suppressing all visible symptoms of rising panic, or even excessive interest in the answer, he asked them if they knew where Miss Seaton was.

"I haven't seen her since soon after breakfast when you were speaking to her," Lady Georgina replied with barely disguised curiosity.

"I saw her through the window on my way here," said her giggling sister. "She was walking through the lower garden toward the lake path."

"Alone?" He *would* strangle her.

"She was with a gentleman."

His heart pounded. "Who?"

"A stranger. I didn't know him."

Tarquin wanted to shake the girl till she stopped tittering. He refrained because he doubted Lady Felicia's ability to provide a sensible description of the man who, he very much feared, might be Constantine. He couldn't even ask whether Celia appeared to be going willingly without provoking undesirable questions.

Striding from the room with an urgency unbecoming to a man of legendary coolness, he almost broke into a run as he passed through the oversized hall, down an endless arched corridor and through the massive scarlet saloon to the doors leading onto the garden front terrace. Damn it, why did these ducal houses have to be so ridiculously large?

From the terrace he had a splendid view of the gardens leading down to the lake, but the only humans in sight were servants. Giving up any pretense of insouciance he caught one of the gardeners who, yes, had seen a gentleman pass this way, with *two* ladies, on their way to the kitchen garden. The presence of a second lady relieved his anxiety for an instant, until he recalled the existence of Mrs. Stewart and her possible part in the mystery of Celia's kidnapping. Yet a kitchen garden seemed a benign enough spot, and likely to be full of laboring outdoor servants.

Nevertheless he hot-footed the quarter mile or so to the ten-foot wall surrounding an enclosure commensurate with the vegetarian requirements of the vast household. Tearing through the wrought iron gate he was greeted by female laughter. He discovered Celia and Minerva between two rows of raspberry canes. Standing in the middle of the trio, stuffing himself with ripe berries, was William Montrose.

"What in the name of Jupiter do you think you are doing, going off like that?" he roared. Three heads turned in unison, three reddened mouths fell open. His attention fixed on Celia's stained lips. Good God in Heaven! It was bad enough trying not to kiss her under normal circumstances.

"I was with Minerva and Will," she protested. Will! She called him *Will*.

"And how was I supposed to know this fact?"

"How was *I* supposed to tell you, since you weren't present when they called?"

"You could have left word."

Minerva broke in. "The duchess knew. We paid our respects to her. Blakeney saw us too."

William Montrose said nothing. He merely folded his

arms and looked quizzical. Tarquin, beginning to feel foolish, hoped the other man's hands were covered in raspberry juice and soiling his coat.

He returned his glance to Celia and, wishing to avoid that tantalizing mouth, fixed his eyes on a small red mark on the bodice of her peach-colored gown. Not a good idea since it was less than an inch from the lace trim on the low neck. Not that there was anything unduly revealing in her dress. A pleated chemisette covered her chest from bodice to chin. But pale rosy mounds gently swelled, veiled but not completely hidden by the sheer gauze, every bit as enticing as an overt display of flesh. He gulped down a breath.

"I'm having the best time in days," Celia said. "All the ladies do here is gossip and practice their accomplishments and take little walks in the formal gardens. The Montroses know how to have fun." She lowered the hand, plucked a fat berry and sucked it into the red oval of her lips. "Mmm. Delicious."

"Does the duchess know you are eating her fruit?" It was all Tarquin could think of to say, like a killjoy schoolmaster.

Minerva looked at him in disbelief. "The head gardener knows me." Trust the younger Montrose girl to make all the right connections, even in the world of fruit.

"Don't let us keep you." William Montrose spoke for the first time. "I'll keep Celia safe and see her back to the house." He looked broad and muscular and confident.

Tarquin drew himself up to his superior height and

flexed his shoulders, contemplating a suitable snub. He knew he was behaving like an ass but couldn't seem to help it. "Thank you, Montrose. There's no need. Miss Seaton is my responsibility. We should return now. The party has plans for the afternoon and we will be missed." He plucked a particular large fruit from the bush and tossed it into his mouth. "Miss Seaton?" he said, crooking his arm.

Her glance was resentful and her pout sullen, but she began to comply when Minerva called her back. "Before you go, Celia, I have something private to tell you. Will, please go ahead with Mr. Compton."

He found himself walking two abreast along the path to the gate with William Montrose. The afternoon sun reflecting off the tall walls exacerbated his discomfort. Behind him he registered a whispered exchange of words.

"You'll want to know," Montrose said, perfectly at ease, even a little amused, "that Constantine hasn't been seen in Mandeville Wallop again." Tarquin acknowledged the information with a nod. "As far as we can tell," William continued, "he hasn't been on the other side of the park in Duke's Mandeville, either, but we can't be certain, though we did our best to describe him to the villagers there."

"Thank you," Tarquin replied. "Until I receive a report from my man in Yorkshire on his inquiries there, there's not much we can do but wait for the fellow to reappear." He clenched his fists, the need to stay and keep an eye on Celia at war with his instinct for action, his urge to go out and track down her kidnapper and beat the truth from the man.

The two girls laughed behind him and as he turned he caught Celia tucking a book behind her skirts. "The bit about the rat was the best," Minerva said. At least, that's what it sounded like.

Chapter 24

*The meaning of polite conversation
is not always obvious.*

"I'm glad you walk at a reasonable pace," she said after a while. They'd been striding along in silence. "I've been aching for some exercise. The ladies here tend to mince along with tiny little steps."

"You don't mince. I'll give you that."

She stopped and dropped him a curtsey. "I'm so gratified to finally gain your approval for something."

He stared at her. "What do you mean?"

She raised her chin. "It's been days and you haven't once commented on my dress. Though I know I'll never be a beauty, I think Diana's maid has made me look nice. But not elegant enough to draw a compliment from the great Tarquin Compton. I am sorry I was so presumptuous."

Stepping back, he subjected her to the practiced survey with which he had assessed the appearance of a hundred ladies: hair arranged in neat curls under a low-crowned Leghorn bonnet trimmed with orange satin; eyebrows artfully plucked to a fashionable arch; peach muslin round gown with long sleeves descending to a fancywork cuff and deeper matching embellishments at the hem; orange kid slippers.

But this was merely surface. He was drawn back to her face: to gray eyes, now stormy with rebellion, that roiled with every emotion; skin like a white peach, and the wide fruit-stained mouth; the strong slim column of her neck. His fingers itched for the warmth of her skin, veiled by thin gauze. Back to the mouth, rapidly becoming the object of his obsession.

"It doesn't matter what you wear," he said.

He'd hurt her, he saw at once. "Oh," she murmured, eyes stricken. Then she thrust back her shoulders and gave her head a brief shake. "I see. I never did have the ability to look modish. At least I no longer resemble a cauliflower."

"No," he said. "Nor any other vegetable. You look very well."

And that was the most he could give her. He couldn't possibly explain that, alone of any woman he'd met, he didn't see her appearance, only her essence. She could be wearing rags—he'd *seen* her in rags—and she'd be the same. Just Celia, the irresistible conundrum, the transparent yet deceiving enigma.

Crossing the bridge over a narrow stretch of the lake, the garden front of Mandeville House sprawled above them. An awning had been erected as shelter from the sun and a dozen or so guests, mostly ladies, clustered beneath it. Her face expressed her reluctance to rejoin the house party.

"Let us sit a while," he said on impulse. A convenient bench was shaded by a spreading elm yet in public view. Half an hour in his company would raise Celia's standing in this critical milieu. It would also allow him private conversation with her under circumstances that precluded him doing anything foolish.

"I'm sorry you aren't enjoying yourself."

"How long will I have to stay here?"

"Until we know something definite about Constantine."

"I wish he'd appear again. I'm so tired of waiting." She exuded tension. Tarquin wondered if it was only fear of the unknown threat, or something akin to the strain under which he labored in her presence. "And I am so tired of the heat!" She fanned herself with her right hand. The left rested between them on the bench. She wore no gloves and her fingers, slender and strong, were lightly tanned and stained with raspberry.

"Mr. Compton," she began. "Tarquin. I don't think I have really apologized to you for my behavior when I discovered your memory had gone."

"No," he said. "You haven't. In fact you made it very clear you thought it entirely justified by my own transgressions."

"In a way I do. But I was wrong to think you'd abandon me. I've learned you are a better man than that."

"Thank you," he said dryly.

Before she averted her glance he saw her eyes glisten and he realized, through everything they'd shared, he'd never once seen her weep. She spoke almost in a whisper. "I was afraid of being left alone."

He wanted to draw her into his arms but in view of the gossiping hordes he couldn't even take her hand. He rested his own on the bench beside hers and nudged her little finger with his. "You've really been alone since your father's death, haven't you?"

Celia nodded. The sympathy in his voice, the gentle touch of his finger, threatened to undo her. She stared down at their hands on the bench and dared not say a word lest she burst into tears.

"You told me of the day you heard the news, when you were waiting at the port for him to join you for the voyage home to England. It must have been a dreadful moment for you."

Home. When the messenger came with news that her father had been killed on the road to Madras, she had to make the trip with only strangers for company, the months-long voyage halfway around the world to throw herself on the mercy of an uncle and aunt she'd never met, in a country she'd never seen. Unthinkingly Tarquin called England her home, but she still wasn't sure it ever would be for her.

She remembered lying in the dark on the moors under her blanket, telling him the story. Was it only a couple of weeks ago? It seemed an age. Nostalgia pierced her. Those days with Terence Fish had been, for all their discomfort, some of the happiest of her life.

"I'd like to tell you about the day I learned of my father's death, of my mother's too."

Her head jerked up as his voice penetrated her sadness. He'd never confided anything personal to her. When they'd been friends and lovers he'd known nothing personal to confide. His dark eyes met hers with a softer gaze than she'd yet seen in Tarquin.

Then he stared ahead. "I was nine years old and it was summer in Yorkshire." He paused, his eyes narrow as though recalling a vision. "A summer day, much like this one. I went fishing with one of the village boys. Dickon, that was his name. Dickon Mossley. He could catch trout without rod or line, using only his hands. He called it tickling."

"I'm grateful to Dickon for teaching you." She strove to keep her voice from wobbling. "That fish was the best thing I've ever eaten."

"It took me a few years of trying, but that day I finally managed to tickle a fish myself. The first and last time until last week. I'm surprised the skill remained."

"Perhaps you wouldn't have remembered it if you hadn't lost your memory." Her remark didn't quite make sense but he understood what she meant.

"You may be right. Of course, strictly we were poaching, or Dickon was, but my father wouldn't mind. I knew he'd be proud of me. But I couldn't tell him because he and my mother were away from home. They'd traveled into Wales to visit relations. Only my two older sisters were home and I knew they'd be bored by my little trout.

Imagine my joy when I saw a traveling carriage drawn up at the front door of Revesby."

Celia wanted to take Tarquin's hand, but she knew how it would appear to the merciless onlookers above. She owed it to him not to further compromise him in any way. A fleeting touch to his sleeve was all the physical acknowledgment she could offer.

"I thought they'd come home early. But it wasn't them. It was the duke and duchess who'd driven over to tell us my parents' carriage had fallen over the edge of a mountain road."

The longing to touch him was almost unbearable. She glared up at the ladies fluttering like butterflies at the top of the grassy slope, blithely unaware of the poignant scene below them, but surely alive to any contact between them. "I'm sorry," she said. Inadequate words. Their little fingers touched again.

"After that I never lived at Revesby again." His voice sounded almost strangled.

"But you could."

"I don't know if I want to."

"It's a fine house."

"I suppose it is," he said flatly, moving his hand to rest on his crossed knee, "if you like things on the rustic side." He was retreating from painful memories—she could understand that—and in doing so she was losing him for he also retreated from their moment of empathy.

In desperation she tried to call it back. "And that trout, and the water from the brook, are the foods from your land and gave you strength. It *is* your home."

"I remember that conversation," he replied. "For the record I have never set foot in Cornwall in my entire life."

He sounded angry again, reminded of her perfidy. Not the least of their differences was that those days on the moors, so happy in her recollection, to him represented humiliation and deception.

Their brief truce was over. She had been tempted to reciprocate his confidence, to tell him her loss that day was more than just that of her father, that she'd known then she'd never see her two young half brothers again. Though she was not, in fact, without family, she had no idea where her father had sent Ghazala and her children. They were lost to her forever, somewhere in a vast continent thousands of miles away.

She wouldn't tell him now. It would be better if he never learned what a scandalous woman he'd been prepared to wed. Especially if he were to marry someone else. The Countess Something-or-Other who sounded quite loathsome with her wonderful Parisian gown. But very suitable for Tarquin who thought it didn't matter what she, Celia, wore because her appearance was hopelessly beneath his standards.

Suddenly she couldn't bear to be in his debt, but the only recompense she could offer was her genuine contrition.

"I didn't finish my apology," she said. "I realize how much harm I might have caused you and I hope you will be able to recover."

"I don't understand you."

"It never occurred to me that you might be courting another lady, engaged even. I would never have . . . lain with you had I known."

"Where did you get that idea?"

"One of the ladies mentioned you were to wed a countess." She peered at him around the rim of her bonnet. She was horrified to find the answer important to her.

Damn.

Celia was not given to profanity, even in her own thoughts. The present inconvenient truth inspired her to worse language, some of the vocabulary she'd learned in the memoirs of Francis Featherbrain, words too wicked to speak aloud.

She was dreadfully afraid that she was in love with Tarquin Compton.

Little wonder she'd been unable to muster pleasure at William Montrose's obvious admiration. She was mad not to encourage the courtship of an attractive man of good character, excellent prospects, and delightful family. And yet she could not because she pined for a man who didn't really exist. And by sharing an important part of his history with her, Tarquin had given her just enough of a hint that Terence Fish was alive and well so that she couldn't contemplate wedding another man.

All the things she disliked about him faded away as surface irritations. She thought only of his strength, the way he'd protected her, both on the moors and now when he refused to abandon her as long as she was in danger. She recalled that Lord Iverley, the opposite of a fashionable fribble and one of the cleverest men she'd ever met, was his close friend. There was much more to Tarquin than he allowed most of the world to see.

But the fact that Celia Seaton remained fathoms beneath his touch made her infatuation distressing. She had to trust it was only infatuation and she would recover as soon as she escaped his constant company. If she truly loved him the future looked bleak. She only hoped she'd be far away from him when he married another.

The beautiful Julia Czerny hadn't entered Tarquin's mind in days. When he did think of her, she still seemed a very desirable bride. But she didn't occupy his thoughts the way Celia did. His urge to confide in her, sparked by her need for comfort, had taken him by surprise. He'd been forced to retreat in good order when she began to ask questions about his past life he wasn't ready to answer. Or even consider what the answers might be.

His guardian, the duke, had educated him in the obligations of the landowner, but at a distance. The duke employed excellent stewards at his numerous properties and made sure the Revesby estate was well run by a good man. But old memories were starting to intrude.

Leaving the house on his sturdy pony, trailing his father's cob as they inspected the flocks of sheep, the condition of the barns and walls.

Fishing in the trout stream, with rod and tackle and Papa baiting his hook.

Cricket in the garden. Through all his triumphs play-

ing for his school and university, he'd let himself forget
how his father first put a bat in his hands and bowled
him easy lobs.

Hugo had always been amused by his sporting pursuits. "At least, dear boy," he would say, "all that exercise helps maintain your figure."

Hugo, to whom he owed so much. Hugo who, unlike
his parents, had never left him.

Hugo who wanted to arrange a marriage for him with
Countess Julia Czerny.

Perhaps it was a good thing Celia had heard gossip
about himself and Julia. It was inevitable that news of
their connection had spread and made him remember
that he might, in fact, have an obligation to the lady.

"I'm not engaged," he said, smoothing out a wrinkle
in his sleeve.

"But you have an understanding?"

Given the confusion of his feelings, he avoided a
direct answer. Although he had no idea of Celia's senti-
ments, he did not wish to give her the wrong idea until
he knew his own.

"Countess Czerny is a charming woman. A distant
cousin. I enjoyed making her acquaintance in London
at the end of the season." Let Celia make of that what
she would.

She took the hint and ran with it. "I wish you joy. And
now I think we should rejoin the party." Jerking to her
feet, she shook out her skirts, leaving a small book on
the bench. "Oh, that's mine . . ."

He beat her to it. "No," he said, checking the spine

lettering of *The Genuine Amours*. "I believe it is in fact mine." He stowed it in the pocket of his coat and offered his arm. "Shall we?"

Celia looked mutinous, but what could she do? She'd been caught, not only reading a most unsuitable book, but also lending it to Minerva Montrose, the innocent seventeen-year-old daughter of her recent hosts. On the other hand, the Montroses were unconventional and for all he knew Miss Minerva had been reading Aretino in the schoolroom, most likely in the original Italian.

He looked forward to finding the bit about the rat.

Chapter 25

The tyranny of affection is hard to withstand.

Mandeville had an apparently unlimited capacity to absorb people. Each day, usually in the afternoon, new guests arrived and the great hall bustled with their accompanying servants, luggage, and sometimes pet dogs and birds. Then they were shown to their rooms, and seemed to disappear into the fabric of the building, leaving the mansion graceful and serene. Only when large numbers assembled in one place did one get an impression of a crowd. At dinner in the state dining room Celia was always stunned to see dozens of people accommodated at the endless table.

Feeling hot and sticky after the day outside, she was passing through the hall on her way to a wash and change of clothing. She glanced without much interest at an arriving party, not expecting to see anyone she knew. A gentleman of advanced age was guided through the massive front door on the arm of an upper servant. Despite his years the man possessed an air of great elegance. Judging by the deference he attracted, he was someone of importance. The Duchess of Hampton herself came out to welcome him and could be heard expressing gratified surprise at the honor of his visit.

Joining in the veneration was another new arrival, a raven-haired beauty who appeared to be his traveling companion. Celia wondered idly if the gentleman was a high-ranking nobleman, another duke perhaps, and she his granddaughter. She was certain she'd never encountered the lady during her London season; she wouldn't have forgotten the combination of exquisite features and perfect figure dressed with a level of sophisticated good taste to which Celia could never in a million years aspire.

She had almost skirted the activity in the hall and reached the stairs when an unmistakable figure entered from the other end. Given the recent revelation of her feelings, it gave her no pleasure to be instantly aware of that dark imposing presence, the buzz in her head, the jolt of excitement beneath her ribs at the sight of him.

Tarquin made straight for the newcomers and took the lady's hand. The pair of them presented a picture of supreme modishness and perfect *ton*. The limber grace of his bow, the refined curve of the lady's wrist as she raised it for his kiss brought an uncomfortable pricking to Celia's eyes. She looked down and saw a small raspberry stain on her bodice. She'd been wearing a soiled gown for much of the day and she hadn't even noticed.

Sniffing and blinking hard, she surveyed the scene below through a mist of unfallen tears. At least Tarquin hadn't lingered over the lady. All his attention was now on the old man who relinquished his servant's arm and transferred his weight to Tarquin's. In a flash she saw the resemblance. Not so much in feature, though they shared the aquiline nose and commanding height. Tarquin's dark handsomeness contrasted with the still-thick white hair of the other. But though the old man was frail, his posture was almost as straight as the younger's and there was an indefinable similarity in their stances.

"Who is he?" she asked one of the lady guests who stood a few steps below her.

She hardly had to wait for the answer. Tarquin wore his rare smile and a look of affection she'd seen only in the days of Terence Fish. "Lord Hugo Hartley," came the reply. "I am amazed. I do not believe he has left London in decades. Something important must have happened to bring him to join his nephew here."

"And the lady?"

"The Countess Czerny."

Tarquin was summoned to Lord Hugo's room thirty minutes before the dinner hour. His uncle had rested from the journey and, while his valet completed his toilette for the evening, they exchanged remarks on the continuing struggle between the king and his estranged wife and the prospects for the coronation. But these days Hugo preferred reminiscences of the past to speculation on a future he might never see. From the man who had been like a grandfather, even a father to him, Tarquin never minded hearing the same old stories.

"Amazing that I should have outlived King George," Hugo said, his voice distinctly smug. "We were exact contemporaries, you know. Born just weeks apart in 1738. I knew him as a boy and attended him at *his* coronation. He was always a dull dog, you know, and priggish. Whoever heard of a straight-laced Hanoverian? After he married I avoided Court."

"Didn't he approve of your clothes?" This question always provoked a response. Lord Hugo had been a dandy for over sixty years, since before the term was invented, or so he claimed.

"As to that, I can't say. He always dressed soberly but in those days we weren't afraid of colors." He sighed. "No one has ever accused me of failing to dress à la mode but I find modern taste sadly plain. Look at us both. All in black like a pair of crows."

"In your case a robin redbreast."

Hugo eyed Tarquin's chaste white waistcoat with displeasure and ran an approving hand over the embroidered scarlet satin of his own. "I don't suppose," he said on a sigh, "that I shall live to see satins and velvets or gilt embroidery and heavy falls of lace return to fashion. I'm sorry I shall never wear pink again."

For the first time he could remember, Tarquin felt impatient with Hugo's conversation. He wished they could talk about something other than clothing and gossip. There'd never been any point discussing the state of the nation, or the business of his estate. Hugo would merely wave it aside with a flick of the wrist and a well-turned witticism on the horrors of rural economy. Come to think of it, Tarquin had often been guilty of the latter himself.

He refused to be diverted any longer. "Are you going to tell me what unprecedented event brings you out of Mayfair for the first time in twenty years?"

Hugo withdrew his hand from the ministrations of his valet who had been buffing his nails. He nodded at the man who bowed and left the room in silence. Probably listening from the dressing room next door. Bennett had been in Lord Hugo's service longer than Tarquin had been alive. He sometimes wondered about the exact nature of the relations between master and servant.

"Hand me that letter, if you please, dear boy." He gestured to the mantelpiece, accepted the folded sheet, then bade Tarquin be seated. "A few days ago I had a letter from Lady Garsington who heard from Lady Amanda Vanderlin who had the news from her brother Lord Blakeney. Let me read part of it."

Tarquin knew what was coming. The extent of Hugo's correspondence made it inevitable he'd hear something.

" 'According to Blakeney your nephew had taken it into his head to rusticate. He is in Shropshire, staying at the childhood home of Lady Iverley. Since Lady I. is expecting to be brought to bed (strangely soon after her marriage I may add, but more on that later) it is odd she should be entertaining guests. Most curious is that Mr. C. arrived in company with a young lady, a Miss Celia Seaton. I don't understand why your nephew, my dear Hugo, should be concerning himself with a young lady of such negligible connections. I know nothing about her at all, aside from her brief appearance in London under the aegis of Lady Trumper, no very great recommendation I am sure you agree. For all I know the girl may have fallen from a tree. These things may be misrepresented at a distance, yet Blakeney seemed to think your nephew on terms of some intimacy with Miss S.'" Hugo lowered the paper. "Well?"

Tarquin refrained from swearing out loud and tried to shrug it off. "I confess myself astonished that Blakeney should have read so much into the bare fact of my staying in the same house as Miss Seaton."

"And now, I gather from the duchess, you are both staying in this one, invited by Blakeney. I was surprised, and naturally pleased, to find you at Mandeville. But why is Miss Seaton here if there is no connection between you?"

"There wasn't enough room at Wallop Hall."

Hugo knew him too well. He merely raised his eyebrows, folded his hands, and awaited the truth. Tarquin considered what portion of the long, involved tale to impart. He wasn't in the habit of keeping secrets from Hugo, but he didn't see the point in distressing the old gentleman with the tale of his attack and subsequent memory loss. He must have been truly concerned to have traveled so far in the summer heat. Tarquin felt a quiver of terror that the unwise journey might have damaged Hugo's frail health.

Whatever his own feelings about Celia, he didn't want Hugo to think the worst of her. Although Hugo was been like a father to him, he couldn't confide in him as he had to Sebastian. Sebastian didn't deal in simplistic moral judgments. Neither did Hugo, to be fair. How could he with his socially unacceptable, not to mention illegal, tastes? But his great-uncle was old and had become hardened in his attitudes, which had something of the poacher-turned-gamekeeper. Tarquin was reluctant to expose Celia to the harsh light of his opinions.

"I won't go into details without betraying a confidence. Let me just say," he equivocated, "that I was able to assist Miss Seaton when she found herself in an awkward situation, and escorted her to Wallop Hall."

Hugo nodded in satisfaction. "Then nothing has happened to change your intentions with regards to Julia."

"The countess and I have no kind of understanding. If you recall I left it to you to make the arrangements, to negotiate an arranged marriage in fact. Very French. I am not sure why I did so and I fear I may have been drunk."

"Not even a little jug-bitten. You acceded to my wishes because of the great respect you have for your elders."

"Have you offered for her on my behalf? I don't know how these things work."

"We have spoken."

Tarquin's temper frayed. "For God's sake, Hugo, stop being so damned opaque. Am I obligated to marry the Countess Czerny?"

"Respect, my dear boy, respect." Perhaps realizing

he'd pressed too far, Hugo shook his head. "There is no agreement."

Relief was preceded by a momentary pang of cowardly regret. If he really were engaged to Julia then he could stop worrying and dismiss his continuing, and most inconvenient, attraction to Celia.

"How did she happen to come here with you?"

"Julia called on me the morning I had the letter. She immediately offered, the dear girl, to accompany me here."

"And a damned bad idea, too. Why you decided to leave London on account of such a rumor, I have no idea."

Hugo smiled smugly. "I could tell she was disturbed by the report and asked a good many questions about Miss Seaton, none of which I was able to answer. I do believe she was jealous. You made quite an impression there. I am pleased to give you both the opportunity to further your acquaintance. There's nothing like a country house gathering to foster intimacy."

An intimacy Tarquin now felt loath to advance. What did Countess Czerny mean, encouraging an elderly gentleman to run around the country in this heat? If the noble lady was truly in pursuit of him, killing Uncle Hugo was not the way to endear herself. Between the two of them they'd managed to make the idea of his marriage to Julia seem quite unpalatable.

He wished he'd never set eyes on either Julia or Celia. He wished he were a hundred miles away.

Good God. He'd rather be in Yorkshire.

Chapter 26

*Dismiss the follies of your youth and
hope others are equally forgetful.*

Celia climbed the stairs determined to look her very
best that night.

So Tarquin Compton thought it didn't matter what
she wore! She'd show him. If she could win the admiration of William Montrose, then there had to be *one*
gentleman among the many at Mandeville who would
flirt with her and she was going to find him. Without
fooling herself that she could compete with the luscious
countess, she would keep her pride intact as Tarquin
demonstrated his intentions to the world.

"I'll wear the green crepe and satin," she told Diana's
maid who awaited her with hot water and the imple-
ments of the hairdresser.

She half expected Chantal, with her very definite
opinions on the proper attire for any occasion, to argue,
to urge her to save the most elaborate of Diana's al-
tered gowns for the grand dinner party and ball planned

for later in the week. But Chantal seemed distracted, though she arranged Celia's hair and helped her into her stays, petticoats, and gown with her usual efficiency.

Then she asked for permission to return to Wallop Hall for the night. "I am concerned for milady. Four days without me and she will look like *une bohémienne*. Lady Felicia's maid will help you undress."

By no stretch could Celia imagine Diana resembling a Gypsy, but she gave her permission readily enough. It mattered little how she appeared when she went to bed, just as long as she looked acceptable now.

Better than acceptable, she decided as she practiced an alluring smile in the looking glass. With a light step and a determined heart she descended from the guest wing, ready to show Tarquin Compton exactly how little she cared for him.

He was one of the first people she encountered when she entered the rotunda, the customary pre-dinner meeting place. While not expecting him to appear bowled over by her beauty, she'd hoped for some reaction. Instead he seemed on edge, not quite the arrogant and overconfident dandy.

"Miss Seaton," he said. "Allow me to present you to my great-uncle Lord Hugo Hartley."

The old gentleman acknowledged her curtsey with a polite reserve that disappointed her. She hoped Tarquin might have spoken kindly of her to his uncle. Though come to think of it, why should he? Just because they'd enjoyed a period of amity and even rapport that afternoon, didn't mean he'd forgiven her. For all she knew, he'd told Lord Hugo the whole shocking story.

"I see our cousin, the Countess Czerny," Lord Hugo said. "Please fetch her while I make Miss Seaton's acquaintance. If, that is," he said, giving Celia a glimpse of his charm, "she doesn't mind keeping an old man company."

"Of course, Uncle," Tarquin said. "Excuse me, Miss Seaton, allow me to remove this piece of fluff from your shoulder." This gross insult to Chantal's diligence was a mere excuse to whisper a quick warning. "Don't tell him anything. He knows we arrived together but that's all." And left her alone with Lord Hugo, who examined her person with a keen eye.

"Allow me to compliment you on your gown," he said in a light baritone overlaid with decades of courtesy.

"Thank you, my lord."

"The shade is most becoming to your coloring."

This drew a gratified smile and a brief curtsey. She could survive this.

"I understand my nephew was able to render you a service."

"I am most grateful to him."

"Perhaps you could enlighten me as to the nature of his assistance."

Celia glanced up at the domed ceiling for inspiration. "I think it would be better," she said carefully, "if he were to tell you himself. I wouldn't wish to betray a confidence."

Lord Hugo's response was very dry. "I rather thought *he* was loath to betray *your* confidence but I am mistaken. I so often am."

She searched wildly for Tarquin, or someone, to save her. All she saw were the full-sized statues of naked Greek men that filled niches at regular intervals in the walls of the oval chamber. For the first time it occurred to her they all had tiddly little pillocks, likely having emerged from cold baths. Her lips twitched at the impropriety of the thought in such august company. In any company.

Lord Hugo looked amused. "They all look rather chilly, don't they?" She made a choking noise. "Standing without a stitch of clothing, I mean."

"Of course we are enjoying a very hot summer," she said. "In winter perhaps they are dressed for warmth."

Lord Hugo smiled. "Perhaps they are. Not in yellow trousers, I trust."

"Yellow trousers?"

"A dozen years ago there was a most unfortunate rage among the younger set for baggy yellow trousers of a violent hue. Of course young men get these ideas and there's no stopping them. But I was disappointed in Tarquin. I thought better of him."

"He must have been very young."

"You are quite right, Miss Seaton. Only fifteen years old and one must excuse the follies of youth. But this was beyond mere folly, it was a crime."

Though not certain she had his approval, she warmed to old gentleman and his obvious affection for his nephew. No wonder Tarquin loved him. She smiled at his droll exaggeration, and the mental image of a youthful Tarquin in the silly fashion. It pleased her to think him a mere mortal, capable of sartorial error. "He must have looked absurd," she said.

"He never bought them. I took measures."

"Oh?"

"I read him an astringent homily on the occasional necessity of distinguishing between high fashion and good taste."

"And that worked?"

"I think so, but I left nothing to chance. I had Tarquin's credit severed at all the best tailors in London until the craze for yellow pantaloons passed."

She chuckled again but he didn't join her. He seemed to be regarding her with peculiar concentration, so she stopped and tilted her chin.

"Are you interested in male clothing, Miss Seaton?" His voice turned grave and she understood this wasn't the real question he asked.

"It isn't something I know much about, Lord Hugo."

"Would you improve your acquaintance with the subject if you had the chance?"

"I wouldn't aspire to such knowledge."

"Excellent, Miss Seaton. I can see you are a young lady of common sense. Pray feel free to call on me if I can serve you. As my nephew cannot, I mean. He is likely to be otherwise occupied."

She followed the line of his sight to find Tarquin and the countess exchanging bright chitchat with the

Duchess of Hampton. Any illusion of adequacy about her appearance dissipated in the presence of the exotic beauty. There wasn't a single point of comparison in which Celia came out the winner, not even in height. True, the countess only held an inch or so advantage over Celia, but her stature was enhanced by an excruciatingly modish coiffeur, gleaming curls entwined with a confection of velvet, satin, and diamonds.

Together, the countess and Tarquin presented a picture of fashionable perfection that drove Celia's spirits down into the soles of her shoes. She was not happy when this ideal couple made their way over to join her and Lord Hugo, who welcomed his dearest Julia with effusive affection.

"Miss Seaton," the lady said in a voice like a clarinet arpeggio. "I have been wishing to make your acquaintance."

"Thank you," Celia said. *The feeling is not mutual*, she didn't say.

"I knew Mr. Twistleton and I was sorry to hear of his death. Pray accept my condolence."

"My late guardian? You knew him better than I did, perhaps. I only lived with him a short time."

"He was not, I recall, a man with a great deal of conversation. In fact he made rocks seem eloquent."

"Did you also know his wife, my mother's sister?"

"I didn't have that pleasure. My acquaintance with your uncle was slight and confined to a matter of business concerning some jewelry."

Celia, who knew even less about her uncle's business

than she had of the man himself, murmured a polite nothing. The countess, however, appeared to be more interested in her than was warranted by the slender connection. A sudden thought increased her discomfort in the woman's presence. If she knew Twistleton, perhaps she also knew about his disreputable brother-in-law. Then she recalled how her uncle had despised Algernon Seaton and warned Celia never to speak of him. Surely he wouldn't have mentioned him to a mere acquaintance.

"I understand you lived in India," the countess said, with a friendly smile.

"I understand you lived in Austria," Celia almost snarled.

She found it impossible to contain her resentment. Probably due to the depressing fact that in the eyes of Tarquin's uncle she was akin to a pair of yellow trousers.

A stir at the entrance to the room saved her from having to hold on to a ragged semblance of good manners. A pair of furiously bowing footmen had opened both sides of the double doorway.

Tarquin observed the exchange between the two women with apprehension, poised to intervene if things got difficult, when he, too, was distracted by the new arrival. "Good God and Zeus," he exclaimed in deep disgust. "It's my aunt."

The Duchess of Amesbury, though not unusually large, possessed too much consequence to enter through a single door. Brushing aside the greetings of people too sycophantic to treat her with the scorn she deserved, she marched through the assembly, straight for the group of people with the least desire for her company.

"Hugo! Compton! What a delightful little family party! Cousin Julia, and Miss Seaton too!"

Her eyes shone with malice and Tarquin guessed she was aware of his bruited engagement to Julia Czerny. Whether or not she knew about the end of his betrothal to Celia, the duchess was ripe for mischief and there was plenty to be made.

As usual, Celia was the one she could hurt the most, the person with the most to lose.

"Duchess," he said, grasping her satin clad arm in a vicious grip. "Please come with me. I have something important of a private nature to communicate to you."

Perhaps because no one ever dared treat her with such indignity, his aunt let him drag her into a corner out of earshot of other guests.

Such submissiveness didn't last. "Let me go," she barked.

He dug his fingers into the flesh. "Only if you promise to behave. You will smile, you will nod, and you will listen to every word I have to say."

"You've lost your mind, Nephew!"

"Just ask yourself, *Aunt*, who has more to lose by making a scene in the Duke of Hampton's rotunda."

He could see the wheels turn in her malicious brain, considering the fact that at Mandeville she couldn't terrorize everyone by reason of her rank. In a bout between the Duchesses of Hampton and Amesbury, Tarquin would back his hostess every time, and his aunt agreed.

"Very well," she conceded with ill grace. "Let go of me. What do you want?"

"Why are you here?" Tarquin countered, relaxing his grip without relinquishing his hold. "Did you learn of my presence here with Miss Seaton and come to make trouble?"

"Certainly not. If you choose to ally yourself with such an insignificant young woman, it's nothing to me."

"But you see, aunt, I have not. Or rather Miss Seaton and I have agreed mutually that we shall not suit. We are not betrothed and I do not wish a word of our connection to get out and damage her good name."

The duchess's thin lips formed a smile to make a crocodile seem melancholy. "Dear me, Nephew. Are you crossed in love?"

"That is none of your business. You shall not make it your business and you shall not mention it to another soul."

"You can't stop me."

"No, I cannot. But if I hear one word of gossip about Miss Seaton's brief and unexceptional sojourn under my roof, I shall not rest until I make you the laughing stock of London."

"Who cares for that?" She didn't back down easily, but he could hear just a hint of anxiety in her question.

"I think you do, Duchess. I think you care very much. You are a bully and you get your way because people are too weak and perhaps too polite, to stand up to you.

I'm not speaking of your inferiors, of course. There's nothing I can do about your servants other than pity them. But look around the room. Look at this gathering of the very cream of the *ton*." He watched her obey, calculate the power assembled under the spectacular oval dome. "And then imagine them all smirking at you, whispering behind their fans, repeating the witticisms I have spread at your expense. Do you imagine, Aunt, that there is enough love for you in this room that even one person will refuse to participate in your mortification?"

"Sticks and stones," she said scornfully. "What is the opinion of anyone to me?"

"If you really thought that, Duchess, I believe I would have more respect for you, but I know you very well. I had ten miserable years under your roof to learn exactly how the mind of a bully works."

"I'll ruin the little tart, and you too," she spat.

"Setting aside, for a moment, the disrespectful reference to Miss Seaton, I'll agree with part of your statement. You can ruin her. But me? I don't think so. I shall be very slightly embarrassed, that is all. You don't have the power to cause me any great harm. But you, you will suffer very greatly from *my* power."

The parrot face was blotched puce with rage as she thought about it. Every word he'd spoken was true and his heart thudded with anxiety. He delivered the final argument and prayed his gamble paid off. "Is it really worth it, Duchess, to destroy a lady who means nothing to you? I'm the one you hate and there's nothing you can do to harm me."

But there was. He kept his face impassive and hoped she hadn't guessed how much it meant to him to protect Celia.

She wavered between rational fear and bitter resentment of defeat. And Tarquin, who knew her so well, found the words to tip her over the edge. He lowered his voice almost to a whisper and spoke close to her ear. "What shall you do? Are you going to give me the very great pleasure of destroying *you*? I'm already sharpening my wits."

She jerked back and shook off his hand. "Very well. I'll say nothing. I don't care if you marry her, or Countess Czerny, or no one. You are of no importance to me."

"Excellent," Tarquin said, disguising his relief. "I am enchanted to find us in perfect accord."

Tense with anger, the duchess stood and surveyed the room, like a bird of prey seeking her next victim. Her glance settled on Celia, who must have taken leave of Hugo and Julia and now stood alone.

"Don't even think of it," Tarquin said.

"Truly," the duchess said, in a tone quite mild for her. "I just wish to reassure Miss Seaton that I wish her well."

"I'll do it for you. If you even go near Miss Seaton my threats stand. Leave her alone."

With a faint odor of brimstone, the duchess shook her ruffled feathers and stalked off to join her husband who, as usual, had managed to enter unnoticed.

Tarquin allowed himself a satisfied smile. Six years ago, when he finished Cambridge, he'd removed every one of his belongings from Amesbury House and moved into his own London rooms, never to return to the detested mansion except for the occasional family gathering. Since then he'd climbed to a paramount position in the *ton*, despite occasionally wondering whether his ascent had any point. Tonight he knew that it did. Finally he'd used his power in a worthwhile cause. Perhaps the only time.

Chapter 27

When attending a house party, the well-bred
young woman stays in her own room at night.

Celia couldn't have pinpointed what awoke her. Perhaps the recent memory of the last such distur-
bance in a dark room penetrated her slumbering brain.
Someone was in the chamber with her.

It hadn't occurred to her to be nervous in the crowded
Mandeville guest wing. Fearing her heart thumped loud
enough to wake the dead, she lay still. She heard the
intruder rooting through the things laid out on the dressing table, mostly the tools of Chantal's trade and nothing of great value save some inexpensive amber beads
and a silver chain lent her by Diana. He moved on to
the chest and slid open a drawer. He wasn't going to find
anything of any value among her undergarments, not
even a scrap of lace. She hadn't wasted Diana's funds
on fripperies.

Even keeping her eyes shut, she gained the impression there was a light in the room, that the searcher

carried a candle or a lamp. It was agonizing to both follow his movements and keep her anxious body from betraying her wakefulness. Something, a change in her breathing, an involuntary movement, must have given her away. As she snapped open her eyes a flame was extinguished without revealing a glimpse of her visitor. She lay under the covers, sensing him in the dark: still and waiting as she was. She took mental inventory of the bedside table and came up with no better weapons than her hairbrush and a candlestick.

Sitting up, she attempted to preempt assault.

"Leave," she said loudly. "I have a heavy candlestick and a loud scream. I could make enough noise to summon help from the other rooms." And prayed he didn't know her immediate neighbors on either side were an elderly spinster cousin of the duchess and an empty room.

There followed a rustling, soft retreating footsteps, the opening and closing of the door. The momentary admission of light from the dimly lit passage wasn't enough to give a clue to his identity. Gathering her courage Celia jumped out of bed and raced to the door. The broad corridor, stretching many yards in each direction, was deserted. The intruder had vanished into one of the dozen or so rooms, or around the corner.

Back in her room she groped for the candlestick, a puny thing that would have made a paltry weapon, and took it out to borrow a flame from one of the sconces illuminating the corridor. She hesitated before returning to bed. Suppose he came back? Suppose it was Constantine who had somehow inveigled himself into the house, posing as a member of the army of servants?

Even with light she couldn't face the rest the night alone in a room with a malfunctioning lock. Tarquin had brought her to Mandeville House on the assumption she would be safe here. He had been proven wrong and she wasn't waiting till morning to tell him. She *needed* him, now.

The guest wing was actually a quadrangle and Mr. Tarquin Compton, though a commoner, had been placed in one of the better chambers facing the avenue, around the corner from hers. Celia wouldn't have known her own comfortable room matched her lowly standing without Chantal's explanation of the order of social precedence as reflected by the assignment of guest rooms. Much of the maid's several tirades on the subject had slipped her mind, but one thing stuck: the exact location of Tarquin.

Tiptoeing down the passage, the emergence of a man from another room made her jump. Before he backed away and slammed the door she identified a portly middle-aged peer, visiting a chamber inhabited by a lady who was not, she believed, his own wife. Suppressing an impulse to giggle, she wondered if he'd recognized her and if so, where he thought she was headed. She reached her destination without further adventure, hesitated before the sturdy polished door, and softly knocked.

No response. He would be sleeping. As quietly as possible she turned the door handle and pushed. It wasn't locked. Offering a quick prayer that she had the right room, she opened the door just far enough to let her slide in, and closed it behind her.

Soft air wafted in through open uncurtained windows, rendering the atmosphere deliciously cool after the stuffy passage. Starlight revealed the shadowy monochrome forms of the furnishings, dominated by a great bed from which emerged the sound of rhythmic breathing.

"Tarquin?" Celia whispered. No reaction. Depositing her candlestick on a chest, she crept to the side of the bed and repeated her call. He stirred but didn't waken. In the gloom his dark head contrasted with the white bed linens. She leaned over and reached for his shoulder and found skin, hot to the touch over muscle that jumped beneath her palm. He slept without a shirt.

Was he naked? Her hands itched to investigate further, to explore the body she'd known for a short while, before it retreated beneath the armor of sartorial perfection. A jolt of desire fluttered through her abdomen and her brain felt fuzzy.

"Tarquin?" she asked for the third time and he came to life. Half sitting, he twisted over and hauled her up. She found herself sprawled over his chest, captured by steely arms. Her halfhearted remonstration was stifled by his lips and she surrendered without a fight.

The taste and texture of his mouth were immediately familiar and kindled the memory of pure happiness. Lovingly she framed his head, looped her fingers through the soft hair to the shapely skull, opened to welcome a deep kiss she wanted to last forever.

An eager moan rumbled in the back of his throat. He drew her closer and she arranged her body to align itself over his. One question was answered: he was indeed naked. Only a sheet and her own nightgown separated them. Every inch of her ached for him. She wanted his skin and muscle, his very soul and spirit to surround and possess her. His arousal pressed against her thigh and she willed the layers of linen and cotton to disappear. Maddeningly, cloth failed to dissolve into the ether so she dragged her lips away and struggled to her knees, straddling his hips. He groaned an incoherent protest.

Tarquin was having a wonderful dream in which finally, at long last, he was kissing Celia again. Better still, it wasn't happening in a dirty hay loft or on the bare Yorkshire ground, but in a soft bed with sheets of lavender-scented linen. Then she withdrew, faded away. *Come back*, he spoke in his dream. *Don't leave me alone.* And woke up.

His heart leaped with astonished joy to find her still there, in all her corporeal reality. Her magnificent corporeal reality, revealed when she pulled her nightgown over her head and tossed it away. Framed by a faint aura of distant candlelight, he could make out only a shadowy blur of her body so he stretched a trembling hand to trace a slender shoulder, down the silky arm, firm for a woman, around the gentle curve of trim waist and across the flat stomach to linger. She wriggled a little when his fingers tickled the indent of her navel. At the shake of her hips his swelling cock arose to make a tent of the sheet covering it, straining toward the curly entrance to her sex. Yes, she truly was in bed with him. Shuddering with desire, he raised both arms to cup the small breasts, feeling her hard nipples tickle his palms and kneading the firm flesh with his fingers.

Her own hands were busy, too, tugging the sheet out of the way until nothing separated their nakedness. He reached for her, planning to roll them over, when she pounced, wresting control of the encounter. She fell on him like a tiger, seizing his shoulders with strong fingers, devouring his chest with her hot mouth, and grinding her pelvis over his erection.

The unschooled fierceness of her loving assault was more exciting than the skill of a courtesan. The ferocious sincerity of her ministrations clawed at his heart. "Yes, like that." He murmured encouragement, tilting his hips and grasping hers to better guide her gyrations. "Oh, Zeus, yes!" he hissed when she took his cock firmly in her hand and lowered herself onto it. It took a little trial and error on her part, but finally he was lodged inside her.

Then she stopped. "What now?" He smiled at the chagrin revealed in the two words. Her ignorance annoyed her. "I want to ride you." She gave it a few seconds of thought then leaned forward to clasp his shoulders. Tentatively she raised herself off him and sank down again.

"You have the right idea," he said through clenched teeth, and thrust back.

"I do, don't I?" she said with a naïve pride that sent a little thrill of emotion through his chest.

In very little time they established their rhythm and worked in harmony, damp bodies burning against the cool linens, urgent hands caressing, hot breath mingling in consuming kisses and barely comprehensible words of bliss. He held back, waiting for her. He had to summon all his strength but it was no hardship; he'd happily spend all night drowning in Celia's scent and skin, the music of her moans. Hell, he'd spend a lifetime doing this. With fierce satisfaction he felt her climb toward climax, reach for her own peak, and tumble over the top in a joyful orgasm. She collapsed on his chest and he drove to his own finish.

He retained just enough presence of mind to roll over in the last seconds, and pull out before he spilled his seed. Then he gathered her close in his arms and murmured her name as he dropped slow, grateful kisses all over her face. He hadn't felt this good in years.

"Tarquin," she said and nipped at his ear.

"Celia," he muttered again, beginning to feel sleepy. "I think you've killed me."

"I'm so sorry."

"What a way to go."

She snuggled closer and kissed his neck. "Riding St. George is fun."

"Where did you hear that phrase?" He refrained from pointing out that it was whore's cant.

"Er, I read it in a book."

"Right. I think I know the volume in question. You shouldn't have read it."

"Oh? Yet it's perfectly correct for you to own it?"

"I am a man. Ouch." She'd punched him in the side, though not hard. "It's not as though it's much of a book. My collection contains volumes of far greater artistic value."

She drew back to look at his face, her gray eyes huge and dark in the half-light. "You own many books about . . . this kind of activity? *Illustrated*?"

"Yes," he admitted.

"I should like to see them."

If they gave her more ideas like "riding St. George" it was a notion with merit. He yawned. "We'll talk about it later."

He pulled her close and tugged the sheet half over them, though the night was warm enough without. She gave a little sigh and laid her head on his chest. He stroked the thick locks draped over her shoulders and felt her breath on his skin. As he prepared to drift into slumber he made a mental note to wake early so he could get back to his room before the servants stirred. Then he remembered. He *was* in his room.

He was in his room *and so was Celia*. Suddenly wide awake, he sat upright, drawing a grumble from her.

"What?" he almost shouted. "What are you doing here? What do you mean by visiting a man's room in the middle of the night?"

She scrambled to kneel beside him, arms folded, lips pouting. "You didn't seem to mind. I came to tell you something and you just grabbed me."

"I was asleep. I had no idea what I was doing."

"If your valet came in while you slept would you pull *him* into bed with you?"

Her comical indignation drew a smile. "No, of course not. What did you need to say to me that couldn't wait till morning?"

"There was someone in my room, searching through my things."

"My God! And you waited till now to tell me!"

"I was distracted."

He could appreciate that. Kneeling in her naked glory, she looked beautiful enough to distract a saint. Grasping her elbows he peered at her face. He didn't know whether to be relieved at her state of calm or worried by her lack of concern for her safety. "Tell me exactly what happened."

Celia was still distracted. The earlier events of the night seemed far off now and somehow unreal, compared with their lovemaking. She feared to ask what it meant for their future. After days of being treated with scant civility, his confidences that afternoon had given her hope he might forgive her, though no realistic expectation that his feelings would ever match hers. But now this. What did it mean? Did it mean anything to Tarquin, or had she been merely a convenient female body taking him unawares? If there was any truth in Featherbrain's memoirs, men were not only capable of lying with women who meant nothing to them, they could do so when enamored of another. The existence of the beautiful, charming, and witty countess loomed large.

Her mouth watered at the sight of his lean, muscular chest set off against crisp, bright white linen. Irrationally, she had no wish to revisit the alarming matter of awaking to find an intruder in her room. What she wanted was to discuss their feelings for one another. But he was looking at her expectantly and she had no idea how to broach the topic.

He misunderstood her sigh. "It's all right. You're safe now." His concerned tone and his touch on her shoulders felt like affection to her infatuated brain. Then he got down from the bed, retrieved her nightgown, which he handed to her, and fetched a dressing robe for himself.

The resumption of clothing diluted the sense of intimacy. Decently covered they sat on the bed, she with legs folded beneath her, he perched on the edge.

"Now tell me," he said.

By the light of the candle, which he'd moved to the bedside table, she watched his clever, characterful face as he listened to her account.

When she finished he frowned. "Are you sure you locked the door?"

"Yes."

"You didn't forget?"

"Tarquin," she said. "I don't believe we've had a conversation since we came to Mandeville when you didn't remind me to lock my door at night. No, I didn't forget."

"What about the window? Was it open? Could he have come in that way?"

"My room overlooks an enclosed courtyard. It's a

steep drop and even if he somehow climbed the wall he'd still have to get into the house to reach it. Besides, he left by the door and when I followed him a few seconds later he'd disappeared. He's somewhere in the house. That's why I didn't want to stay alone in my room. Do you think Constantine could have broken in?"

"It seems unlikely. And even less likely he could have talked his way in. As you know, there are servants everywhere and a stranger would be spotted at once and questioned. I doubt it was Constantine."

"Who, then?"

"I don't know, but more likely one of the servants or guests, or a servant of one of the guests. Are you sure it was a man?"

She narrowed her eyes, reliving the nocturnal visitation. "No, I assumed it was Constantine but it could have been anyone."

"I'll ask Blakeney if anyone unusual has arrived at the house, anyone who one might not expect to see here."

"I think I'm the only guest who answers to that description."

"I'll take him into our confidence if necessary, but I'd much rather not explain the situation. It won't do your reputation any good for our journey across the moors to be known, even if we are engaged."

His tone was so matter-of-fact she almost missed it. Her heart jolted but the expression on his face was equally detached. "We are not engaged," she said, hoping for a fervent contradiction.

"You should have thought of that when you came to my room."

"You know why I came, and no one saw me."

"And look what happened."

"That wasn't my fault. You started it."

He took a deep breath and exhaled slowly. "Yes I did. And since I am not in the habit of seducing respectable single ladies, we shall have to marry. I'm sorry if you don't like the idea but that's all there is to it. Prepare to be married."

"We lay together before and you didn't think we had to wed. No one need know."

"Last time you took advantage of me when I was out of my mind. I have no such excuse. I may still not be entirely sane but I take full responsibility for my actions."

"That's stupid. You still don't want to marry me and you can't make me." She was desperate for him to argue with her. It wouldn't take much for her to agree. Just a tiny indication that their marriage would mean more to him than an unfortunate necessity muddled into by mistake. Instead he barely looked at her. "Is this something to do with the duchess?"

"No. The duchess need not concern us." In this case the confidence in his voice gave her all the assurance she needed.

"What about the countess? What about Lord Hugo? He wants you to her marry her, doesn't he?"

His face, which hadn't cracked a smile since the subject of marriage had arisen, looked grim. "If he does, I shall have to disappoint him."

"I know how important he is to you."

"You may not be my uncle's first choice as my bride, but he'll recover. Now," he continued briskly, "we need a plan. We can't announce our betrothal tomorrow. It would appear odd when we've spent so little time together. I'll have to court you for a few days first. It'll also let me stay close to you so we don't have any more little incidents like tonight's."

Celia felt she was giving in too easily, but there wasn't any point arguing, for now. Nothing irrevocable would happen immediately and she had to acknowledge she'd enjoy being courted by Tarquin. Perhaps she'd convince herself he meant it.

Perhaps he *would* mean it.

"Are you going to stay close to me all night too?" she asked. She intended the question flirtatiously, fishing for a further compliment on her appeal as a bed partner.

She stood with her hands on her hips, head tilted seductively, and Tarquin wanted nothing more than to accept her invitation and return to bed, together.

Resisting her wasn't easy, but soon he would legitimately sleep with her, every night. The resumption of his betrothal to Celia felt right, much more so than last time. No need to examine his feelings closely. He still had Hugo to deal with, but he'd worry about that later.

"Your maid will have to sleep with you," he said, "and I'd better get you back to your room now, before the servants are up and about." Dawning light through his window told him that wouldn't be long.

They crept back along the passage to Celia's room.

Within seconds they determined the small chamber was deserted.

"I'm afraid I have to leave you," he said, keeping his voice low. "Do you wish to send for your maid?"

"She's not here. She returned to Wallop Hall for the night but I expect her back later this morning."

"Good. I don't want you alone at night."

"No more than I want to be alone." She bit her lower lip and he read the strain on face. "I hate having to wait for his next move. I want to know what's going on. When he comes back I'd like to catch him in the act."

"I like that idea. Unfortunately he may have already been. Your room has been empty for an hour or two and if he was watching he'll have had time to search every inch."

"He won't have found anything because there's nothing to find." Celia shook her head in frustration. "What does he want? I have nothing, nothing at all. Every single thing I have with me was either lent to me by Diana or bought in Shropshire."

"Whoever is after you thinks you have something of value."

"Constantine took my luggage, my reticule, and my clothing. Whatever it was, I don't have it anymore." He was about to offer her a comforting hug when she stiffened. "Wait! The rattle, the silver rattle I gave to Diana for Aldus."

"Why would anyone want that?"

"I don't know. It's not valuable, but it's the only thing Constantine didn't take. That, and my shift."

He couldn't restrain a grin. "I remember that shift."

"I think Chantal burned it."

"Pity," he said, mulling the situation. Like Celia he had the urge to force the mystery into the light. Only when it was resolved would Celia be safe and they could proceed with their lives, together. The prospect was distinctly pleasing.

"I think we could take advantage of your maid's temporary absence. Do you think you could tell as many people as possible that some possessions, perhaps a piece of baggage mislaid on the journey, have just arrived at Mandeville?"

Chapter 28

Things aren't always better in the morning.

"I am so thankful the missing bag has appeared."
If she said it once, she said it a dozen times and most members of the house party must have heard it by now. If they wondered why the generally reserved Miss Seaton was suddenly twittering trivial facts about her personal affairs to all and sundry, she didn't care. She'd had to listen to enough nonsense from them.

Getting attention wasn't hard. Since Mr. Compton had seated himself beside her at breakfast and appeared rapt in admiration of her wit and beauty, she'd been the subject of much speculation on the part of the ladies and curiosity from the gentlemen. Both sexes, she thought ruefully, found Tarquin's apparent attraction to her puzzling.

She drifted toward another group, containing a couple of ladies who might conceivably remain in ignorance of the imaginary adventures of her luggage, when a stirring and rustling among the assembled females indicated the arrival of men, come in from the morning's masculine entertainments. Celia couldn't help observing that courtship didn't keep Tarquin away from his regular exercise.

Everyone noticed when he came into a room. She used to believe his influence in the *ton* derived from fashion's fickle whim: admiration for one who was taller, ruder, and better dressed than any other gentleman. Hard to please, he must be worth pleasing. Now she no longer resented him, she understood his allure. Tarquin possessed a commanding presence as much for his strength of character as for his appearance.

His presence certainly commanded *her* attention. The sight of him at the door aroused a prickling awareness that started in the back of her neck, spread to her shoulders then downward through her body. She was breathless without the least exertion. His gaze swept around the room and settled on her with one of his heart-stopping smiles. He made his way across the room, brushing off the appeals of two peeresses and the wife of a cabinet minister.

A dozen pairs of curious eyes watched him bow low over her hand and murmur her name. "You look delightful this morning." A dozen heads tilted in their direction, trying to overhear. "Have you had a good day?"

"Thrilling. And you?"

"Very dull. But it's getting better now."

"Instead of going out and doing whatever you gentlemen do, you should stay with the ladies. The embroidery! The piano practice! The exchange of beauty secrets! So much excitement is enough to give me palpitations."

"I can always use a new beauty secret."

"You're quite exquisite enough. I'm keeping them to myself."

"Forget them! You don't need any."

She looked at him uncertainly, in case this was one of his remarks like "It doesn't matter what you wear," but the admiration in his eyes seemed genuine and he sounded sincere. For the moment she decided to forget he might be acting a part and revel in the enjoyment of being courted by Tarquin. The heat in his gaze reminded her that while he might not love her, he enjoyed bedding her. Perhaps that was sufficient basis for a successful marriage. She looked back at him with what was doubtless a smitten grin.

He raised his voice a notch or two. "Did your belongings arrive from Wallop Hall safely?"

"Yes, thank you. I was so thankful." She launched into her tale for the sixth time. "I had that box sent by carrier from Yorkshire and I feared it was lost."

He shook his head mournfully. "Carriers can be so unreliable. And Yorkshire is very large and quite wild. There's no saying what one may lose there."

"How true. It's not the only thing I've lost in Yorkshire."

"Really? Anything in particular?"

Her toes curled in her slippers and she pursed her lips to stifle her laugh. Also, to stop herself from acting on the sudden urge to kiss him. He leaned in and his breath tickled her ear. "You'll have to tell me all about it. Or perhaps you could show me. Again."

She stepped back, afraid she *would* kiss him in public, and reapplied herself to the task at hand.

"My maid—she's really Lady Iverley's maid—went to Wallop Hall last night and, fancy, there was the box. She brought it back with her this morning and I am so happy to be reunited with many things, including precious family treasures. I feared them lost forever." Not knowing what she was supposed to have that was so valuable, she was deliberately vague about the contents of the illusory box. Family treasures covered things she might have acquired in India, or during her brief tenure as Mr. Twistleton's ward.

Since the object was to have people overhear, her annoyance at the interest of those around them was irrational. She wanted Tarquin's undivided attention and she was loath to share it with anyone, least of all Countess Czerny. She didn't know how long the countess had been there, a few feet away. Not long. Although the lady moved quietly, adding a serenely swanlike glide to her many perfections, she had a way of making her presence felt. Tarquin was apparently feeling it. He stared at her in a way that made Celia's heart plummet.

"Miss Seaton," she said, looking odiously beautiful. "I hope you won't mind if we borrow Cousin Tarquin from you." By "we" she meant herself and two of the best born, best-looking, and best-dressed lady guests. Neither one of them had ever given Celia more than the time of day. And, yes, Celia minded very much.

"Mr. Compton may do whatever he likes," she said.

"I hope, then," said one of the ladies, an extremely

wealthy marchioness, "he will like to tell us what he thinks of Julia's costume. It's the latest fashion from Paris and though I like the fuller skirt I find the sleeves very ugly. Do you not agree, Tarquin?"

Julia emitted a carillon of tinkling laughter. "It is a truth universally acknowledged that the latest fashions are never ugly when they come from Paris."

"Very true," Tarquin said. "I wouldn't dare criticize such an objet d'art as your gown." He looked her up and down with total absorption, no doubt taking in the details of the countess's dark red dress made from some rich material Celia couldn't even name, though she was sure Tarquin could. "But I can safely predict, Jane,"—he called the marchioness by her Christian name—"that in a few weeks, perhaps only two or three, when Cousin Julia's gown is no longer new, that I shall be able to agree with you that, yes, the sleeves are very ugly."

Another carillon. "I've always heard that no one can slip an insult past one's guard like you, Cousin."

"Tarquin is a master of fencing," said the marchioness.

"Not just verbally," piped up the third lady, the Honorable Mrs. Someone whose name Celia had forgotten. "He defeated my husband handily yesterday. Poor Edward is practicing for the rematch. You'll have to join us in the gallery, Julia."

As Celia had suspected, some of the more favored ladies, those belonging to the inner circles of the *ton*, joined the gentlemen for their mysterious activities. The bubble of excitement engendered by Tarquin's flirtatious wooing popped, dissipating her sense of well-being and leaving her depressed and ill-tempered.

This was Tarquin's world and not hers. She mustn't forget that the lives they found comfortable were oceans apart. She could never be at home in his milieu. To believe otherwise was delusional.

Chapter 29

*The presence of a man hiding in
your bed may be misconstrued.*

Tarquin finally made his way to Celia's room without interruption. At the agreed-upon signal—two
short knocks, then a pause, then one more—she opened
the door, dragged him in, and turned the key.

"Why did you take so long? I've been waiting over
an hour." With hands on her hips in her simple cotton
nightgown and her hair a halo of pale fire in the candle-
light, she looked wonderfully fetching. Also grumpy.

"Each time I tried to leave my room, someone else
was in the passage. It's like Charing Cross out there.
Does no one in this house sleep in his own bed?"

"Apparently not," she said, her mouth twitching into
the grin he found so alluring.

He pulled her toward him by the waist. The idea of
their marriage seemed less a dutiful necessity and more
a pleasure by the hour. The joys of night would make up
for many daytime annoyances.

Not that the days were so bad. He hadn't felt angry

with her in a while and his pretended "courtship" today had been fun, positively a delight. He drew her closer and ran his hands down her back to cup her buttocks and press her against him. Her skin was warm and soft through the thin material and he felt overdressed in his breeches and shirt under a knee-length banyan.

She pulled away from his embrace. "That's not what we are here for," she said.

He groaned, adjusted the ties of his robe, and looked around the room, which was small, bordering on mean in comparison to his own spacious chamber. It drove home for him how lowly Celia was regarded and how her stay at Mandeville must have been less than enjoyable. He might not suffer the pinpricks of the *ton* but he was aware of them. He had, he acknowledged with shame, administered a few himself.

"Where shall I hide? Behind the bed curtains, I suppose." The most prominent feature of the room was the old-fashioned bed.

"I don't think it matters. If he comes in with a light, he's going to see you wherever you are and you'll just have to overcome him."

He cracked his knuckles in anticipation.

"And if," she went on, "it's dark, then it will be even easier for you. Let's hope he isn't too strong."

"If he's anyone resident in this house, I'm not worried. There isn't a soul on the premises half as large as Joe and he didn't give me any trouble."

"Ah, Joe! If all else fails I can always return to him. He really appreciated me."

"I appreciate you, too, and I'd be happy to give you a demonstration, later. Now we wait. And I think I'd better hide. We might learn something before I am overcome by my feelings and beat him to pulp." His fists itched. Alas, it was unlikely their visitor would be Constantine, but any cohort of his late assailant would be good for a little payback. He loosened the ties that held back the bed curtains on the side facing the door and pulled them closed. "Will you join me?"

She looked reluctant, shy even, which surprised him for in none of their various adventures had she ever appeared timid. And modesty seemed absurd under the circumstances.

"I think I'll let you suffer alone in the heat," she said with a careless air he found unconvincing. "I'll wait out here next to the window, where it's cool."

Perhaps she was being coy about getting into bed with him, playing a game and asking to be wooed. Fine. He was quite happy to woo her.

In three strides he was at her side and scooped her into his arms. "Please come." He dropped a kiss on her surprised lips and stepped back to deposit her on the mattress. "You'll be much more comfortable here." He climbed up beside her. "And so shall I." He tucked her into his embrace and snuggled them down into the burrow of the bed, enclosed on one side, open to candle-light on the other.

"No!" She struggled out of his arms and backed up against the pillows. Apparently she had not been feigning reluctance.

Naturally he wouldn't do anything against her will, but so far she'd welcomed his embraces. True, it wasn't strictly proper for them to lie together before they wed, but they were betrothed and they'd already done it, twice. As far as he was concerned there wasn't any reason not to continue.

"What . . ." he began.

She shushed him with a whisper. "Let's preserve the element of surprise."

So, side by side, they sat in the dim light and waited, the silence broken only by the sound of their breathing. He sensed a tension in her beyond the natural anxiety about her nocturnal visitor. After a while, five or ten minutes, he reached for her hand but she snatched it away. There was definitely something wrong. Before he could insist on discussing it, he heard a soft knock on the door.

He covered her wrist as a warning to keep quiet but there was no need. She sat stock still and barely breathing. After a brief interval he identified a different noise, someone tinkering with the lock. Their visitor was a picklock of some skill and before long he heard the quiet sweep of the door opening, muted footsteps, the click of the latch shutting the intruder in the room. Tarquin braced himself for attack.

"Miss Seaton? Are you awake?" The voice was female, low and musical with a slight exotic intonation.

What in hell was Julia Czerny doing in Celia's bedroom?

Celia's first thought was that the countess had come to take Tarquin away from her. She was going to storm in and accuse her of stealing her betrothed husband. Celia suspected all along that things had gone further between them than Tarquin had let on. How right had been her instinct not to get further enmeshed with him until she determined his true feelings.

She looked at him in mingled panic and accusation and he shook his head. An expression of exaggerated bafflement, palms-out gestures with both hands, told her he had no idea why the countess was there. He put a finger to his lips then pointed it through the closed curtains, indicating that she should go out and confront the visitor. Whatever the reason for her visit—it might be quite innocent—it would be better if the countess didn't know Tarquin was there.

Wait a minute. She had picked the lock, quite skillfully. Celia's upbringing might have been irregular, but she knew breaking and entering wasn't a common ladylike skill. The countess wasn't that innocent.

She thrust her legs through the curtain opening and walked to meet the lady, who stood next to the dressing table.

"Countess. To what do I owe the pleasure?"

The countess looked quite unabashed. "Miss Seaton. Isn't it rather warm for bed curtains?"

"I am susceptible to night chills," she improvised.

"I see. That explains why your window is wide open."

Celia refused to be interrogated by someone who had, after all, invaded *her* room. "I would have invited you in had I known you wished to see me. There was no need to pick the lock."

"I did knock. I thought you must be asleep, as you were last night."

"Then that was you."

"At your service," her visitor said with a curtsey.

"What do you want?"

"You truly do not know, do you? Did you really receive a long lost box, or was that a ruse to draw me in?"

"I don't think I owe you an answer to that question until you respond to mine. What do you want?"

"It's a long story. Shall we sit?"

Celia removed a light wrap from the only chair in the room and arranged it about her shoulders. Though not remotely cold, her nightgown put her at a disadvantage when compared to the other who was elegance personified in an evening gown complete with the larger Parisian sleeves. She gestured to her visitor to take the chair and sat on the stool next to the dressing table. She didn't want the countess too close to the bed.

"Have you ever heard of the Mysore ruby, a pigeon's blood gem of legendary size and quality?"

"Is that what you think I have? You must be mad!"

"Bear with me. This concerns your father. I told you a little untruth before. I knew your guardian only by reputation, but your father and I were well acquainted."

"How? He hadn't left India in years, and he certainly never went to Austria."

"No, I knew him in India. In fact, we were by way of being partners. I act as an agent in the acquisition of various valuables, mostly antiquities but occasionally gems, particularly those with interesting histories. The

Mysore ruby is *very* interesting. It's reputed to have belonged to both Tamerlane and Shah Jehan. Your father was very good at—how shall I put it—persuading people to part with their treasures. That's how he was able to afford your magnificent house."

"He worked for the East India Company."

"My dear girl, don't be naïve. He was barely tolerated by the Company. By the end he had almost no connection with it, unless there was dirty work to be done on strictly unofficial terms."

Celia would have liked to argue but the countess only confirmed what she'd instinctively known for years, that they'd left Madras with her father under a cloud. Or more likely a monsoon. She wished Tarquin wasn't hearing every word.

It got worse. "We worked together on the ruby and we had been paid in advance for the price of its acquisition by a generous but very demanding customer. Then Algernon became greedy."

Celia was startled. She'd never heard her father called by his first name. She wondered exactly what had been between him and the countess. It was hard to guess the latter's age, but she couldn't be much over thirty. Relative youth, however, had never deterred her father when it came to his bedmates.

"He decided to keep the ruby. He had a buyer in England and he stole it from me. A very unwise decision."

Celia's blood froze. She was intensely thankful for Tarquin's lurking presence, even if he did learn the secrets of her disreputable past, including some that were new to her. "If he did, he certainly didn't give it to me."

"It took me months to work out what happened but it's the only explanation that fits. He sent you ahead to Madras to wait for him. You were to travel to England together."

Celia nodded.

"Why didn't he accompany you to the city?"

"He had some details to see to. I was staying with a family in Madras when I heard the news of his murder." Her voice trembled, bringing the countess out of her chair to kneel beside her on the floor.

"I'm sorry, Celia." She took her hand. "May I call you Celia? I always think of you that way. Your father spoke of you. Hearing of his death must be painful."

"Did you kill him?" She had to ask.

"No! I swear. I had nothing to do with it. But it wasn't brigands. I wasn't the only one he robbed. It was our principal in the transaction, and that's why I must find the ruby. Algernon knew he'd be pursued so he gave it to you while he took care of his other business."

"My father gave me nothing, except enough money for emergencies and my passage. And if he hid it among my possessions it's long gone. Everything I owned was stolen from me, as you very well know."

"When were you robbed? How? Did you lose everything?"

"If you don't know," Celia said sharply, "I'm not going to tell you."

The countess's manner was now one of supplication. Taking both Celia's hands she looked her in the eye and spoke fiercely. "You don't understand. The man your father cheated is very dangerous, but I'm acting for him. I'm trying to get the jewel back to pay my debt. If you were robbed, it's someone else after the ruby. Does he have it? I *must* get to it first."

A quality of desperation in the countess's voice gave Celia the urge to trust her, at least in a limited way. "Countess," she began.

"Call me Julia."

"Very well, Julia. First of all, I never heard of any jewel and I certainly never possessed it. After my uncle died I was penniless. If I'd owned a valuable ruby I assure you I'd never have worked as a governess."

"That explains why I couldn't find you. I've been searching England for you. It was pure chance that Lord Hugo told me you'd arrived in Shropshire with Mr. Compton. I couldn't believe my luck."

"You came to Mandeville to find *me*?"

"I originally called on Lord Hugo in London because I wanted an introduction to the Duchess of Amesbury. As England's most avid collector of jewelry, she was the most obvious buyer for the ruby. I'm a distant cousin, but not close enough to warrant the notice of the duke. I made up to her because I wanted to know if she had word of the ruby in England."

"Did she?"

"Not recently. There's a certain disreputable London dealer who was rumored to have it at one point, but nothing came of it."

Celia knew she ought to be curious about the priceless jewel, but the whole story seemed too outlandish to be true. She was much more anxious to get to the bottom of Julia's relationship with Tarquin.

"So you never really meant to marry Mr. Compton." She hoped Tarquin was taking all this in.

Julia gave her a quizzical smile, suggesting she knew Celia's interest went beyond the impersonal. "I didn't say that. If I can't lay hands on the ruby I shall need all the protection I can get and marriage to a member of a powerful English family would provide it. Quite aside from that, he's an excellent match and a *most* attractive man."

Hmm. She hoped Tarquin's ears were blocked with wax. She'd been feeling almost friendly toward the countess, finding her quite charming, until the last remark.

She stood up. "I wish I could help you, Julia, but I'm in the dark. I will tell you this. If someone else thinks I have this ruby, he still does. The man who robbed me of all my possessions is still pursuing me."

"And was the tale of the lost luggage a ruse?" Julia looked about the room. "Please be honest. If it's true we must search it."

Celia shook her head. "You guessed it. After last night I used it as bait."

Unfortunately Julia Czerny wasn't at all stupid. She gave the bed a considering look then got to her feet. "I have too much respect for you, Celia, to think you'd risk luring a possibly dangerous criminal into your room when you are alone. I won't ask who is lurking behind those curtains. I do hope he—or she—isn't suffering excessively from the heat."

Tarquin knelt on the bed and peered through the crack in the curtains to watch Julia leave. Several times during her recitation he was tempted to jump out and interrogate her, but opted for discretion. There was no need for her to know he'd been in Celia's room, as long as the latter wasn't in danger.

Locking the door behind the countess, Celia returned to the bed and tore open the curtains.

"What do you think of that?" she asked.

"I think I shall ride over to Wallop Hall tomorrow and have a good look at that rattle."

"A ruby might just fit inside the ball part," she said, creasing her forehead. "My goodness! The rattle itself is very dull and there's a crack."

Tarquin nodded in satisfaction. "I wager your father hid it in there."

"It makes sense that he would. It's the only thing I had from my mother and he knew I'd never let it go."

He put his hands on her shoulders. "Yet you gave it to young Aldus Iverley. That was quite a sacrifice and an act of generosity far in excess of its worldly value."

Celia stepped back, shrugging off his touch. "I had to do something to repay Diana's kindness."

"What a piece of luck you gave it to the baby. Otherwise Julia might be long gone with it."

"Perhaps that would be for the best."

"Why? I should think you'd be glad to find yourself the owner of such a valuable gem."

"It's not mine."

"That will be a matter to decide if and when we find it."

Celia walked over to the window and ran her hands down the open curtains. When she turned to face him, her expression in the dim light appeared uncertain.

"Are you very upset about the countess?" she blurted out. He didn't understand her. "Are you upset that her main reason for being here is to look for the ruby?"

He did believe she was jealous.

He got down from the bed, took her hand, and smiled. "The only thing about the countess that upsets me is how she dragged my elderly great-uncle up here. Otherwise, I don't much care what she does."

"But you did think about marrying her."

Tarquin trod carefully. "I considered it. Mostly to please Hugo. He wants to see me married and a father before he dies. But he should live forever as long as he doesn't do mad things like undertaking a journey of one and hundred and thirty miles in excessive heat."

"So you intend to marry. For your uncle's sake."

"And so I shall. I am going to marry you."

"Lord Hugo won't be happy. He doesn't like me."

"He'll get over it. He's old-fashioned. Now," he said, thoroughly sick of the subject of Julia, Hugo or anyone else when he was alone in a bedroom with Celia and only one garment lay between him and her naked body. "Come here."

When he started to kiss her neck she pushed him away.

"What's the matter? I could tell earlier something troubled you."

Folding her arms she eyed him fiercely. "I don't think we should do this. I don't think we should be married. If pleasing your uncle is the only reason, you should find someone who *will* please him."

"I can think of several excellent reasons why we should marry." He leaned in for another kiss. "Starting with this. I find you extraordinarily desirable."

"Extraordinary, indeed," she said, stepping away.

If kisses and compliments weren't going to work, he decided to try logic. "Marrying me is the best thing for you. You have no money or friends. You might find another position as a governess but do you really wish to return to being an underpaid drudge? I'm not rich but my income is more than adequate. As long as we avoid fashionable excess I can maintain you in comfort for the rest of your life."

"And I would be grateful to you for the rest of my life. I never had any doubt that marrying you is to *my* advantage. What will you be grateful to *me* for?"

"You would be my wife and the mother of my children." That's what women did when they married, after all. What was all this gratitude nonsense about? He couldn't understand what she was worrying about.

"If that was all marriage entailed I'd accept. I can fulfill those requirements of the position of wife as well as anyone. At least I assume I can have children. But what about the other aspects of your life? If there's one thing I've learned during my time at Mandeville it's that I am not cut out for the fashionable existence. I floundered in London last year, although I made every effort to be accepted, and I'm still a fish out of water."

"We don't seem to be able to get away from fish references, do we?" He intended the remark to be conciliatory, to show that he could joke about his former identity.

"This isn't funny."

"You could learn to fit in," he argued. "Anyone can. Especially with my patronage."

She stood next to the empty hearth, as far from him as the small chamber would allow, and raised an arm to hold on to the mantelpiece. The position stretched the cotton of her modest nightgown across her small, shapely breasts. With one strong leg thrust forward, her wild curls glowing in the candlelight, and fierce resolution set in her features, she lacked only spear and shield to complete the image of a warrior queen: Boadicea, perhaps, or Britannia.

"Perhaps I don't want to. Perhaps I don't care to win the good opinion of others thanks to your *patronage*. Perhaps I am bored witless by life among the *ton*. You belong here. No, you don't just belong. You *lead* these people. Even if I were interested in following, I wouldn't be any good at it. I'd end up a millstone around your neck and an object of pity. I can imagine the remarks, whispered behind fans as we enter a ballroom. 'Mr. Tarquin Compton and his very peculiar wife. She's so plain and shabby compared to him. There must be some kind of scandal behind the match for she didn't even have any fortune.' And after a while, perhaps, your power would fade. 'He used to be such an elegant creature but why did he marry *her*? It makes one question his taste.' "

He listened in amazement to the gathering force of her tirade. Did she believe him so shallow? "Do you think I care what they say?"

"Yes, I do." He opened his mouth to argue but she cut him off. "And even if *you* don't, I would care on your behalf. Knowing I was dragging you down would heap guilt on top of gratitude. I cannot imagine a worse combination."

"Celia," he said softly. If reason wouldn't work, he'd try seduction. He stood over her and trailed his fingers over her face, along the line of her jaw, and down her neck. She trembled at his touch. "What can I say to convince you that you are wrong? That we would have a happy marriage? What can I *do* to convince you?"

"Tell me one thing I could do for you that would make *you* grateful to *me*. And I don't mean sharing your bed and bearing your children."

Tarquin thought bed-sharing an excellent argument. The best in fact. But he began to accept it wasn't going to happen tonight and the fact made him edgy. "I don't understand you. You are making a big fuss and over-complicating things. I want a wife, you need a home, and we have lain together. I would like to do it again, tonight if possible, but if you prefer to wait until after we're wed I respect your wish. Let's do it soon. No need to arrange an elaborate wedding. Just a quiet ceremony with a few friends then we can take a wedding trip back to Revesby. I still have unfinished business there."

"That's it!" Celia waved her clenched fists and shook her hair in a frenzy. "You can leave now. And please make sure no one sees you leaving this room." She stamped over to the door, pulled it open a crack, and peered out. "No one, for now. Not that anyone would find it unusual to find you wandering the passages. It's a popular sport around here. But I don't want you to be spotted near my door, giving you another excuse to condescendingly insist we need to be married."

"I can't leave you alone. Julia Czerny may return."

"And do what? Torture me with hairpins until I reveal the location of the Maharajah's ruby?"

"Don't underestimate her. I suspect the lady could do quite a lot of damage if she thought it necessary." He raised a hand to fend off further infuriated invective. "I'm not staying against your wishes, but—"

"I know! Lock the door."

"And move this chest against it. Here, let me make sure you can move it."

Celia flexed her arms and Tarquin remembered the muscles of her upper arms. With some pleasure. It was a shame she was proving obdurate. But little as he was accustomed to placating angry women, he was confident he could do so once she cooled off.

Celia woke early and unrefreshed. The uncertainties that whirled around in her brain most of the night re-

mained present and active. The best thing for her headache would be a brisk walk, but she'd promised Tarquin
she'd stay safely in the house and not allow herself even
to be alone in a room with anyone.

"Trust no one," he'd said as he slipped out into the
empty passage. Withstanding the urge to call him back,
she'd barred the door and settled into bed to toss and
turn until the sheets were hot and creased.

Was she mad not to accept Tarquin's proposal of
marriage? It wasn't as though she had any other alluring prospect. The only alternative was Diana's offer of
assistance. The thought of returning to the governess
trade held no appeal, and marriage to another even less.
She ought to be casting every lure she possessed in William Montrose's direction. But to do so when she was
in love with someone else would be fair to neither. She
no longer found a marriage of convenience, or even of
friendship, an acceptable solution.

How frustrating to have the man she loved propose
marriage to her yet feel there was no chance of being
happy. She didn't ask to be loved equally. She knew Tarquin to be an honorable man who would treat her with
respect and kindness. In the rare optimistic moment she
thought he might learn to love her back. He might even
already. He'd said nothing, but she sensed he'd forgiven
her for the Terence Fish episode. When the two of them
were alone she felt more than amity: a true connection
of their minds.

The illusion fled in the company of others. Every
hour at Mandeville House taught her afresh how out of

place she was in the world of fashion and power where she swam upstream, a sad minnow waiting to be swept away by the currents or torn apart by the teeth of vicious pike.

Celia had been a minnow all her life. Without aspiring to whalehood, she'd like to spend her life a little higher up the piscine hierarchy. A humble perch, perhaps: a plain fish, large enough to avoid most predators and too bony to attract the gastronomer. Terence Fish had been a match for a perch; Tarquin Compton navigated the shoals of the beau monde like a sleek glittering salmon.

Breakfast gave her further opportunity for fishy thoughts. In Tarquin's absence she was invisible again. Either the disturbed night had made him oversleep, or he'd taken her arguments to heart and swum away. Melancholy recollections of another breakfast and the taste of wood-smoked trout intervened. The lavish display of dishes prepared by the Mandeville kitchen staff offered nothing as delectable.

The Countess Czerny sat at the other end of the table, the fashionable end. As usual she appeared to be entertaining her neighbors vastly with admirable vivacity. Julia, she suddenly realized, was not the person she presented to the world. She had no way of knowing how much of the countess's public story was true, but at the very least she wasn't as rich as rumored. Otherwise, why would she be running around India engaging in shady transactions in partnership with Algernon Seaton?

Celia no longer disliked her. Instead she felt a kinship

with the alluring adventuress. They both presented a false front to the world. And both, if she could believe Julia's tale, were threatened by mysterious and dangerous men.

At the moment she was far more annoyed by Tarquin who should be here to escort her to Wallop Hall. She couldn't wait to see if their speculation about the rattle was correct. If it contained a valuable ruby, could she sell it? A vista of riches opened up before her. Such a jewel must be worth a huge sum for so many people to take such extreme measures. Would it be enough to keep her without recourse to the unreliable support of men?

"Very lovely, isn't she?" The courtly voice made her jump. Lord Hugo Hartley was assisted into the chair next to her by a footman.

"Countess Czerny? Certainly."

Celia, who had barely exchanged words with him since he discreetly warned her off Tarquin, eyed the old gentleman with apprehension. Whatever he wanted to say to her, she had a notion she wouldn't like it.

Her efforts to frame a tactful reply were thankfully forestalled by the appearance of a manservant.

"Excuse me, miss. Her Grace requests your presence."

"Me? The duchess wishes to see me? Why?" Since her arrival, Celia had received no more than the occasional nod from her hostess, the Duchess of Hampton. She looked at her neighbor as though he would have the answer.

"You are a guest in her house. I should think that

would be sufficient reason," Lord Hugo said, reminding her of Tarquin at his most supercilious.

The servant, whom she judged by his lack of livery to be a retainer of some status, helped her pull back her chair. "I am to escort you to Her Grace's private quarters."

Mystified, she rose to her feet and prepared to follow. On impulse she turned back. "Lord Hugo. If Mr. Compton should come in, please tell him where I am. We had arranged to meet this morning," she added, deciding her request needed an explanation.

Lord Hugo nodded. "I'd hoped to further our acquaintance, but the pleasure must be postponed."

Mandeville was a very large house. Although she knew the route from the guest wing to the public rooms, she had no idea where the family quarters were located and soon lost track as she followed the servant though a maze of passages. The transformation of the decor from polished double doors with gilt plasterwork architraves and marble floors to simpler fittings might have struck her as surprising had she been paying more attention. When her guide opened a door and gestured for her to precede him she obeyed without question.

Instead of a duchess in a sitting room, she found herself in a deserted three-sided courtyard, confronting a familiar sight: Nicholas Constantine, a cart, and a horse.

Chapter 30

*Don't judge a book by its cover,
or a lady by her title.*

Constantine dragged her, gagged and sneezing, from the back of the cart where she'd been rolled up in a dusty blanket and tied like a parcel. Blinded by sunlight, she caught no more than a glimpse of stone pillars before being shoved down a short steep staircase and through a door. While the Yorkshire cottage had been stifling hot, her new prison was freezing and grew chillier still as her captor urged her along a dark narrow corridor. With his lantern at her rear, she could see little. Her feet stumbled over uneven ground, her bare arms brushed against rough walls of stone or masonry, and ahead she could hear the sinister echo of slowly dripping water.

Gooseflesh arose on every exposed inch of skin. What was this place? She envisioned a dreadful dungeon in a Gothic romance. They reached a circular chamber roofed with a brickwork dome on which the lantern cast giant, looming shadows. Celia reminded herself that they were merely those of herself and Constantine, not supernatural beings.

"Now," he said. "Let's sit down here and have a little talk."

He maneuvered her onto some sort of stone or brick wall surrounding a dark pit, her feet dangling free. Damp penetrated her petticoats and cold seeped up from below and pierced the thin leather soles of her slippers. Constantine stood behind her. *Don't let him push me in*, she prayed. What else but a deep well would emit such a chill?

"Where is it?" he asked.

She shook her head and made furious denying noises.

"The gag'll have to come off," he said and rested the lantern beside her on the rim of the pit. "Don't try anything funny while I untie it."

As if she would! Her nails dug into the slimy stone surface and her muscles tensed in the effort to keep her balance and avoid pitching forward.

"Now," he said as she worked her jaw in relief, "talk."

"I have no idea what you want," she said, opting for ignorance. "As you well know, you stole everything I owned the last time you kidnapped me."

"But I heard tell you had some more things delivered from Yorkshire just yesterday."

Someone in the house had told him about her false report.

Constantine crouched beside her and slung an arm about her shoulders. "Look here, Miss Seaton. You and

I are all alone here." His slightly foreign accent took on a sinister tone. How could she ever have mistaken this criminal for a Yorkshire rustic? "The walls are thick, thick as the Tower of London, and even if they weren't, we're a long way from anywhere."

A long way was probably an exaggeration given the time she'd spent in the cart. But the journey had been long enough to get them well away from the house and the Mandeville Park stretched for miles. The chances that anyone would save her seemed slim. Even if Lord Hugo delivered her message, and she wasn't sure he would, Tarquin wouldn't be able to find her.

Dear God, she prayed. *Don't let him hurt me. And if he does, give me strength not to tell him about the rattle. And if I do tell him, don't let him hurt the baby.*

She sensed Constantine reach into his pocket, heard a soft click, saw a flash of metal, a blade pointed at her throat. His breath, visible in the dim light, warmed her ear. "No one's going to hear you scream."

"Oh for heaven's sake!" The voice, loud, forceful, and female, came from the passage. "Why did the Governor ever entrust an important task to a melodramatic fool?"

When Hugo told him Celia had been summoned by the duchess, Tarquin felt the first twinge of alarm.

"Did you recognize the servant?" he asked, wishing he'd told Hugo about the threat to Celia.

"Why would I? I don't know the people here." Hugo gave the matter some thought. "Now I think of it, the man did seem familiar. Perhaps I've seen him at Amesbury House. There is more than one duchess in residence, after all."

Tarquin looked up eagerly as a group of ladies entered the room, including their hostess the Duchess of Hampton. Celia was not among them, neither was the Duchess of Amesbury.

Damnation! If only he hadn't gone riding this morning, then let curiosity draw him to Wallop Hall. He should have waited for Celia to come down.

If his witch of an aunt was bullying her, he'd strangle the woman. It would be a boon to society and someone should have done it years ago.

He strode over to interrupt his hostess's conversation. The possibility that Celia was suffering something worse than a verbal pummeling had him sweating with fear.

Good manners be damned.

Finally Celia was in the presence of the duchess, but not the one she expected. Rescue came in the unlikely form of the Duchess of Amesbury.

Or not so unlikely. Julia Czerny had mentioned that Tarquin's aunt was also after the ruby. Relieved that the duchess's methods were less crude than Constantine's, Celia feared she might be just as ruthless.

"Really, Miss Seaton," she said, striding to the edge of the pit, "I am most displeased. Had you told me when I saw you in Yorkshire that you had the Mysore ruby, I wouldn't have had to go to all this trouble."

"I am so sorry, Duchess, to have discommoded you.

But I had no idea you were looking for it and, as I keep telling Mr. Constantine and everyone else who asks me, I don't have the ruby, I never had the ruby, and I never even heard of the ruby until yesterday. So Mr. Constantine can torture me but I won't be able to tell you a thing."

"Torture? Miss Seaton. You've been reading too many novels."

"There's nothing fictional about the fact that I've been kidnapped, bound, and threatened with violence. More than once, I may add."

"You can blame my nephew for that. He forbade me to speak with you so I had to take measures to get you alone. I've been trying to buy this gem for over a year. Since Constantine and his employer have proven utterly inept in obtaining it from you, I shall enter into direct negotiations. I am willing to pay you thirty thousand pounds."

Constantine emitted a furious growl and tightened his grip on Celia's shoulders. "You wouldn't know where the ruby was if it wasn't for the Governor. I won't let you cheat him. I'll kill her first."

Celia closed her eyes and prepared to die.

"Don't be silly. If she dies none of us may ever find the jewel. Your Governor will be paid for his information. More than he deserves."

Celia breathed again.

"Much more than he deserves considering his agent stole it from me." A new voice entered the discussion. The Countess Czerny stepped into the chamber, a lantern in one hand and a pistol in the other.

If she wasn't so horribly aware of the gaping abyss beneath her and Constantine's grip on her shoulder, Celia would have laughed. This chamber—whatever its purpose—was becoming crowded and the duchess was regarding the new arrival as she might a naked footman.

"I don't know what you are doing here, Countess."

Julia, on rough ground and with both hands occupied, dropped a curtsey that left Celia breathless with admiration. "I followed you, Duchess, to prevent you obtaining something that belongs to me. Or rather, to my principal in the matter."

Feeling a little safer in the presence of Julia's weapon—she couldn't see any reason for the countess to shoot *her*—Celia tried to shake off Constantine. He removed his arm from her shoulder and instead, still crouched beside her, took her upper arm in a painful grasp.

"Let me get this straight," she said. "My father was working for the *duchess* when he stole the ruby from the countess?"

"Certainly not," said the duchess. "I never engage in lawless transactions with unsavory characters."

"You wouldn't call the Governor unsavory?" Julia asked. "He's merely the most successful receiver of stolen jewelry in all London."

"I don't concern myself with the petty concerns of those I buy from. I had no reason to believe this gem stolen, merely mislaid when the agent entrusted it to his daughter then had the temerity to die. Once I heard the whole story I had this man"—she nodded at

Constantine—"arrange a meeting between me and the young woman in possession of the Mysore ruby so that we may come to terms."

In a sudden move, Constantine hauled Celia to her feet. She swayed on the rim of the well, desperately clinging to him until she steadied her balance. "Neither of you gentry bitches is getting it," he said, drawing an indignant gasp from the duchess, who'd probably never heard herself referred to so vulgarly, though many must have thought of her that way. "Missy here is coming with me."

He pushed Celia forward, twisting her arm behind her back. When Julia raised her pistol, he swung Celia around so she was between him and the gun barrel. "Don't think of it," he advised, "because you'll likely hit her instead."

Celia's look of entreaty was answered by a nod from the countess. She kept her gun pointed but she would not, she sent the silent message, endanger her.

Pushed inexorably toward the exit and then who knew where, Celia made a final desperate attempt at reason. "I do not have the ruby and I don't know where it is!"

"But I do!" This time it was a male voice and an exquisite masculine figure that ducked through the archway. "And if you ever want to see it you'll let her go. At once."

Tarquin Compton regarded Constantine as though he were an encroaching mushroom at a London ball, the effect only slightly spoiled by his having to bend to fit beneath the sloping ceiling at the edges of the dome.

"Come and get her, you puny dandy," Constantine responded. "I knocked you cold once and I'll do it again."

Though confident of Tarquin's ability to defeat the villain in a fair fight on open ground, Celia was terrified he would end up in the pit during a struggle in these confined quarters. With a desperate pull she twisted around and managed to free her arm from Constantine's distracted grasp.

"Get out of the way," Tarquin yelled at the same time and, with a grace that looked effortless, launched himself into the air.

"No!" Celia shrieked at she was flung aside and landed on her behind, her back to the brick wall.

The next moment both Tarquin and Constantine tumbled together into the abyss. "Tarquin," Celia cried, crawling to the edge of the pit with some mad idea of jumping in to save him from drowning.

Instead of bodies flailing in inky water, they were on solid, though uneven ground, apparently beating the blazes out of one another. She snatched up Constantine's lantern and looked down into the pit. Several feet down, the floor was covered with straw and the fall of their feet caused strange crunching noises. Tarquin rained a succession of punches at Constantine who, though a more worthy opponent than Joe, succumbed to superior power, crashed against the brick walls of the pit and slid onto his rear. She lowered the light below floor level, the better to see that her kidnapper was bloodied and unconscious.

"Are you all right?" she called.

Tarquin put his hands on the rim of the pit and pulled himself up with ridiculous ease. He stood before her, rubbing his hands together. His coat was soiled, his waistcoat had lost its buttons, revealing a tear in his shirt, his neck cloth was in disarray. With a cut on his nose and a half-closed eye, he grinned from ear to ear and never looked better to her.

"I enjoyed that," he said.

She choked up with tears.

"I thought it was a well!" she managed with a gulp. "I thought I would drown. I thought *you* would drown."

"Idiot girl," said the duchess, who along with Julia had moved to the edge of the pit, the better to follow the fight. "Haven't you ever been in an icehouse before?"

"Icehouse? Is that ice down there?"

"Of course."

Celia took in the long entrance tunnel, the thick walls, the midsummer chill. "We didn't have them in India, she said."

"Of course not," Tarquin said, and looked at her with tenderness she couldn't mistake, despite the injured eye. "Did he hurt you?"

"Not much."

His face darkened and his glance shifted. "I should have killed him."

"I was mostly worried I'd fall into the pit. I feel foolish."

"I was afraid I wouldn't find you in time."

"How did you know where I was?"

"When Hugo told me you'd been summoned by our hostess, I went to find you. Once I learned you'd disappeared, I asked Blakeney to help. While we were searching, I heard that a cart had gone to the icehouse. Since ice is usually fetched at dawn, I decided to look here first." A beautifully manicured hand, a little gritty from grasping the edge of the pit, cupped her cheek and her heart melted. "Thank God I was right."

"Compton!" She'd forgotten about the duchess. "Now you have the ruby we can settle this nonsense. Where is it?"

Tarquin turned to his aunt. "You'll never find it." He nodded at Julia. "And that goes for you too. And you." But Constantine was out cold and unable to hear.

"What do you intend to do with it?" Julia asked. "As I am sure you know by now, it should rightfully be restored to me."

"The way I see it, the jewel is Celia's. She's suffered enough for it and I shall abide by her decision."

Celia found herself in an unaccustomed position of power. "I feel like Solomon," she said with a dazed laugh. "Should I slice the gem in two?"

"No!" Two female voices united in agony.

"Shall I keep it to wear?"

Tarquin considered the matter with mock gravity. "I do not believe rubies are the best gems for your coloring. You could sell it and buy emeralds instead."

"Now we're getting down to business," said the duchess. "I've offered her thirty thousand."

"Paltry. The stone is worth twice that at auction. I'd

be glad to conduct the sale on your behalf, Miss Seaton. Countess, what is your bid?"

"Fifty thousand, and not a penny more," snapped the duchess before Julia could speak.

They all looked at the latter, who walked around the edge of the pit and placed her arm on Celia's. "You know why I need the jewel," she said softly.

"Make your best offer, then," Tarquin said. "Didn't Count Czerny leave you wealthy?"

"He left me virtually penniless."

He looked down his nose at her in his most Tarquin-ish manner. "That's something you have in common with Celia. Her father left her with nothing. So did her guardian. And you are asking her to give up her only asset."

"Fifty thousand," repeated the duchess. "And my patronage. With such a fortune and my support you could marry anyone."

There was only one person Celia wanted to marry. With fifty thousand pounds she wouldn't come to Tarquin a penniless nobody. She had a dazzling vision of herself as an heiress once more, as she had been during her London season, only with better connections and better clothes.

"Celia." There was no mistaking the entreaty in the countess's voice. For the first time in their acquaintance Julia Czerny sounded less than confident. Perhaps it was the yellow light of the lantern, but the polished beauty looked haggard and ten years older. "I can't equal that offer." She bit her lip. "My God, I can't come near it. I am throwing myself on your mercy."

Celia looked at each of the women, the duchess glaring like a power-mad parrot, the countess pale and pleading, then at Tarquin. She tried to read his face. She knew he had no love for his aunt, but did he favor Julia?

"What shall I do?" she asked. "What do *you* think I should do?"

"I think it's entirely up to you, my dear."

She thought about the Mysore ruby, the legendary gem that Tarquin must have retrieved from the rattle. She wondered what it looked like, this famous treasure that had caused so much trouble. Incredible that she'd been carrying it with her ever since her father had packed her off to Madras. What an insane risk he'd taken, hiding it in an unused child's toy. Despite the rattle's sentimental value to her, she could have lost it a dozen times. Of course, he'd expected to join her within a day or two, had never thought his theft of the jewel would prove fatal. His greed had cost him his life and it had cost Celia her family, not just her father but her father's other family.

Suddenly she wanted no part of it. To profit from her father's crime seemed sordid. The vision of riches melted away, but after all, she was no worse off than she had been.

She took Julia's hands and smiled at her. "The ruby is yours by right. Tarquin shall return it to you."

He nodded with a grim smile.

Chapter 31

*When it comes to a book, the good bits
are always worth reading again.*

Blakeney, together with a platoon of servants who
had been searching other buildings in the park,
arrived before Constantine regained consciousness and
hauled him away. Tarquin would have preferred to accompany Celia back to the house, but he needed to lay
information with the magistrate against the kidnapper.

He would happily have subjected the Duchess of
Amesbury to the same treatment, but he wouldn't disgrace his uncle. The duke thanked him for his forbearance while looking a little wistful at the notion of his
wife in jail. He cheered up when he learned he wouldn't,
after all, have to pony up for the ruby. He even talked
about putting his foot down when it came to future
purchases.

Tarquin had no opportunity to speak to Celia before
it was time to dress for dinner. Never had he found the
nightly ritual more tedious. He upset his valet very

much by refusing to take an interest in his choice of waistcoat. The man almost burst into tears when Tarquin tied his neck cloth at the first attempt, glanced in the mirror and said "good enough."

On a sudden whim he hurried to the writing desk in his bedchamber to scribble a note. What was it she said she wanted from him? *Gratitude.* He didn't entirely understand her need, but that didn't mean he couldn't provide it.

"I need a box."

"A box, sir?"

"Something small. Empty out those cuff buttons."

"But sir . . ."

"Never mind about them. Just put them somewhere else."

It was unwise, perhaps, to send Celia the ruby. But he didn't believe her any longer in danger. Besides he had no intention of letting her sleep alone tonight.

She'd never seen a famous ruby, or any other famous gem. Pigeon's blood, Julia had called the color. Celia wondered idly how the blood of a pigeon differed from that of any other bird. She held it up to the light but it left her curiously unmoved. She didn't regret for a moment that she wasn't to keep it. Tarquin's note was much more interesting.

My dear Celia. How she treasured the endearment. *I am deeply grateful to you for thwarting the duchess, and so is my uncle. T.*

She sat at her dressing table while Chantal arranged

her hair, pondering his meaning. She'd demanded his gratitude as a necessity for an equitable marriage. Was that what he meant? If so, she'd prefer him to state it with less ambiguity. The single sentence could just reflect his delight in his aunt's displeasure. The duchess had flung her some very unladylike epithets while they waited for a carriage to carry them the half mile or so from the icehouse to Mandeville House.

The mention of the duke suggested that his sentiment had no very deep meaning, let alone a hidden one. But he did call her "dear." And he'd done so in the icehouse too. In front of other people.

She wished she had someone to discuss it with, Minerva perhaps. But that rational young lady would no doubt tell her to be direct and just ask Tarquin what he meant. She might know more about parliamentary tactics and the nation's foreign affairs than any seventeen-year-old on earth, but she'd never been in love. Only one in the throes of that inconvenient passion could understand the wild pendulum swing of her emotions, cleaving her into two personalities.

Sensible Celia wanted Tarquin only if she could be sure their marriage wouldn't leave her a sad neglected shadow in his godlike glory. Besotted Celia just wanted him, at any time under any conditions.

Where is your pride, girl? demanded Sensible Celia. *You have no worldly advantages to bring to a union with a man who exemplifies worldliness: no fortune, no family, no beauty.*

But he likes *my looks!* shrieked Besotted Celia, fastening on the only point she could argue with. *Why else would he wish to lie with me?*

Because he's a man and in both cases you were there, and willing. You think he'll want you forever, when he has the choice of real beauties?

Like Countess Czerny, you mean?

Like Julia.

If he wants her, he should have her. I only want him to be happy.

Wait a minute, just now you said you wanted him under any conditions.

I do! But I want him to have what he wants.

But if we are being sensible we'll accept his offer because we've just whistled away fifty thousand pounds and we have nothing.

I won't be married for pity.

You're mad.

And there both sides of Celia, Sensible and Besotted, agreed. Quite, quite mad in the head.

There was also the unseemly physical effect Tarquin had on her. When he was in a room she was struck down with a strange kind of partial blindness by which everyone else faded into a blurred grisaille compared to Tarquin's vividly etched presence. The affliction was getting worse. Just the thought of him now had her hot and bothered.

The second package arrived as Chantal prepared her for bed, after a long tedious evening playing charades in which they'd been on separate teams and had hardly a chance to exchange a word.

It contained a book, a very familiar volume. A strip of paper marked a particular page. *I fear there may be a rat in your room.* She read the passage, one that had been recommended by Minerva, she recalled.

Apparently charades weren't over for the night.

He entered her room to find her seated on a pillow on the floor with her back to the door. The room was well lit by four candles. The scene was, after all, supposed to take place in broad daylight on a river bank. Some of his best moments with Celia had taken place next to running water. Though unfortunately covering her legs, her simple nightgown was quite reminiscent of a fondly remembered shift.

"May I sit with you, *madame*?" She nodded without looking up and waved him down onto another cushion, placed on the floor beside her own. Her nose was buried in a small octavo volume covered with a paper wrapper. He tilted his head to examine it. "Pray tell me, what are you studying so assiduously? A work of piety, no doubt."

Naughty eyes met his over the top of the open book. "What else, sir?" She showed him the wrapper on which she'd written in ink "Fordyce's Sermons." A nice embellishment. His Celia had imagination as well as a sense of fun. He silently commended her success in suppressing her laughter and only hoped he could match her restraint. She'd made quite an impression that evening at charades, displaying a thespian talent he should have suspected. It had given him the idea for the little drama they now enacted.

Damn it, he loved that she'd understood his suggestive note.

He removed the book from her hands and arched away in mock indignation. "You, madam, are a hypocrite. Why, these are no sermons! This is that notorious work of depravity, *The Memoirs of a Lady of Pleasure* by Mr. John Cleland."

Celia buried her face in her hands. "Alas! I am discovered."

"And I took you for a lady of virtue!"

"I am so ashamed!" And, just like the pious widow in Featherbrain's memoirs, she shifted to a kneeling position and buried her face in her cushion. "Alack, sir!" she moaned. "I cannot look at you."

The sight of her well-formed rump drove away the urge to laugh. Dropping to his knees behind her he stroked the taut linen-covered cheeks then pressed a hand between her thighs. Heat and wetness told him she was as excited as he. She might be able to control a laugh, but a happy little gasp escaped her. With a big grin he reached under the skirt and walked his fingers up her long, strong, shapely limbs.

Zeus, but he loved her legs.

"Oh, sir!" she cried. "What has happened?"

"Do you feel something crawling up your legs?"

She emitted a muted but most convincing shriek. "Yes! For heavens sake, what is it?"

"I saw a big water rat escape from the river and I fear it's hiding in your skirts. I think I'd better take a look."

Alas, once he got his head under her skirts his recollection of the prescribed scene unraveled. Her smooth skin touching his face, the heat and musky scent of her sex sent his senses swimming and his brain sailing off into the ether. A particularly luscious piece of inner thigh being offered to his mouth, he licked and sucked on it.

"The rat bit me!"

That she could still remember elements of the playbook, even when delivered in a squeak, told him she wasn't yet as crazed as he. He'd have to see about that. With a little vigorous rearrangement he had Celia on her back, gasping with delight as she succumbed to the ministrations of his mouth.

"Oh lord," Celia sighed happily. He kept two fingers inside her and she could feel herself continue to convulse around them. "Francis Featherbrain never did that."

"Francis Featherbrain was an idiot." His face lay on her belly and the movement of his mouth tickled. "Also fictional. I am real and therefore my repertoire is unlimited."

"But Tarquin," she began, enjoying her prerogative to toy with his short silky hair. Then she became distracted tracing his ears with her fingers. She'd never noticed how beautiful they were, just the right size for his head, the whorls neat and even.

"What?"

"We didn't finish the bit with the rat. I want to see how the scene ends."

His head popped up with conspicuous speed. "I'm ready if you are. Do you mind if we omit some of the dialogue?"

"It was rather long."

"And very badly written."

"In this particular work of literature . . ." the word drew a snort from him " . . . the plot surpassed the quality of the prose."

She pushed him off and returned to her previous position on knees and elbows. "You can go hunting under my skirts anytime," she said, giving her rear a provocative wriggle.

Her grateful ears detected the rustle of discarded garments. When he pushed up her nightgown and enveloped her from behind she quivered at the touch of warm skin, the rasp of his chest hair on her back, his hard cock pressing against her bottom. Already she ached for its entrance and pushed back against the rock hard muscle. But in addition to the physical excitement generated by the silly, titillating game, her leaping heart answered the strength and protection of his powerful body.

Two other times he'd held her from behind against his chest: ducking on the hillside, hidden by a boulder, when they first escaped from the cottage, and in the loft in Joe's barn. And each time she'd been safe in his arms, she realized, even the first time when he was half out of his mind from a blow to the head and she was filled with anger at everyone in the world, including him. Whether Terence Fish or Tarquin Compton, and despite the fact he had every reason to dislike and distrust her, he'd never once let her down. A dozen times over the past weeks he could have washed his hands of Celia Seaton, and more than a few times he'd wished to, she knew. But he'd stayed and met his slender obligation to her without flinching, and she had grown to expect it.

She had not been nearly as frightened as she should have been in the icehouse that afternoon. In the depths of her heart she'd known Tarquin would come for her.

Heat welled behind her eyes. Giving an incoherent keen, half laugh and half sob, she reached clumsy arms back to grab hold of a thigh, a handful of buttock, to pull him closer, to embrace the only person in the world who hadn't failed her. And lost her balance to land ungracefully splayed on the cushions, more laughing than crying. She managed to roll over and throw her arms about his shoulders and neck and tug him close as though to never let him go. "Make love to me, Tarquin," she whispered fiercely. "Love me."

His expression took her breath away and made her feel beautiful. Waiting tears escaped at the sight of such eager tenderness. He kissed away a trickle that damped her cheek.

"You are crying," he whispered. "Why?"

Not knowing how to explain her feelings, or whether it was wise to do so, she shook her head and pulled his head down to hers. Since he was, as she had learned, easily distracted by physical advances, she took control of the kiss, drawing him in, sucking on his tongue, devouring him. He gave up asking questions and kissed her back until the distinction between his mouth, his taste, and hers blurred and she felt as close to him as she had to any living soul. When at last he entered her, through her spiraling frenzy of excitement she felt a never-experienced peace, like a weary traveler who tops the crest of a hill and sees the road home. And her climax, when it came, was an earthy echo of the sentiment.

Afterward they lay on the carpet, Tarquin on his side propped up on his elbow. With his other hand he finger-combed her hair, spreading it over her pillow with absorbed concentration.

"Like fire," he said.

"Huh?" She basked in the compliment, however absurd. "Ginger, you mean."

"You. You warm me."

She grinned in delight and was rewarded with a quick kiss. Then a frown creased his brow. For a moment she saw his familiar haughtiness then realized it was something different, an expression she'd never seen on the stern features of the leader of the *ton*: doubt, anxiety even.

"Do you forgive me?" he asked.

"What for?"

"For comparing you to a vegetable and ruining your life."

"You haven't ruined my life," she said softly.

By asking for her pardon, she believed, he offered his own. But she'd wait until he was ready to speak it.

His smile sent her heart into its usual somersaults.

"Good. Let's go to bed." Pulling her up with him, he stood, and tossed her onto the mattress. Instead of continuing the conversation she gave a half-suppressed shriek that was still, she feared, loud enough to awaken the deaf cousin in the next room. The pillows from the floor landed beside her, followed by Tarquin himself.

He'd forgiven her, completely, but he didn't say so, perhaps because he wasn't entirely sure why. Her greatest offense had been allowing him to lie with her under the illusion they were engaged. Under the circumstances he could no longer summon even the memory of his previous anger. He was too happy and lazy after the best lovemaking he'd ever experienced. After disposing of her nightgown, which was rucked up and half falling off, he stripped off the covers and they stretched out on the sheets, on their sides facing each other.

"It's too hot for blankets," he said, ogling her from neck to toe.

She ogled him right back, her gray eyes delightfully lascivious. Idly she trailed her palm along the route from his collarbone to navel. "We still never finished the rat scene."

"Give me a little time."

"Oh, right. Tiddly pillock."

"It won't stay tiddly for long if you look at it like that."

She ran a playful finger along its gradually stiffening length.

"Or touch it."

"You told me you have many books like that." She gestured in the direction of the discarded volume.

"A good number."

"How did you come to collect such things?"

He put an arm about her waist and drew her close, her head rested on his shoulder. "I suppose it started by accident. As boys grow up they speculate about these things among themselves. A school friend lent me a volume ascribed to Aretino's nephew."

"Who is this Aretino, anyway?"

"An Italian poet who wrote some obscene sonnets and a very smutty book called *The Dialogues*."

"And the *Genuine Amours*."

"Definitely not. There are dozens of books ascribed to Aretino's authorship but written by others. His name on the title page tells the reader what kind of book to expect."

"The kind you like."

"I'll never forget that first book. It had the most amazing illustration of a couple on horseback, fully joined."

"You cannot be serious! Could one do that?" He loved the awed eagerness in her voice.

"I wouldn't like to try, but I wish I could show you the book. I lost it and never found another copy."

"How did you lose it?"

"The nursery maid discovered it hidden under my mattress and gave it to the duchess."

"Trouble?"

"I can still remember the beating," he said with feeling. "After that I started to buy as many such books as I could, just to get back at her. A foolish defiance, I admit. And it became a habit. At Cambridge I became friends with Sebastian Iverley, who was already a bibliophile. I discovered a taste for poetry and started to collect early editions. But I continued to add to my collection of 'curious' books."

"The contrast is an odd one."

"Between poetry and profanity? You are not the first to point that out."

"I meant between your exterior elegance and more . . . earthy activities."

He was surprised that had never occurred to him, but also a little offended. "Do you find me disingenuous, then?"

"Does anyone ever present the whole truth to the world? I shouldn't think there's a soul on earth who doesn't have things they prefer to hide."

"Isn't that dishonest?"

"How can it be? Are you telling me that you are the way you look and your clothes represent your essential being? If that is so, then you are nothing and nobody without your valet and your tailor, a puppet in fact."

The words shook him because he feared they might be true. He removed his arm from her waist and withdrew a little. "You're very philosophical all of a sudden, Miss Seaton."

She twisted her neck to meet him eye to eye. "Let me tell you something, Mr. Compton. I prefer you without your clothes. I liked you in a farm laborer's smock and I like you even better naked."

He hadn't known how wound up he'd become until he felt the tension snap like an over-tuned fiddle string. With a crack of laughter he rolled her over onto her back. "I like you naked too."

She smiled back at him. "You told me it doesn't matter what I wear so I suppose I may as well wear nothing."

"When I said that, I meant it as a compliment."

"It didn't sound like one." Though her pout was mocking, she sounded cross.

"When I look at you, I see only Celia. Your exterior trappings are of no importance."

She blinked. "Thank you. That may be the nicest thing anyone ever said to me."

He'd offered her the truth and found the response alarming. She sounded moved and he wasn't used to communicating with people on terms of emotional candor. Irony and detachment were his usual currency.

He watched her face as a look of understanding dawned. Had she read his ambivalence correctly? Even Celia's expression couldn't be read infallibly and it occurred to him that he could just ask her what she was thinking. But as he pondered this novel way of dealing with uncertainty, she turned the weighty moment into a light one. "So it won't matter if I get dressed again." She pushed at his chest to escape but a saucy smile sent the opposite message.

He laughed with relief and gratitude and with . . . something unacknowledged. Snatching her wrists he pinned them to the mattress above her head. "Don't you dare," he said into her lips and swooped in for a kiss that grew long and deep and went on and on until he found himself hard again. Celia shook off his restraining hands, reached between their bodies and grasped his pillock, far from tiddly. Fatally weakened by her touch, he let her reverse positions, straddle him, and ride St. George into mutual oblivion.

She swam in warm waves of happiness as the night passed in talking, dozing, lovemaking. She didn't know what would happen on the morrow, but for the first time she felt a timid optimism about her future. She knew just what she wanted. And, if she sensed Tarquin hadn't quite reached the same point, she was willing to ignore the warning in the back of her mind that she deluded herself, believing she knew his feelings better than he did.

In the weeks they'd passed in varying degrees of intimacy, she'd always been—or felt like—the follower. Poor plain, untidy, helpless Celia, trailing in the glorious wake of Tarquin the tall, the strong, the clever, the moneyed, the well-dressed, the witty, the monarch of society.

But not tonight. Tonight she was in charge because she knew something he didn't: that they loved each other and belonged together. And if it turned out tomorrow that she was wrong, at least she'd had this night.

"What did the duchess do with that book?" she asked idly as they lay entwined, bodies damp. "Do you suppose she acted out the scenes?"

Tarquin's body shook with mirth. "I would love to think so. On the other hand, have you seen the duke?"

It was impossible to imagine Parrot Lady doing *any* of the things so enthusiastically described by Master Featherbrain, not with her fat little nobleman husband, anyway.

"With someone else, perhaps. I thought all great ladies of the *ton* took lovers."

"It would need a very brave man to take her on." He grew serious. "I don't believe most 'great' ladies are faithless and if so I do not condone it. For myself I believe in fidelity after marriage."

"And before?"

"As I believe I told you when I couldn't even remember, I have had other women. It isn't at all proper for me to discuss them with my future bride."

"It's isn't at all proper for us to be naked together in my bedchamber." Celia couldn't leave it alone. "Did you love them?"

"I've never been in love, but I've never bedded a woman I didn't like."

She was overcome with loathing for an unknown number of likable ladies and tortured herself by picturing them—beauties to a woman—with Tarquin. "Have you tried all the different things suggested in your books, apart from the horseback one?"

"All of them! What an idea. Some of them sound downright painful, if not anatomically impossible. However, I'm always ready to experiment. And since it looks like you're going to be my bed partner for the rest of my life, I'm delighted to find you equally adventurous."

Feeling much better, she decided to find out what it was like to bite his neck. Tasty.

"Is there anything particular you'd like to try?" he asked.

"Well, there's this thing in a chair . . ."

Chapter 32

Money isn't the most important thing in life, but large sums can be very nice.

Tarquin left her room at first light, recommending she catch up on her sleep and remain in bed until noon. After a few short hours, wide awake, she joined the house party for the eleven o'clock breakfast. She saw by his absence he'd taken his own advice.

This morning invisibility seemed a particularly desirable quality. She quietly sipped tea and stared at a plate heaped with ham and eggs and buttered muffins. Lovemaking had famished her but, after two bites, she found love had stolen her appetite. She both longed and dreaded to learn how the next days would play out.

Her best hope was a happy wooing followed by a blissful betrothal. Yet the possibility remained that all the things that made her doubt her happiness as Tarquin's wife would come flooding back. Naked he was loving, vulnerable, and entirely at her service. Clothed in the midst of the beau monde, he might revert to the terror of the *ton*. She reminded herself that more of life was spent clothed than naked, more of the day abroad than in bed.

For the tenth time Celia checked the reticule hanging from her wrist. Carrying a ruby worth fifty thousand pounds tended to prey on her mind, but she dared not leave it upstairs. The sooner she handed it over the better.

At each new arrival at the table she looked up. Longing for Tarquin, hoping for Julia, and dreading the Duchess of Amesbury, the guest who claimed her attention was Lord Hugo Hartley.

She stood at the venerable old dandy's approach.

"Lord Hugo," she said. "May I summon a footman to help you to a seat?"

"Thank you, Miss Seaton, but I breakfasted in my rooms. I hoped for your company but I see you are still eating."

Apprehensive about his motive for seeking her out, she glanced at her plate. "I've had enough, thank you. I have little appetite this morning."

Might as well find out what he wanted and get it over. She prepared to be compared to a pair of pantaloons, or some other garment in dubious taste. Hosiery, perhaps this time.

"Excellent. Perhaps you would join me for my morning constitutional. My doctor insists I exercise every day."

Lord Hugo refused to take her arm. He made his own

way to the terrace, assisted by an ebony walking stick with a polished ivory handle. He kept up a steady stream of gossamer small talk and she couldn't fault his courtesy, but in his company Celia was unable to appreciate the impeccable summer day. Despite his great height and erect posture, she worried the slender figure would be blown away in the light breeze. Taking tiny steps to match his slow ones, she watched him anxiously, ready to step in if he tottered.

"Thank you for your forbearance," he said. "It must be dull for such an *active* young lady to be restricted to an old man's pace."

Somehow she didn't feel complimented. She was not looking her best that morning. When Chantal complained her hair was unmanageable she couldn't offer the excuse of a busy night. Quite *active* come to think of it. She choked back a laugh that she would be quite unable to explain to Lord Hugo.

"It's a pleasure, my lord. I've heard much about you from Mr. Compton."

"And I heard of you before I came here."

"You surprise me, sir. I thought I was quite obscure."

"I'm acquainted with Lady Trumper," he said. "In fact I saw her the day before I left London."

"I see." She did indeed see. She had no doubt that her former chaperone had left Lord Hugo in full possession of every fact she knew about Celia's history.

He said nothing more on that head, but there was no need. "Has my great-nephew told you how we met?"

The phrasing stuck her as odd. How did one meet ones relations? Of course, having none she wasn't in a position to know. She shook her head.

"He came to London as a boy, to live under the guardianship of my nephew, the Duke of Amesbury. Since I rarely set foot in Amesbury House, being unable to abide the duchess, I never saw Tarquin until he'd been there two years. A sadder sight I'd rarely encountered than the gawky beanpole of a lad, hunched in the corner of the duchess's drawing room. He'd just finished his first half at Eton and he had no idea where to put his oversized feet. And naturally no notion of conversation. I don't know why I noticed him, except he seemed to have attracted the especial venom of the duchess."

"I've met her," Celia said.

"So we understand each other completely. I have every confidence we shall continue to do so." A hint of emotion rippled through Lord Hugo's urbane tones. "I decided on a whim to do something about the boy, so I took him to be measured for a coat. Thinking back on it, taking an eleven-year-old to visit a tailor might not have been the greatest treat. I daresay he would have preferred a confectioner's shop or a menagerie. But it was what occurred to me." He paused and his face shone with affection.

"I think it was very thoughtful of you," Celia said. She felt a little choked up. "And Mr. Compton proved a worthy pupil."

"He is like a son to me. There is nothing I will not do to ensure his happiness."

And having thrown down this elegant gauntlet, Lord Hugo proceeded to the duel.

"I'm a very old man, born the same year as the old king, you know. I'm over eighty and in my life I've known almost everyone."

Everyone from a certain stratum of society, he meant of course.

"And though I've never married," he continued, "I have observed numerous marriages. People wed for many different reasons. Often they are worldly goals: dynastic needs, money, or social advancement." He'd reverted to his languid conversational style, as though his observations were no more momentous that a comment on the weather. "Then there are the marriages formed for reasons of sentiment: companionship, passion, or love. Not all marriages are successful." He paused and looked at her.

"I would imagine not," she said, since he seemed to expect a reply.

"I have given the matter a good deal of thought and I believe I know the most important ingredient of a happy lifelong union. It is certainly not passion, neither is it love. The most important thing is for a couple to understand one another. And understanding comes from a common background, an equality of position."

"Do you not believe in love, Lord Hugo?"

He stopped walking and placed a hand on the stone balustrade. "Love matches can be the best of all, but not without that shared experience." His eyes met hers, perceptive and not without sympathy. "I do not believe that a marriage between a prince and a beggar maid, however much they love each other, will succeed. I've seen too many unequal matches end in unhappiness to believe in fairy tales."

He looked out over the rolling parkland of Mandeville, then behind him to the soaring pillars of the mansion's south front.

"What a beautiful morning," he said. "I very rarely leave London these days but this is a magnificent spot. I'm glad to see it again. Perhaps I should visit Amesbury Park again, too. I grew up there, you know. Very different from Mandeville, being Elizabethan. A shade smaller? Perhaps not."

And this, he meant but didn't say, was Tarquin's milieu. As a duke's nephew he was miles above Celia Seaton.

She had to hand it to Lord Hugo, in fifteen minutes of excruciatingly polite conversation he'd managed to enumerate every reason she was utterly unsuitable to be Tarquin Compton's bride.

He'd be gratified to know she agreed with him, or almost. She did not believe that she was unworthy. None of his reasons had anything to do with her character and her value as a person. But she was, by any worldly definition, unsuitable. Instinctively she knew Lord Hugo was right about a couple needing something in common besides love. He only repeated her own concerns.

Tarquin might belong in a ducal mansion but she did not and she was leaving, that very morning. Leaving the field to Lord Hugo was a risk, but one she needed to take.

* * *

Arriving at Wallop Hall in one of the Mandeville carriages, she was greeted with affectionate delight by Minerva and dragged off to the nursery to visit the baby, who was little changed. So much had happened since she last saw him, he might have grown old enough to be breeched. She duly admired him and agreed with his doting mother that he showed signs of uncommon precociousness. It might even be true, if a red face and lusty squall were indicators of intelligence.

The Iverleys showed her the rattle Tarquin had broken into to retrieve the ruby.

"We'll have it repaired, of course," Sebastian said. "And we're anxious to know what happened."

At the end of the tale they all exclaimed and applauded her decision to give the jewel to Countess Czerny. "The Duchess of Amesbury is an impossible old harridan," Diana crowed. "I wish I'd seen her face. And the countess sounds quite fascinating. I hope I'll meet her sometime."

"You may get the chance this very day," Celia said. "I haven't had a chance to give her the jewel so I sent word that she could come here for it. I hope you don't mind."

"Not in the least. Is she very beautiful?"

"I think we're about to find out." Minerva spoke from the window embrasure. "There's a lady in an absolutely gorgeous bonnet getting out of a carriage."

Celia and Diana joined her at the window. "Oh goodness," said the latter. "Where did she find that pelisse with the ruffed collar? I've never seen anything so elegant."

"I'm told all her clothes come from Paris," Celia said. "I suppose I'd better go down and see her."

She received Julia in the Montroses' small morning room.

"Here," she said. "No, wait."

The box in which Tarquin had sent her the ruby, a simple affair of polished blue leather, rested on her palm. She carefully removed the lid, stamped in gilt with a crest and a curly letter *C*. The huge red stone sat in a nest of linen that emitted a faint hint of Tarquin's unique scent. Celia inhaled appreciatively then extracted the jewel, held it up, letting it catch the sunlight pouring through the window.

"I think I'll keep the box," she said and tossed the gem to the countess.

"My God!" Julia cried, clutching it in her fist against her chest. "You almost gave me an apoplexy. Do you have any idea how valuable this little rock is?"

"I know almost nothing about precious stones. A fact that strikes me as ironic since I gather my father was not so ignorant. Will you do something for me, Julia?"

"Anything in my power. You could have sold the ruby to the duchess and I might have ended up dead like your father."

"Will you tell me what you know of my father? I've never understood why he decided to leave India."

"He was recommended to me as a man who could get things done. Unfortunately for me that wasn't the whole story, or I would never have used him for this commission." She paused at Celia's flinch. "I'm sorry to have to say that about your father."

"It's all right. I'd rather know the truth at last."

"From what I learned later," Julia continued, "he'd offended too many powerful people and it was time to get out. He decided to use the gem to make a fresh start. In England I supposed, but who knows what he planned?"

"Do you know what happened to the household?"

"I'm going to speak bluntly. His bibi and children and their servants had already left the house when he was killed."

"Do you know where they went?"

"I never learned that, but I gather he raised as much money as he could for them. When his killers searched his body he had almost nothing left. That's why I was so certain you had the ruby."

"Were they safe?"

"My informant believed that they were."

"Thank you. I've always wondered and worried about that. It means a great deal to me to know."

"Is there anything else I can tell you?"

"What will you do now?"

Julia gave a knowing little smile. "I haven't quite decided what I shall do once I restore the ruby to the owner's agent in London. As we discussed before, I've been considering marriage."

"You're still interested, then?"

"Perhaps. However, I'm not sure Mr. Compton is still

interested in me. If that should change, who knows? He's such a terribly intriguing man. What do you think?"

"I have no opinion."

"If you say so, my dear Celia, of course I believe you. And what do you intend to do with yourself?"

"If nothing better comes up, I expect I shall seek another position as a governess. But I fear the whole world is about to be privy to the fact that I spent my formative years living in the same house as my father's mistress and my two Indian brothers." Even if Lord Hugo kept quiet about the tale he'd heard from Lady Trumper, the Duchess of Amesbury must also know the truth.

Julia nodded. "That kind of narrow-mindedness is one of the disadvantages of English life. You may be sure I will never mention it."

Celia believed her. Though she still had reasons to resent this woman, she also felt kinship with one who had an understanding of her own checkered experience. Unlike Lord Hugo who'd made no secret of his disgust with her background.

"Others may not be as discreet—or forbearing," she said. "I envy you. You seem to have found a way to make a life on your own. I wish I could do the same."

The countess tilted her head and looked at her for some little time, as though trying to come to a decision.

"I have a better idea. When I hand this jewel over to its new owner I shall receive the final payment of ten thousand pounds. Since half of it was your father's share of our profit, you shall have it."

"I don't think he deserved it."

"No, but you do. And five thousand is not a great fortune, after all."

It sounded a vast sum to Celia. It represented her independence. "Can you afford it?" she asked.

Julia waved aside her concern. "There's always more money to be found. I spent most of my capital on my Paris wardrobe so I could present myself in London as a rich Hungarian widow. Not that I ever find it a sacrifice to spend money on clothes."

"Who are you, truly?"

"I never tell unnecessary lies. I was born a Hartley and I am the widow of a Hungarian count, but not a rich one. Don't worry about me. Five thousand pounds is ample to start me off on my next adventure."

"Then I accept your offer with gratitude. Thank you." She held out her hand but instead Julia gave her a quick embrace, saluting her on both cheeks. "Do you think you will remain in England?"

Julia laughed. "Why of course? How else am I to marry Mr. Compton?"

The door opened to admit William Montrose. "Celia," he said. "Min told me you'd come back to us."

He strode across the room toward her then stopped dead. His welcoming smile froze and his blue eyes grew wide. "And who is this?"

"Allow me to present Countess Czerny. Julia, this is Mr. William Montrose."

William looked as though he'd been hit over the head with a large blunt object. "Countess," he gasped and took her hand. "I am honored to make your acquaintance." He kissed her hand.

"I am happy to make yours, Mr. Montrose. I was just leaving."

"I'll see you to your carriage."

Without another glance at Celia, he took the countess's arm.

"Tell me," she heard Julia say as they left the room. "Are you related to Rufus Montrose? I met him in Athens once . . ."

Good thing about the five thousand, Celia thought. Marriage to Will Montrose was clearly no longer an option. Much as she liked Julia, it might be better if she did leave the country.

The lovely adventuress was not, however, going to take Tarquin from her. Not if Celia had anything to do with it. On the other hand, it was time to put Tarquin in possession of the unvarnished truth. She sat down at the writing desk and found pen, paper, and ink.

Chapter 33

*Those who have your best interests
at heart may not be right.*

"What have you done with Celia?"

"Good afternoon, my dear boy. Yes, thank you, I am very well today."

Since Hugo set great store by polite forms, Tarquin would not normally burst into his uncle's chamber without ceremony. He bit back his impatience. "I beg your pardon, Uncle. I understand you walked with Miss Seaton after breakfast."

"Do sit down. May I point out that the symmetry of your neck cloth is off by a few degrees." Hugo was more than usually languid, but Tarquin, who knew him very well, detected an undercurrent of unease. He was in no mood to investigate the cause.

"I don't give a damn about my neck cloth."

"My dear boy! Are you quite well?"

Tarquin dragged an ottoman next to Hugo's wing chair and tried to contain his impatience. "After she spoke with you, Miss Seaton packed her belongings and left in one of the Mandeville carriages. I would like to know what you said to cause her to depart."

"Nothing to upset her, I am sure. Perhaps she merely felt she had stayed long enough. These country house parties can be so fatiguing."

"What did you talk about?"

"Oh, this and that. We may have broached the topic of marriage and what makes for a happy one. We found ourselves in agreement."

"Hugo," Tarquin said in a warning tone. "Have you been meddling?"

Hugo looked aggrieved. "I have nothing against Miss Seaton. She seems a nice enough girl, though without much elegance of dress or manner. And she has no fortune."

"Are those your only objections?"

"Her upbringing. Not only did she live in India until a year or two ago, so that she has no experience or connections in English life, I gather from her former chaperone Lady Trumper that the circumstances of her upbringing were somewhat scandalous."

"Such intolerance is unlike you. I daresay her father was a little disreputable, but that's hardly her fault."

"I'm afraid it's worse than that."

"I don't care and I don't want you to tell me. It all happened in India so who's to know?"

"Now you are being naïve, my boy. People always know."

"This has nothing to do with Celia, does it? It's about Julia Czerny."

Hugo nodded. "Julia is clever and beautiful, witty, and modish. Just the kind of person we enjoy."

Tarquin had never felt so much at odds with Hugo. Yes, Julia Czerny was a dazzling woman but Celia was also clever and witty and beautiful. And frankly he didn't care whether or not she was modish. The heretical thought crossed his mind that perhaps he didn't enjoy the same kind of person as Hugo.

"I think you'd like Celia very much if you gave her a chance."

It would be too much to say he slumped, but Tarquin's practiced eye detected an infinitesimal slackening in Hugo's perfect posture. His voice grew serious, without his usual witty flourishes. "I was very fond of Julia's late father but I also owed him a debt of gratitude. Without him I would have been ruined. Jonathan Hartley helped me out of a tight spot involving a moment's indiscretion on my part and a blackmailer."

Tarquin squeezed the old man's hand. "There's no need to tell me the details, unless you wish to."

"Thank you, I won't. Suffice it to say I would like to repay my debt to his daughter. And I can't think of a better way than to see her wed to the man I regard as a son. And I believe a lady of wit, elegance, and fortune will suit you far better than a harum-scarum former governess of dubious antecedents."

Unable to dispute Hugo's assessment of Celia's worldly position, Tarquin wondered how much of *Julia*'s he should reveal. At the very least the countess was guilty of considerable sins of omission: she might still be the widow of a rich Hungarian nobleman (though Tarquin wouldn't want to lay money on the accuracy of that description) but it wasn't all she was. Having castigated Celia for her lies, he'd come to believe in her fundamental honesty. He wouldn't bet sixpence on Julia's.

Not upsetting Hugo, however, was a priority for him, however much he might be out of charity with his dear uncle in this instance.

"I have reason to believe," he said carefully, "that Cousin Julia may be a bit of an adventuress."

Hugo actually smiled. "I shouldn't be surprised if she took after her father in that regard. Jonathan was a Hartley by birth but too far down the line to come into a Hartley fortune. He lived abroad mostly, traveling around. He died a few years ago, somewhere in the East Indies. I never inquired too closely how he managed to live."

"So you have no particular objection to me marrying an adventuress. I'm very glad to hear it."

Tarquin felt slender fingers tremble as they rested on his own, papery skin reminding him of Hugo's age and frailty. His uncle spoke with indubitable sincerity. "As I have always said, I only want you to be happy."

"In that case, Hugo, you must accept Celia. She makes me happy."

Hugo looked into his eyes, long and hard. Finally he nodded. "Very well. Just as long as she loves you."

"I believe she does." Doubt assailed him as he realized something. "She's never actually said she will marry me."

"Did you ask her?"

"Of course!" He paused. He wasn't sure he'd ever rendered a proposal in the form of a request. "Perhaps not."

"My dear boy! This is not a matter on which I can advise you from experience, but I am tolerably sure it is good *ton* to make an offer of marriage in a humble and beseeching manner."

As happened numerous times over the years, Tarquin and Hugo exchanged looks of complete mutual understanding. "Thank you, Uncle. Your guidance in these matters has never failed me yet."

A knock at the door preceded the entrance of a footman with a letter. For Tarquin. Ripping off the seal, the first words relieved his anxiety with the news that Celia had traveled no farther than Wallop Hall.

Her missive filled two full sheets. He'd never seen her handwriting before. It reminded him of her: idiosyncratic and slightly disordered, the product of an interrupted education. The letter spelled out in detail exactly how she'd lived in the years after that education was cut short.

He swore viciously as he took in the final piece of news. The last veil of uncertainty was ripped to shreds and his feelings were clear as summer noon.

"Bad news?" Hugo asked.

Tarquin wanted to kill Julia Czerny. "It appears that Miss Seaton has come into a nice little independence. She no longer needs to marry for her own security. She can manage without me."

Chapter 34

Never get into a cart with a strange man.

By late afternoon Celia began to fear Tarquin wasn't coming, the chance she'd taken when she set him free.

Still, he might have risen very late. The night had required a great deal of energy on both their parts and she wished now she'd been able to sleep. Fresh air, she decided was what she needed to counter her own fatigue.

Enjoying her freedom to venture out without fear of another kidnapping, she turned down Minerva's half-hearted offer of company. The latest edition of *The Reformist* had come in the day's post and the younger girl was fully engrossed. In a heady abandonment of convention, Celia left off bonnet and gloves and set out at a brisk pace, making believe she was back on the moors.

Refusing to cry because the companion of her Yorkshire adventures was absent, she scarcely allowed herself to hope she might meet him on his way to Wallop Hall. She turned out of the drive into the lane and reached the back gates to Mandeville but refrained from peering through the iron bars. So far she'd walked the best part of a mile without seeing a single living creature not propelled by wings. Resolutely undisappointed, she carried on, refusing to look back. Then she detected the clop of a single horse moving at a slow walk, clearly not a gentleman on horseback or in a smart carriage. Instead, as it drew nearer, she judged it to be pulling a cart and glanced over her shoulder to find her guess correct.

Her heart thudded. The driver was a dark man wearing the rustic smock of a farm laborer. Thus had the adventure begun. She stopped and waited. The vehicle drew to a halt. A voice hailed her in a miserable facsimile of a Yorkshire burr.

"Can I give you a lift, miss?"

"Why would you do that?"

"So I can take you off to a lonely cottage, tear off all your clothes, and ravish you."

"In that case," she said, putting a hand on the seat and hoisting herself up beside the driver, "by all means."

He had come. It remained only to discover if she read the message of his costume correctly.

He gee-upped his horse, turned around, and drove back into the Mandeville park, tossing a coin to the gatekeeper.

"Where are we going?" she asked.

"Wait and see."

They followed a grassy ride though a stand of trees, away from the road to the house. She waited for Tarquin to speak first.

"Tell me about your brothers," he said.

She took a deep breath. Apparently her letter hadn't been enough. He wanted the whole story. "When I was twelve we left Madras. I never knew why, but I think my father had disgraced himself with the Company. That's when I discovered he already had another home where he kept his bibi. That's what the Indians call a mistress."

"I assume, even in India, it was unusual for a man to take his daughter to live with his mistress."

"All the English, in India and here, were shocked about this. I learned to accept it. We had separate quarters and servants, but I was lonely when my father was away so I'd cross the courtyard and visit Ghazala and later the children, when they arrived."

Beginning with the missionary and his wife who'd accompanied her on the voyage to England, everyone had cautioned her to silence, advised her to forget that she'd spent seven years in such scandalous circumstances. Now she could finally speak about this part of her life, Celia found she couldn't stop. She poured out her memories of the graceful compound with its well-tended gardens, the lovely girl, only a few years older than herself, who was the true mistress of the house, and above all of Arthur Akbar and George Ghalib. Her beautiful little brothers, whom she'd held in her arms as newborn infants, had been only five and three years old when she'd bid them farewell, weeping bitterly that she'd never play with them again.

From time to time during her narrative, she looked at Tarquin, dreading to encounter the distaste she'd seen on the faces of the few who had heard the story. She'd never dared tell Bertram Baldwin.

While driving the cart Tarquin could do nothing more than listen. But he sensed it was a tale Celia needed to tell, one she'd locked inside herself for too long.

"I understand now why your first impulse when we met was to make up a story. It's been a habit for you, hasn't it?" At her stricken look he took her hand and held onto it. He could drive this placid mare with one hand. "I didn't mean that as a criticism. Since your father's death, everyone has encouraged you to lie about yourself."

"But I didn't have to," she said. "I should have had more courage."

"It's easy to be brave when nothing threatens you."

"I'm sorry it took me so long to tell you the truth. You deserved to hear it."

He swallowed, proud that she had brought herself to confide in him and resolved to be worthy of her trust. "Have you ever heard what happened to your brothers?" he asked.

"Never. But Julia told me today they and Ghazala were safe and my father had provided for them. I know now that he was not at all a respectable man, but at least he didn't abandon his family."

"Perhaps she could help us find out where they are. I expect you'd like to write to them."

Us. He'd said "us." Celia hadn't known her heart could be this full. All she could manage was a strangled "Thank you," from a throat tight with rising tears.

"It's funny that you have two younger brothers," Tarquin said, squeezing her hand. "I have two older sisters, you know. I don't see them often but we write to each other. We'll have to visit them. Claudia has six daughters and Augusta a boy and a girl."

Celia recovered her voice. "Did they live at Amesbury House, too, after your parents died?"

"For a while. The duchess tolerated them better than she did me, but she still married them off quickly. Claudia was seventeen and Augusta only a little older."

"Are they happy?"

"Happy enough, I suppose. Neither one of them made a love match."

Her heart beat faster. "So you don't believe love is important in a match?"

"I used not to. But as Uncle Hugo pointed out not so long ago, I appear to be, at heart, a romantic."

"Does Lord Hugo wish you to make a love match?"

"I believe he does. Hugo loves me and wants me to be happy."

"I see. He thinks you are in love with the countess."

"If he ever did, he knows now he was sorely mistaken."

Hardly daring to believe the evidence of her ears, Celia fell silent and paid attention to their whereabouts. Tarquin had driven them to a distant part of the vast walled park, with not a classical temple, nor any other building in sight. Instead they approached a stream of middling size. Celia guessed it must eventually feed the lake close to the house, though neither was in view. Around them no signs of human life or habitation were visible and the only sounds were birdsong, the hum of insects, and the trickle of running water.

Tarquin stopped the horse, descended, and helped Celia down. While the tranquil beast lowered his head to munch on grass, he led her to the edge of the stream, to a gentle bank under a willow tree. Oblivious to the danger of grass stains on the pale breeches he wore beneath his smock, he settled on the ground.

"Sit with me," he said, guiding her down beside him.

Side by side, leaning on their bended knees, they gazed at the water. Were it not for the peaceful domestication of the landscape with its soft meadows and picturesque stands of trees, they might have been in Yorkshire. "I miss those days on the moors," she said. "We were hungry and dirty and uncomfortable and they were the happiest of my life."

"I've missed them too."

Courage, she decided, should become a habit. "I've missed Terence Fish," she said. Her heart raced as she learned that truth could be a heady quaff. "I loved him."

His hand glanced over her hair and came to rest, warm and firm, on her neck. "Do you think there's any chance you could love Tarquin Compton as well?" His breath was a warm buzz in her ear.

Her throat clenched and her voice emerged in a croak. "I do love him, and just as well. No, I love him more."

"Thank God for that. I love you too."

She finally looked at him and was rewarded by an expression of heart-melting tenderness with not a hint of cynicism or reserve. Then he pulled her into his arms and tumbled them down till he lay on his back with her sprawled on top. Holding her head fast, he joined their mouths into a deep kiss that lasted an age and left her reeling with joy.

"Are you sure?" she had to ask, when they came up for breath. "Are you sure it's not just duty because we shared a bed? Now you know all about me, you understand why I don't have quite the same feelings as a proper English lady would have about that."

"One of the things—the many things—I love about you." He kissed her again.

"Stop," she said before things got out of hand. Despite his protests she rolled off him and sat up again. "I have something I want to say."

He gave an exasperated sigh, but she could tell he wasn't serious. He sat beside her again and put his arm around her. "Yes?"

"I have five thousand pounds and you don't need to worry about me. I can manage without you."

"That's how I knew I loved you," he said. "I kept telling myself I couldn't leave you alone while you were in danger. As soon as we resolved that threat, I knew I'd been lying to myself and I had no intention of letting you go. But I wanted to kill Julia Czerny for giving you the means to live without me."

Celia wanted to laugh for joy then fall into his arms and do something Featherbrainish. "One more thing . . ." He was trying to kiss her again. She put her fingers to his mouth but he shook them off.

"What more is there? I love you, you love me, we'll be married and live happily ever after."

Pulling herself free, she got up on her knees beside him and folded her arms to stop herself touching him. "There's still my background, which everyone is bound to find out about. Moreover, I'm still shabby Celia. Well not shabby, perhaps, but I'm never going to be fashionable and elegant and witty and I don't even want to be. And you? Well, you know what you are. And you know what people will say."

"My darling love, I think you have a fundamental misconception about what it means to be a great dandy. I have better taste than anyone else so I don't care what anyone else thinks about anything. I am right and they are wrong."

Celia didn't know whether to laugh or hit him. She did both, softly. "I always knew you were the most arrogant, toplofty beast ever born. How could I live with you?"

"Because you are the exception, the one person whose opinion matters to me."

"Truly? You mean you'd take my advice on your clothing?"

"Probably not, but I'd listen. And I would care what you think."

She grinned down at him and fingered the collar of his smock. "I like your costume today. Is it the same garment?"

"Yes."

"It appears to have been laundered." She ran her palm up his sleeve, feeling the contours of his arm beneath the rough linen, now starched and ironed to a state of smoothness. "Very nice."

"I brought it with me from Revesby. When he found it in my bags my valet didn't know what else to do with it."

"Why did you bring it?"

His smile contained a sweet humility she'd never seen in him before. "I didn't know why, not then."

"And now?"

"I realize I didn't mind being Terence Fish. But, if I have to be a country bumpkin, let me at least be a well-appointed one."

"Do you have to be a country bumpkin?"

"I'll be anything if it makes you stay with me. I don't want to live without you in London but perhaps you'd be prepared to share Revesby with me."

"I loved Revesby. I thought it was perfect."

"Well, come with me to Yorkshire and we'll go fishing and restore my mother's garden and I'll learn to be a country gentleman and a good landowner."

She desperately wished to credit the sincerity she read in his eyes. They held her gaze, dark, earnest, pleading. "I'm going anyway," he said. "With or without you. It's time I went home for good. But it would make me very happy if you would come with me. Will you marry me? Please? I beseech you humbly."

Tarquin waited for her answer. He hadn't realized he had tensed up until she hurled herself into his arms, knocking the remaining breath out of him. "I will, I will," she cried. "I'll marry you and go with you, to London, or Yorkshire, or anywhere in between." And started kissing him again.

With soaring spirits he put her aside, for the moment, and hauled her to her feet. "I brought you here because I thought I'd try and catch us a little supper. I'd like your help."

"Are you going to teach me to tickle trout?"

"First you have to undress. You can't lie on the bank and dip your arms in the water in that modish morning gown."

"Really?" she said. "Do you find it à la mode?"

"How would a country bumpkin like me know that?"

"Would a country bumpkin like you know how to untie a lady's stays?"

"We rustics are equipped with natural ingenuity."

"Very nice," he said once she had stripped to her shift, which was made of fine cambric and with the low sun behind her revealed much of her figure.

She puckered her forehead. "There's something wrong," she said, reaching for his cheek and jaw. "Too smooth."

"My apologies. If I'd known I was going fishing I wouldn't have shaved today."

"And you're wearing boots."

"I cannot believe you mentioned that fact," he said. "Do I take it you are volunteering to remove them for me?"

"Later, perhaps. How do we fish?"

"Come. Lie beside me."

She chuckled as she settled down on her stomach, chin propped on her elbows.

"What?" he asked.

"Francis Featherbrain. He consorted with one of his many lady friends on a downward slope. He found it—ahem—enhanced his pleasure."

"Interesting. Would you like to try it?"

"Another time."

"Did you get to the end of the book? What happened to our Francis, anyway?"

"It was very sad. The love of his life died."

"There was only one love of his life? I had the impression there were many."

"Oh no! He truly, truly loved Nancy. Stricken with grief at her passing, he assuaged his pain by seducing other men's wives."

"I think I understand," Tarquin said gravely after giving the matter some thought. "He was merely sharing in the happiness of those who had married their loves."

"That's a line of reasoning worthy of Francis."

"And did he end up catching a pox and dying alone and penniless?"

"Not a bit of it. He wed a girl with a large dowry, gave up being a dissolute and abandoned rake, and became a sober, honest, industrious, virtuous, and constant husband. I believe those are almost the words he used."

"A most edifying tale. I wonder if there's a sequel."

"I'm glad you carried a great work of literature with you that day." He was too. "If you'd chosen some lesser opus, like Shakespeare's sonnets or 'The Rape of the Lock,' I wouldn't have learned nearly as much."

And Tarquin sent up a silent prayer of thanks to Nicholas Constantine and Joe. Had either of them realized what a treasure they'd been offered in *The Genuine Amours*, he and Celia would have missed out on some excellent experiences.

They lay in silence for few minutes, watching the water flow by. Celia felt the sun on her back and her bare legs. "Tarquin," she said, "I don't think there are any fish in this stream."

"I'm afraid you are correct."

"If we can't go fishing we'll have to do something else."

"Can you think of anything?"

She flung herself onto him with a joyful laugh, rolling them down into the stream.

Splashing, spluttering, flailing about, they ended up laughing in a shared embrace, barely covered by the shallow water. Tarquin's mouth scorched her chilled lips, initiating a voracious kiss as they fought to devour one another and their bodies burned, even with the intervention of cold wet garments. She clawed at his sodden smock and felt him try to find his way to her breasts through her clinging shift.

"We have to get out of here," he gasped, dragging his mouth from hers for two seconds. "It's not going to work," he said a minute later, tugging the tangled ribbons at her neck.

"Of course," she said. "Cold water, tiddly . . ."

"No," he interrupted, guiding her hand so she could feel for herself. "That is emphatically not the problem. We need to get out of the water and out of these clothes."

They scrambled up the bank and gazed at each other, dripping wet and grinning like idiots.

"I'm a fool," he said. "I should have had you remove these damned boots."

Epilogue

Revesby House, Yorkshire, six months later

Celia Compton sat with her morning caller in the small parlor. An unseasonably fine February day had brought Mrs. Stewart over from Stonewick.

"I'll be back from Cheshire in a month," she said, "assuming all is well with the children."

A few weeks after their wedding, much to Celia and Tarquin's surprise, Mrs. Stewart had returned to Yorkshire after an extended absence attending her daughter's confinement. It turned out she was just who she had claimed: the widow of an East India Company official who remembered both Algernon Seaton and his late wife with fondness, despite Algernon's later vagaries.

Celia found great satisfaction in her acquaintance with someone who could talk about her mother. Tarquin was so grateful to Mrs. Stewart's daughter for taking her mother away at that time, and therefore leaving Celia on his hands, that he sent the child a silver rattle.

"We may be in London then," Celia told her. "The postman brought a letter from Lord Hugo."

As always, she waited impatiently for Tarquin's return from the fields, where he'd been checking on the progress of the lambing with his agent. It was hard to believe he'd settled down to be a concerned and contented Yorkshire landowner.

He was also, without doubt, the best-dressed one in all three Ridings. If she'd feared removing to his estate would cure Tarquin of his dandyish ways, she needn't have worried. It was true, when he came in, his boots were splashed with mud. But his everyday country gentleman's garb of buckskin breeches, wool cloth coat and matching waistcoat were impeccably cut and his neck cloth almost undisturbed by a morning on horseback.

"How many sheep did you dip?" she asked, putting her arms around his neck and sniffing appreciatively. It was a standing joke. Tarquin hadn't changed enough that he engaged closely in the messier aspects of farming, certainly not those that would affect his clean scent. She nuzzled his smooth jaw and pulled his head down for a kiss.

"There's a letter for you from Lord Hugo," she said after an interval that, as usual, left her rumpled and him pristine. She never could work out how he managed that.

He slid a knife under the seal. "He wants us to come to London for the season," he said.

Celia had expected it. Since attending their wedding at Wallop Hall, Lord Hugo had written her two perfectly courteous letters. Tarquin insisted his great-uncle was quite reconciled to their marriage. "He wants me to be happy and I am."

Celia wasn't so sanguine. Surely, she reasoned, Lord Hugo must blame her for taking his beloved nephew away to live in the wilds of Yorkshire.

"He wants us to stay with him in Bruton Street," Tarquin said, continuing to read his letter. "It's a delightful house and very convenient." Her husband had given up his London rooms which were too small and didn't allow women.

"How kind of him," Celia said. "And if we're going to stay with him, it had better be this year, before the child arrives. I expect Lord Hugo has lots of fragile things for an infant to break."

Tarquin grinned. "You wouldn't believe the bibelots he's amassed in a lifetime of collecting."

"I'm sure I would."

He looked at her with concern, not fooled by her effort to sound delighted at Lord Hugo's invitation. "We don't have to accept," he said. "Sebastian and Diana would have us. Or the Chases have a huge house in Berkeley Square. Or we can just stay here. There's no law says we have to spend the season in London."

This Celia would not allow. She knew Tarquin

missed London and there were aspects of a trip south that appealed to her too. Tarquin had assured her they had no need to attend every assembly of the *haut ton*, and she'd always enjoyed theaters and other pleasures of the capital. How bad could things be when she had Diana and Minerva as friends and Tarquin's constant companionship and support?

"Nonsense, love," she said. "You simply must go to your tailor's. You have nothing to wear but rags."

"I couldn't have put it better myself. Here." He handed her a folded sheet. "Hugo encloses a letter for you."

My dear niece,

I believe you may think I disapprove of you and I wish to assure you that nothing could be further from the truth. Since the day I first saw Tarquin (an occasion I described to you at Mandeville last summer) I have been concerned only for his happiness. I thought I knew what would achieve it, but I was wrong and he was right. He chose the wife he wanted and he chose well. It distresses me that you should doubt your welcome from me. I hope you will make Bruton Street your London home while I live. It will of course be yours afterward, but that is to look ahead. I have no intention of shuffling off the mortal coil until I have met your children and I look forward to entertaining them too. My valet tells me it's best to put away small fragile objects when there are children in

the house. Next season I will do that, but this year
I shall enjoy showing you my collections and get-
ting to know my niece.

> *Yours very affectionately,*
> *Hugo Hartley*

She set aside the letter, blinking back tears.

"What is it?" Tarquin asked, drawing her into his arms. "What did Hugo say to upset you?"

"Nothing. Nothing at all. We shall go to Bruton Street. I look forward to it very much."

"I'm glad," Tarquin admitted. "Once you know Hugo better you'll appreciate him."

"How could I not love the man who made you who you are?"

Author's Note

Quite often in historical romance, our innocent heroine learns about sex from a book. How else is a well-bred virgin going to get out of the missionary position? I thought it would be fun to use a real publication of the period.

In researching my series on the Regency book collectors of the Burgundy Club, I read quite a lot of eighteenth-century pornography. (It's okay, you know, if it's historic, especially if it's in French.) I came across *The Genuine and Remarkable Amours of the Celebrated Author Peter Aretin* in the British Library catalogue. I don't know if it is the only copy in existence, but I've found no record of another and I doubt there are many. Every quotation and reference in *The Amorous Education of Celia Seaton* comes straight from this badly written and exceedingly prurient little novel, which bears a publication date of 1796.

Some of the other books in Tarquin's collection no doubt had greater literary merit. In pre-Revolutionary

France a number of distinguished writers wrote erotica as a subversive act. Pam Rosenthal's *The Bookseller's Daughter* is an erotic romance set in the world of these illicit publications. *The Genuine Amours* has none of the philosophical pretensions of these French works. It's smut, pure and simple, with enough outrageously purple prose to make me laugh out loud in the British Library rare book reading room.

As usual, I have lots of people to thank for helping me with this book, more than I will remember to list here. Thanks to these writers for historical research assistance and/or moral support and entertaining e-mails as Tarquin and Celia's story took form: Gaelen Foley, Shannon Donnelly, Kalen Hughes, Courtney Milan, Alleyne Dickens, Jenny Brown, Janet Mullany, Anna Campbell, Caroline Linden, Pam Rosenthal, Cara Elliott, and Christine Wells. Thanks to Jill and Kathy for being my faithful and perceptive first readers. Thanks to Meredith Bernstein and Esi Sogah, my ever helpful and supportive agent and editor. And thanks to my friends and family for normal life.

Miranda

Next month, don't miss these exciting new love stories only from Avon Books

A Night to Surrender by Tessa Dare
Spindle Cove is a haven for the women of England looking for something more than the brute air of pig-headed men. So when Victor Bramwell, the Earl of Rycliff, breaches its borders, Susanna Finch is hell-bent on protecting her utopia. But as the two collide, their friction becomes fiery. Who will back down when both of have so much to lose?

In the Arms of a Marquess by Katharine Ashe
Knowing the fire that Lord Ben Dorée once set off in her heart years ago, Octavia Pierce has had little interest in anyone else. Though she claims to have put her lust for the rogue behind her, she now needs his help with a most dangerous, clandestine matter. But as they fall in league with one another, their reunion proves to spark a hotter flame than they ever imagined.

One Night in London by Caroline Linden
After Edward de Lacey hires away Lady Francesca Gordon's solicitor to help save his inheritance, she demands he rescue her niece in return. He agrees to her proposal, but is determined to keep the beauty at arm's length. And still…their arrangement quickly ignites a passion too hot to tame.

Star Crossed Seduction by Jenny Brown
Miles Trevelyan is looking for temporary, unattached bliss when he meets Temperance, a skilled pickpocket. Not sure what to make of the wily vixen, he falls for her. As love blooms, their desire unlocks secrets of the past better left unopened. With betrayal and treason in question, will love rise above?